A Light so BLINDING

II

ALSO BY EMMA HAMM

Deep Waters
Whispers of the Deep
Song of the Abyss
Echoes of the Tide
Call of the Fathoms

Seven Deadly Demons
The Demon Court
The Demon Crown
The Demon Prince
The Demon Mark

Dragon of Umbra
Fire Heart
Bright Heart
Brave Heart
Torn Heart
Taloned Heart

and many more...

Emma Hamm

Copyright © Emma Hamm 2025

Visit author online at www.emmahamm.com

Cover Design by Feyspeaker
Underside Dustjacket by Andrea Corsini
Hardcover Design by BookishAveril
Interior Artwork by JaneDark7

You made it through this year.
You'll make it through the next.
But fuck this one was real shite.

Chapter 1

Priestess of High Regard,

It has come to our attention that you are seeking your lost sister. Rose is safe with us, but we need your help if you ever wish to get her back.

There is a troll locked in that labyrinth. We're aware of it, yes. There are those in this kingdom who know the dark desires of your king and all the terrible deeds he is willing to do to satisfy his own malicious desires.

A troll with horns and dark green skin, that is who we want.

We offer you a trade. Your sister, for that troll. Otherwise, we will do with her as we see fit.

Signed,

King Egil, son of Olaf Witch-Breaker

The words flickered in candlelight that made the ink seem illuminated through the thin paper. Astrid stared at the letter in her hand and didn't know whether she should laugh or cry. Countless letters had been sent to her just like this throughout the years—people who swore they had seen Rose. Some had told her they were the only ones who could bring her sister back. Stories that always led her down a rabbit hole to nowhere.

But no one had ever claimed to be a troll before. At least this person was original.

Although... she hadn't the faintest idea who would dare to mention the labyrinth so glibly, or who would even know about it. The king was very secretive, and hand chose which nobles and their families were allowed into that dark place.

Staring at the paper in her hand, she had to notice as well that it wasn't the same texture as the paper she was used to. Sure, it could all be planned to make her think this had actually been sent by trolls. But there were claw marks at the edge, and the writing was harsher, almost rudimentary, like the person wasn't used to writing at all. And then there was the smell, almost musty, like it had been written in a cave.

A knock on the door resounded throughout her room, and she jumped. Astrid whirled toward the door as though expecting someone to walk into the room at any moment and see her clutching a letter from trolls.

"Our lord would like to see you!" A feminine voice drifted through the door. "He said to tell you he has little patience today."

Of course he had little patience; the man never had such a thing. He wanted what he wanted when he wanted. Such was the life of a rich man.

Standing, Astrid realized that her room was unfortunately in chaos. She'd been so wrapped up in her studies, remembering all the names of all the nobles and making sure that she memorized all their secrets, that she hadn't cleaned in weeks. Her bed was piled high with all the silk and satin dresses that had been delivered a week ago. Her dresser was similarly drowning. And then, of course, her mirror was nearly entirely covered by the veils that would hide her face from all those who might dare to look at a priestess standing with her nobleman.

"He's not patient today?" she shouted, rushing forward to at least grab a reasonable veil. And then she saw herself in the mirror.

"Damn it," she hissed under her breath.

"I'd even go so far as to say he's angry," the priestess on the other side said. "You had better hurry. What is taking you so long?"

Her hair was wild. Her eyes were sunken and hollow. She looked like a wraith, and that wouldn't do. Lord Tolly prided himself on beauty at all costs. He made sure that everyone knew his power and wealth simply by what he surrounded himself with. He'd take one look at her and send her away.

Frantic now, she rushed for her desk and picked up the paper that very well might have been the only connection to her sister that she would ever get. She read it one more time, her eyes dancing over the strangely scrawled words, and then held it to the candle on her desk.

It didn't take long to light on fire, nor did it take long to burn. Astrid kept hold of it until the very last second and then dropped the paper onto the floor, stamped out the last bit of flames and kicked it under her desk.

"Help me!" she shouted. "Come in and help me!"

The door opened, revealing a much younger priestess, who had just joined their sisterhood. Her name was Marten, a strange name for a woman, but she was pretty enough to be here. Her blonde hair gleamed in the candlelight that made her horrified gaze turn red.

"Priestess!" Marten said, her hands flying to her mouth. "What happened to you?"

Stress. She had a lot riding on her shoulders at all times because she was the closest priestess to Lord Tolly, and there were many things expected of her. Political meetings, knowledge of everyone attending, meetings with other priestesses and bartering secrets, not to mention keeping all of it straight for a lord who loved his alcohol more than his own people.

Gesturing with her hand, she ushered the younger woman into the room. "Enough with that. Just help me get dressed."

"Yes, yes, of course. I will do my best."

Together, they rushed to make her look presentable. Astrid stripped out of her clothing and yanked another dress on. This one was stunning in white and gold. The gossamer fabric was nearly entirely transparent, although there were strips of golden fabric over her breasts that narrowed to a V between her legs. It hid enough, but would do its job as a distraction. Lord Tolly would be looking at her body more than her face. Beading covered the entire thing, tiny gold beads that dripped down her shoulders and hips.

A single bead pinged off as she moved awkwardly. It skittered across the floor, rolling underneath her desk, where she could see a portion of the letter hadn't entirely burned.

The portion that still said King Egil.

Sucking in her breath when Marten moved to get the bead, she hissed out, "Leave it! We don't have time."

Harsh words, but the last thing she needed was the sisterhood assuming she was communicating with trolls. She'd learned long ago that it was better to be known as mean than someone who could be taken advantage of.

Marten hustled back to her, finishing brushing her hair with a harsh pull that made her scalp sting but got the job done fast enough. "Which veil? The partial face covering?"

No, she knew the veil she would use. Lord Tolly was a simple man, after all. Beauty was the only thing he cared about, and he certainly did not care if he saw the faces of the priestesses he housed.

She reached for the gold chain veil. It was little more than strategically placed links, ones that revealed her eyes and allowed glimpses of her red lips. It would bedazzle him with the tiny stones woven in between the gold. He wouldn't look at the hollows beneath her eyes, or the way she could barely keep them open. He'd be too busy staring at her body and the wealth that dripped from her.

Astrid took one last look at herself in the mirror before nodding. "Where is he?"

"He was last in the parlor. He said he was entertaining a few other noblemen, and that's why he needed you."

"Shit," she muttered before rushing out of the room.

As a priestess, her job was to keep all the secrets that Lord Tolly couldn't remember. She stood beside him and told him all the things he needed to know, so he didn't have to waste his time remembering anything about anyone. He was the figurehead, and she was the whispering snake wrapped around his neck.

If he were alone with any nobles, he likely had already made a mistake she'd have to fix later. Foolish man. He should have waited for her. Or at the very least, come for her himself.

The halls of this home were stunning, but she didn't have time to marvel at their beauty. She often did, because Astrid reminded herself every day where she had come from. As orphans, Astrid and her sister had grown up in squalor. She knew what it was like to go hungry.

This house was everything she hadn't had as a child. Thick rugs cushioned her feet, making her footsteps nearly silent as she walked. The portraits on the walls had all been hand-painted by the greatest artisans alive, and the frames were gold. Actual gold. The walls were plastered with wallpaper that had also been hand-painted. Everything in this building dripped with luxury and wealth that had no right to be spent the way it was.

She rounded a corner and headed toward the parlor, where she could already hear men's voices. The murmuring tones didn't seem overly upset, so that was a good sign as she headed in.

Astrid didn't knock. She did not need to. She was Lord Tolly's personal priestess, not just some acolyte who was trying to catch the attention of another nobleman. She was renowned throughout the kingdom for her work with her lord. No one questioned her.

The parlor was lit with oil lamps that filled the room with a peculiar smell. She'd never liked being inside a windowless room, but all of Lord Tolly's rooms were like this. This one was decorated with the colors of her lord, greens and yellows, some of them rather sickly. The chairs were all in a circle, with a large table in the center. Already, maids were entering with food and drink for the visitors, and they would keep those options coming even though their own kitchen was a little bare at the moment.

Three men sat in the parlor. Two Astrid did not immediately recognize, although she would have to remember them soon enough. One man had silver hair that was slicked back against his skull, and the other... Ah, this was Lord Harwick and his son. Her mind raced to catch up with all the information she knew about the two of them.

Harwick was one of the king's favored noblemen. He was not known to be a good man and had gone through three priestesses already. He did not favor the opinions of women, and he was rumored to be teaching his son to take over for him. An illness was what some people assumed plagued him, although no one had confirmed it as of yet. Astrid would have to talk to the neighboring priestess, as she did not believe Harwick would reveal anything himself.

She strode toward Lord Tolly, where he sat in his usual plush chair. The man had been handsome when she'd first been given to him. She'd been a bright-eyed, new priestess who had sworn she would do whatever she could to serve him well. Now he was old. His skin was wrinkled. His hands shook when he reached for a cup of tea. He looked less like the man she knew and more like someone else she barely recognized.

He used to tell her everything. Now, it was a rare moment for her to be called into his parlor.

His voice did not waver as he murmured, "Ah, there you are. I was wondering when you would join us."

She stood beside his chair and leaned down. Their conversations were expected. A lord always had a private conversation with his priestess when she entered the room. "I came as soon as I knew they were here."

"Anything I should remember?"

"Lord Harwick is training his son to take his place; that's why he's bringing the young man everywhere. Rumors are of an illness that will take his life quickly, nothing confirmed."

He patted her hip as if they were merely glad to see each other, before turning to the nobleman before him.

But Lord Harwick knew this game. All the noblemen did. He

lifted a glass of brandy to his lips and saluted her, not her lord. "So, what does your priestess know of me?"

"I don't know what you speak of," Lord Tolly said. "I was merely about to ask after your health."

Harwick's brow lifted. "She's only got that? Perhaps your priestess is losing her touch, Tolly. You should get another."

These were the hardest times for her. Astrid wanted to reply. She wanted to argue that there were few people who were capable of finding out anything regarding other noblemen, and she happened to know that was damn good information. The favor she now owed to the man in his employ was sizeable indeed, and she'd been assured that no one else knew that Harwick was sick.

But she wasn't allowed to say anything at all. Priestesses talked to no one other than their Lord, at least within sight of the man who employed them. So she bit her tongue and hoped that Tolly would stand up for her.

He didn't, of course.

Lord Tolly just laughed and sipped at his tea, even though his shaking hand made that difficult. "Ah, you know I wouldn't get another. Unlike you, I get attached."

"A weakness."

"Indeed."

They talked of nothing for a while after that. These three men had no business to attend to. She listened to every word though, spending time peering through the veiled threats and the laughter of men who knew that they could end the other person's career with a single word.

Until Harwick started speaking of the labyrinth itself, and she felt her blood run cold.

"It's just that the king knows the labyrinth could be so much more than it currently is. Understandably, we're all aware that some people will find it distasteful to watch what we do. But others will be very interested in it. Those with money should be brought into the fold without fear of what would happen if the rest of the kingdom found out." Harwick gestured to his son. "Even my boy can see the reason in that."

The labyrinth was what had been mentioned in the letter, wasn't it? If that letter had been real and the trolls did have her sister, then they had wanted her to go to the labyrinth and release a particular troll.

But no. She wasn't receiving letters from trolls. How would they even have gotten the letter to her? It was another cruel trick by someone who knew her story.

Harwick's son spoke up, unusual for the young man who was known as oddly silent. "The king is right. The efforts in the labyrinth can only be expanded upon. There are a great many things we could do with it, and the money that would come from the betting is impressive if you look at the expected revenue."

Tolly rubbed a hand on the back of his neck. "Gambling? That's what the king wishes to push for?"

Wait, no, they couldn't gamble. Tolly's house was already lacking money. They had convinced people everything was fine, and no one would guess that he was struggling, but this household couldn't afford to be anywhere near Tolly's greatest weakness.

Gambling.

Astrid leaned down and murmured, "It does not sound like a good idea. The noblemen of this kingdom already struggle with debts to each other. Betting more in this kingdom would only put everyone into ruin more quickly."

Harwick spoke over her though, and she wondered if Tolly was listening to her at all. "The king would like to personally invite you to the labyrinth show this weekend. He said you would be a good investor if I could convince you."

And she watched her lord crumble. That easily. He ignored everything she told him, all because a more powerful man had complimented him.

This was going to end poorly. She could feel it. But if it got her close to the labyrinth, then perhaps this was a blessing in disguise. She wouldn't argue too hard, because she still had faith that she could control her nobleman. It wasn't like Harwick could hover over the man the entire time they were at the labyrinth. She still had Tolly's ear.

Leaning down one last time, she had to try to get control over the situation. "My lord, perhaps we should speak on this matter privately—"

Again, Harwick interrupted her. "Tolly, I don't believe I've ever seen so much of a priestess's face before. Do you usually allow her to shirk her duties so often or is this a personal choice of her own?"

Lord Tolly looked up at her, and she saw his eyes narrow, his jaw clench, and she knew in an instant that the game had changed once again. He had been a man who enjoyed seeing her beauty flaunted, but now another man had told him that he should not.

Therefore, he did not.

Lifting a hand to her face, she covered her lower features with her palm. "I will replace the veil before we leave, my lord."

"Do that, Priestess," he spat. "I will not tolerate the king's disappointment."

"Of course not, my lord." She bowed low and headed out of the room, her heart thundering in her chest.

She had to sway Tolly to her side, or she'd be back out on the streets. But perhaps the labyrinth was an opportunity. That letter still burned in her mind.

Perhaps she was one step closer to her sister, no matter how dangerous it was.

Chapter 2

Bjorn's world had narrowed to pain and relief. That was all. There was nothing else in his life. He lived for the brief moments when no one was watching him, when he could feel like himself again, or even allow the hope in his chest to build.

They would come back for him. They'd promised.

Ragnar was the most trustworthy troll he knew. He'd been a dear friend for many years, and more than that, he'd been the man to come and find him. After all the years Bjorn had spent in this place, after all that he had destroyed within himself, the other trolls had found him.

All he had to do was stay true to who he was. He had to remember that he was a person. He was not just the Bull who killed anything and anyone who was put in his way. He was Bjorn, son of Dag the Destroyer. He had a family, a life. There were memories in him that were gentle. He knew what it was to be a good man.

Even if the humans didn't want him to be.

The games had changed since Ragnar had escaped. King James now knew there were ways out of his labyrinth, and he wasn't happy about it. But it had given the humans an excuse to change every rule and fight. After all, the labyrinth had been about the spectacle.

Which was why Bjorn had been dragged out of his cell and out here. It used to be that the trolls had only walked past these rooms before they'd entered the labyrinth. Lavish, lush rooms where the humans had eaten and drank before he'd be forced to kill his own people. Now, the trolls were within them.

Someone had installed hooks in the ceiling and floor. The humans had figured out how to create impressively strong chains that even he could not break free from, which were wrapped around his wrists and forearms, stretching his limbs far over his head. Then they chained his legs to the ground, sometimes allowing him to stand, other times in a kneeling position so he was at chest height for the noblemen of this kingdom.

Today, they had him standing. Specifically, because the moment he'd walked in, an announcer had declared, "Today we have a feast for your senses! The Bull is here, and you are allowed to touch as much as you wish!"

He'd had to grit his teeth. He ground his teeth so hard his tusks ached, and his hands gripped the chains with such force he thought the metal would bite through the flesh of his palms. He didn't want them to touch him. He hadn't fucking said they could do that.

But then they swarmed him. Disgusting humans with their greedy hands and their wide, staring eyes. It was mostly women at first, their hands sliding over his chest and down his stomach.

"Look at how big he is!"

"I've never been this close to a troll before."

"Green skin! Can you imagine? Having skin like this always? He looks like a frog up close!"

Over and over, they remarked on his body without ever looking up into his angry eyes. Rage dotted throughout his vision, sparks of red that warned he was losing control. It was how he had lived this long. Bjorn had a rage inside him that ate him up but promised he wouldn't have to remember any of the horrible things he had done.

His father had the same beast, as had his grandfather and all the other men who had come before him. Legendary warriors with a demon that lived inside them.

It whispered into his ear that he could kill every person in this room. All he had to do was jerk these chains. Surely they weren't so strong that they could hold a troll like him. But he held himself together, because though these human women wished him harm, he had not lost himself so thoroughly that he would harm them.

And then the men came closer. They held drinks in their hands, the acidic scent biting at his nose. One of them, a man with a twisted mustache, tapped him on the side. "Do you think these muscles are from fighting? Or are all trolls born so disgustingly... toned?"

"I think it's the fighting. No man would be born like this without a life of hardship. Unless all trolls live in hardship." The man beside him sipped at the alcohol, his greasy hair sliding out of its careful curl at the top of his head. "Do you think they could be useful in the fields? We could make them pull the carts with the cattle."

They chuckled before turning away from him, and all that rage threatened to bubble up again. They really only saw trolls as monsters or beasts who had no reason or thought.

And then came the next. A nobleman Bjorn recognized. This man was always at every single fight, no matter how often they were held.

He was an older man with white hair, and he had a son who had eyes just as harsh as his own. But this time it was just him. He held a plate of food in his hands, and the smell made Bjorn's mouth water.

How long had it been since they'd fed him? He couldn't remember. All he knew was that he shoved food into his mouth whenever it was offered.

"A beast like you deserves to be tied up," the man said, lifting his steak knife from his plate. He placed the blade against Bjorn's ribs and looked right into his eyes. "Does it shame you that I could kill you right now? No one would care, troll. We'd all just laugh as your blood ran out."

Rage burned through Bjorn so white-hot, it was hard for him to think. He couldn't remember their language right now, only his own language. The one they called the black tongue. "I would sooner kill you, human, than allow that tiny blade to be the one that ends me. You have no idea what I could do to you." He tugged on the chains around his wrists, hard.

The man took two large steps back, creating space between them at the cracking noise that filled the room. While the chains held, Bjorn was too far gone. He raged at the man, spitting insults and swears at the human who thought he was worthy enough to fight a troll.

The metal bit through his wrists, just as he'd feared it would. But he wasn't even aware of the pain as he pulled and tugged at them. If he had to rip his own hands off to get to that idiotic creature who stood before him, then that was what he would do. Blood dripped down his forearms, landing on his shoulders and face. The scent enraged him even more.

He could see nothing but the prey that stood before him. A man who had claimed to have such bravery and yet refused to stand close enough for a drop of Bjorn's blood to land on him.

He would make sure this man died screaming in pain. He would rip out his intestines and watch the man's features as he stared down at his own guts. Only then would Bjorn feel peace.

The man who would soon die said, "Look at him! With just one threat, he goes into a rage. It's no wonder he's the king's favorite fighter. Don't you think?"

Another voice barely broke through Bjorn's anger. "They are all like this, Harwick. Must you toy with them?"

They were talking about him as though he couldn't understand them. As though he wasn't even real. He hated them. Hated every single human who had ever stepped foot in this room, and someday, he would kill all of them.

Then a voice. A cool splash of water that eased the rage inside his chest. A promise of quiet and solace that made even the raging beast inside of him pause and look around.

"My lord," she said, her voice so quiet he didn't think anyone other than him and the man she spoke to could hear her. "Surely you have more important things to do. Cruelty is beneath someone of your station."

Bjorn wanted to tell her cruelty was why these men were here. There wasn't a single person in this room who wasn't walking a knife's edge between masochism and sadism.

But then Harwick, the man he wanted to kill, snorted. "So you'll break the rules of speaking for an animal, Priestess? How curious. You think you could control him?"

"I think anyone would react better to kindness than threats of death."

"Prove it, then. You think you can make this beast calm? Then do it."

No. No, he was a risk. No one should come anywhere near him. Hadn't she heard of what he had done to so many women who'd been gifted to him?

Bjorn shook his head like a bear, trying to piece together the truth in his mind, rather than what they had told him. The rumors were that he killed women, and he did. But only because they had asked him to. They'd begged him to kill them because of what their life had been. Not because he enjoyed killing them. That wasn't who he was. He didn't hurt women, not maidens, not wives.

Then, a woman stepped in front of him, and he was blinded by her beauty. Golden hair fell straight down to a silver dress that left little to the imagination. It clung to her shoulders by what looked like only pearls, each of them in little clusters that held the sheer fabric slinking down her body. More pearls concealed most of her form, but it showed just as much. Tucked into a tiny waist, caressing flared hips, and stroking legs that were so long it made his head spin.

She wore a mask dotted with pearls that covered her face from the eyes down, but he could stare into that ice-blue gaze forever.

"Princess?" he croaked, the rage disappearing into shock as she looked up at him.

"No," she murmured quietly, clearly not wanting anyone to overhear her. "A fair lookalike, though."

She lifted a cup to his mouth, and he didn't think. He just drank. This was likely how they poisoned him, getting rid of him for good in a show that was embarrassing. He'd never join his ancestors if he died like this, but... He drank.

It was cold, clear water. Crisp as a mountain spring, fresh as the first snow melting from the peaks. He drained the cup that she offered, desperate for the relief of water that wasn't collected from condensation in his room or dirtied by the hands of so many other fighters in the labyrinth that it was more mud than liquid.

Then a hand. A chilly hand pressed against his cheek as she took the cup away. "I'm sorry they've done this to you. You deserve better."

"It is my life, bright one." His breathing was ragged even to his own ears. The common tongue. So he did remember it after all.

He could see clearly again. No more red. No more anger. Just her. He could see the difference from the princess now. This woman had hollows under her eyes, and her gaze wasn't icy blue but more cerulean, like a calm lake on a quiet day. Her hair wasn't the color of gold, but more like wheat.

Her soft expression wasn't one that he'd ever seen on the princess's features; he knew that. He'd met that witch a few times, and she enjoyed watching other's pain, just like her father. This woman, though... Her eyes were so blue, he could feel himself drowning.

Harwick's voice laughed, breaking through the small bubble of peace. "Look at how she toys with him! Tolly, you've trained her well. A priestess like that should know how to make a monster bend a knee. We could probably release him, and she'd have him wrapped right around her finger."

"Well, you know my priestesses are always the best."

Bjorn didn't care to pay attention to these men. He had eyes only for the woman dripping in pearls.

"Priestess?" he asked.

"That is what they call me."

"Why?"

Then he could feel it. The slightest pulse of magic at her touch, as her fingers slid away from his jaw, and then the magic disappeared.

"That is why."

His anger nearly came back. He could still feel the remnants of her spell, a lingering calm that she had pushed into his body without his permission. But it was more than that. She had sought out the calm within him, the man who wanted to be in control, and she'd simply pulled that emotion to the front of his mind.

"What are you?" he asked again.

"They call us priestesses, but that is not something you need concern yourself with." She leaned a little closer, as though proving to the people surrounding them that she wasn't afraid of him. But then her voice, that quiet voice that was so hard to hear, murmured, "Are there other trolls looking for you?"

His entire body stiffened. He clutched the chains above him again, holding on to them harder. The sound of his squelching blood reached his ears, and he jerked the chains forward even more.

"Speak nothing of what you know," he snarled. It was a warning that she needed to adhere to.

The people in this room would kill her if they thought for even a second that she was working with the trolls who had escaped. Bjorn was chained up. He could do nothing to help her if they all turned on this priestess, who was far too brave for her own good.

But she merely smiled at him, the barest ghost of a smile, before turning back to the men behind her. She said nothing, but her "lord," as she called him, turned to Harwick and said, "What was it you wished for her to do? Calm the beast? He seems very calm now, Harwick."

Harwick snorted. "Yes, it is rather easy for a pretty woman to do that. Especially a priestess of her breeding. Come, Tolly. There is much for us to talk about, and I don't wish to do it here."

Bjorn watched them walk away, but he couldn't tear his eyes away from the woman decorated in pearls. She was so beautiful. So light in this dark place. What was she doing here?

Another woman approached him, this one done up in fabric that had far too many colors. Her face looked... odd. As though there were a layer of something on top of it, garishly painting her features with vivid colors.

"Keep your eyes away from that one, troll. The king doesn't take kindly to anyone looking at his priestesses, let alone one such as yourself."

He blinked, words coming back to him as naturally as they had with the priestess. "Who are the priestesses to the king?"

"Mimics of his daughter. Women who would be as powerful as her, stolen right out of their beds as children. They are pitiful things with more power in their right pinky than most of us have." The woman sniffed. "Decorated dolls, used as secret keepers for the rich and famous of our kingdom. Sad to see, really. They have no life, no future, just the knowledge that they must serve. But don't stare at them. No one can even speak to them except their master and others like themselves. They'll take your eyes and tongue for such a thing."

They could do that, but he didn't think they would. Bjorn was their strongest warrior, and the king had use for him. Besides, no one had said a word when he'd spoken to her just moments ago.

He kept his gaze on her regardless, watching as she walked across the room and through a door. He was left alone, facing these women and men as they crowded him once more.

The priestess might have left, but the calmness she had brought to him stayed.

Chapter 3

Her heart had never thundered like that before. Astrid could deal with intimidating men. She'd done that her entire life. But that troll had been massive.

She'd stared up at him, shocked and awed by the sheer power that had been forced into submission before her. It had made something inside of her ache. She'd never questioned what her people were doing before, especially the king. He was charged with keeping their people safe, and he had promised that he would always do that, but something about this felt wrong.

The trolls were talked about as if they were another species. Her people believed they were creatures who had refused to serve the elves and therefore must've been evil. Elves were the only reason why so many of the humans had magic, and why so much of their lives had become easier. Magic made living simple. The elves were the saviors of the humans, and yet...

That troll had spoken to her. Not in the black tongue, but in her own language. He had seemed reasonable, warned her against talking about the trolls who wanted him safe, and there was something odd about that.

He shouldn't care about her at all, or even have the ability to do so. And he certainly wasn't supposed to protect someone he had every reason to hate. It was confusing. Very, very confusing.

She followed Lord Tolly into the back room, her mind whirling with the possibilities of what her conversation had meant. She shouldn't even be thinking about this. Trolls were beyond her worries. She needed to focus on the here and now.

A rival had the lord she served in a back room in the labyrinth, and all she could think about was the troll tied up in the room beyond. Saving him wasn't her job. Her job was to keep her own people safe. The priestesses and acolytes who lived with Lord Tolly at her request were real people, ones she had vowed to serve as well. The town that relied on its lord to keep them safe was her task to keep running.

And yet... That letter had mentioned getting a troll out of this labyrinth who looked an awful lot like the troll who had been angry at Harwick.

"Did you see his horns?" Harwick said as they entered the sitting area. "I have never seen the likes of them on another. The creature is clearly more animal than man. No wonder they call him the Bull. I've never been so close to him, but I always know to bet on that fighter before any others."

Lord Tolly chuckled. "I have bet against him myself, and I know how foolish that was now. He is an impressive creature, absolutely."

The room was filled with food and drink. She didn't know why they thought this would be a private place to talk. Anyone could walk in here during their conversation. Surely one of them was concerned about that?

"Lord Tolly," she murmured, stepping closer to him. "I believe there are observation rooms that are more private than this."

He hummed low under his breath, then loudly declared, "What observation room are we going to, Harwick?"

"Oh, we're having our conversation in here, old friend. It shouldn't take very long."

She prided herself on always knowing what was going to happen in meetings like this. Astrid had spent the past week preparing for every possible outcome. Harwick would not trap her with any of his foolish plans, because he simply was not as smart as she was. Nor did he have her connections. She'd spent far too long ensuring every detail was perfect. She knew what he was going to say.

And it wasn't, "Your debts have not been paid in a very long time, Tolly. Unfortunately, it is time to pay up."

Four more men came through the door they had just entered. These were the king's men though, each of them wearing armor and decorated with weapons. None of them even looked at her as they walked through the door, standing at attention and waiting on...

Harwick's order.

What had gone wrong? How had she missed this? She could feel Lord Tolly's gaze on her, but she had no knowledge of this plan. Harwick's own people had always shared what they could with her, and they had never lied before.

Desperately, she looked over at Lord Tolly, hoping that he would see just how much she had tried, but he... he didn't look surprised. If anything, he looked resigned.

"Debts?" she breathed, her voice perhaps too loud in this room where so many could hear her. "What debts do they speak of?"

His expression didn't change as he looked at her. "I may have been attending some of the fights..."

"Oh, come now. Don't lie to her, Tolly, not when she's already seen it all. Priestess, your nobleman has been attending many fights and betting all that he does not have."

Her mind raced with all the details Tolly had explained away. "The food storage you said was going to a neighboring lord?"

"I could not afford more."

"The missing paintings?"

"Sold so I could pay off some of the debt, although clearly not all of it."

Harwick snorted. "Not even a small fraction, if we're being honest. You owe enough that I could take your title and town, Tolly."

That couldn't happen. The Tolly line had been in that manor and managing that town for the better part of five hundred years. She'd vowed that she would protect it at all costs, not that she would... would...

Let it fall because of a man she couldn't keep under her thumb. She was supposed to be one of the best. A priestess who had been trained to perfection with power that could assist her lord beyond any other. She knew how to draw emotions out of people, how to make them feel good or scared or tired. Anything that would aid her in her cause.

Turning her gaze to Harwick, she intended to do just that. But the moment she stepped toward him, one of those guards grabbed her shoulders.

She reached into his soul, feeling around for the emotion that she wanted. It wasn't that she was just a calming presence, like these men thought she was. If she wanted to fight them, if she wanted to make them hurt, then she could.

Her elven bloodline had been cruel. The older priestesses told her stories about her suspected grandmother, a half-elven woman who had been as cold as steel. She'd known how to manage her family. That much was certain. She would have killed anyone who didn't keep the magic strong within all of them. And she had done it before.

Although Astrid had never wanted to be like that rumor, she knew damn well she could be.

The guard holding on to her didn't want to be here. His emotions were all over the place, swinging wildly from excitement to guilt to anger. She used that to her advantage. Weaving around his mind, she tied his guilt like a noose around his neck. He didn't want to hurt her. He didn't want to hold a defenseless woman down, especially not a priestess who should be revered. He knew better. He knew that she deserved his respect.

The man released her almost instantly.

It should have made every man in the room tremble, but it didn't. Instead, Harwick just rolled his eyes. "Really, priestess? Using your magic feels a little out of hand, doesn't it?"

"Not for the likes of you," she snarled.

She wasn't supposed to talk to anyone other than her lord, but damn it, this felt like the right time to do it. Tolly did not need to be punished just yet. She could still fix this.

Scrambling, her mind started working in overdrive. "There is plenty for us to give you in exchange for his debt. Tolly hasn't sold nearly enough of the household objects. Half of my dresses alone should cover what he owes. Why he has not spoken with me about this situation, I do not know. But I am willing to work with you, Harwick. We'll get this paid off."

Lord Tolly stepped up to her and grabbed her arm. "That's enough,

Priestess."

By all the gods, she was so tired of men talking to her like that. Like she was nothing more than her title, rather than a woman who had thoughts and expectations of her own life. She had served him for years, and he'd trusted her for that long. Didn't he see that her reasoning might be better than his own?

She ignored her own lord and instead kept her attention on Harwick. "I'm telling you, I can make this work."

"But can you keep him out of the gambling dens?" Harwick shook his head. "I'm afraid we're going to have to kill him for this."

Kill him?

No, no, no, she couldn't allow that. If he were killed, then she would be sent far away from here. She'd pushed so hard for this job with Tolly because he was close to the city where her sister had been. And then when her sister had gone missing, she'd pushed to stay here because of Rose's disappearance. This was where her only surviving family was. If she weren't here, then Rose would be gone forever. She had to stay here and keep searching.

Harwick leaned forward, a wicked grin on his face. "I already know who you're going to be working with next. As a priestess of your ranking, you should serve a lord with considerable power and recognition among our peers. Don't you think?"

Did he mean... himself?

Absolutely not. She would not be his personal priestess. She'd rather die. She'd rather take whatever punishment was coming to Tolly than service Harwick for the rest of her days.

"That's quite enough, Astrid!" Her name snapped through the room, and she turned to Lord Tolly in shock.

He knew better than anyone else that he wasn't allowed to say her given name in the presence of others. She was to remain as anonymous as possible. A figurehead of his wealth, nothing more, nothing less. Priestesses trained their entire lives to serve men like him, but never, never, had he broken a rule so blatantly.

A fine sheen of sweat covered his brow. She could see a single bead of it dripping down his temple as he implored her with his gaze. "Stop talking," he said, but she could sense the nerves in him. "I'll fix this."

Astrid stared at the man she'd thought she trusted and realized... she didn't. She didn't actually trust him to do anything because, time and time again, he had proven to her that he was unworthy of her trust.

Lord Tolly turned his attention to Harwick and the guards. "I understand the debt I have is great, and to many of you it seems that there is nothing I could do to pay it back."

What was he doing? Why was he coming at this like it was a bargain to be made? She was going to kill him. She was going to wrap her hands around his neck for threatening all that they had and then... it hit her.

She could fix this. She had the tools now to discover where her sister was, and this situation was the final piece in that puzzle. Yes, it would be difficult. She knew that everyone in this room would think that she was insane, but she could do everything she was brought up to do, and she could still get her sister back.

All she had to do was play this right.

Tolly was still talking. "My priestess is correct. There is much I could sell, and I will ensure that the money gets to you quickly."

"The king doesn't care about money anymore. What he cares about is a spectacle in the arena, and you are going to be a perfect spectacle indeed. A nobleman fed to the trolls! I'm sure they're going to love ripping you apart."

Astrid opened her mouth, no matter how stupid it was for her to do so. "What if I could offer you a better show?"

Tolly scoffed. "Priestess, there is no show you could offer him that would convince him to change his mind. We need to pay him—"

But Harwick's gaze had already narrowed. "What is your offer?"

"Me."

Silence filled the room like a bubble about to pop. She hadn't expected them to be quite so surprised. But then again, they had all been assuming that they would need to fix this problem themselves. Even Tolly.

"What?" Harwick asked.

Even her lord was quick to say, "What are you even offering?"

It was time to make them believe this offer was merely self-sacrifice.

"My entire life has been dedicated to Lord Tolly and the people who call him their lord. I will not see him fed to trolls and all my work disappearing in seconds." She knew they might think her insane, so she had to make this even more believable. "My life has been yours for longer than it was mine, Lord Tolly."

"Astrid," he murmured.

She turned toward her lord. Reaching for his hand, she slowly got onto her knees. "Please. Allow me to do this in your stead. It would be my greatest honor to know that my last gift will keep you alive."

Tolly stared at her helplessly, his hands shaking in hers. She could feel the turmoil within him. At his core, he was still a good man. He didn't want to be the reason for her death, nor anyone else's. But there was a part of him that feared what would happen to him in that labyrinth, as all of them feared what would happen if they stepped foot in that realm of warriors.

Harwick was muttering something to a guard, who then left the room. Likely to confirm it was all right for him to change plans, but she knew what she had offered him.

A feast.

A massive amount of money, as well as countless men and women would rush to the arena knowing that the prize or the prey was a priestess. They had all seen her people for countless years. They knew exactly what to expect from her. It was poise, silence, and mystery. Now they would see what was underneath the veil that so many of her people wore.

Harwick understood that, but he eyed her desperation with mistrust. "You would do all that for the lord who gambled away your home?"

"I would do anything to keep the people in my home safe and happy." That was the truth. She would do anything for those acolytes and priestesses who deserved to be safe and warm and not traded about as she had been early in her journey.

He snorted. "Then you're just as stupid as your lord. It is ridiculous, but I'd be willing to give you up for the money that would come in. We'll think up quite a battle for you as the prize. The men in that arena haven't seen anything as pure and untouched as you in... well. Since before they ended up here."

She knew that. But she also had hopes that one in particular would fight for her harder than all the rest. If she could get to him, then that was one step closer to getting him out.

They all forgot that she had been here many times with her lord. The labyrinth was right in front of her nose, and no one watched a priestess. While the others had reveled in the bloodbath, she had been wandering these halls. The only area she did not know very well was where they kept the prisoners.

Given time, she could figure a way out of this place. And if she did that, then maybe she would finally find her sister.

The guard who had left entered the room again and stepped up to Harwick. Within seconds, she watched that evil man's face brighten with pleasure.

"Priestess, you have yourself a deal. Your lord's debt in return for your sacrifice." He held out his hand. "To the dungeons with you. We'll see just how frenzied the warriors get when they realize you are what they will win tonight."

Chapter 4

Bjorn traveled back to his cell in a daze. The blood loss from his wrists was likely the cause of it, and the exhaustion of his arms being stretched over his head for hours.

He thought he might have passed out a few times. It was hard to tell, really. Part of him thought that he had, because he blinked and he swore all the people in the room had changed positions. But it was hard to keep track of the humans, anyway. They all looked the same to him. All primped, dusted, and painted creatures that moved in the same eerie way.

All he had to do was make it back to his cell, and then he could lie on his back and relax for a little while. He needed to rest. If he'd had water, then he would have rinsed off his hands and arms as well, but there was no water here. They hadn't provided him with anything to heal the cuts that he had caused himself.

That was a bad sign.

The jingle of the keys at the head guard's waist kept him focused. At one point in his time here, he had been determined to steal those keys. They made sure there were ten guards with him at all times, each of them carrying swords that were at the ready and pointed at his throat. But some part of him still thought he could fight them off. It wouldn't take much to twist, surprising most of them, before sacrificing the cords of tendons at the back of his neck. If he was fast enough, the humans wouldn't know what had hit them.

He'd always saved that plan for the worst-case scenario, though. Perhaps the other trolls would still manage to save him, because fighting off ten men with swords at the ready was likely suicide.

For all that he had suffered, Bjorn had never gone to that place in his mind. Not yet, at least.

The cells were small. Too small, some might even claim. He could walk from one side to the other in four strides, and such little space was torture for a troll. His people were used to wide open lands, wild and untamed forests, not a small little hole in the ground with no consistent food or water. But this was where his life had been for over ten years now.

Bjorn was ashamed to admit he'd gotten used to it. The tight spaces were reassuring these days. They meant he wasn't in the labyrinth, with all its winding corridors and attackers in every open area. At least in his cell he knew he wasn't going to be hunted.

The door unlocked and swung open with the wrenching grind of metal on metal. The guard turned to him and gestured to the room. "Get in."

As if he was going to argue. He slipped into the room while somehow managing not to cut himself on the countless swords pointed at him, and then stood there quietly as they closed the door.

There were few trolls left in this place. Most of them had escaped with Ragnar and his people, but those of them who were still here had been locked up in the same hall.

The troll to his right had been quiet ever since they'd been moved to these cells. But the one on his left liked to talk, even if it was quietly through the walls.

"You made it back, Bull." Today, the troll's voice was raspy. Perhaps they had taken him for some kind of experiment. The king liked to toy with their kind whenever he could, so it wouldn't surprise Bjorn.

"Hello, Rabbit." They used the names that the humans had given them. It was just... easier that way. At least then they didn't forget where they were. Who they were. Or why they were here.

Rabbit was remarkably fast in the labyrinth, which was what had earned him the name. Quick footed and somehow perfect at remembering all the twists and turns, he was the most difficult one to catch. He could run for hours on end, too. It had become a bit of a challenge to the humans to see if they could confuse Rabbit as they moved the walls and changed the patterns of halls in the labyrinth. So far, they hadn't succeeded.

Bjorn sat down on the edge of his cot. There wasn't much to it. Just a rickety frame and a moth-eaten blanket that he'd thankfully remembered to take with him from cell to cell. But it was home, as much as he could have one. A small dented cup sat in the corner where the walls met. At least there the condensation slid down the wall and he could gather some water.

Two doors, just like always. One leading out into the hall beyond with a tiny window to look out. The other, windowless, leading into the labyrinth.

"What did they do to you this time?" Rabbit asked, his raspy voice sliding through a crack in the wall beside Bjorn's cot.

"Ah. They wanted a show for the nobles. They hung me up by my arms and let them do whatever they wished."

"They grab your cock?"

He flinched. "No, they did not. Too many humans around for that."

"Lucky you."

There was a long pause of silence, and again Bjorn wondered what Rabbit had been doing today. He supposed it wasn't worth it to ask. Whatever the male had done, it was traumatic enough to wreck his voice and he didn't likely wish to talk about it again.

Bjorn didn't like talking, anyway. He'd learned a long time ago that it was foolish to want to hold on to that part of himself. The part that used to talk all the time, to everyone who would listen. He remembered holding conversations for hours on end. He'd talked through feasts that had gone on until the sun came up the next morning, and he had never slowed. Not once.

Shaking his head, he leaned back on the cot, lying down to rest. "Tell me a story, Rabbit."

This was what they did every evening. The humans did whatever torture they could think of, and then he and Rabbit came back together to relive the lives they once had. Before Ragnar had broken into the labyrinth, Bjorn never would have entertained this. Remembering home in those ten years had been a weakness he could not show. Home was a soft place, a safe place, a hidden spot in his mind that he only visited at his worst.

But now, he wanted to remember. Now he wanted to be assured that he was going to be all right when he finally made it back to Trollveggen.

"Have I ever told you the one about how my sister met her

husband?" Rabbit asked.

He had. Countless times.

Bjorn loved the story all the same.

He grunted for the other man to continue, and let himself spiral into a world he barely remembered. A story with a young troll woman, her coloring a lovely deep violet so dark her skin was almost black. And how she had found solace in the arms of a bright turquoise troll, much smaller than her. A lean man who had been kind and soft when she'd needed that.

Rabbit's sister had been a warrior in a warband that had traveled beyond Trollveggen. He'd never shared where she had gone, or where she'd met her husband, but it must've been the same place Bjorn was from. He remembered leaving the mountain for months on end in the summer to see his mother and her people.

His father had been a cruel man. Dag the Destroyer had always been a fighter, and nothing could have prevented him from battle. But his mother had been softer, more afraid. So they had only visited her on the rare occasion, though it had been enough for Bjorn to love that gentle side of her.

The story wove around him like a spell. He could almost see the lands that Rabbit spoke of. The emerald green hills on the other side of Trollveggen. The wild that was so untouched by humans, it was like the only paths to be found were the ones that had been carved by animals. It was hope that allowed him to dream of it again. Hope that someday, he would return to those emerald meadows without fear of what he might bring with him.

The story ended as it always did, startling Bjorn out of his own memories and back into a story of a couple that had lasted forever.

Rabbit always ended with a flourish. "And that bastard loved her until the day I left. I assume he'll love her until the day he dies."

"Why call him a bastard?" Bjorn asked, the same as always. But the repetition made both of them feel better.

"Because he loved her so much it was hard to watch," Rabbit muttered. "She's my baby sister, and seeing him with her like that... well, it reminded me that she wasn't a baby anymore."

Bjorn hummed in agreement.

"You're talking a lot more than you ever have, by the way. Does that have something to do with those other trolls we met?"

They hadn't talked about that, but hadn't really had the chance either. Trolls were meant to be silent here. The less they talked, the better. Bjorn and Rabbit had gotten into the habit of it, but only through the crack in the wall.

A commotion in the hallway caught his attention. Bjorn had no idea how long it had taken Rabbit to tell the story this time. It seemed every time he told it, there were more and more embellishments that turned it into a fantastical tale he was certain was mostly untrue. But a commotion at this time of night? It was unheard of.

Then he could hear words as the guards walked through the halls once more, too late for it to be anything good.

"Prisoners! Behold your newest prize! The fight tomorrow evening will be the greatest you sorry lot have ever seen." Then a loud clang as a sword met the openings of a window on the door. "Don't try to touch her, you animal! Tomorrow, if you win, you get to touch her."

Her?

"Oh no," Rabbit muttered, and Bjorn heard the sound of him getting up and heading to his door.

Often the warriors were given the opportunity of a woman for their prize for winning in the labyrinth, but no one had ever gotten this much fanfare. Whoever the poor soul was, they were going to be torn apart by whatever man was "lucky" enough to win her.

Bjorn got up as well, curious to see who they had brought in. Usually the women were...

Dark thoughts battered against his mind. So many necks that he'd snapped. So many women he'd held the hands of as they drifted away into that realm where no one else could follow until it was their time. Death dogged his footsteps. Death they begged for, and only he could give it to them without punishment.

Shaking his head to clear those old, guilty thoughts, he headed to the window with the others.

The person in the cell across from him was a man he tried to forget. The human had been caught doing all manner of terrible things, and as such, his punishment was to be in here. Bjorn had heard him bragging about murdering a man who had been living on the streets and made it a point to target him in the labyrinth. Unfortunately, the human was an unreasonably good fighter and a large man who could hold his own against even trolls.

That man peered out at him through the window in his own door, and flashed a grin of missing teeth. His lank, greasy hair had once likely been a shade of brown. But now the oils had made it so stiff and dark it was hard to tell what the color even was. His face was getting paler every week he was in here, revealing a fish belly shade that wasn't the same as his tanned skin when he'd first come in through the door.

"Who do you think it is?" he asked Bjorn, his voice practically vibrating with excitement.

Bjorn didn't talk to the humans. None of them had earned that right.

He merely turned his head to look at the guards who were walking toward them. They made it difficult to see who was hidden behind them, but he knew the type of woman. She'd be terrified. Curled in on herself, her arms around her waist, trying to make herself seem smaller because all of this should frighten her. The men in here weren't anyone they wanted to be gifted to.

The guards had watchful expressions on their faces as they parted to reveal...

Her.

The woman he'd seen when he'd been tied up. The one kind enough to give him a drink. The one who looked nearly identical to the princess, but who had a softer heart. He had been able to tell just by looking at her. She'd hated that he was in pain and all his rage had disappeared at the first cool touch of her magic.

Shock made him grip the bars of his door, staring at her as she walked by. She wasn't afraid. This woman held her head high as countless men jeered at her, reaching through the bars to touch a lock of her hair, doing everything they could to get her to even look at them.

Her dress of pearls had a single section on the right hip that was ruined. Some might not even notice it, but he did. The pearls rose in eight strands, each of them an arc that accentuated the curve of her hip, and one of those strands had broken. He wasn't sure why that made him so angry, but it did. She deserved to be adorned like she had been. And now, someone had ruined that.

As the guards walked her by, he noticed she turned her head just slightly to look at him. Recognition flared in her eyes. She knew him, or at least, she knew of the monster she had seen hanging by his wrists. Like a dolt, he almost lifted his arms over his head as though that would make it easier for her to know that he was the same troll she had seen.

The priestess swallowed hard, and Bjorn knew he was the only one she allowed to see how frightened she was. For a few moments, the mask dropped. She wasn't the proud woman who feared nothing. For a few moments, she was a prisoner thrown into a dungeon with starving men.

Bjorn wanted to rage. He would rip the door from its hinges if that would get him to her faster. She didn't deserve this. No woman did.

What the guard was shouting finally broke through his thoughts. "The king has decided you lot deserve a gift! Fight hard tomorrow, and you'll get yourself a priestess. For keeps!"

For keeps?

What the fuck did he mean for keeps?

A million questions burned in his mind as she was moved forward. The priestess glided across the floor, her dress only barely skimming the dirt and blood that caked the room. He watched her go, terror burning in his chest until his gaze locked with the man across from him. And then it was rage that ignited inside him.

The human grinned, his remaining teeth bared with glee. "I'm going to get that one, Bull. I'll keep you up all night listening to her screams."

Bjorn knew damn well that wasn't going to happen. She was his, he decided. His to protect.

His to win.

Chapter 5

They kept her in a cell overnight. And throughout it all, she didn't sleep. Astrid knew better than to let her guard down around men like this. She had lived with them for years, but always with the barrier that she was a priestess who couldn't be touched. Now, all that had been stripped away.

This was her plan, though. She had known what she was getting into when she'd offered to take this role.

That troll was the one written about in the letter. She was certain of it. Looking at his features through the bars of his door, she knew it was him. Dark green skin, like pine trees in the shade, and horns that looked devilish in that low light. She'd nearly shuddered in fear at the sight of his eyes that glowed in the darkness. Some of them had eyes that reflected the light of the guards torches', remnants from when they'd been more animal than man. But she hadn't expected to see it just walking to her own cell.

Now, she had to figure out how to remove him from this place. She knew the setup of the labyrinth well. The dual-door system, how the gladiators were marched past all the nobility who would watch the coming fight, these features never changed.

It took her all night to figure out what they would do, but she wasn't surprised when the guards came to get her the next evening. Her stomach grumbled for food, and her mouth was parched from a full day without water. But she knew she looked exactly how they had left her.

With her mask covering her mouth, the only thing they would be able to see were the hollows under her eyes. But those were always there. The guards found her still in the pristine dress that had remained exactly as it was yesterday. Her hair was still perfect because she hadn't ever lain down.

"Come on, Priestess," the guard at the windowless door said. "Time to march you past the peepers."

"Peepers is a good name for them." She stood and smoothed her hand down her dress, making sure everything was in place before striding up to him. "Should I expect touching?"

"Not from anyone until you get to the labyrinth. Then who knows what the warriors will do to you." He looked her up and down, and she swore there was a flash of pity in his gaze.

She didn't want his pity. Not if he wasn't going to help.

So, she straightened her shoulders and walked out after him. The hall was empty, but she had suspected as much. The guard couldn't keep her safe with a bunch of warriors around her, and they wouldn't want a brawl to get out of hand when they needed her for the show. But she hadn't expected how horrible it would feel to walk by the nobility.

The whispers were easily ignored. But it was the sight of Lord Tolly himself. He stood close to the bars, wringing his hands as she walked by.

"Astrid," he said, trying to get her attention. "Astrid, please look at me."

The short walk here had sodden the hem of her dress with mud and blood. It had once been a piece of artwork, and all because of his stupidity she was now forced to ruin it. Along with herself. If her plan didn't work, everything could fall apart spectacularly in a way that would ruin her life. This was a risk she had to take, but all he knew was that it had been for him.

She paused and turned her head to look at him. Coolly, she replied, "I am Priestess to you. You do not have permission to use my given name."

Gliding forward, she followed the guard through the winding tunnels. She could see there were hundreds of feet that had passed in this direction, until the guard paused before a locked door, unlocked it, and brought her into a newer section.

"I shouldn't tell you anything," he muttered. "But it feels wrong to say nothing. The king wanted a show. I'm bringing you to a raised platform, and the warriors will fight to get to you. The one who reaches you first and who manages to hold you the longest, gets you. For good. Not for a night, like normal. You'll be their bedmate for... for good."

Well. That certainly made her plans a little more difficult. Hopefully, she had gotten the Bull's attention enough for him to fight for her then.

Nerves churned in her belly. What if this had all been a grave mistake? What if she ended up with the wrong person and she had to suffer through whatever they wanted to do to her for... however long it took her to escape. Or die.

She needed to have faith in her own abilities. Astrid had gotten through harder situations than this in her life. She was a priestess of all things. She could trick a few meathead warriors who thought they would own her if they fought hard enough.

"Fine," she replied to the guard, who was still staring at her. "Are you expecting me to thank you?"

"For the warning? Yes."

"You are doing nothing to save me. You are telling me what my future will be while feeding me to the wolves. No thanks are required for someone who isn't helping me." She walked past him onto what she assumed was a podium. She'd seen them used before in the few games she'd attended. Unfortunately, these podiums had been used to give certain warriors an advantage back then.

All she could hope was that they were taller this time. They'd only been about three feet tall when she'd seen them, and she struggled to see how that would keep a prize above their heads.

Standing in the center, she turned toward the guard and took a deep breath. "I am ready. You can do whatever you need to do."

He muttered something under his breath, perhaps about how icy priestesses always were, before he reached for a chain on the wall and began tugging on it. Slowly, ever so slowly, he lifted her out of the pits and into the arena.

Some days, the arena was lit by the sun. The king would order the false ceiling to be removed so that the warriors were blinded by the light. Not today. Today, it was all shadows and fire that raged in a circle above her head. Red banners decorated the ceiling, but not hanging over the arena itself. No, the king didn't want to obscure anyone's view of what was to come.

She was shocked to see that it wasn't a labyrinth laid out before her. They'd removed all the walls. Instead there was a blank, open space about the size of a field around her. The podium continued to lift, raising higher and higher until she was at least ten feet above the ground. The seats where she had sat with her lord were all filled to the brim. So many people who had once welcomed her among them now were bloodthirsty enough to watch her fall.

The sound of their voices made her head spin. Vertigo struck her quickly, but she remained steady as she forced herself not to react. She had practice in smoothing her features so no one would know what she was thinking or how she was feeling. That was her entire life. Astrid knew how to stay calm and quiet and collected.

So she stood there, looking out at the massive amount of space and knowing it would soon become a bloodbath. The king didn't just want a spectacle. He wanted this to be a night to remember.

And there he was. King James strode out onto a platform extending out over the blank arena and lifted his hands for silence.

"Tonight, we have a show unlike any other! This priestess before us has sacrificed herself in the greatest act of humility for her lord and her people. She gives her life so that our warriors might have a banquet tonight!"

A cheer rose, deafening from the stands. But more than that, she swore there was a cheer that came from beneath the floor as well.

Again, King James lifted his hands like a conductor, and the crowd was his orchestra. They fell silent, waiting to hear what he would say next. "Humans and trolls will fight for her tonight. To the death. But I couldn't just allow anyone to fight for her, oh no. These are our best. And tonight, we will see if a beauty can tempt the Bull."

More shouts, more screams, and her stomach churned with fear.

This wasn't right. She shouldn't be fought over like this, and yet, this was the only way.

Astrid folded her hands primly at her waist, clutching her fingers in a way she hoped no one could see as the king shouted, "Let the games begin!"

Doors opened everywhere. All along the walls, the floors, men surged out of them or yanked themselves onto the battlefield. There were so many of them, she had a hard time believing the king would actually risk all of their lives.

He had only so many fighters. She remembered Lord Tolly claiming that the king went on regular hunts to find more, but he was churning through them at a pace where this just wasn't sustainable. They needed to use fewer of the warriors and more difficult showcases so perhaps they would be able to make more money.

But tonight, the entire arena was sold out. So she understood why the king would risk so many of his best fighters. The people wanted a show, and he was going to give it to them.

Astrid had thought she would be prepared for what would come, but she had been wrong. The brutality these men showcased made her heart race and her palms grow sweaty. Some of them had been given weapons, and they used them to their advantage.

To her right, a man swung an axe that caught in another man's shoulder. The scream the injured man let out couldn't even be heard over the sounds of so many others yelling. Another man had a sword, and he lopped off a man's arm with ease before getting tackled to the ground by another.

There were trolls in the mix, too. They stood two heads taller than all the human men in the crowd, but they didn't seem to be fighting to get to her. They were fighting to keep the humans away from her. For that, she was grateful. It was the human men she feared. Their hungry gazes cast to her on the podium multiple times, and she could feel the malice radiating around them.

Where was he?

The king had even said the Bull would be here, so where was he? Her gaze searched the crowd, but she didn't see anyone with horns on their head. Which made little sense to her, considering how much the king had bragged about him being here in this fight. He had to be here. That was her entire plan.

A man reached the bottom of her podium, wrapped his arms around it, and started to climb. Astrid's breath caught in her lungs. What was she to do? He couldn't catch her. She refused to go with him. If she kicked him when he finally made it to her, would that be considered tampering? Would the king simply choose who she went with?

The ground rumbled as another door opened. This one was held by chains, and everyone in the arena froze as they looked at the massive door. Fog rolled out of it, as though it was so cold that the air touching the heat in the arena changed form.

And then he emerged. Face creased with rage, head down and horns first, like the Bull they had named him. He came into the arena seeking a fight. His head connected with the first man near him, then his hands found another.

She turned her face away from the carnage as the Bull ripped the man's head from his shoulders. So easily. He'd just twisted that man's skull and popped it off. Though his biceps had bulged and his body had appeared to show some strain, it had been far too easy for him to do.

The man at the bottom of her podium struggled to get higher. He climbed frantically, an expression on his face that was close to adoration. She could barely make out the babbling noises he was making.

"Priestess! Look at me. Cast your gaze upon the unworthy."

A fanatic, then. She'd always known there were some, but she'd never had to suffer through the attentions of one before.

The man with the axe approached the Bull, and she wondered if he was going to get to her in time. But then the troll's gaze flicked to her. His shoulders squared, and she swore she watched a huff of breath leave his nostrils before he started fighting in earnest.

Men flew into the air wherever he walked. Like he was grabbing them and just tossing them away from him rather than fighting. He was wading through countless soldiers, men who had fought for ages in this arena, all because of her.

Why did that make her heart beat so quickly? Was it fear?

She didn't think she was afraid of him. Of all the men here, she didn't believe he would do anything to harm her. And even if he did, she was prepared to do whatever it took to get her sister back. This troll would want his freedom just as much as anyone else. But he was her leverage. He was the man who would get her sister back to her, back to the life they should have had for all these years.

Breath tickled her feet. She looked down to see the frantic man had successfully made it up the pole, and was now trying to figure out how to get onto the podium with her.

She would not make room.

"Priestess!" he called out, his breath yet again fanning across her feet. "I have made it to you."

He didn't have long to look at her. A massive, green clawed hand landed on his back and ripped him off the pole. He screamed before he landed on the ground and fell silent, either stunned or dead. She didn't know.

Now she was staring down into the Bull's harsh features and wondering what she was supposed to do. Go with him? Of course. But there were men fighting all behind him. Men fighting…

Trolls, she realized.

The trolls were surrounding him. With their backs to her, they were fighting the humans off so he could stand unencumbered and look up at her.

"The king said whoever can keep me in the arena can keep me for good," she called down to him. "Do you think that person is you, Bull?"

She wondered if her voice had been amplified. It seemed there was an answering gasp that echoed among the watchers in the stands. As though everyone was holding their breath at the battle before them that seemed all too easy.

"I do," he rumbled, that deep voice making every hair on her arms stand straight up.

He lifted his arms like this was something they did every single day. He didn't seem to care about the carnage happening behind him, or that there was blood running down his hands and claws. He had eyes only for her.

For the first time in this entire mad plan that she'd somehow thought up, she wondered if this was the wrong thing to do. She had no idea who this troll was. Astrid had never even talked to a troll before him, and all of this had just been in her head because of a questionable letter that could very well have been a prank.

Her desperation for her sister had always been her weakness, but…

She had no choice now. He gestured for her again, and even though she was terrified, she leapt into his arms. He caught her with ease, like she weighed nothing, before turning and shouting, "Now!"

The trolls converged around them. What had once been a wide circle was now tightly knit. She was pressed against troll bodies, the stench of their sweat and the metallic bite of blood filling her nostrils as they moved her toward a wall. Closer and closer until they could spread out further and suddenly she was pressed against the worn stone.

"Stay here," came a deep rumble, before the trolls parted.

He charged out of that opening with a roar that seemed to shake the stones beneath her feet. Astrid weakly leaned against the wall, watching as he tore through the human men like they were nothing more than paper. More and more of them, countless bodies in pieces that littered the ground at his feet and bathed his entire form with blood. He looked like a monster standing there, taking the life of any person who dared come near him. Even a group of men was no challenge for the rage that poured through him.

A lean troll whose ribs protruded dangerously turned to her and said, "He's from a line of destroyers. Berserkers, you might call them."

"Is that what's happening?"

"Not even a mortal wound will stop him when he's like this." There was a lot of pride in the troll's voice, and then immediate concern. "You don't look so good."

"Do I not?" She could feel the blood draining from her face and a faint coming on. It was so much blood. She'd never seen that much blood in her life and all those dead people...

A thin, narrow face the color of yellow vomit appeared in her vision, preventing her from seeing the pile of bodies that littered the ground. "Breathe in through your nose, girl. You'll pass out if you keep holding your breath like that."

"They're all dead," she whispered.

"They are. He killed them so they wouldn't do horrible things to you." The troll tried to smile, but it looked wrong on that gaunt face. "My name's Rabbit. What's yours?"

Before she could respond, another roar echoed out of the Bull. She flinched, and in doing so gave herself a view of him.

He still had his back to her, but his arms were now at his sides. He'd thrown his head back, every muscle flexed and taut with rage. Blood poured down the muscles of his back as he raged at the ceiling. Firelight gleamed around him, turning the entire world red.

But she remembered he'd been like this before. He'd been so angry when she first walked into that room where they'd tied him up, but something about her had calmed him. It wasn't just her magic. It had been more than that.

He tilted his head back again and let out that sound once more. A screaming, echoing cry that dared anyone to come near him. Anyone at all.

As if in a dream, she walked through the gathering of trolls on shaky legs. She might have stumbled once or twice; she didn't know. Astrid refused to look at what she was stepping over. But then she reached up and pressed a hand to his blood-slicked arm. Just a single touch, and something that might have ended with him turning on her.

But then his arm shuddered in a ripple of muscle like touching the hide of a horse before he looked down at her and seemed to ease.

The Bull gave her a nod before he pierced the king with his gaze. "I will take this one!" he shouted.

And she thought it might have been the first time anyone in the arena had heard him speak. There were murmurs from the crowd, and the king appeared angry as well.

Until he replied, "Then take her, Bull. We've all been waiting to see what you do with a prize like that."

Chapter 6

What had the king said?

Bjorn stared up at the man he knew was evil to his core, but it was still hard to believe that he'd heard him right. They'd been waiting to see what he would do with a prize? He knew what the others did. He was forced to listen to it, night after night, while he was in his own cell. He knew what the warriors who were given women did to purge themselves of the darkness that hid within them.

But he had never done that. And everyone in this arena likely knew. If the rumors among the warriors were that he killed women, then it would likely get out to the rest of the kingdom, too.

So, the king wanted this priestess dead. Why? Bjorn could only imagine she had done something to anger the man, but now he wanted to know what it was.

He stood there, covered in blood, glaring up at the king who dared order him around. Some madness welled up inside him because all he could think to say was, "You are not my king. I do not take orders from you."

Even a few of the trolls hissed out sounds of warning. It wasn't the safest thing to say. He heard the danger in it too. But it was the right thing to say. This man did not get to order him to perform just because he was a king.

The man who loomed over them all smiled, but it was a slow, menacing look. "You believe you have the right to say no to me? You? Look around yourself, troll. If I wanted you dead, then I could have you killed this instant."

"Then who would fight for you?" Bjorn knew better than to test King James. His next fight would be so much worse than he had ever experienced, but it was worth it for this moment.

A small hand on his back reminded him that he wasn't standing alone. There was a gem of a woman, a golden creature who, for some reason, had ended up in this pit with him. And she was the one who murmured, "Whatever he asks us to do, we should do it."

"I will not."

"I need to make it out of here alive." Those fingers flexed against his spine. "And if that requires whatever King James asks, then that is what I will do."

Damn it, she was right. But he wasn't going to kill her, no matter how much they wanted to watch that. Glaring at the king, he stood there and waited for King James to make his move.

The king merely spread his arms wide. "Did the priestess talk some sense into you?"

"I will not kill her."

The priestess sucked in a harsh breath. Perhaps she hadn't been aware of what King James was suggesting. Maybe she didn't know the rumors about him after all, and something in him unraveled. A knot that had been tied so tightly, wondering what kind of woman would choose to side with a killer.

King James chuckled, and the sound echoed through the silent arena as though it had been amplified by magic. "That's fine. Fuck or fight, I don't care what you do. But all these people came here for a show, troll, and you're going to give them one!"

Bjorn didn't know which was worse. This woman would likely prefer death than to have his hands on her. She should. He had killed more people with these hands than she could count. He would continue to kill people for as long as he was lost in this labyrinth as well.

Dirty hands shouldn't touch pretty things.

He turned to her, his mind spinning with how to get them out of this situation. But he couldn't think through the red rage that still tinged his vision. Bjorn was built to fight. That was who his father was, and who he had become in this labyrinth. He knew how to get out of situations with his fists and his horns, not with... with...

Rabbit's voice broke through his thoughts. "Do what I tell you, and I think we'll all get out of this alive."

"Rabbit," he hissed. "Stay out of this."

"Stop talking and turn toward the woman, you fucking nitwit."

The hissed words were clearly said through lips that weren't moving. Some of the words were lisped, harder to say around their tusks. He was speaking in the common tongue, though, likely for the woman to understand what they were saying.

Body stiff with displeasure, Bjorn turned toward her and froze. She was blinding.

A smear of blood had splattered across her cheek at some point during the battle. Her perfect hair was still smooth as silk, not a single strand daring to go against the rest. Her crystal blue eyes looked up at him with so much trust, and she shouldn't trust a troll like him. He was unpredictable. Even now, his hands were shaking as he stood in front of her, trying to pretend this wasn't happening to either of them.

Rabbit whispered, "Touch her, for the love of all the gods. Make it seem like you're going to do what King James told you to do."

"I will not hurt her," he growled.

"No one is expecting you to. Just touch her for a few seconds." Then Rabbit seemed to hesitate before adding, "If the lady doesn't mind."

A peculiar expression traveled across her face. It was a bit like surprise, but he couldn't guess at what she was surprised about. Maybe it was that they'd asked. Maybe she assumed they would be as animalistic as her own people.

She nodded demurely and said, "Whatever we must do. You have my permission to touch me, Bull."

He hated her calling him that. Hated it deep to the marrow of his bones. He couldn't stop a word from blurting out of his mouth.

"Bjorn," he said as he haltingly stepped toward her.

"Your name?" she asked, again in that almost pristine voice that shook ever so slightly. "I'm Astrid."

He nodded and then reached for her. Damn it, his hand was too big to touch her. He could have palmed her entire head in his hand if he wished, and there wasn't a safe place for him to lay his hand without ruining her dress. Bjorn had forgotten that he was coated in the blood of her kind.

So instead of grabbing her like Rabbit likely wanted him to do, he ran a trembling claw down the line of missing beads over her hip. He stepped ever closer, until a breath would have pressed their chests together, and something in him yearned.

He wanted to touch those beads. He desperately needed to graze his finger along that line of exposed flesh that he knew would be soft and velvety. For once in so many years, he wanted to know what something delicate felt like.

His talon scraped along the sheer fabric underneath, but Bjorn had long ago forgotten how to be gentle. He was horrified to see his claw had left a red mark in its wake, and there was nothing he could say that would excuse such a touch. She deserved better. She shouldn't have to subject herself to the vile touch of a man like him.

Except... she grabbed onto his hand and pulled him a little closer to her.

"I think I have an idea of what your friend Rabbit is suggesting," she murmured as she stepped so close he could smell the mint on her breath. "But I do believe we'll have to be much closer for it to work."

"She's got the right idea," Rabbit said, before he lunged in front of the crowd of trolls. "High king! Trolls do not do this in front of the eyes of so many."

"He will do it if he wishes to live," King James shouted back.

"I believe we can still save the honor of this warrior and woman! May I suggest you shall hear only the sounds of their pleasure rather than watching? It will keep our people... happier." Rabbit bowed low and swung out a dramatic arm.

The sounds? What the fuck was Rabbit going on about? Bjorn wasn't going to fuck her in front of all of these humans, and he certainly wasn't going to put on a show for them all. This was wrong. This was what evil people did, and even though he had been a murderer for years now, he had never considered himself evil.

But the priestess, she seemed to understand the plan. She called out, "The order of priestesses forbids sexual acts! I will not have my honor destroyed by being seen doing this. You would be dishonoring not only me, but my entire sisterhood."

Murmurs erupted throughout the crowd. It seemed there were many who agreed with her. They wanted her honor affected. They wanted her torn down. But they did not wish to see it happen before their own eyes. Typical.

So many of these people wanted the outcome of ruin, but they only wanted to see the aftermath.

The king seemed to think about this before he finally nodded and waved a hand, as though that was all that was required in this moment. With a wave of a hand, a woman's life was ruined.

"Thank you, oh marvelous king," Rabbit called out, before whirling upon them. "Trolls. Hide them."

Suddenly, a wall of trolls surrounded the two of them, facing inward. They all took the order very seriously, pressing their bodies so close together that he didn't think anyone would have seen through the wall of flesh. A hand pressed against his shoulder, shoving him down onto his knees so the trolls could bend over them as well, preventing anyone in the highest seats from seeing what happened.

His people, at risk to their own lives, created a bubble of safety with their bodies. The priestess was crouched on the opposite side, looking up into troll faces that were likely terrifying to see. Most of these men and women were covered in blood and mud. They were multicolored, with tusks that arched up from their faces. Many of them were splattered with not only blood, but organs and meat that hung from their teeth.

They had fought hard and long. They deserved rest after what they had done, and had every reason not to help him, but... they did.

For Bjorn.

For a woman they did not know.

A spark in his chest burst to life, brighter than he had ever felt. This was what his people stood for. This was why he had loved them fiercely and never fallen into madness like he so easily could have.

Rabbit wrestled his way through the group, his yellow face appearing through the folds of skin and muscle. "Well? Make it sound believable!"

What the fuck was he going on about now? Bjorn was having a hard time keeping up with this, but maybe it was the rage that was still making his fingers shake with a need to tear the king's head off his body.

"Oh!" Astrid said, her face turning scarlet. "I don't know how to make it sound that loud."

One of the female trolls next to her snorted. "Have you ever eaten whipped cream?"

"Like... milk beaten until it's frothy?"

"With sugar mixed in."

"Right, yes, of course I have."

"Over strawberries?" The troll woman's eyes went a little glassy at the thought, and Bjorn hated that she'd been kept away from something she so clearly loved.

The priestess opened her mouth, closed it, and then nodded. "Understood. That's easy enough."

She settled onto her knees. She looked very much like she was about to pray, with her bottom resting against her feet and her hands neatly settled onto her thighs. Even smeared in mud and blood as she was, he understood why they called her priestess. She looked like she was made of starlight, a being sent by the gods themselves for him to remember that he did not deserve to touch perfection.

Then the priestess let out the loudest, most ungodly moan he had ever heard in his life.

His mouth dropped open at the pure pleasure that seemingly ripped out of her. It was a moan unlike anything he'd ever heard. Although there were perhaps sparks of memory where he knew that was the correct sound for a woman to make, not the screams or cries for mercy that he heard echoing down the cell halls.

He was staring. Most of the men were as she closed her eyes for concentration and did it again.

Bjorn was suddenly very, very uncomfortable.

Until Rabbit hit him over the back of the head and hissed, "Now it's your turn! No one's going to believe you're just silent through the whole thing. You're damn loud killing people, you might as well be loud here too."

But he didn't... He didn't know how to do that. He had no memory of pleasure, only pain. And it felt wrong to make sounds of pain when she was making sounds like that.

Perhaps one of his brothers understood that Bjorn simply wasn't going to be able to make that noise. Another troll did it for him, groaning deep in an exaggerated fashion that was as ridiculous as it was embarrassing.

And then another troll wriggled their arm into the midst of them all and started smacking their thigh. Mimicking the sound of... of...

He was certain he turned a very deep shade of green. This was horrible. This wasn't the first impression he wanted to give her of himself or his people. When he had first seen her in that room, he'd thought she looked like the kind of woman who could become a troll wife. She was made to be decorated in jewelry that had been created with careful hands, as only trolls could do.

But now, they were pretending to fuck so a king wouldn't kill them, and this was just... all wrong.

His breathing escalated. The rage that always seemed to get him in trouble bubbled up again. He couldn't breathe with bodies so close to him. The only thing he knew to do in situations like this was to kill. His claws suddenly ached, whispering that he could get out if he wanted. All he had to do was hack and slash at these bodies, it didn't matter if they were trolls. He'd done it before. He could do it again.

But then she reached out and grabbed his clawed hand. He stared down at her pale little fingers, wrapped around his, avoiding his claws with such deft expertise. She squeezed his fingers, and he swore there wasn't even a touch of magic in her grip, but he could feel his anger melting away.

Bit by bit, she eased the fear that threatened to burst inside him. All by just being there. With him.

He stared at her, watching her lips shape around the sounds of those moans, growing faster and more frequent until they stopped. The troll making noise for him let out an answering, deep guttural sound, and then someone had to press their hand over his mouth as he chuckled afterward.

Rabbit leaned forward, running clawed hands through her hair and messing it up. "That's... No. One more thing."

Bjorn growled under his breath as Rabbit hooked a claw beneath the delicate pearls at her shoulder and snipped them. They tumbled onto the ground, little pings that were all he could focus on. He hated that they were ruining her like this. Hated that her pretty things were now broken.

Rabbit turned to him next, tugging on his loin cloth and tilting it a little bit. Then he looked at his hair and sighed. Clearly he wanted to tussle that as well, but there wasn't much worse it could get.

And then they all parted, revealing a mussed priestess who looked like she had just been unraveled by a troll. How had she made her cheeks so pink?

Oh, she was pinching them. She lifted her hands, and it looked like she was trying to cover her face so people couldn't see her, but she was pinching her cheeks so hard they were getting redder and redder.

King James started clapping, and the entire stadium applauded what they thought was the rape of a priestess.

They applauded.

Snarling, Bjorn shook his head like an animal and chuffed out a loud exhale. "Open the doors, King. We are done here."

For once, the human king didn't mind the order.

67

Chapter 7

Astrid wasn't sure what she had expected from these trolls who had spent years fighting in the labyrinth. Perhaps cruelty and enjoyment in harming others. Perhaps she had thought they enjoyed killing, as so many warriors ended up doing. But the trolls had helped her. They'd helped each other as well.

The humans? The remaining few alive were all knotted together in little groups. They watched her with hungry eyes, but she was no longer worried that they were a threat.

The troll dripping in blood beside her certainly made it far more difficult for those humans to lay a finger on her.

Clutching the threads that held her dress together at her shoulder, she kept herself covered while the doors opened. It seemed the warriors knew what to do as they turned as one and trudged out of the arena. Clearly, they were tired. It was like all of a sudden the fight just drained out of them. Shoulders hunched, energy gone, they moved listlessly through the open doors.

This was the part she had never seen from above. No one even looked at the arena after the fight was over. Those watching all turned to each other, talking as they always did about work or politics or new marriages. She hadn't ever looked to see what happened with the bodies, or noticed that there were people coming out of the doors as well. Workers who were...

She gagged, turning her face away from the carnage as she realized those people were here to drag the bodies away. They looped their hands under armpits or gathered up lost limbs and just walked off with them.

"Do not look," Bjorn said. He even lifted a massive hand and covered her face so she wouldn't be able to see what they were doing.

But then all she could focus on was the blood coating his fingers that was starting to dry. Astrid tried to look anywhere else, but then she looked down at herself and saw all the red that stained her dress. Splatters of it had sprayed up during the fight or dripped off the trolls that had been looming over her.

Her head swam. Sparks floated in her vision, making it difficult for her to see what was around her. So much blood. So much pain. The injuries that were in this room were all mortal, it seemed, and many of them were caused by the troll she had tied herself to.

This was dangerous. Far more dangerous than she had thought.

He gestured for her to follow him, nodding toward a door that led into darkness. Astrid knew she didn't have a choice. She'd trained her entire life not to fall apart like this, and that training was what she drew around herself like a veil.

She paused only when he reached for the mask covering her face and gently nudged it up over her nose. When had that fallen? She didn't remember. Perhaps when she'd been making a fool of herself, moaning like a harlot.

"Hide your face, Priestess," he said. "For a little while longer."

Following him into the pitch black was horrible. Her heart beat so fast she thought she was going to pass out. Her legs were shaking, and she knew that wasn't a good sign. What would happen if she hit the dirt? Would those workers gather her up with the rest of the dead bodies, uncaring that she was still alive?

For a moment, she regretted this decision. But there was no going back to her old life. She had been so rash in thinking this was the right thing to do. Astrid knew better than to make decisions like this without thinking. She was the one who always took her time to ensure that every plan would work out, no matter the outcome. But in this, she had rushed right in.

Berating herself didn't help. Especially walking by the rooms still full of noblemen. Lord Tolly stood very close to the bars, his face nearly white with emotion as he watched her stride past. She could feel his gaze on her face as she held her head up high and walked with the trolls and bloodied men, all the warriors trying hard not to bump into each other.

The guards led the prisoners to the doors, but she did not go into the one she had originally left. Instead, the guard out front just gave her a little shake of his head and then pointed for her to go with Bjorn.

The troll didn't even look at her. She had to follow the silhouette of horns ahead of her as they meandered through what felt like a second labyrinth before he finally stopped. The guard pulled his cell open, and then she entered the domain of the Bull.

It was hard not to shudder. Or maybe that was just the chill in the air. She wore barely anything to keep her warm, and last night she had been so terrified, she hadn't been thinking about how cold she was. But now, she couldn't stop shivering.

Wrapping her arms around herself, she noted the single cot, the threadbare blanket on top, a cup in the corner, and a bucket at the opposite end. Quite a life she was meant to live here.

The door with the bars beckoned. She immediately went to the window, looking out into the hallway and praying that there would be a view of anything useful. Keys. A marking. A way for her to get her bearings because she had no idea where they were.

There was nothing but the same view as the other cell. Doors that were endless as they traveled down the hall, and guards that stood at attention.

A pale face appeared in the opposite cell. A man who looked at her with pity in his eyes and cruelty on his lips. "What a sad thing that a creature like him won you. You know that he's known for killing his prizes, don't you?"

She stared at him, saying nothing. A man like this didn't deserve her attention, but it was hard to ignore him.

"I've heard them every time he wins a fight. The women beg and plead, but he doesn't listen to them. You hear them shrieking and crying, then a quick snap and it's all over with." The man's hand reached through the bars of the window and pointed at her. "You're next."

Warmth settled over Astrid's shoulders. She flinched back from the window, grabbing onto the blanket that Bjorn had settled over her shoulders. He shook his head at her, then retreated to the back of the room. "Don't listen to him."

"Is it true?"

He stared at her, those eyes reflecting the meager light from outside of the room before he lifted one shoulder. Crouched as he was, with his back pressed against the wall, he appeared to be some creature out of a nightmare. Like a warped shadow she would see hunched there after waking from a nightmare.

She was frozen where she was. Unsure how to proceed now that she was not only unsafe but also in his domain.

"Then what does he speak of?"

"The women in here…" He hesitated before continuing. "Life is not good for those who are given to people like me. They beg. I give them what they want."

"They begged you to die?" She needed to be clear about this. She needed to know that those women had asked to be killed, and he'd just…

If she wasn't careful, she was going to vomit. Astrid hadn't eaten or drank anything in the better part of a day, and she'd be lucky if she could force anything out of her body at all. She needed to rest. Just for a few hours. Uninterrupted sleep would help her think, but she wasn't sure she would ever get that in this place.

"They asked for a way out," he murmured. "I gave it to them."

There it was. The entire world tipped over until she had to grope for the cot and sit down heavily. The blanket slipped off her shoulder and pooled in her lap as she stared down at her shaking hands. She could feel how pale her face must've been, how little blood was in any of her appendages because he just admitted to killing many women.

Women like her. They'd been looking for a way out of this labyrinth, just like she was going to ask of him, and instead, he had killed them.

She really had made a foolish mistake in trusting him. He was a killer, and she had known this before she had ever thought of this plan. Everyone in this place had long ago lost what made them men and women. They were animals now, through and through.

He moved slowly. Like he didn't want to startle her, not just that he didn't want to catch her attention. He reached for the cup in the corner, precariously placed in a strange way, until she heard the slosh of water as he lifted it.

He shuffled a little closer, and she marveled at his posture. His shoulders were curved in, and he kept himself somehow lower than her, even with the massive horns on his head. He looked at the ground, not her, as he held out the cup for her to take.

"Why are you giving me this?" she asked, although she took the water because she desperately needed it.

There wasn't much in the cup. Just enough for three mouthfuls, most likely. She sipped as much as she dared before handing the cup to him.

He shook his head, then tried to give it back. "Drink, Priestess."

"You need water as well."

"Not as much as you."

"You were the one who fought off countless men for an evening with me." She swallowed. "More than an evening, I suppose. From what the guard said, I am yours now."

Bjorn seemed uncomfortable with that. He shuffled where he was, the muscles of his shoulders bunching and releasing before he set the cup down on the ground by her foot and retreated back to his corner.

His movements were awkward, so very inhuman but also unlike the trolls she had seen before. Even now, he tapped his head with a fist right below his horns and said, "People can't own people. I remember that much."

She was about to argue that the king quite literally owned all of them, but his words made her thoughts catch. "You remember? What do you mean by that?"

He shook his head, more animal than man. Anxiety seemed to

ride him so much she could see the little wavering lines of emotions pulsing out of his body. There were lines of tension around his mouth. His brows were drawn down, and his movements were still odd. Twitchy, even.

She wanted to use her magic to peek inside his head. She didn't need to know what he was thinking or how to fully manipulate him, but this was a different version of the Bull than she knew. The man she had seen in the arena was terrifying, bloodthirsty, capable of killing anything and everything in front of him.

This man crouched in a corner, desperately trying to make himself seem smaller, was not the Bull. Perhaps who she was seeing right now was... Bjorn.

If she was going to get anywhere with this, she would need to confirm if there were trolls looking for him. Or, at the very least, if there was a way for him to know if her sister was with the others.

Perhaps now wasn't the best time. But she'd already taken the leap into being locked in this dungeon. She could at the very least tell him why she'd done it.

He had killed for her, after all.

Removing her mask, she reached down for the cup of water, noting that it was dented many times over. She sipped again, and the muscles on his shoulders seemed to release. As though the mere act of her accepting his care was important.

"I do not know your culture or your people," she said. "If I do something wrong, or if I somehow insult you, I need you to tell me."

He nodded. "My memory is not what it once was. But I know that a good troll takes care of women before himself and that a priestess's needs are far more important than my own."

What a strange way to say that. "Do you have priestesses where you come from?"

He nodded. "We do."

A voice came through the wall, startling her so much she almost dropped the cup. "They're terrifying."

Bjorn reacted as if someone had slammed open the door. One moment he was in the back corner and the next, he'd launched himself at the cot. She froze, uncertain if she'd done something wrong, only to realize he wasn't coming for her at all. He had put himself between her and the wall, his teeth bared and a snarl ripping out of his throat.

Was he protecting her? From someone on the other side of the wall?

"Hush," the voice said, and she realized it had to be the strange yellow troll who had come up with the plan that had gotten them out of whatever the king had wanted from them. "It's not like I can ignore you."

Bjorn seemed to deflate a bit, but there was still rage running through his body. In this small space, it was so much harder for her to be brave. A voice in her head told her to place her hand on that rippling back. She could convince him to relax beneath her, though. But then another voice, one much louder, shouted that she needed to keep herself safe.

So Astrid shifted away from him. She gave him enough space that if he was going to explode again, then she wouldn't be caught in the crossfire.

He didn't. Bjorn pulled himself back together, piece by visible piece. She watched him as he struggled to get himself under control. But then he looked over his shoulder at her. His gaze swept from the top of her head down to the bottom of her feet, and she had the distinct feeling he was measuring to make sure that she was all right.

Then he grunted. With slow movements, he pulled the blanket up over her shoulders again and then retreated to his corner.

"I, uh…" She tucked the blanket around her shoulders a little tighter. "I didn't just end up here. I received a letter from, um…"

She hadn't struggled to speak like this in such a long time. She had to just blurt the damn sentence out.

"I was contacted by who I believe to be trolls that know you. They said you need help to get out of this place, and that if I do, they'll return my sister to me." Her heart stuck in her throat. "My sister's name is Rose. I had hoped that maybe… maybe you would know her. Or know if she was really with them."

He stared at her, his eerie eyes glowing in the dark. "You sacrificed yourself to find out if I knew your sister?"

"I want to know if the letter is true."

"You could have just asked when you saw me hanging from the ceiling. There was no need to come here." There was a hint of anger in his voice, as though he was upset with her.

"I had no other choice. I need to get my sister back, and if that means helping you escape from here, then that's what I'm going to do. All I'm asking is if you know if it's true that she is with the trolls." She wanted to pace, but there was no room here.

He stayed where he was, at least. Giving her all the room she needed to breathe. "She's with the trolls who escaped from here. Your sister was in the labyrinth with the rest of us. She was one of the women gifted to the warriors who won. She was never gifted to me."

Astrid's heart shattered.

She'd known Rose had been taken somewhere. She hadn't realized her sister had been right under her nose all this time.

If she'd known, she could have saved her. Rose had been so close.

She might have even seen Astrid in the stands if she looked through her cell or... or...

Astrid pressed her hands to her suddenly hot face. "She was so close this whole time."

"There is no way out of this labyrinth now," Bjorn said. His gaze caught on her face, as though he was seeking a way to ease her torment, but that didn't help at all. "I gave your sister the last way out. If the trolls asked for your help, it is because they are going to try to come for us. If they succeed, we will leave. If they do not, then we will all die here."

She needed a moment. This was wrong. None of this was going as she had thought it would go, and Astrid was never wrong.

Until now. Until...

"Sleep, priestess," his deep voice rumbled. "Tomorrow will be a better day."

She rolled onto her side on the cot and tugged the blanket over her head. Maybe tomorrow would be better.

But she doubted it.

Chapter 8

Bjorn's memory was foggy at best. He used to be a good man. He knew that. He'd seen so much of his life in his memories, replaying them in his darkest hours there, that it almost felt as though they weren't his memories at all. Ten years. Or more. That was how long he'd been in this nightmarish place and, unfortunately, that had whittled away at whatever sanity he'd once had.

Crouched in the darkness, he stared at her. His hands twitched every now and then, but that was the only part of him that could move. Not even his eyes.

Astrid had fallen asleep far too easily in a place like this. It made his stomach twist with fear and his heart race. This woman should have known how dangerous it was to rest in the labyrinth. Someone would notice that she was weak. Someone would see that she was an easy target.

He'd keep her safe. Keeping women safe was one of the few things he remembered. Troll men were tasked with ensuring their women were not attacked by humans or anyone else. Their job was not to provide, but to be a shield between all they loved and all who would take that from them.

But his mind had fractured long ago. Those memories, whether his or not, had faded. He knew that he was expected to care for her, but he did not know how to do so. Human women were different. They weren't trolls. She clearly had no way to protect herself, and he didn't even have a way to clothe her and hide the skin revealed by the dress that continually fell off her shoulder now.

So delicate.

So breakable.

And a voice whispered in his head that it was better if he did the breaking. The same voice that told him the women who'd begged for their freedom into the afterlife could only be helped by him. It was a darkness that existed inside him now, bred and conditioned by the never-ending drip of water that slithered down the walls of his cage and the echoing howls of wounded men that he had cut up and torn apart.

"Bull?" Rabbit asked, his voice quietly floating through the wall.

"What?"

"Is she still sleeping?"

It was hard to tell. His eyes hadn't moved from her small form underneath the blanket, but her breathing hadn't yet changed. It was slow and even, deep as if she were in her dreams. Sometimes she shifted, and one of the last times that movement had dragged the blanket halfway down her head. Golden hair spilled off her pillow and hung off the edge of the cot.

"That or dead," he replied.

"Let's hope she's still alive. You just won her, after all." A shifting could be heard through the wall, as though Rabbit was getting closer.

"Keep her fed. Keep her watered. Keep her warm. That's all humans need, really."

"Why are you telling me this?"

There was a long moment of quiet. He wasn't sure if Rabbit was trying to get his own bearings, or if something was happening in that room. That was always the question. No one knew when the guards would enter their cells, or what would happen if they did. Their lives were full of uncertainty and hardship without knowing how or if anyone of them would survive.

Bjorn did his best not to think about it. He didn't want to make attachments that would fall apart if he thought too hard about them. He didn't want to believe that his people were dying around him.

This prison had become somewhat of a liminal space for him. Nothing was real. That was how he survived.

Shifting a little closer to her, he reached out a slow, shaking hand and gently brushed a claw through the tangled, golden waterfall of her hair. It felt soft against the pad of his finger. Which... No, it wasn't right. Couldn't be right. It was a tangled mess and therefore, should have been snarled like his own hair. It couldn't be soft. Not like the silk he'd once touched when a woman walked by him as he was hanging from the ceiling.

Rabbit's voice came through the wall again, quiet and lulling as though he knew what Bjorn was doing. "They are delicate creatures, humans. Sometimes they are hard to manage, but from what I've seen, their females are far more breakable."

"Why does it feel like you're warning me to be good?"

There was another shifting sound from inside the cell beside him. "She's a priestess. We have to care for them even more than the others. A priestess sees the future, you know."

He didn't know if the human priestesses were the same as theirs. In the troll realm, women like her were revered. He still remembered the blood witches he'd met, the bone readers, all women who had unnatural talents that should have seen into his future and predicted this.

Maybe they had. Maybe he still remembered his mother's whispered fear to his father. "His path is wrong," she'd said all those years ago. "Twisted. It should be a straight line."

His father had taken him away after that conversation. Yes, that was what had happened. He'd thought perhaps his father had wanted to train him all on his own, but that wasn't how it had gone. His mother had been rambling about twisted paths and how they needed to alter his future. She'd wanted Bjorn to stay with her in the Outlands.

"The Outlands," he murmured, testing the word on his tongue. He hadn't thought about that place in ages. But now that he was thinking of it, he couldn't stop.

The valleys were beyond the mountain. Far from Trollveggen, which the humans knew about. They were so far away that no human could ever traverse their lands, and that was where there were other trolls. Wild trolls. Those of his people who refused to be trapped beneath rock and stone, even though it was safer for them to do so.

The people who were more connected to their roots of mud, and fur, and scales. Hardier folk who cared little for the calm and safety of the mountain home and instead, lived beneath the sun.

"The Outlands?" The voice that broke through his memory was soft and quiet.

He looked down to see her eyes had opened, and she'd tugged the blanket down to her chin. He was caught in that icy gaze, unable to think past the terror of what that gaze did to him.

"You look so much like the princess," he said. The words were ripped out of him, a fear that burned in his chest because she did. She looked like the worst extension of the king, and a woman who had tormented many of the prisoners.

She blinked up at him. "As I said, that is by design. The king himself picks those of us who are to become priestesses. He chooses us out of a group of girls who have been abandoned by their families. I am a priestess because he made me one, or at least, deemed me worthy to become one."

That was not how it worked in troll culture. Some were born with talents that others did not have.

Frowning, he stared down at her. "Your power should have been enough to encourage training. Your people do not allow talent like yours to build on its own?"

"I don't have much talent, really. I just... pull." She blinked up at him. "My apologies, Bjorn, but you are looming over me, and it is not very comfortable. Would you mind taking a step back?"

It was a very reasonable request, but said in such a way that made him think she'd practiced it. Or perhaps that she had a lot of practice asking people to give her space in a way that wouldn't anger them.

It made rage burn in his belly. She deserved to not have to ask anyone for space. She deserved so much more than what it seemed like she had gotten.

Bjorn shifted back to his corner, slowly crawling on his knuckles so he wouldn't look quite so large. He didn't want to frighten this woman, who had more bravery in her pinky than most human men.

She'd come here after all. How many of her people had faced him in the labyrinth and turned white with fear? How many of her kind had tried to flee when they realized he was running toward them?

But she had stood there, waiting for him to reach her. Even perhaps begging him to reach her with her wide eyes and smooth features.

No, that wasn't what had happened. He shook his head to clear the thoughts, and then froze when she shifted.

He watched her as she sat up on the cot, and the blanket fell to her lap. Those pretty pearls had scattered even more while she'd slept. Perhaps the tension hadn't helped, because more strands had broken. As she moved, they popped, sending cascading pearls onto the floor that scattered in his direction.

She caught the dress before it fell with the blanket, but he watched her features turn scarlet. She moved her face to the side and grimaced before her hands flew to her face.

Was she looking for the mask? Of course she was. She'd been wearing it every time he had seen her, and obviously that was a huge part of who she was. The mask helped hide her reactions when they might be inappropriate.

He reached for it where it had fallen onto the floor at the same time she did. Their hands bumped against each other, and the zing of electricity that moved up his arm made him wince. He didn't want to feel that way. It wasn't appropriate to feel anything for a priestess, and certainly not for one like her.

He flinched away from her touch and moved back to his corner, where he should have been for a while now. Staring at her, he watched as she brushed some of the dirt off her mask before letting it fall into her lap. It, like the rest of her outfit, was very broken.

"I barely slept," she said. "All I could think about was that my sister was here the whole time, and I didn't know. We might have been in the same room together. All it would have taken was… was…"

He reached for her. It was a stupid thought. Bjorn hadn't tried to comfort anyone in years. Although he had attempted to comfort Ragnar's troll wife when she'd been in this same cell and he thought maybe he had helped her.

First, his hand found her thin fingers. His massive paw enveloped hers, and he gently squeezed in a way that he hoped wouldn't hurt her. "You could not have known she was here. And getting her out would have been impossible."

He watched her expression harden. "Nothing is impossible for a priestess. I had the favor of a lord. I could have done anything I wanted, and I would have gotten it."

"I have had the favor of a lord. I was sponsored by one of them when I first came here. They did nothing to help me." He released her hands and reached for the blanket in her lap. She stiffened, and he wondered if she was afraid he would take it from her.

But he had no interest in doing so. Bjorn pulled it off her lap, and then gently draped it around her shoulders instead. At least now she wouldn't need to hold her dress at her shoulders, and he would not see anything she didn't want him to see.

Warmth, Rabbit had said. Humans needed to be warm, and they needed water and food. He didn't have any food here, but he did have water.

Moving back to his corner, Bjorn grabbed the water container and brought it back to her. "Here. Drink this. There won't be much in such a short amount of time, but there will be enough for you."

"Don't you need to drink?"

He shook his head.

It was a lie, of course. He needed some of the water for himself, especially if he was going to fight. But he didn't want to take the water from her. He'd figure out another way to get it. Perhaps he would get lucky in his next fight and someone would have a weapon that looked similar to a cup. He could steal it and bring it back to his room, like he'd done with the cup she drank out of. The opposite corner worked for gathering water as well. It was just slower.

She finished, her throat working in a swallow before looking at him. "You don't have to move like that while I'm in here, you know. You can stand."

"The previous women found my height frightening."

She winced. "The previous women were likely frightened for many reasons, Bjorn. I have seen your kind before. Your mere existence does not intimidate me."

He thought this was a terrible idea, but she was telling him to stand, and he hadn't done so for hours. So he stood.

As his height continued to go up, and up, and up, he watched as the blood drained out of her features. One of the women who had been in her same position told him that the humans feared creatures with horns. She called them demons. Monstrous beings that took souls in the middle of the night and who hunted humans down whenever they could.

He could see the same thought on Astrid's expression. The woman was so pale, he thought she might pass out. Instead, she stared up at him, swallowed, and then held out the cup for him to take.

"Thank you for taking care of me, Bjorn." The words were said so calmly, he wondered how she was so good at lying.

"You are welcome, Priestess." He bowed his head, even though he knew that would bring his horns closer to her. Perhaps she wouldn't be so frightened of him if she could see them up close.

They weren't sharp or pointed. His horns were more like a ram's. Blunted, rounded, smooth to the touch. They were good for battering through things, and that was all.

He was suddenly very aware of how thin he was. How his ribs showed and how there was dirt smeared across his body and in places he wasn't proud of. He knew without a doubt that he looked like a monster. But he didn't want to look like a monster. Not to her.

Some part of him remembered to be ashamed. There was so much more to being a good troll warrior than just what he was offering here. But he couldn't remember what the right thing to do was.

The door without a window banged loudly. An armored fist hit it ten times before falling into silence.

He watched as she flinched with each sound, drawing deeper and deeper into herself before suddenly all that fear was wiped clean. As if she had never been afraid, she lifted the mask to her face, and turned her attention cooly toward the door.

"Are you going to answer that?" she asked, barely even there in the words.

"There is no choice but to answer it," he murmured as the door banged open.

The guard on the other side peered into the shadows of the room, and then appeared surprised to see her sitting there with a blanket around her shoulders. The man didn't acknowledge Astrid, though. He looked at Bjorn and blurted, "You decided to keep this one?"

Bjorn hunched his shoulders and headed toward the door. "I keep all of them."

"You kill all of them," the guard snorted, before waving at Astrid. "Looks like you're the lucky one, Priestess."

He didn't think, just reacted. He reached forward and slammed the guard into the wall. The man wheezed, and Bjorn leaned his weight even more into his hand that compressed the man's ribs. It would be easy to crack them. So easy to shatter those thin bones even through the armor the guard wore.

With a snarl on his lips and tusks close enough to graze the guard's face, he snarled, "You gave her to me. Don't look at her. Don't talk to her."

The guard nodded frantically, but he would have done that no matter what. He just wanted to live.

A blade brushed against his side, sharp enough to do damage. He looked over to his right and saw all the guards who normally brought him to the arena at the ready. They wouldn't kill him—he knew that from experience—but they would do their best to make him bleed.

Bjorn released the man and started down the hall. He didn't look back at the priestess in his room, but he didn't have to. He knew without a doubt they would leave her alone while he was gone.

Chapter 9

Y ou're certain it curves to the right?" Astrid asked, barely avoiding tapping her mouth with her dirty finger. She did that when she was thinking, but she couldn't do it now. Her hands were smeared with dirt and whatever else covered the floor of this cell.

Rabbit chuckled on the other side of the wall. "Yes, Priestess. We've all gone that way more times than I can count. We go to the right."

"So the left leads out of the labyrinth, and the right goes deeper." She shook her head and changed the lines she'd just drawn. "I could have sworn we went the opposite way."

She'd been trying to keep track of every turn they had taken to get to her cell, but it was damn near impossible. Whoever had created the labyrinth, and cells that were attached, had designed it to be difficult for even the guards to find their way around. She had seen a couple of the guards with rolled-up maps in their pockets, and she assumed those were the guards who were newer.

Of course, that led her to the point where she was. Scratching her own map on the floor with their combined memories, hers and

Rabbit's, to try to figure out the best way out of here. She backed up to the door with the window, pressing her spine against it so she could see her work.

The floor was covered with scribbles, growing larger and larger the more they both remembered. It was daunting to look at it and try to even imagine a way out. No one had managed before, and it would take quite a bit of ingenuity to get out of here.

Giving up, she tapped her finger on her cheek, where she knew she had left smudges. The mask was back on the cot, considering no one had bothered her in the hours after they'd taken Bjorn.

Rabbit was already talking before she could say a word. "They probably took you in the opposite direction. There are parts of this labyrinth that none of the prisoners have been to. I think it's fairly obvious that way will lead you where you want to go, but we have no idea after that. You'll have to improvise." He seemed almost excited by the idea.

She pressed her hand against the door behind her. "Rabbit, I don't think..."

"I know you can't bring me, Priestess. I'm just happy to think he'll be getting out. A lot of staying sane in here is just dreaming. Dreaming of what could be, the outside world, anything to keep you out of the darkness that nips at all our heels."

Astrid's heart broke even further. Being down here, hungry, dirty, thirsty, she now realized what conditions these warriors had been kept in. Some of them were bad people, at least the humans down here were. But the trolls? She knew they were stolen from the battlefields. They were the ones who'd been left behind, or who had been presumed dead but weren't.

Someone rattled their door down the hall. The cells exploded into commotion all of a sudden, shouts and cheers echoing so loudly it was hard to think. She spun, holding on to the bars of her window and peering out into the hall.

All she could see was a group of guards walking down each and every cell. They were carrying something, but she couldn't see it just yet. And it wasn't like she could hear anything other than the angry shouts of prisoners.

"Rabbit?" she called out, but no one answered her.

Instead, all she could see was the grin on the face of the man across from her. The same greasy man with missing teeth who loved to stare. Without Bjorn in the cell with her, the feeling of her skin crawling from his attention came on even stronger.

He waved at her, and she ducked away from the window until a guard's helmeted features filled the space she had just stared out of.

"Bowl?" he asked.

"I don't have a bowl."

"Then no food."

He started to move past until she shouted, "Wait!"

Apparently, some people still had pity. The guard paused, looking through her window for just a few more seconds. Astrid grabbed the cup next to her cot and raced toward him, holding it out through the bars.

He grabbed it, looked over the dented cup a bit before shrugging and then...

Oh god.

She gagged, watching as he used his bare hand to dunk the cup into a bucket of what looked like vomit before holding it back to her. "This is what food is down here, Priestess. Eat up, or starvation will kill you before your troll's lusts will."

"This isn't food," she hissed, her decorum forgotten over the chunks of... whatever it was that floated on top of that sludge.

"Troll whores get the same as the rest of the prisoners." He spat through her window, and she narrowly avoided it.

Thankfully, he didn't look beyond her into the cell. Otherwise, he might have noticed the giant map she had drawn out on the floor. Not that he would have cared. The guards here all seemed to be very certain that no prisoner could escape, despite a few of them having done so only months ago.

But that had been within the arena, and no one had ever escaped from the cells. She was going to change that.

Glaring as they walked by, she held the cup in her hands and waited until everyone quieted down. It sounded like maybe people were eating, which was... horrific. She couldn't imagine eating what was in her hands.

"Rabbit?" she tried again.

He grunted, clearly through a mouthful of food.

"What are you eating?"

"Scraps. Whatever they eat up above, they scrape the plates and leftovers into buckets for us." He made a little "ooh" sound. "I got a bone!"

Her stomach rolled at the crunching sound that came after he said that. Was he... eating the bone? It sounded like many of them were. The horrible sounds of men eating made her even more nauseous than she had been before. She couldn't even hold the cup because looking at it, smelling it, knowing that other people's mouths had touched this food made everything in her revolt.

She would go hungry. She would starve. She wasn't this desperate.

Setting it down next to the cot, Astrid crouched down in the corner where Bjorn usually was. Planting her hands over her ears, she tried to block out the sounds.

Her feet were on the cold ground. There was air in her lungs. She could breathe in deeply, but then all she could smell was that fucking food. And it did smell like food. It wasn't an unpleasant scent, and that was even more confusing. Her stomach was clenching now, desperate to eat something that wasn't leftovers from other people who didn't deserve to eat as lavishly as they did.

Panic set in. She couldn't control her heart rate, and she had always been able to do that. Her carefully cultivated control was now gone. She had nobody, was no one, and nothing she did or begged for would be given to her.

Back to the street rat.

Only good enough to be a whore.

Warm hands covered hers, and then all the sound was actually gone. There was just silence, blissful silence without the constant sound of eating that somehow slipped through her fingers.

She blinked a few times, focusing on her breathing until she looked up. Bjorn must have returned at some point, although she couldn't guess when. Crouched in front of her, wearing but a tattered loincloth to cover his lean, muscular body as he used his hands to block out the sound.

He watched her with dark eyes that saw far too much. It was like he knew she needed these few seconds of silence before she could pull herself back together again. And she did. She forced herself back to calm, even if it felt like she was kicking and screaming the whole way. Astrid rebuilt the shield she always kept up until she could be herself again.

She was the priestess who was affected by nothing. That was

who she was. That was who she had always been. If she could just get control of her emotions, then she had control of something. Her fear eased enough to be reasonable again. She was Astrid. High priestess. Capable of handling this situation just like she had the moment he'd left. She had a map on the floor. She had a plan.

Except then she looked at the ground and all of her map had been wiped away. There were footprints through the whole thing, most likely his, because they were huge and claw-tipped. She'd spent hours on it. Hours and hours of work that were now destroyed.

Breathing in deeply, she pulled her hands away from her ears, forcing his hands to drop.

"It's all right," she told herself. "I can redraw it."

He looked down at the markings on the floor and grunted. "Maps are no good."

"Maps are helpful when you're planning an escape."

"I know how to get out of the labyrinth." He stood, and once against she was faced with the looming man over her. He was massive. Far bigger than anyone she'd ever been close to, and all that glistening muscle...

Not shiny with sweat, she realized. With blood.

At her horrified expression, he glanced down at himself and winced. "Not mine."

"Not your blood?"

He shook his head, then headed toward the cot where there was that single cup of food waiting for him. Dropping down onto the edge of it, he sat heavily. As though he had weights on his shoulders that curved him forward.

He didn't reach for the cup. Instead, he just stared at her. It seemed like he did that a lot, and she wasn't sure if it was a good thing or an act that should make her nervous.

Astrid curled her legs under herself, tucking the blanket a little tighter around her shoulders before pointing at the cup. "There is food for you."

"You should eat first."

"All I have done is sit around in this cell all day. I do not need the energy." She pointed at it. "Eat."

He just slowly shook his head. Those eyes stared at her with a certainty that she knew he wouldn't accept her argument. No matter what she said, he wasn't going to eat until she did, and she just... couldn't. No matter how hard her stomach growled, she knew she was going to vomit the moment that food touched her tongue.

Rabbit's voice broke through the wall. "She doesn't want to eat it because it's their scraps. Probably looks disgusting to her. It looked disgusting to us too, once upon a time."

Bjorn's gaze seemed to sharpen. He looked at her, then at the cup, and then reached to pick it up.

She was miserable that what Rabbit had said was the truth. It really was the issue of where the food came from, who had prepared it, and how little she wanted to put that in her mouth. "I feel like the most difficult prisoner to keep," she said. "But it's been years since I ate anything that wasn't prepared for me."

There were times when she had. When she and Rose had scrounged through garbage cans to eat, but those memories were so deeply buried, she couldn't even remember reaching into bins for food that had likely been in there for a day or two. Astrid most certainly did not remember getting so sick that it took weeks for her to get better. She didn't. She didn't have those memories because they were from a different time, a different person. Now, she was a priestess. She was used to fine dining and foods that most people had never even seen in their lifetime.

The massive troll seated on the cot had started cleaning off his hands. He used the loincloth covering his lap, so she averted her eyes the moment she realized what he was doing. Why was he cleaning his hands, though?

She gave him long enough to reasonably clean the blood off, then looked back at him. He seemed to be waiting for that. He'd been staring at her again before he gestured for her to come closer to him.

"Sit with me, Priestess." That low voice was a bit of a siren call, even if she was terrified of what he was going to try to do.

"I can't eat that food," she said, moving to sit next to him and giving up on preserving the map on the floor.

He shook his head at her and then nodded over his shoulder. "Sit behind me."

"I... what?"

He stared until she did what he ordered. Did he not want her to watch him eat? That seemed... odd. Maybe trolls ate differently, though. He did have those tusks, and maybe that made eating a rather stomach-turning sight to watch.

But the moment she sat down, primly folding her hands in her lap with the blanket wrapped around her shoulders, he said, "Hold out your hand."

"Why?"

No response.

She did so, preparing herself to be sick the moment something touched her. But what he placed in her hand was... a perfect slice of tomato. Sure, it was a little soggy around the edges, but it was a perfectly round tomato slice.

"Oh." This wasn't so bad. She could eat a tomato.

Even though her mind screamed at her that it had just been in the cup, it didn't look like it had been. With a quick nibble, she could say it didn't taste like anything other than a tomato either.

Swallowing it down, she waited for her gag reflex to kick in. It didn't.

"Good?" Bjorn asked, not even looking at her. He was fiddling with the cup again, and she realized he was using his body to block the sight from her. If she wasn't looking at the food, it wasn't so bad. Not to mention, she couldn't really smell it. All she could smell was the metallic scent on him and the strange warmth of his body. He didn't smell terrible, just not like the food.

Taking a deep breath, she replied, "I suppose it wasn't so bad."

"Take this, then."

She reached out her hand, and he handed her half a carrot. Then a piece of broccoli. Three strangely savory grapes that she didn't like all that much, and a few slices of chicken breast that were rather impressively good. By the time she was done, she wasn't full in the slightest, but her stomach didn't hurt quite so much.

And then when she finally looked around the massive back that prevented her from seeing anything, she realized there wasn't much left in the cup. Just what had made it look like slop in the first place.

"Bjorn, you need to eat," she said.

He grunted, turned the cup back and slugged it down. All of it. In one big gulp, like it wasn't a big deal that there was just mashed food and the juices of other things inside of it. He just drank it down and then used his claws to clean the cup out the best he could. Without looking at her, he brought it back to the corner where water was gathered, and set it down.

"They usually bring water soon after feeding us," he murmured. "I need to rest, but if you'll get water from them, there will be enough for both of us."

She stared at him, unsure of what to say with this massive creature who had just made sure she'd eaten while he'd gotten nothing in return.

"All right," she stammered. "I'll stay awake so you can rest."

He was limping as he returned to the cot, then patiently waited while she stood. He fell down face first onto the cot, sprawled out like he hadn't a care in the world.

"Do you want..." She fingered the blanket around her shoulders before starting to pull it off.

He didn't even look at her as he replied, "Keep it. Humans need to be kept warm."

She had no idea what that meant as the troll drifted off to sleep. But she kept her eyes on the hall, just as he asked, ready to get water for them. And while she did, she made a plan.

Astrid didn't need a map to escape this place. All she needed was her wits and the troll locked in here with her.

Chapter 10

Bjorn watched the priestess as she worked on her map once again. She should've known it by heart now. She'd been in this cell with him for nearly five days, rotting away with the rest of them, and nothing had changed. The reality was that they were not getting out of here.

He had spent years figuring out the weakness in the wall that had given Ragnar and his people their escape. Bjorn knew without a doubt that that exit had been the only way to leave this place.

He knew the halls well. He was the only one who had been in here for this long. Ten years was enough to remember this labyrinth by heart. He'd played Astrid's game for multiple nights now, pointing out flaws in her plans to leave and nudging her hand when she made the mistake of turning a hall in the wrong direction on her floor map. But none of it would help.

Even if they could get out of this cell, they wouldn't be able to leave. There were too many guards. Too many chances for things to go wrong.

They were stuck here, just like he had always been. Nothing was going to change that.

"You can't go in that direction," Bjorn said, sitting on the cot and picking through the scraps they had been given for dinner. This was a rare opportunity for them to eat twice in two days.

She didn't like the look or smell of it, so he tried his best to pick out what he could find that didn't seem too mashed. Tonight was harder though, and he was going to have to figure out a way to get her to eat. She was already shaky. He'd noticed how she had to hold on to the walls when she was upright, and how pale her features got when she stood. There was something wrong with her, and he suspected it was that she wasn't eating enough.

He'd tried to make this place tolerable for her, but there was no comfort here. The cells were cold and damp. Her clothing had not been created for a place like this. Soon enough, she would beg him for release just like everyone else had done.

He wasn't sure how to feel about that. Killing any woman had always felt wrong, and especially so now that Ragnar had awakened something in him. Bjorn wanted to take care of her. The memories that had been so buried were now screaming at him that no matter what he did, he had to keep her safe. That was his job. His duty.

His honor.

Picking out a half-eaten carrot, he whittled away at the end with a claw so she wouldn't notice someone else had already bitten into it. "Not that way, either."

Astrid blew out an angry breath and glared at him. "Are you going to be helpful?"

"I am being helpful."

"You're just pointing out flaws. If you have an opinion on the best way to get out of here, why not share it?"

He speared the carrot onto the tip of his claw and held it out for her. Good enough. If she wanted to be snippy, she could eat the damn thing with someone else's teeth marks. "There is no good way to get out of here. We are trapped."

"I refuse to believe that."

Bjorn could see he'd made her angry. Her ears were bright red, and she wouldn't even look at him, which he had come to learn meant that she didn't want to deal with him at the moment. Which was fine. He didn't need her attention all the time.

He just liked it. Maybe a little more than he should.

After years and years of being alone or handed women who only feared him or begged him for death, it was nice to be around someone who treated him like a person. Even annoyance, without immediately flinching as she waited for his fists, meant more to him than she knew.

Everyone was resting at this point, although none of them knew if it was nighttime outside. He could hear it throughout the dungeon, even if she couldn't. The restful breathing. The quiet sounds of sadness that only happened during this time of their night. This was when only a few were awake, and if they were awake, they were having a moment that needed no one else's intervention.

And here his little captive was, making a map on the wall because she was so certain they would escape.

The sound of footsteps caught his attention. They were not from a guard. Those footsteps were always intentional and loud. Whoever was walking down the hall didn't want anyone to know they were here.

Bjorn turned his head toward the window on the door, keeping his gaze on the small gap that would reveal who dared walk through the dungeon while all the warriors were sleeping. A few other trolls were stirring, and he could hear them turning toward the sound as well. Even Rabbit, who usually was asleep at this time of night.

Flickering light illuminated the corridor outside their cell. Someone was walking with a torch, which was an even worse idea. There were rounds made by plenty of guards this time of night. They'd be caught if they weren't supposed to be here. Then the shadow of a person was revealed, wearing a cloak.

Astrid moved toward Bjorn, hovering by his side as she stared. So quietly it was hard for him to hear her, she whispered, "Who is that?"

The shadow stopped in front of their door, lifting the torch so it cast light into the room. His guts twisted. Were the guards coming for him, or for her? It wouldn't be the first time that he'd been taken out of this cell in the middle of the night, but now he had her to worry about as well.

Bjorn stood, nudging her behind him so that whoever this person was wouldn't see her. A low rumble started in his chest, the growl as impressive as it was terrifying. If he had to, he'd keep her right where she was. Guards or not. This cell was his domain.

Then a whispered, "Priestess?"

Astrid darted out from behind him before he could catch her. She ran to the door, wrapping her fingers around the bars and holding herself as close to the person as possible. "Lawrence?"

The hood was yanked back, revealing a young man with wide eyes. "He sent me. We have to go. Now."

"How?"

"Put this on." He handed a bundle through the doorway.

Bjorn watched as Astrid unraveled it, revealing yet another dress that was far too nice for a place like this. It was like molten silver, dripping down her arm and reflecting the torchlight like metal. But she didn't question what the man told her. Instead, she held it out to Bjorn.

When he didn't immediately take it, she hissed, "Hold this!"

He did, even though he was terrified his claws would scratch the pretty fabric and ruin it for good. Bjorn turned his attention to the door while she stripped out of her clothing, glaring at the young man who likely would have otherwise watched her. The clinking sound of her pearl dress hitting the ground tortured him, as well as the cool feeling of the dress slipping from his fingers.

The young man gulped before whispering, "Lord Tolly wished for me to tell you that he has not slept since you were traded away. He feels terrible for his part in your downfall, and simply could not stand to hear that you were still here with this beast. I am to bring you out of the labyrinth, and then it is his greatest wish that you slip away. We will tell the others that the Bull killed you."

Bjorn would never do that. Not to her. But when his gaze slid back to her, seeing that molten silver dress caressing her curves, he knew that he'd let her go. She didn't belong in a place like this. And if they had to lie and say that he had killed her, then that was what he would do.

One more death on his shoulders wouldn't surprise anyone. They were all shocked she'd lasted this long.

"It's so good of my lord to help me. He is truly an honorable man," she said.

He almost saw red. Honorable? The man had sold her into this life! There was no honor in him. It stung that she would even think of saying such a thing. Especially not to the man here to save her.

Unlike Bjorn. Who couldn't get her out of here, no matter what plan he might come up with.

He took a step back as the sound of keys rattling came from the other side of the door. This man had keys to get her out. This Lawrence could walk her right out of the labyrinth, and then she would live. There were other ways to find her sister. He was certain. She didn't actually need Bjorn. At this point, he was only holding her back.

Resolving himself to being a mere moment in her life that she would likely forget in the months to come, he stepped even farther away from the door so the man wouldn't be nervous to open it.

The door swung open, and Astrid stepped out. She looked like a goddess in this light, her dress reflecting warm tones while the rest of her was icy. She was the only person he'd ever seen who looked like that. Truly, it was a holy experience to look upon her. Bjorn committed her to memory as she grabbed the face covering that the man held out to her. The fabric was little more than a veil with a metal circle attached to it, but she settled it on her head and suddenly it was a crown with a silken sheet that only she could see out of.

"Thank you, Lawrence," she said, her voice almost simpering. "You are brave to have trusted him."

And then she punched the young man square in the face. He went down like a rock. Standing one moment, and then falling over the next. His body hit the floor with a heavy thud that echoed down the corridor, and then she reached back inside the cell.

Astrid held her hand out for him to take. "Come with me."

He wasn't sure what was happening.

"Bjorn," she said, and his name jolted through him like an electric shock. "This is our only chance. I need you to get my sister back."

Her sister. Of course, this was about her sister. For a moment he'd thought that maybe she just wanted him to come with her because she would miss him. That all of his care and effort had proven he wasn't the monster that this place had made him.

But of course it wasn't that. She needed a protector, a shield between her and this world. After all, she was a priestess. She had been delicate her entire life. Someone needed to be hard for her.

He did not take her hand. Instead, he stalked through the door and out into the hallway. Eyes darting from side to side, he took in their surroundings. The guards usually came from the right, so they would go to the left. The labyrinth had many passages that connected with each other, and if they could avoid some of the guards, then that would be best for them. He'd still kill anyone who got in their way, but the fewer people who knew they were out, the better.

Heading to the left, he left the torch where it was. He didn't need it to see.

"Wait!" Astrid hissed. "Rabbit!"

"Leave him."

"We can't just leave him here! He's been so helpful, and he saved both of us in the arena." Her tiny hands grabbed onto Bjorn's arm, trying to tug him back.

But he knew they didn't have time. Just finding the right key from that ring would take enough time for the guards to find them. His neighbor poked his hand out of the window and waved his fingers. Rabbit said nothing, but he gestured for them to go. The less commotion, the better.

He knew there would be a commotion. The moment someone in a cell recognized they were out, the floodgates were going to burst open.

Rabbit knew. He had always known that if anyone was going to get out of here, it likely wasn't him. And as much as that broke something important inside of Bjorn, he knew that Rabbit would be uninterested in him sacrificing this chance.

"Guards," Rabbit hissed. "Get going."

"We can't," Astrid said, tugging his arm again.

But the choice had already been made. He looked back one last time at the yellowed hand reaching through the bars of his cell before wrapping an arm around Astrid's waist and heading in the opposite direction. They rushed through the halls, faster and faster until he swore he could almost feel the fresh air on his face.

Until he found the first group of guards. Already he bristled, knowing that this would be a difficult fight. He had hoped not to get bloody. It was easier to carry her without worrying about dripping through the silver dress, but it would have to be done.

He put her down, readying himself for a fight. He'd have to get a weapon first. That was the safest choice. The guards were carrying their own weapons, so if he could take one…

"Gentlemen," Astrid called out, her voice a lashing whip in the darkness. "Good, I need you to direct me how to get out of this dastardly place."

"What are you doing?" Bjorn snarled, trying to grab her arm, but she stepped out of his reach and into the torchlight of the guards.

They had all turned to look at her. Too late for talking now. But she spread her hand behind her back, clearly signaling him to stay where he was.

The man in the front hesitated before saying, "Priestess. He's not allowed out of his cell."

"In this case, he is. Lady Faraway has requested an evening with him. We have the king's approval, and the beast has proved docile thus far. However, I was meant to have a contingent of guards assist me in bringing him out of the labyrinth." Astrid's voice got sharper and sharper as she spoke. "I have yet to see that provided to me. And while

I am a patient woman, the longer I am standing in these halls with the keys in my hand, the longer I am realizing this place is not safe for a priestess alone. I will be speaking to your superiors about the lack of safety for one such as myself."

The guard wasn't quite convinced yet, but a few of the others had already stood at attention. The man asked, "Who do you serve?"

"Lord Faraway, you imbecile," Astrid snapped. "Now get out of my way, or bring me to the exit."

The guards didn't even convene about the matter. They all just pointed swords at Bjorn's neck in warning and then... turned away from the cells. He was shocked. Was it going to be this easy? Really?

Astrid walked ahead of them, her hips swaying in a way that was clearly calculated. Every guard around him was distracted by her looks, by the pristine silver clinging to her beautiful body.

But then they paused, the same guard speaking up one last time. "There was a priestess in the room with him, now that I think about it..."

He could almost sense the unease that ran through the group. The realization that they had perhaps done something wrong.

Except Astrid turned toward the man and without any question in her voice stated, "Dead. He'd killed her last night, by my guess. He was eating when I arrived. Her body was mangled, neck snapped and face bloated, but I recognized her. The high priestess who served Lord Tolly was renowned among our ranks. It is a shame she had to die like that. You will not speak of her until her soul has been laid to rest."

A rumble went up, but Bjorn was just shocked at the detail she had conjured. How did she know that was how he had killed the others? How did she know that he had been horrified by the sight of their features slowly turning purple even though he knew they were already dead?

She sniffed and then pointed to the right. "That's the way out, isn't it? I can take it from here."

"We can escort you to Lord Faraway's home," the guard said.

"No." Disdain colored the word. "I have my own guards outside, thank you. They are more than capable of handling a troll."

More words were hidden in her statement. More than capable was clearly more capable. And though the surrounding guards were insulted, they dropped their weapons and let them walk up to the door that left the labyrinth and then... out.

Chapter 11

The problem was that she had no idea where to go from here. Astrid had been born in this city, and living on the streets with her sister had been one thing, but she'd never actually left the vicinity of the castle in all her time as a priestess. She'd had no reason to leave when Lord Tolly ruled one of the castle districts. He'd always had visitors come to him, never the other way around.

She closed the door of the labyrinth behind herself, sealing all those bad memories inside. She'd poke and prod at them someday, just to get the haunting images to stop, but for now she needed control.

Where were they going? She had no idea. How were they going to get food? That was also a very good question she didn't have an answer to. How were they going to get her sister back?

Her hands were trembling against the wood of the door. They never trembled. Tucking them into her sides, she curled them into fists so no one would see her weakness before turning to look at Bjorn.

He'd tilted his head back, eyes closed, just soaking in the moonlight that played along his features. Bliss, she realized. That was the expression on his face as the air cooled the sweat on his brow and tried to stir the greasy hair that tangled around his horns. Out here, she could see how poorly he'd been treated.

They had exited through a side door. It was the discreet exit, so no one would see them behind all these bushes with a stone wall behind them that extended up to the castle itself, easily fifty feet or more. But the moonlight could still play across his features, and the wind could still touch him.

The shadows cast by his ribs alone were concerning. There was a hollow above his belly as well, where his skin dipped in heavily toward his spine. But he was still massive. His muscles were still bulging as he lifted a hand to his head and smoothed his hair away from his horns. Those tangled locks needed far more than a good brushing. She'd prefer to cut it, but maybe with patience his dark hair could be saved.

As she stared, a single tear leaked out of his eye and dripped down his cheek. It left a track of clean skin in the grime that covered his face.

Her magic stretched out, brushing against his skin just to see what he was feeling. And it broke her heart to see that he was glowing with a bright white light. Hope, she realized. Hope was nearly bursting out of him.

She'd never seen anything more beautiful than him. The moonlight turned his horns and figure into a silhouette outlined by the moon. A warrior, a survivor, a man who had been through so much and came out alive.

She removed the veil on her face, feeling the wind with him. It cooled the faint sweat on her face as well. Perhaps both of them could be free from their shackles now.

They didn't have much time, though. They had to keep going before someone came to look for them. She tucked her shaking hands against her sides and resolved to take charge.

"I don't know where to go now," she whispered. "I didn't... I should have thought this far ahead."

She always thought ahead with every plan that she had ever conjured up in her mind. Why hadn't she done it this time?

Astrid had been so wrapped up in trying to get them out that maybe she hadn't really thought this would happen. Maybe some part of her had believed this was an impossible task and that no matter what she did, she was going to be stuck in that dark cell for the rest of her life.

But now they were out in the moonlight, and it all felt far too real. She was standing beside a troll. A creature who would be hunted down in this city if anyone saw him, and then they would both be thrown back into that dungeon before they had a chance to escape.

He took a deep breath, those harsh ribs flaring wide before he opened his eyes and looked at her again.

She hadn't realized his ears were so big. She hadn't really looked him over in the cell, or couldn't in the shadows. But his ears were large and pointed, and as she looked, they twitched toward some sound she couldn't hear.

"We go," he said, turning confidently away from the bushes and toward a small path that led toward the village and away from the castle.

She supposed it made sense they would go that way, but it still made her heart skip a beat.

"Where are we going?" she whispered.

"You said you don't know where to go," he rumbled. The path led downward, and she was certain it popped out in the heart of the villages that surrounded them. But that wasn't good, because people were always walking around the villages.

If he were any of the other trolls, she might have hidden him. Tall men existed here, and she could easily claim he was her guard. A priestess wandering about in the middle of the night was a woman on a mission, and no one would question what she was doing, at least until they figured out who she might be.

But with those horns, there was nothing she could do to hide him at all. He would stand out with any covering, any helmet—even a blanket tossed over his head would be ominous. People would either think they were dreaming about some demon appearing on their doorstep, or they would run away screaming, troll.

Both of which would get them caught.

"Bjorn, I don't think—"

He turned to look at her with a scowl. Placing a finger on his lips, he made it very clear that she was supposed to keep her mouth shut. So she did. She trusted he would get them out of here, even though it made every part of her quake and shiver.

This wasn't what she had thought it would be. The threadbare slippers on her feet made it hard for her to walk over the pebbles that covered the path. She tried to do so without complaint, but soon enough she could hardly keep the little grunts of frustration from escaping her lips.

It seemed every tiny pebble was getting underneath the edge of her slipper and jamming itself between her toes. She had to stop to shake them out, and then Bjorn was just moving farther and farther away from her. Astrid hadn't done all of this to lose every part of her life she'd fought for and then not get her sister back. So she rushed after him, inevitably getting even more rocks in her shoes.

When they reached the back of the first building, Bjorn went right into its yard. She tried to hiss a warning, but he completely ignored her.

He moved on his knuckles and haunches, looking almost ape-like as he traversed the person's yard. Strangely enough, it did keep him very low to the ground. No one would see him even if they looked out their window. The moonlight guided him, apparently, because she could barely see now that they were in the village. Everything was shadows and darkness.

The moon didn't cut through buildings, and no matter how hard she tried to peer around the shadows, her eyes simply could not get used to this level of darkness.

Bjorn appeared at her side, looming out of the darkness with a sheet in his hands.

"I don't think anything is going to cover your horns believably enough that someone won't realize you're a troll," she muttered, glancing around them to make sure no one had seen him.

But he was already wrapping the sheet around himself. He'd folded it so it looked like one long string, and then he pulled another sheet out of seemingly nowhere. What was he doing? He bound them around his chest, crisscrossing them around each other, and then gestured for her to come closer.

"Get on my back."

"Excuse me?"

"Get on my back," he repeated, but slower this time, like she didn't understand what he was saying. "Put your legs through these."

She realized he was holding the sheets out at an odd angle. They had crossed along his lower back, creating almost a cradle for her bottom, and her legs would go through the sheets at his side.

She'd seen mothers walking around the market with slings like this. Their children were secure on their backs, and then the mother's arms were free to gather whatever produce they needed from the market. She'd always thought it was a rather ingenious way to get around with a child.

He wanted to carry her like a toddler.

Cheeks burning with embarrassment, she did exactly as he said. After all, there was no way for her to deny what he wanted. She was slowing them down, and any minute people were going to start waking up. At this rate, they'd likely only get through half of the village before people woke, and then what would they do? They needed to move faster, and not waste so much time on her pebble-laden feet.

Astrid made quick work of climbing onto his back, although everything in her wanted to grumble about it. Hiking her skirts up as high as she could, she tightened her legs around his waist and wrapped her arms around his massive ribs.

His hands reached back, sliding up the bare skin of her thighs, and they both froze. She had never had a man touch her like that. The calluses on his palms abraded her skin, leaving behind what she was certain would be a red mark. And his claws trailed up her skin so gently, leaving streaks of heat in their wake. She'd never had such a visceral reaction to another person's touch. The danger in his grip made her entire body light up, and she... she didn't know what to do with that.

Bjorn seemed to stop breathing entirely. But her palms were on his ribs, and she could feel how hard his heart thundered.

He ripped his hands away, holding on to the thin fabric strips at his chest that held her weight. "Hold on tight," he murmured, before darting off at a speed that left her breathless.

If anyone in the village woke and saw them running past the

homes, she wouldn't know. The only sound she could hear was the wind moving past him as they bolted through town. And then he was leaping over a fence, using one hand to launch himself over it. Cows lowed at them as they ran by, one of them leaving an image in her mind of white, rolling eyes.

Then, more cobblestone streets that echoed with the sound of his running footsteps. Suddenly, he turned just slightly, using his arm and shoulder to bash through a door. She had only the slightest image of horse stalls with the creatures shrieking in fear before they were bursting through the next door and out into the fields beyond.

Fields, she realized, that surrounded the castle limits.

The wheat had long ago been harvested, and it was all flat planes as far as the eye could see. No animals were out here grazing, but on the horizon the sky had turned just slightly pink.

They had run out of time.

Bjorn's chest heaved with exertion. She could feel every breath thundering out of him, and how sweat slicked his body. And yet, even though the sun was coming up and someone would soon see them, he pushed himself even harder. Faster. They were moving so quickly that everything turned into a blur.

She hadn't realized anyone could move this fast. Definitely not after he had been tortured in a dungeon for years on end. But Bjorn was running with all the speed of a man who had tasted freedom and who refused to be denied it for even a moment longer.

Astrid pressed her palms against his chest, holding on to his heartbeat as though she could keep the organ in his chest. The trees were so close. The shadows there would hide them if they could make it.

"Troll!" someone shouted. "Troll in the fields!"

Bjorn spun suddenly, twisting his body toward the voice so quickly she squeezed her eyes shut. He let out a grunt before spinning again and running into the forest. They had made it, she realized. They had made it into the trees that he now dodged with the deftness of someone who had run past trunks and leapt over fallen logs his entire life. She didn't know how he was doing it, but he was.

There was so much grace and beauty in his movements. This was not just a man running. He was running toward something. Freedom. Home. She didn't know what, but she could feel it rumbling in his heart.

It felt like they ran for hours before he slowed. His footsteps changed from a quick sprint, to a light jog, and then he was walking.

"Are we safe?" she asked as he finally stopped.

"Safe enough."

Astrid struggled out of the bindings that had glued her to his back and then landed on the forest floor in a heap. Her tangled hair obscured her vision of the forest, but she shoved it all back to stare in awe at what surrounded them.

Emerald moss had cushioned her fall, and the same moss climbed up the silver trunks of the surrounding trees. The morning sunlight shone through the leaves, leaving a dappled texture all along the ground. It was beautiful. Marvelous. Remarkable.

And then something red dripped onto the back of her hand.

After looking down at the droplet, she turned her gaze up to see that Bjorn had an arrow sticking out of his chest. The fletching was crudely made, clearly created out of chicken feathers. But it had done its job all the same. The arrow stuck into his chest farther than she would have thought, the arrow head so far beneath his skin that she couldn't see it.

A spike of fear lanced through her chest, right where he'd been hit.

"Bjorn," she whispered. "What happened?"

He looked down at the arrow and shrugged. "A farmer saw us. It's fine."

As though it didn't bother him at all, he reached up to the arrow and snapped it in half. Only a small portion of the stick stuck out now, and he left it where it was as he crouched next to her. His gaze wasn't on her, a rarity, as he surveyed the forest. "There should be a cottage here. Somewhere."

No, he wasn't going to change the subject just like that. "You're hurt."

"It's nothing."

"There is an arrow in your chest, Bjorn. We need to get it out of you."

"The humans will hunt us." He finally turned his gaze to her, and she saw the worry in them, the fear that plagued them both. "They will follow us into the forest. I have taken us deep into the trees, but I do not know how long it will take before they follow my tracks. I did not hide them well so that we could move faster. Now we must hide until they give up searching for us."

Astrid nodded along with the words. She had no idea how to survive out here, and he did. She wasn't going to question him.

"But you still have an arrow in you," she stammered. "What are we going to do about that?"

He gave her a look that clearly said he couldn't care less about the arrow. "It's fine, Astrid. I've had far worse wounds than this one."

"Bjorn," she whispered, her voice broken.

He gave her one look and then sighed. "Fine."

Then he reached into his chest with those ragged claws and pulled it out. It wasn't pretty, nor was he gentle with himself. He just cut and sliced and tore until the arrowhead dropped onto the ground. "Now, we find the cottage."

Astrid thought she might be sick. She stood on shaking legs, so uncertain of how she had gotten to this point in her life. He'd just dug an arrowhead out of himself like it was nothing. Like pain didn't even bother him. She was in the forest, reliant entirely on this troll to care for her, with people hunting them down. Shouldn't she be considering rushing in the opposite direction and begging her own people to take her back?

Lord Tolly would. He had gone to the trouble of releasing her from that prison. Surely he would hide her away, keep her safe, make sure that she was comfortable and fed for the rest of her life.

But her sister would never be free if she did that.

Her mind volleyed back and forth between what she wanted to do as she wandered through the forest after Bjorn. A cottage should be easy to find, she thought, but it wasn't. Until he shouted, "Here!"

She turned to see what looked like a mound of earth. It was little more than a hill sunken into the ground. Moss covered the top of it, and the door was so close to the ground, deep inside a hollow that was covered by a fallen tree, she never would have guessed it was anything more than a naturally made hump.

"What is this place?" she said as she walked toward him.

Bjorn reached for what looked like a tangle of wooden sticks, and opened them like a door. "Here is the cottage, Priestess."

What had she gotten herself into now?

Chapter 12

Bjorn pushed the door open and stepped into his past. It was so strange to walk through that door of twigs, knowing that the person who had once lived here was long gone.

It was exactly as he remembered, although covered in dust and perhaps rotted from years of no one being here. The cottage might've looked like a hovel to some, but he'd grown up around blood witches. He knew what their homes looked like, and he knew what to expect.

"This was the home of a blood witch," he murmured as he stepped across the threshold. "Her name was Embla."

Like saying her name had awakened something in the home, all of a sudden there was light. The shadows were banished by hundreds of will-o'-the-wisps who had served this blood witch for centuries. Suddenly they could see that while it was a small single room, it had once been very comfortable. On his right were walls of old spellcrafting materials. Bones of every kind of animal safely kept in jars that were always where she had left them. Although all the jars were now covered in a fine layer of dust.

Beyond that, at the back of the room, was a small seating area. Although a few clods of dirt had fallen onto the couches, Bjorn knew they would be very easy to clean off. They were facing an old fireplace that was only lit when Embla had known she was safe. The stone hearth stretched all the way up to the earthen ceiling.

Her kitchen was in the back left, a homey part of her abode that had always been full of light and life. As though the ghosts of his past had awoken, he saw trolls wandering there. His mother and her sisters, another blood witch who had come to visit, all of them vibrant as they were the day he'd seen them here. They were all huddled around the stove, joking with each other and pushing to be the first person to taste what Embla had made.

And then to his left, a bed that had broken in half from crumbling age. It was still covered with the same patchwork quilt he remembered from his childhood, though. The same one that had always made him lift it to his nose and deeply inhale, because it smelled like home, and memories of when everything in his life had been calm.

The entire room was illuminated by wisps decorating the ceiling, dotted about so they looked like stars. They were so pretty, hundreds of them in glimmering golden light that made the entire room far more welcoming than it likely seemed to her.

He moved aside and allowed Astrid to explore. She didn't seem ready to do so, however. She stood next to him, her hands clasped at her waist in that prim and proper way that set his teeth on edge.

She was nervous. He could tell that much. But why?

This was home. This was a place where she could feel safe. No one would find them here, and perhaps she needed to hear that.

"No human has ever discovered Embla's house," he said. "We are safe here. Safer than any other place in the forest while they hunt us."

"I..." She took a deep breath. "I don't think we see the same place."

He glanced around, trying to see the room through her eyes. But he really couldn't. "What do you see?"

"The home of a witch. The bones give it away, of course. The herbs hanging from the ceiling. The smell of mildew and musk in the air. This place is probably cursed, and I know the feeling of witchcraft on my skin when I feel it." She ran her hands up and down her arms. "There is more danger here than in sleeping on the forest floor."

That was ridiculous. "This is my aunt's home. Embla was family. If there are any of her spells still alive, they certainly would not react to me."

Perhaps she was merely reacting to seeing the home of a troll. He was certain this was not what she was used to, and she looked out of place here. With her pretty silver gown, she looked like someone had pasted her into this space. The discomfort practically radiated out of her. Even when he pointed to the chairs, she refused to move away from the door.

At least she'd closed it behind her. He'd mark that as progress.

"Are you thirsty?" he asked.

At her slight nod, he got to work in the kitchen. Fortunately Embla's piping still worked. He turned the water spout on and let it run for a while, since dirt had clogged it in the time since anyone had used it. Soon enough, the spring water would be drinkable, and he could use it to start some tea.

Wood still sat in the corner from the last time Embla had brought it in. Some spell must have been placed on the woodbox, because it didn't look all that old. It should have been rotten at this point, but it would burn nicely in the stove.

It hit him then. Not when they'd been running through the fields, not even when he'd stepped foot into this house. Only in that instant, making tea on a stove, did he realize he was free.

He was no longer in that horrible place. He was no longer subjected to fighting or killing whenever humans pointed him like an arrow. He was here. Back in the same place he had been as a child, and now he was...

Free.

A low laugh started in his chest before it burst forth. The sound must've sounded manic, or perhaps insane, but he couldn't stop laughing because he was *no longer in the labyrinth*. And all it had taken was a priestess, just like the beginning of his life.

The sound ripping out of his chest was equal parts humor and grief. He laughed until tears ran down his face, mourning the ten years he had lost in that place. But he also laughed because he had given up hope that he would ever be free again. Those emotions spilled out of him until his ribs ached, his stomach burned.

He no longer had to sleep with one eye open, waiting for a guard to prod him awake in the middle of the night. He didn't have to fear what they would ask him to do next. No more killing. No more unwanted touches from unwanted people.

He was free.

Bjorn finally got control of himself, although it took some time. The joy and relief that burned through him were nearly impossible to grasp. Freedom such as this was only gifted once or twice in a lifetime. A part of him didn't think he deserved to be free. But another, much larger part, was just glad that he was offered this opportunity.

Finally, the water turned clear, and he filled the old teapot with it before putting it onto the stove. He made the fire and then turned to see she was still in the same spot. Standing by the door, like an outsider who had no right to be in here.

"Come," he said. "Let me tell you about Embla."

"You are a man of few words, Bjorn. I didn't think you knew how to tell a story."

Perhaps he had been in the labyrinth. He'd had to be that person to keep his sanity and not lose his mind amid all the death and destruction there. But pieces of him were returning now, even the large piece that had enjoyed telling people stories.

He gestured again for her to come near the fireplace, although he could not light it. The stove would already be putting off smoke above the cottage, and he could only hope the humans were as dull as he thought they were. Hopefully they wouldn't notice.

"Blood witches are similar to your kind. We do not fear them, although I understand your people might."

"Anything labeled a witch is to be feared," she murmured, but she took a few more steps into the room.

"Are you not a witch?"

"I have elven blood. A high and revered bloodline, although nowhere near that of the princess." She brushed her hair away from her ears, showing him the rather prominent points. "Like you."

He reached for the tips of his own ears, stroking the long lengths thoughtfully. "Ah, but trolls are far from those bloodlines. The elves made it so."

"I have heard the stories that you were made from mud and scales."

"We were made from all that were animals. The elves created us. They crafted slaves and gave us thoughts in the hopes that we would be more biddable if we could worship them." If she wasn't going to sit, then he would. He took a seat on the couch, remembering all the other times he'd been here with his family. Loud and boisterous memories that felt so muted now. "The trolls are far from that these days, though. Our king pushes us ever more toward our elven bloodline, rather than the animals we were made from. At least, he did in the years I was there."

"How long has it been?"

He glanced over at her, seeing those wide eyes staring at him with what he hoped wasn't fear. "Ten years. Maybe more than that. I lost track of time in the darkness. But if Embla is gone, it was at least ten years."

At her inhalation, he knew she understood how hard his life had been. He didn't want her to pity him, but some part of him wanted Astrid to own what her people had done as well. It wasn't her fault. And yet, something inside him still wanted to punish her for what had been done.

She licked her lips, turning those wide eyes toward all the bones that hung on the wall and the jars of questionable things. "A blood witch, you said?"

"They use their magic to identify power within people. It is a ritual many of us partake in throughout our lives." He held up his hand, showing her a small scar that traced along the meat of his thumb. "This is the mark I earned when I was a boy. We meet with a blood witch to test our powers and our magic."

"You have magic?" she asked, her voice suddenly surprised.

"I am elven, am I not?"

He watched as she turned scarlet. Bjorn had thought it was rather obvious, given his ears. All those with elven bloodlines had magic. Just like she did.

"I have felt your magic," he said as he leaned against the couch more comfortably. "But I do not know how to describe what you can do."

"I am sensitive to emotions." Astrid moved closer to the bones on the walls, her gaze focused on the skull of a snake. "I have always been able to use those emotions to my advantage. It's not that I can make someone feel anything. All I can do is amplify or pull certain emotions to the front. It's not much, but it is something."

"Useful in your line of work, I suppose."

She turned her focus to him. "What do you know about my line of work?"

"Only what I saw in the dungeons. I would hang from the ceiling while your people worked in the shadows. I saw how the priestesses controlled the nobility like puppeteers. It was as impressive as it was terrifying to see that those in power were so dangerously controlled by another group." He leaned forward, bracing his elbows on his knees while staring at her. "Your people have the real power."

She snorted. "If only that were the truth. Perhaps I would not have been sold into the labyrinth to pay off a debt."

But then she... hesitated.

And it made him wonder. "He sold you into the labyrinth? You made it sound like it was your own doing as well." He wanted to know the truth. He had to know the truth. If that man had really sold her off, then he wanted to kill him someday. Bjorn would hunt him down and make the lord suffer for not taking care of what he had been gifted.

"It's fine," she said. "I offered."

"You... offered?"

Suddenly she seemed even more uncomfortable. She cleared her throat a few times, shuffling back and forth on her feet as though she didn't have the same balance as she had before. "I mean, isn't it obvious?

This was the easiest way to get to you and my sister. Lord Tolly... Well, he wouldn't have done it if I hadn't suggested such a thing."

"Why would you do that?" he snarled. "You took your own life into your hands! The labyrinth is not somewhere for someone like you."

"It was my only chance. I had to take it."

"You didn't have to take it! You could have figured out another way to talk with me. If Lord Tolly got you out of the labyrinth that easily, then you could have done the same with me. All you had to do was lie about that Lady... whatever her name was!"

He was getting heated, and he could feel it. The ugly side of himself that always seemed to come out when he was angry wanted to throttle her. He had told himself that he would protect her because she had saved him. How was he supposed to protect her from herself?

The woman had willingly gone into one of the most dangerous places in the realm. She had tied herself to a troll she did not know, risked her life staying in the cell with him, and all of that had been done with the hope that he would even help her.

What if he hadn't been so kind? What if he had been more interested in raping her, killing her, and all the other horrible things the human guards had expected from him?

Astrid moved closer to the wall of bones, clearly pretending to be interested in what was there to distract him. "These were used in her work?"

"Don't change the subject."

"I'm just curious what they were for." She reached for a large raptor talon. He could tell even from a distance that the curved edge was sharp.

"Blood witches have many instruments for many things. Don't touch anything." He leapt to his feet, heading in her direction because she couldn't keep her hands to herself. "Put it down, Astrid."

She turned the claw, reading the words off the side in damn near perfect black tongue. Not that his language was all that hard to read aloud, but she clearly had no idea what the words meant. And then he watched in horror as the claw tilted. She lost her grip on it, and the sharp edge sliced through her palm.

The bright red line horrified him. Again, he was supposed to be taking care of her, and now she was hurt. Really hurt. The amount of blood pouring out of her palm terrified her.

He reached for the claw at the same time as she did, and somehow that ended up with both of them fumbling it between them. He hissed out an angry breath, managing to grab it for a few seconds before it sliced across his palm too. The beaded blood rang a bell in his mind. Something was wrong. Something about this wasn't supposed to happen without him doing something, or avoiding it, or...

"Bjorn," she snapped. "Now you've hurt yourself too!"

As if time had slowed, he watched Astrid reach for his hand and grab it with her own. Their blood mingled together, slipping as she tried to see how badly he'd hurt himself.

Then there came a spark. A spark of red magic that he knew was his own floated up between the two of them, and a spark of her own. Light blue and delicate, it twirled around his own as he stared in horror. And then, just like that, the two lights combined into something that was a purple abomination.

"No," he whispered, staring at the light.

Bound, he remembered. The word burned through his mind.

Now they were more than just bound. They were...

Mated.

Chapter 13

Astrid watched the glowing lights that had erupted out of their blood glimmer right in front of her face. She couldn't hazard a guess at what they were, but they were certainly pretty. Although the red ball illuminated Bjorn's face in a rather terrifying manner that she shouldn't have noticed. He'd been a good man. He'd protected her. Kept her safe. He was not the monster that red light painted him to be.

And then the blue light surged toward the other, twining in tighter and tighter circles until they were combined into a lovely purple light. Deep amethyst, the color of royalty.

It truly was a beautiful thing to behold, even if she had no idea what it meant. But as she stared, she realized that Bjorn's dark green face had turned a rather interesting shade of greenish gray. He looked like he was going to throw up before he muttered, "No."

No?

What did he mean by that?

She released his hand, feeling the slickness of their blood sliding across each other as she did so. She needed to wrap her hand. The blood was surprisingly already slowing, but she didn't want to take a chance at infection. Especially considering it was clearly a spell that she'd read off the raptor claw.

Silly girl. She shouldn't touch things in a witch's hut without knowing what they were. Now she had likely cursed the both of them.

Oh, no. Was she going to lose her hand? Was that what terrified him?

The lights still glowed in front of them, so it was hard for her to see his expression as he turned away from her. The brightness turned the entire room into a rather comical hue of purple. Every blanket, every rug, every piece of furniture.

"No, what?" she asked, her stern tone hopefully snapping him out of whatever strange mood he was now in.

"No, this was not meant to happen," he snarled. A clawed hand slashed through the colored lights, revealing the anger on his expression that chilled her to the bone.

She really had done something irreparable, hadn't she? That was the only reason he'd be looking at her like that. With rage simmering underneath the surface, so powerful that she was certain he would kill her now.

"What did I do?" she whispered.

"That is..." He huffed out an angry breath, and she couldn't stop focusing on his tusks.

She'd seen trolls with much larger ones, but they were still deadly weapons. There was a time in the arena when she'd watched one of his kind rip through a man's belly with his tusks. The sharp tips had parted the soft flesh there all too easily. And then there were his claws, of course. Dagger tips that she would prefer he use if he was going to kill her.

Shaking, she took a step back from him. "I don't know what is going on, but I need you to take two steps back."

Astrid had used that tone with men many times. Humans were quick to anger as well. All it took was an order like that, snapping them a bit out of whatever had angered them, and the men usually would do one of two things. They would fly at her in anger, in which she would use her power to control them, or they would do as she told them to do and then seem a little confused about why they had.

Bjorn was the latter. He took two massive steps back, making sure to keep his eyes on her as he did so.

"Blood witches..." He exhaled again, the sound nearly like the snort an animal would make. "We bring our children to them to see their magic. That was what the lights were."

"The red was yours," she said. "And the blue was mine."

Hers. She had never thought to see her magic outside of her body, and now she wished she could see it again. She hadn't gotten a good look at it before they had merged.

Blue like the sea, she remembered. Blue like the sky on the clearest of days and it had been stunning. How did she get it back? Could she converse with it? Could she ask the magic questions? How to strengthen it would be her first, of course. There had to be a way to encourage power like that to grow naturally without having to cajole it out of her body. Perhaps they could work together, rather than be so separate from one another.

He shook his head as though trying to clear it of dark thoughts. "Listen to me. We also bring our chosen partners to a blood witch. She measures the weight of our magic, looks at them together, melds the powers before we are... mated."

She blinked at him.

"Mated?" she repeated. Perhaps she hadn't heard him correctly. "That sounds rather animalistic."

He looked at her with so much despair in his expression that she realized where she had gone wrong in saying that. Of course it sounded animalistic. His people had been created by using pieces of animals to make them who they were.

"Our powers combined together. It has meaning for my people. It binds two people together because it means they are..." Again, he shook his head. "It doesn't matter now. We are bound."

"Bound?"

"Bound," he said again. "Do you not understand what I mean by that?"

Some part of her maybe did. That was the screaming voice in her head arguing that she needed to get control over this situation, and fast, or her entire life trajectory was going to change. But she didn't know how to say that to him without looking weak.

Groping for the back of the sofa, she held on to it so he wouldn't notice how shaky her knees were. "Please explain it to me, Bjorn. I would like to make sure that I understand what you're saying correctly."

He seemed to struggle a bit with how to say the words before clearing his throat and replying, "It is similar to a marriage for my people. But more binding than that because our magic will seek out the other. We should be able to use each other's powers, sharing our magic until it changes the fundamental basis of what we can and cannot do. It is more than just a marriage. It is a melding of souls."

Fuck.

Fuck, no, she didn't want that. Astrid had been very glad that he had saved her life. That much was certain. She owed him for taking care of her in the labyrinth, but she didn't want to pay for that with her soul.

She had to sit down. Perched on the back of the sofa, she curled her arms around herself and shook her head. "I don't even know what magic you have. And I don't want to be bound to you, no offense."

He shook his head. "That is understandable."

"It's nothing to do with who you are or what you stand for, Bjorn. You seem like a good man—"

"I am not," he interrupted. "You should not be bound to a creature like me. My life has not made me a good man, nor do I expect you to wish to remain locked together with me when you did not choose this. It is an unfortunate circumstance that we will need to remedy as soon as possible."

She swallowed hard. Bound to a troll. That wasn't something she thought she'd ever have to endure. "So it is... reversible?"

That was good. That made things perhaps a little less scary. She wasn't locked into her relationship with him or into the knowledge that at some point, she was going to be so tied up in him that her magic wasn't even hers anymore.

But then he hesitated, and all the anxiety bubbled up again. Why was he hesitating? Why wasn't he talking to her?

Finally he said, "It may be. But it will require us to change course."

"Change course?"

"Your sister has been the object of your desires. You wish to see her more than anything. It was why you risked your life and ended up in the labyrinth. But if we wish to undo this, then we cannot see your sister first."

He had to be wrong. She needed to get to Rose. "I'm afraid that won't be possible. Rose is being held captive by your people. They made it very clear in their note that they were not going to keep her for long before they disposed of her."

He shook his head. The dim light in this hut played across the edges of his horns, revealing ripples that she hadn't been able to see in the darkness of the labyrinth. "My people will not hurt her. They may have lied to get your attention on them, but she is as safe in Trollveggen as she would be anywhere else."

"She was kidnapped out of her 'safe' bed, brought to that labyrinth, and gifted to men who did god knows what to her," Astrid snarled. "She was never safe, so those are not words that reassure me."

She still remembered waking up that night and seeing that her sister's bed was empty. She'd run throughout the entire building that housed the acolytes. That building was supposed to be impenetrable. No one was allowed to get in or out without the knowledge of the king himself. So she had thought that it would be impossible for anyone to grab Rose right out from under her nose.

Nerves made her hands shake again. She'd only just gotten them to stop doing that, and now they were back to it. She tucked them into her lap harder than before, and took a deep, steadying breath. "I need to see that Rose is all right."

"We don't have that kind of time." He gestured between the two of them with a clawed hand. "What just happened between the two of us is binding, like I said. There is very little time to undo it if it was a mistake. Blood witches don't make mistakes like that. Therefore, it is unusual to have to unravel the ties that just happened."

"Then why was it so easy to do?" She almost shouted the words before clearing her throat.

She should never have raised her voice like that. Astrid knew how to keep control of herself. She knew how to be better than this.

He looked at her with pity in his gaze. "Most people cannot perform the spell unless they are blood witches themselves. But those with magic that could be one of our own priestesses, like you, certainly possess the ability to cast the spell. You read the words on the claw."

She had read them out loud. Astrid wasn't even certain why she had done so. After all, she knew that magic was dangerous. Something in her heart had whispered that it was meant to be read aloud, and so she had. The words had flowed off her tongue as if she'd said them a thousand times.

She hadn't known what they meant. She hadn't known what it would do if she read them aloud.

Her stomach twisted, and she swore she was going to vomit. But they hadn't eaten anything in a very long time, and she knew that if she threw up, all that would come out of her was thin, meager bile.

So she clamped her mouth shut, turned her face to the side, and tried to get herself under control.

A sharp whistle filled the hut. She flinched, and Bjorn cursed as he rushed back to the stove and pulled the tea kettle off the top. The steam wheezed out a dying breath, and then there was just the two of them alone with the sound of their ragged, angry breaths. She heard him pour water into two cups that were likely dirty, and then the soft sound of metal clinking as he added pinches of tea into metal tea balls.

What was she supposed to say? That she was going to give up on her sister's well-being just because she'd made a mistake? It wasn't going to happen. She'd sacrifice herself if that was what it took, but she was getting her sister back.

But then he handed her the handmade mug and sat down on the sofa to her right, while she was still leaning against the back of it. Back to back, they both sipped their tea while staring off into the distance, mulling over their predicament.

She swallowed far too much of the boiling water, feeling it burn on its way down to her stomach. "How do you know so much about this?"

Some part of her hoped it was all rumor. Then she could point out that this was a fool's mission, and he knew nothing. The logical thing would be for them to go wherever Rose was and find an expert.

"I was raised by people like you," he murmured. "My mother is a smoke breather. She inhales the future through smoke and breathes it out like a dragon while telling prophecies. People like her only have children rarely, but when they do, they are raised among all those with gifts their children might not have."

Her heart squeezed in her chest. Such a childhood must have been hard for him. "Why do you not share her gifts?"

"The goddess only blesses women with such things. I was born to protect people like you. That is the only reason my mother kept me." His hand clenched around the mug so hard she heard the ceramic creak. "But my father was born to do the same, and he renounced those ways. I was brought to Trollveggen more than I was trained to protect my mother and her sisters of power. My brutality comes from him."

Her hand twitched. She wanted to offer him comfort, and her offending fingers desperately wished to settle on his bunched shoulders and ease some of the tension there. But she did not. Instead she said, "It seems you were trained well. You kept me safe."

Bjorn glanced up at her, his mouth slightly open in shock and his brows raised. It looked like he wanted to say something to her, and she wondered what those words could be. Would he thank her for her kindness? Would he argue?

Instead, the thoughts cleared from his expressive features, and he replied, "The priestesses in my world see beyond what you or I can see. The future is theirs to wield as a weapon, and as such, they are the only ones who can sever the bond between us."

"Are they in the same place as my Rose?"

"No. They do not choose to remain in Trollveggen with the others. They hear too many thoughts. The mountain is crowded with those who would ask their opinion, drain their magics, and they are..." He waved around the hut. "Solitary creatures."

"Then where are they?"

"Beyond the mountain," he replied. "Where I grew from boy to man."

Beyond the mountain? She'd never thought of going that far. He'd talked about it, of course, but she hadn't ever thought that this journey would bring her there.

"What happens if we don't?" she asked.

"Then we are bound for life. Perhaps you will find another, but I..." A muscle on his jaw jumped. "I will endure without you."

So there really wasn't a choice. They had to take this detour, or they would be tangled together forever.

Chapter 14

Bjorn argued until the wee hours of the morning. Astrid was bound and determined that they were not going to go anywhere but to see her sister first, and he kept pointing out that if they did that, they were stuck together.

A part of him whispered that it wouldn't be the worst thing in the world. Even if she left, he would still have the memory of her, the feeling that there had once been something bright in his life.

Bjorn knew a life without his bound mate would be torture. He'd seen a few males who had either lost their wives too early, or who had been denied after the binding. He knew their lives were less without those women. Their souls always searched for the one they were bound to, even if it was only to feel the brush of their magic for just the barest of seconds.

He didn't necessarily want to live like that, but... being tied to a woman like her wasn't the worst thing that could have happened.

Eventually, she fell asleep in the broken bed. He could still see the anger radiating through her body even at rest. Her fists remained clenched. Her jaw worked continually. He was certain he'd get an earful about this again once she woke and her mind had had time to consider the options. Their problem was simple. They needed to find her sister to appease her guilt and heartbreak, but they also needed to take care of themselves.

He wondered if Astrid had ever done that. She seemed so firm that she needed to take care of everyone other than herself. Even in their escape, she'd wanted to bring Rabbit when that was the absolute worst thing they could have done.

She still hadn't asked for food. And when his own stomach rumbled, he realized she'd be starving before they left. Too many days without food would leave her weak, and he needed her strong for this journey.

There was no safer place for her than this hut. He hoped she had enough foresight to stay inside as he slipped out into the night. Soon enough, the sun would rise, and he would miss his opportunity to find the warrens that used to be plentiful in this area. When he was a child, he'd hunted rabbits for Embla.

She'd been old then too, he mused as he crouched down on the ground and sought the signs he was expecting to see. Footprints, droppings that would lead him to where the rabbits would leave their homes soon enough to start the day.

He crouched near what he suspected was a warren. Bjorn was a silent, dark figure who never moved until he saw the barest hint of a whiskered nose that was just starting to come out of its home. This area of the woods had always been plentiful with their kind, although he felt bad taking them right out of their home.

He made quick work of it. And though he was saddened by the loss of life, a thrill ran through him. He hadn't hunted like this in a long time. Not for death and destruction, but to stay alive.

Part of his mind whispered that he was dreaming. Soon enough, he would wake up in his cell and realize his mind had conjured up a grand story to escape the horror of what was being done to him there. He had only needed a break from what he knew would continue until the day he died.

But then Bjorn felt the breeze on him again. It played through his hair, greasy and lank now that he'd had yet to bathe for days on end. There was no reason for cleanliness in the cells. The worse he looked, the better the humans liked it. The guards didn't torment him as much if he looked like he had been abused. All the trolls knew that.

But now, as he took in a deep breath of the forest surrounding him, he couldn't smell the moss or the loam. All he could smell was the stink of his body and the sweat that still clung to him. Even the metallic aroma of blood still lingered on his body. Perhaps that was why he hadn't been able to smell her reactions or her emotions. Sometimes he could.

He had been able to with Ragnar's woman. Maia, he remembered. Her name was Maia, and she had been a flame in his darkness that had lit up his cell. She had been hope, and now he was seeing all of that come to fruition.

Both his dear friend and his wife would be disappointed to see that he had become such a monster. Bjorn took great care in cleaning the rabbit and then headed off to the stream he could hear nearby. At the very least, he could wash himself before he returned. There was plenty of time before Astrid would wake.

The stream quickly came into view. It was a bubbling, happy brook with water that didn't rush too fast and stones that had been softened by years of the water's travels. Hanging the rabbit up on a tree for safety, he stripped off the loincloth that had kept him barely hidden from the eyes of so many humans who'd been all too happy to peek at what he hid beneath.

He'd lost so much of what he once was. As he waded into the icy water to the deepest part, he stood there with it up to his hips and took quick, short breaths before dunking himself completely under. Running his hands along the hollow parts of his ribs, down his empty stomach to the jagged edges of his hip bones, he wondered what it would have been like if he'd avoided being captured.

Would he still have muscles here? Would he weigh at least a stone more?

Running his hands through his greasy hair, he took time to get some of the tangles out, at least. What a mess. His mother would be so disappointed with him, let alone all the other women who had raised him. They had impressed upon him how important it was to be clean, and here he was, ignoring everything they had ever told him.

Flashes of memories returned to him bit by bit, as he washed away the years of torture and torment. Memories of home with his mother and her sisters, and how they had brought so much love into his life. Years of him in their grotto, with the emerald green hills that had rolled as far as the eye could see, and animals all roaming freely.

Another memory sparked there too. A reason the animals had been able to roam like that without any fences or barriers. But that one was still gone, just as much as the others were. He still had a long way to go before he was himself again, but he was pleased that at least now he could try. He was closer to who he had once been all those years ago.

Finally clean, he started planning as he got out of the water and rinsed off the loincloth the best he could. There wasn't much he could do with it. It was threadbare at best, but there should be some clothing still in Embla's cottage. He wasn't sure if it would fit him—likely not—but at the very least he could make do.

Heading back home with a sopping wet loincloth and a dead rabbit, he paused to grab some wild carrots on the way. There were a few places he used to gather them, and they were now overrun with options. Wild carrots were abundant here, perhaps a good reason why the rabbits were plentiful as well. And then he headed back to the house.

She was still sleeping. But then again, the rays of the sun were only just peeking over the horizon. So he made quick work of sneaking back into the house to paw through the small chest at the foot of the bed.

That took some skill. Astrid stirred when he first opened it, and he froze at the shrieking sound of the hinges. But she settled again, so he rummaged through the small wooden box until he found some old pants that used to be his. They were tied on the sides, so he would be able to make them cling to his thighs well enough.

Grabbing those, he closed the box as slowly as he could to avoid the shrieking hinges again, and then headed outside.

Here, he could cook the rabbit for her. Along with the carrots. He highly doubted the king's soldiers were still looking for them, and even if they were, he would hear them long before they made it to the cottage. So he got a fire going outside, threw the rabbit onto a spit above it, and waited.

And waited.

And waited some more.

The sun was higher on the horizon than he'd anticipated before he gave up. Was the woman dead? Surely she should be up by now, and yet, she wasn't. He poked his head into the darkened house, seeing that she was still underneath the covers.

Neither of them had slept well in the cell. He knew that. But Bjorn had never met someone who could sleep so long into the morning.

"Astrid?" he called out, trying to keep his voice at least a little quiet so he didn't startle her.

She snorted in her sleep, rolled over, and then turned to look at him. "What?" Her voice came, quiet and still half asleep.

"We need to get going."

"Oh." Again, that higher pitched, soft voice that he'd never heard.

Sleep still clung to her as she sat up. Her hair was a little tangled, a billowing cloud around her head that looked more like a bird's nest than actual hair. Her eyes were slightly swollen, and her lips were cracked. She looked anything but a priestess in this moment.

He'd never seen her look prettier. How strange it was to find someone in their most base form so sweet.

She rolled out of bed, barely functioning even though it was well into the morning. She blinked a few times before joining him outside. "Is that... food I smell?"

The poor dear was barely managing on her own. Maybe it was the binding that made something in his chest squeeze, or maybe it was just that she was pathetic looking as she staggered over to the fire and sat down next to it.

Her dress was all rumpled and wrinkled from a night's sleep in it. One shoulder had fallen down, leaving her skin bare to the early morning sunlight as she breathed in the scent of cooking rabbit. "What is it?"

All the soft thoughts in his head ground to a screeching halt.

"What is what?"

"That." She pointed at the animal rotating on the spit. "I can't tell without its…"

Skin, he filled in for her. She couldn't tell what a skinned rabbit looked like. This might be a harder journey than he'd originally thought.

"Rabbit," he replied, hurrying to the fire before she did something stupid. Like grab it with her bare hands.

He made quick work of taking it off the spit, and setting it on the plates he'd found inside as well. That with the steamed carrot would fill her belly far better than anything he'd found so far. Although now that he was looking at the food, he realized he wasn't likely to eat anything himself.

He should have hunted more rabbits, he supposed. But he'd gone longer without food than this. She needed to eat more than he did.

Astrid tore into the food like a woman possessed. He handed her the thighs first, and she ate those without any hesitation. The carrots she ate three of before she pressed a hand to her belly and shook her head. "No more. I've eaten so little for so long, I think my belly shrank."

A good troll would have argued. He would have told her that he was going to hunt even more for her, because the thighs of a rabbit and three carrots weren't enough. But he wasn't a good man right now.

Bjorn tore into the food with a vengeance. He didn't care what part of the rabbit he ate, because he ate all of it, even licking the bones clean. The remaining three carrots he wasn't even sure he chewed before swallowing them. And when it was all gone, he definitely thought he should have hunted more. There was not enough.

But it would get him through the day. He knew this journey would be long, arduous, and risky. Looking at her, he doubted she'd be able to make the trip all that easily.

"Do you still wear those slippers on your feet?" he asked.

She poked them out from underneath the long length of her dress. What was on her feet were the remains of slippers that wouldn't last half a day, let alone the week-long journey this was going to take.

Frowning, he ordered, "Come with me."

Together, they headed back into the hut. Embla's clothing wouldn't fit her. She had been nearly as tall as Bjorn, but maybe there was something of use in here.

Rummaging through the clothing, he was disappointed to find nothing that would suit. Everything was far too big. It would fall off Astrid's frame, and he didn't need her to be picking at her clothing constantly on the journey. That would only make things even more difficult, but...

He leaned down to pick up one of Embla's old shirts. It was just a white, long-sleeved shirt. Nothing special. But the buttons would make it easier for Astrid to cover herself, and the length was almost like a dress. Turning, he handed it to her with a belt. "Wrap the belt twice around your waist. This should cover you on our journey. Your feet I will bind in leathers."

His feet would be fine. Bjorn had been barefoot for years now and the bottoms of his feet were like leather. There was enough leather here to create rigging just like he had before, as well. This time, he could make it out of more comfortable straps, perhaps using blankets as cushioning so she wouldn't be so uncomfortable every time he had to sling her upon his back.

This would work. It wouldn't be pretty, but it would work.

Something hummed in the back of his mind. An old memory, he thought. Trolls were meant to decorate their troll wives. Not to take away the beauty that covered them.

Turning back to the crate, he reached in through the mess and found on old bracelet that he remembered had once decorated Embla's wrist. It was too big for Astrid's, but...

"For your arm," he said, holding out the golden hoop. It wasn't much, but there were pretty stones set on it. About ten of them, clear stones that would glitter in the light.

"I can't take this."

"Wear it so I don't feel as bad about putting you in a shirt rather than a gown." He ducked his head before she could look at him and piled his arms with the leather that had gone to waste in the trunk. "I will work on creating something comfortable for you. We leave this afternoon."

"How far are we going?" she called out as he headed out of the cottage.

"A week of travel. Some three hundred miles."

"That's... that's impossible to travel in a week on foot."

He paused in the doorway, glanced over his shoulder, and tried not to sound smug as he said, "Not for a troll."

Chapter 15

Astrid stared at the rigging he'd wrapped around himself and wondered what he was expecting her to do here. She certainly wasn't going to be seated on his back like cargo for the entire trip, was she?

It had made sense when they'd been fleeing the castle. She couldn't run as quickly as he could, and there had been people chasing them. If she had slowed them down any more, someone would have caught them. But they hadn't heard any soldiers since they'd been in this witch's hut, and surely she could travel without being carried like a misbehaving child?

"Are you sure I cannot walk?" she asked, eyeing him with no small amount of distrust.

She really didn't want to climb onto him and swing in that strange little sling for days on end. Not to mention she was wearing just a shirt.

Astrid had done what she could with it, of course. There had been plenty of belts inside the trunk, and she still wasn't all that certain what the trolls had used them for. But she'd managed to loop a few of them around her stomach to give a sort of corseted look to the ensemble. She'd worn more revealing clothing in her time. All the priestesses did, so she didn't mind her legs being bare. But it was nothing like any other garment she'd ever worn, by far.

Bjorn merely grunted at her question.

She would not let him respond to her like an animal, though.

"I'm serious," she said, leaning into the words. "I don't want to ride you like you're a horse. What if I walked with you?"

"You remember how many miles I said we had to traverse?"

"Of course I do."

"You think we can do that with you walking?"

He... had a point. She didn't like the point, but it was correct nonetheless. Grumbling, she walked toward him. "And you're sure I won't fall right through this?"

He had already slung it across his chest with multiple straps that looked sturdy enough. The back was cushioned by what looked like rolled up blankets.

Bjorn nodded and then helped her in. It was impressive that he could pick her up one handed like that. His massive hand gripped her thigh with a surprising strength that made her feel suddenly flushed and a little speechless.

No. She refused. She wasn't going to focus on how strong his hands were, or how capable he was as he hefted her easily onto his back. This time, it wasn't quite so much an uncomfortable harness as it was last time. This was more like a swing. She was cushioned well, and nothing felt like it was digging into her thighs.

"All right," she said. "I suppose this will do."

And then they were off.

The world became a blur as he ran, and Astrid realized that he'd planned more than she'd thought. Slung around his hips were other sacks, each of them secured so they wouldn't bounce while he ran. These she could only imagine were filled with supplies.

She was proven right a few hours into his running as he reached into one and pulled out a skein of water. He took a sip and then handed it back to her.

"We aren't going to stop to drink?" she asked, nearly yelling the words so he could hear her.

Bjorn shook his head, only slightly out of breath as he responded, "Not until we have to! I plan to put as much distance between us and the castle as we can first."

They didn't talk again for some time. She would have liked to marvel at the world that blurred past them, but really it was hard to see any of it. Pressed against his back, she was lulled into a sense of security. She thought she might have even slept for a little while.

She blinked, and suddenly the light had faded from the world. They had paused, apparently, as he looked up at a sheer cliff before them. His hands were on his hips, only the finest sheen of sweat coating his lean body. She had assumed he would be far more out of breath than this, but he didn't seem to have exerted himself at all. She looked worse after running up three flights of stairs.

He eyed the mountain before reaching up and hauling himself onto it. He climbed as if he had been born to do this. Like there wasn't an ounce of fear in his heart in the slightest, but as the ground suddenly dipped away from them. She had never been more terrified in her life.

Astrid wasn't even sure she could talk without screaming. She clung to him harder, almost climbing out of the sling around his back as she tried to get away from what was a drop to her death.

At one point, he hung from a single arm to reach back and pat her side. "I've climbed my whole life, bright one. I will not let you fall."

Bright one?

It was almost enough to distract her from the fact that the next time he reached for a new handhold, it crumbled in his grip. They swung wildly from a single arm that had just been holding them, and she saw her entire life flash before her eyes.

She'd tried her best to be a good person, but losing her sister had been a major mistake. She'd helped people. She'd given them a chance in a kingdom where people weren't given chances. At least, not regularly. But now she was about to plummet to her very early demise, without ever seeing the one person who had meant something to her.

But then he got it under control. Even though she was still staring at the ground that was so far away from them, at least she knew he wasn't going to lose his grip.

Again.

"Sorry," he muttered under his breath as he reached for what she hoped was a better handhold. At least this one didn't turn to dust.

Bjorn kept climbing. Higher and higher until she swore it was hard for her to breathe. She turned her gaze away from where they had stumbled, and her breath caught. The view from up here was impossible to describe. She'd never been so high in her life. She could see the castle, and all the human lands that had been her home for years. But she could also see beyond that. Toward other kingdoms that were dotted about the landscape like she rode on the shoulder of a giant.

Night fell across the kingdom. The castle was illuminated by thousands of candles, like sparkling stars in the distance that mirrored the ones above their heads.

"Are you going to stop and rest?" she asked.

"Not until I'm tired."

So they kept going.

They climbed to the highest peak just as day broke around them, and then she realized they were still going. They had to traverse an entire mountain range, and it was a journey he did with ease.

They spent the better part of three days moving from peak to peak. He'd let her down to relieve herself and sometimes to stretch her legs, but it wasn't ever for very long. He said they needed to move, and she was going to trust him on that. She had no idea where they were going, or who was following them. But Astrid noted a few times that he looked behind them with a frown and then kept moving a little faster.

On the fourth night, though, she could sense a change in him. His body was shaking, his hands weren't gripping as strongly, and he slipped multiple times as he hiked over a rather impressively scraggly peak.

This one looked more like the mountains she had been told existed. It wasn't a sharp-edged area that she feared they would tumble off of. This was flattened by age and weather, much more manageable if they were going to stop.

"You need rest," she said, placing her hand on his shoulder and trying to press the words into him.

A spark of her magic ignited, and she knew it was foolish to even consider using it. She didn't want to force him to do what she wanted. That was beyond rude, but also unreasonable.

And yet... maybe magic wasn't needed.

"I fear for your safety," she said. "You are not making decisions you usually would. You're tripping over rocks, and this is a fine area for us to rest. It may be cold, but you can start a fire. We will be warm for the rest of the night."

And for the first time since they had started traveling, she felt the muscles in his body ease.

"Aye," he muttered. "They are likely far enough behind us."

Bjorn got to work removing all the straps that had held her to him, and all she could think about were his words. Astrid hopped down from his back, frowning at the thought that there had been people following them this whole time.

"They?" she asked, rounding him and smacking his hands as he worked on the buckles of the straps. His hands were shaking. She could make faster work of undoing them. "What do you mean they are behind us?"

"We have been followed." He stared down at her with those large, dark eyes, and she tried not to look into them. Being around him did something to her chest that was uncomfortable.

It was a familiar feeling. She was getting closer and closer to him, and that made her want to protect him. Even now, removing these buckles and letting the straps fall off of him, felt like she was finally doing her part in all this. She wanted to take care of him, too.

"Are you sure they're following us? We've been moving too fast for humans to follow." She removed the last buckle, and somehow her hand ended up flat against his chest.

He took a deep breath, and Astrid could feel the air expanding through him. It was hard to focus on anything other than the sensations of him, the powerful bellows of his lungs and the heart that beat against her palm. Her lips parted slightly, and she looked up at him to see he was staring not at her face, but at her hand.

She looked too, startled by how small her touch looked against his grayish-green skin. Then, his hand lifted to cover hers. Her nails were long and delicate. Her fingers thin and graceful. His hand was tipped with rough edged nails, some of which had cracked down the center during one of his many fights. His hands were calloused, rough, and so much larger than her own.

Her heart thudded a little harder against her ribs, and she could feel his heart doing the same. Beating harder. Faster. Whispering for them to stand just a bit closer because they had gone through so much together.

She lunged away from him, heading toward a small outcropping with a scraggly tree on top of it. "This seems like a good place, yes?"

"You have good eyes, Priestess."

"I'm afraid that's all I'm good for. I don't know how to start a fire." She tried to stabilize herself with what she could control. "Wood. You'll need wood, won't you?"

"I will gather some."

"No, I can do that." She looked back to see Bjorn standing in the same place she'd left him, with his hand still over his heart. "I have been doing nothing for days on end. It will be good to use my legs."

He nodded slowly, a frown crossing his features. "Stay close. I want to be able to hear you if you scream."

"Unsettling," she muttered as she headed off in search of wood.

She just needed to get her head screwed on straight again. This was a very classic case of her not knowing what to do and how to do it right. This was why she had to have control.

Astrid didn't have feelings for anyone. That wasn't how she functioned. She was calm and collected. She was the person everyone went to when they were struggling because she flourished in chaos. She knew how to control herself.

Picking up an armful of wood, she added more and more sticks to her bundle. They probably weren't big enough, but he hadn't given her any specifics on what size to get. Likely, he knew that she needed some time to herself.

"You were bound to get distracted," she muttered as she bent and picked up more. "You were plastered to him for days on end. That's all. Physical contact isn't something you're used to."

It was an excuse she could get behind, after all. Priestesses might look like objects of sexual desire, but that was the point. They were untouchable creatures who were made to be looked at. That was all. If she had wanted to, she could have had lovers across every single town or kingdom, but she had chosen to remain focused on her own lord. Perhaps that had been foolish of her if she was getting confused by the touch of a troll.

She flinched and flattened herself to the ground as another voice crackled through the air. Deep and low, it was not a voice she recognized.

"Listen to me. I'm telling you that we're fine. The trolls down there don't come up here. And the trolls in the mountain stay in the mountain." Rougher and with an accent she didn't recognize, she feared these men would find her.

Scream, Bjorn had said. He needed to hear her scream, and he'd come running. But she didn't want to let the men know where she was.

Astrid couldn't see them. But she was a lone woman with blonde hair in a white shirt. They'd see her far sooner than she would catch them.

Crawling over to a bush that had seen better days, she pressed herself into it. The twigs dug into her skin, tearing at her flesh until there were red lines dripping down her arms and legs. She didn't even feel the pain and terror that lanced through her.

She could hear their footsteps now. Another man, this one with a higher pitched voice, said, "Yeah, but we have trolls with us. You don't think they track their own kind? I heard the last raid was attacked by a whole warband. No one made it back."

"Then how did you hear they were attacked?" The sound of a smack echoed through the night. "Dolt."

Orange light illuminated the two men as they walked toward her. She could see now that they were in clothing that looked as rough as they did. The clothes on their backs were threadbare and worn, but they wore many weapons. So much glinting metal at their hips, strapped to their thighs, covering their entire forms in a way that made her wonder just how confident they were that they were going to be attacked.

The torchlight drew closer and closer to her hiding spot, and she could feel in her gut that they were going to find her. She pulled at the wells of her magic, tugging it into being so that she could send it at them like arrows from a bow. They wanted to return to their camp. The darkness was frightening, and the sound of skittering rocks could easily be trolls hunting them down. They were safer together.

The man holding the torch shuddered. "Perhaps we should return. It would be safer."

But the man next to him, the one with the high voice, froze. She realized he was staring right at her. And that was when she realized the torchlight had reached her feet.

He could see the leather straps around her feet. She hadn't tucked them in enough.

Astrid's heart skipped in her chest. She slowed her breath, forcing herself to remain silent and quiet. She was in control. She wasn't terrified. She wasn't going to... to...

A roar split through the air. She could feel it vibrating the stones around her as pure rage sliced through them all. It was the sound of an animal who had finally found the creature it was hunting, and all who heard the sound should scuttle away into their hiding places.

"What was that?" the torch bearer said.

The other replied, "Troll."

He was still staring at her. Looking at the bushes like he knew there was something that needed to be done here, but he didn't know what. Should he attack her? She could feel his thoughts stretching across the short distance between them. Whoever was in the bush, it was his duty to find them, report them... kill them.

She pushed harder at the fear in his mind, stretching it like spun sugar. Then, as his friend turned toward the sound, she allowed her face to emerge into the torchlight.

Pale and ghostly, she used his own fear to warp her features. She wasn't just a woman in a bush. She was a specter, a warning.

She whispered, "Run."

And the two men did so as another angry roar split through the air, shattering what little calm she had left. She knew that roar. She'd heard it in the labyrinth before.

Chapter 16

Bjorn heard sounds shortly after Astrid had left. But the noises weren't coming from the direction she'd gone in, so for a little while, he ignored them.

The mountain allowed sounds to echo. He'd heard noises that he would have sworn were the souls of the dying this far up the mountain. He and his father used to travel this way often to visit his mother. Bjorn had stories from those travels that would make the hair raise straight off the arms of any person listening. He knew damn well that there were hauntings here.

But as he made the stone circle that would contain their fire, he continued hearing the noises. They were strange sounds for spirits. Words that continued slipping through, both in the human language and in the black tongue. Words that whispered of travel and others of torment.

For a time, he wondered if it was merely his mind playing tricks on him. Maybe he was back in the labyrinth after all, listening to people talking in the other cells. But no, he knew he wasn't there. Bjorn even tapped a rock hard against his bare foot. It hurt, but it didn't fracture what he saw in front of him.

He had to see what was making the sound, even if it was spirits who called out to him. He'd met them once before.

It hadn't gone well.

Crouched low, he clambered over the stones and followed the sounds until a nightmare unfurled before him. There were human soldiers here, all of them armed to the teeth and setting up a ring of fire around their campsite. Nothing would come close, and nothing would approach them without them seeing who it was. But within that circle, there were cages.

Cages that were as tall as him, but thin and narrow. They held crouched figures within them.

Trolls, he realized. Trolls that looked a lot like him. Trolls with jewelry in their ears, decorating their fingers and wrists, and clothing that was far finer than the humans wore.

These weren't warriors. These were civilians. Men, women, and a little girl who was hiding her face against her mother's belly because she was so terrified. These mercenaries had hunted his people down on the other side of the mountain. They had taken these people from their homes and were now carting them over the mountain in cages for what reason?

A group of mercenaries had gathered together, bottles in their hands lifted to the skies for a moment before drinking from them. One of them shouted, "Drink up! The king will be pleased with us in a week's time. You'll see more riches than you ever dreamed of!"

Someone smacked him upside the head, hushing him. There were more words then, but they flowed through Bjorn's ears without any real recognition. Words that warned of trolls in the mountains. Hunting grounds. Warriors who would rip and tear with their claws.

His own claws sank into the stones that he gripped, and then all he could see was red.

These mercenaries had come to his home. They'd stolen his people. They took and broke and bit until there was nothing left but blood and pain. He was so tired of humans thinking they could claim whatever they stood on and suddenly, his body moved without him.

Bjorn recognized what was happening. This was his father's blood. It was anger and rage that had been passed down to him through generations of trolls. Dag the Destroyer himself had once told Bjorn that the rage was a gift. Berserkers were the ones to hold the rage for all the other trolls, so others could go about their lives without this red mist overtaking them as well.

But to him, it was a curse. A curse where he did not remember or even know what he was doing until it was too late.

His anger passed in fleeting moments of clarity that only provided him with the ability to see what was happening. Briefly. Only a flash of what he had done.

A mercenary raised his sword, rushing forward with a yell that Bjorn knew he would catch on his claws. He plunged the sharp tips underneath the man's jaw, feeling his tongue move against his fingers before he threw him to the side.

Again, another break in his madness to see a young man on his hands and knees, frantically trying to grab his sword that was somehow on the ground. Bjorn was no kinder to him. He stomped hard on the man's back, hearing the snap of his spine before he did the same thing to the base of his neck.

Then screaming. So many screams.

He hated it when they screamed. The sound scratched the back of his skull, and he clutched his head to get the sound out of it. He heard the shrieks of those who had died before, who would die soon, the calls of his people begging him to save them, but he didn't know how.

Bjorn had just been a child. The screams had been echoing then too. The sound of his father rampaging through the humans who had attacked them was hard to forget. He had seen the blood splatters, the way it had coated his father nearly from his head to his toe. What had once been his dad was now Dag the Destroyer. That monstrous creature had once held Bjorn's hands when he was scared of the dark. That beast had once promised his son that he would fear nothing because Dag would always be there to chase away the nightmares.

Then he had become one.

Bjorn fought through the sound of the screams, killing anyone and everything that stood in his way. In some sense, he knew he was as coated as his father had been. He could feel the warm liquid dripping down his chest in rivers of unending pain. There were more though. More people to kill, because there always were.

Except those who were still standing were behind barriers. Bjorn could still hear them screaming, and he wanted it to stop. He couldn't handle the screams. He remembered being terrified underneath that cart, begging for his father to stop killing people because Dag had turned toward his own kind. The rage that burned through Dag the Destroyer was renowned. But he had always targeted humans. He'd never hurt trolls.

Until he did. And then no one could stop him. Not the warriors. Not the people who begged for mercy. No one.

All Bjorn could remember was the screams. Just like the people screaming right now. He needed them to stop.

A cool breeze played along his back. Rage still pushed through him, and he knew that he was pounding on something metallic, trying to get through whatever it was. But then that breeze caught his attention again, and he slowed.

He hadn't felt a wind like that in such a long time. He'd been stuck underground, where he knew most trolls enjoyed their time. But he had never liked it underground. He'd always wanted to feel the wind in his hair, feel it cooling the sweat of his brow, easing the torment of heat in his body.

Finally, he felt the rage in him ease. Like a candle flame blown out by a breath. It was peace. It was hope. It was…

Her.

He knew that hand on his back, and the soft feeling of it tracing down his skin. He closed his eyes, focusing on the feeling. Her hand was dry and cool. His skin was slick with sweat and so overheated. But her touch and that breeze cooled his blood.

"Are you with us?" she asked, her voice quiet even as she stood so close to a berserker.

What bravery it took for her to stand where she did, without quaking in fear. She must've known he could turn at any point and kill her. Some part of him was still screaming at him to do so. But he didn't. Bjorn held on to that cool breeze and soft touch, clutching it against his soul like the lifeline he knew it was.

He let the rage go. When he opened his eyes next, he could see that he had been standing in front of one of the troll cages. The inhabitants were terrified, all watching him with mistrustful eyes that stared deep into his soul. They were the picture of who he had been as a young boy, hoping that his father would return to himself before the monster found him underneath that cart.

Bjorn turned away from them, unable to look into those gazes that were so like his own. Instead, he turned to her. To his bright one. To the woman who gleamed in the moonlight like a fallen star.

She stood there with her hand still raised, her palm bright red with blood. And yet, she did not quiver as she met his gaze. "Are you with us?" she asked again.

He didn't recognize his own voice as he brokenly asked, "Did I hurt anyone?"

Her eyes widened, but he knew Astrid would tell him the truth. She wasn't a liar, or at least, it didn't seem like she was. Slowly, she nodded her head and replied, "Only those who deserved it."

"Good."

Then he noticed all the bodies. So many dead humans, strewn about like a bear had found them and tossed them aside. Swallowing hard, he turned back to the cage and inspected the people within it. There were four trolls in this one. Two young women and two young men. They'd likely been a hunting party who had gone out to get food, considering the clothing they wore. The more lavender-colored female spoke up. "The guard at your feet, he had the keys."

Astrid jumped into action. She rummaged through the dead man's pockets like it wasn't the first time she'd done so, and started trialing keys in the lock.

He watched her until she found the right key, and then the trolls were free. The young woman who had spoken reached for the keys. "I will take care of the others. You keep your berserker calm."

Astrid gave her an odd look, then it was just the two of them as the trolls freed the others. And Bjorn was still thinking about what she had done.

He pointed at the body. "That doesn't make you uncomfortable?"

She glanced down at the dead man. "It does. Horribly, in fact. All I can think of is the labyrinth and watching those people die in front of me."

"It does not seem to bother you."

Her pretty eyes flicked up to him, and he saw the horror in them. He saw the fear that rocked through her. But if he hadn't been looking in her eyes, he never would have known.

"I'm very good at hiding what I'm feeling," she said.

He watched her walk away from him, picking through the dead bodies as she reached for the first troll that listed to the side. She gave them a body to lean against as they headed away from the carnage that he had created. Bjorn realized he had killed them all. So many men that it was hard to count them.

But he knew his role well. His father had taught him everything, after all.

Squaring his shoulders, he got to work removing the bodies from the campsite. One by one, he stacked them into the cages that the trolls had previously been in. Then he hauled those cages away. He heaved his body into it, putting every ounce of effort into the movement as he could. Alone. Berserkers were always alone.

Until he looked up to see Astrid sitting on a rise. A glowing beacon for him to know that he wasn't entirely alone. Though she did not help him, she sat in vigil as he removed all the proof of his anger and rage.

Bjorn staggered up the rise toward her. His entire body ached, and he wasn't sure it was wise to carry her tomorrow, but he would do it. They had lost precious time, and all he wanted was to rest tonight. It did not appear that was going to happen.

"The others started making food," she said as he got close. "They're starving."

"They found food here?"

"A group of them went hunting." She remained seated where she was, her arms wrapped around her knees, and then she asked, "Are you all right?"

"I am fine."

"I don't think you are." Those light eyes stared right through him, and he hated how correct she was. How shattered he felt. He wasn't meant to be this weapon and monster who had been sharpened, honed by years of fighting others. He was not who many expected when they saw him.

And still, she sat there looking up at him as though she knew what he was feeling. So he admitted, "I do not know how I feel. It is uncomfortable to have done what I did."

"You don't like screams. You said that to me before."

"When I was a child, I watched my father do exactly what I did there. He killed everyone. Not just the humans, but the trolls too. Cutting through every living being in the area near him while I was hiding under a cart. I waited there for two days until he finally calmed down. Lying in my own piss, and shit, and tears, hoping that my father would come back." He took a deep breath, breathing out through the ache of those memories before finally admitting, "I fear I will someday become him."

"That sounds… horrific."

"It was."

"And is that the only troll you've ever met who was like you?"

He nodded. The silence that came after only hurt even more. He had been right. She would think of him as a monster, just as he thought of his father as a monster. He should never have said anything at all.

She dusted off her knees, stood, and then reached out her hand for him. "I cannot stop you from becoming him. But I think I can help you ease an old wound, if you'll come with me."

He would go to the end of the world for her. She just didn't know that yet.

Bjorn slipped his hand into hers and allowed her to tug him back to the others. They were all huddled in groups, some recognizing each other and others who did not. She set Bjorn down by one of the fires that was surrounded by many trolls. He settled in, trying his best not to look at the others. Some trolls were uncomfortable around trolls like him.

But the young man to his right reached forward to rotate the rabbit on a spit and asked, "She yours?"

He shook his head. "Bringing her to the other priestesses. Seeing if they can sever our bond. It was a mistake."

The young man handed him water and then nodded toward his hands. "Clean up. You'll need to eat to get there. You have many days of travel to reach that distance."

"I know." He washed the blood off his hands, though. Soon enough, he'd have to sniff out a stream to get the rest of the blood off him.

Then he saw Astrid again, this time tugging the little girl with her. The troll was nearly up to her shoulder already, and he knew the child had to be terrified. She was quaking the moment his eyes locked on her.

But Astrid brought her right up to Bjorn and then sat down beside him. She was still holding the child's hand, who now stood before them, as she said, "Did you have something you wanted to ask him?"

He looked at the girl, not moving a muscle. He didn't want to frighten her any more than she already was. She was a cute little thing, with a fine dusting of feathers on either side of her nose and through her hair. Very little elven blood, then. But still beautiful nonetheless.

"Did it hurt?" the little girl asked.

"Did what hurt?"

She nodded toward his hands.

Now he could see all the wounds covering his hands. Slices in his palms where he must have caught blades and knives. His claws were cracked even worse. Bruises already mottled his skin.

Sighing, he shook his head and held them out for her inspection. "I hardly feel it. I've fought my whole life, little one. These are just scratches."

"You saved us," she said, and his heart stopped in his chest.

"I'm sorry I scared you while doing so."

The little girl looked him over intently, her gaze marking every single one of the cuts before she nodded. "My mum is a healer. I can have her look at you."

And just like that, he was home again. Surrounded by trolls who would do anything to help their own. All because one priestess had brought a child over to him.

The child in him, the one who had been so alone for such a long time, settled down beside him. He swore he could almost see the boy he used to be, sitting on the wooden log with him. But now, that child wasn't quite so afraid.

Chapter 17

They stayed the night with the other trolls, but Astrid couldn't sleep. The people they had saved continued to call him "berserker", just like the people in the labyrinth had. But she didn't know what that meant.

She knew what it meant in terms of her own people. That men sometimes were overwhelmed with their own anger and bloodlust, that they were suddenly able to perform feats they shouldn't have been able to do. Except, that couldn't be what Bjorn did. She'd seen him fighting. She'd followed after the men who'd run to save their own people, and Bjorn hadn't even been a troll in those moments.

Yes, he'd been angry, but he'd been bloated with that rage. His body had seemed larger, stronger, and more capable. He'd been terrifying in the way he'd moved through crowds of human men like they were as fragile as sticks that he'd shattered with his massive fist. And then he'd turned upon his own people.

She understood why he was afraid he would become his father. Whatever overtook him when he was fighting was clearly uncontrollable, even to him. Without her touch, he might have kept bashing himself against those cages until they'd finally snapped under his grip. They were all lucky that he had been so enraged that he wasn't thinking straight.

If he had, then he likely could have peeled those bars open, and there wouldn't have been anywhere for those people to run. They'd have been stuck in that cage, just waiting for the swipe of his claws to reach them.

She pretended to sleep for a while, but then sat up to watch the faces of all the trolls around her. It was surreal in the moonlight to see all of their features. Some of them had horns, like Bjorn. Others were feathery. Some even had a fine dusting of scales up and down their backs. They were not like the trolls she had seen in the labyrinth.

Astrid was used to the trolls who were, for lack of a better term, more human. They had prettier features. Less angular and more pointed. They were clearly creatures who had been honed by magic and softened by time. But these were harder beasts. Trolls who were more used to bashing themselves against the world and chipping away at their own souls.

Then her gaze turned to Bjorn, and she was confused all over again. In his rest, he didn't look like he was capable of what he had done. His body was so thin, his face so troubled even in sleep. He looked like a man tormented by actions he could not control, and she wanted to shelter him from that.

No one had been kind to him. Clearly.

In the middle of the night, he moved in his sleep. Restless and murmuring, he was clearly fighting a struggle that he'd never win.

But she was here. He wasn't alone. So Astrid shifted herself a little closer, just enough that her thigh touched his outstretched hand. She didn't move, or even breathe, as he hauled himself closer in his sleep and wrapped an arm over her hips. His head landed on her thighs as he clutched her close.

And his nightmare abated.

He quieted down, this massive beast with his head in her lap, like he had never been touched so gently in his life. Astrid told herself not to move. She was just doing this because she didn't want everyone else to wake.

Her hand moved on its own. She stroked her fingers through his hair, clean after he'd found a stream before lying down and falling asleep. It was nearly dry, and she worked through a few tangles as he rested deeply in her arms.

The sun rose on the horizon, and she watched the daylight blossom into something beautiful. The entire realm unfurled in front of her, illuminated bit by bit with the sun. Astrid hadn't realized how high up they were. The clouds seemed so close over her head, and everything was cast in rays of pinks and light blue as the world seemed to wake.

The surrounding trolls stirred. One of the bigger males rolled onto his feet, seemed startled that she was awake as well, and then sheepishly waved at her before heading off to do his morning business.

Astrid extracted herself from Bjorn's arms before he opened his eyes. It was probably better he didn't know that she'd spent the entire night keeping vigil over his nightmares.

She followed the trolls to where they were going, as it seemed like they knew how to get around this wild landscape far better than she did. The other women were quick about their business, so Astrid tried her hardest to look like she wasn't just copying their movements before returning to the bloodied campsite.

Bjorn was up by then, talking with a few of the tallest figures. As she reached his side, she was surprised to see they were both women. Not men.

The male trolls were watching intently, of course, but it didn't seem like they were taking part in the conversation at all. They were waiting for the women to make the decision about what happened next.

Bjorn waved his hand for Astrid to come to his side quicker, and when she reached them, he gestured to the two tall troll women he stood with. They were pillars against the sky, dark figures wearing silk and fur. They were otherworldly to her, but Astrid knew better than to be rude. She inclined her head to both of them.

"They are returning to Trollveggen," he said. "I have told them why we cannot follow, but they wish to bring a message to your sister."

It was as if the world ground to a halt. Tears burned in her eyes, and for a second she couldn't even see. Her sister was not going to be within her grasp, but in a sense, she could still get to her.

"Would you?" she asked, trying to control the emotions in her voice. She knew that most people would use desperation like this to their advantage. They had to understand that she would do anything to get a message to her sister.

Rose was everything to her. Always had been. They'd been inseparable as children, and if Astrid could rush off with these trolls to see her, she would. It was maybe the smartest thing to do. Bjorn was... tolerable. It wouldn't be the worst thing to happen to her if she had to stay bound to him for the rest of her life.

But logically, she knew they couldn't do that. She wasn't going to ruin his life as well as her own just to see her sister. If Bjorn was right, then no one would harm Rose until she got there.

The tall troll woman on the right nodded. Her skin was a lovely shade of blue that blended in with the sky, and there was the faintest hint of spots on her skin, like a leopard. "We will gladly bring your message to your sister."

"Bjorn said… I received a letter that stated the trolls had my sister and that they were using her as ransom to get Bjorn back. I want to make sure they are keeping her safe." Astrid swallowed. "The two of us have been prisoners long enough."

She wasn't sure if she was talking about herself and her sister or her and Bjorn.

The troll woman nodded. "They will take good care of her there. The trolls within the mountain are kinder than many of your people give them credit for. I can promise you, your sister is in no pain."

That was good. That was reassuring.

Nodding, she swallowed hard and said, "Then can you please tell my sister I'm coming for her? I'm keeping my promise. I never stopped looking for her, and I won't stop looking. Not until I have her in my arms again."

As though she was hanging on every single word, the troll woman was so focused on her words that Astrid didn't think she even breathed. She repeated the message, and then nodded. "I have it. I'll make sure to tell her exactly as you told me."

Then she headed out. The trolls all gathered together and headed off down the mountain, as though they'd done this a hundred times before. As though they hadn't just been kidnapped and forced to travel in cages with humans who'd likely planned to sell them to the king. None of them knew what would happen to them if that had occurred. Maybe they didn't want to think about it.

Once they were gone, it was just her and Bjorn, surrounded by the remnants of last night's carnage. She watched as he took a deep, relieved sigh and started packing them up as well.

"Why does it seem like you don't want to go back to the mountain?" she asked, blurting the words out before she could think better of asking them.

He hesitated only briefly before continuing to place all of their items back in the pouches around his waist. "Because I don't want to go back."

She blinked. That was oddly easy for him to say, and she had thought it would be more difficult for him to admit it.

"But... why?"

He started placing the straps over his shoulders and waist, readying himself to carry her across the mountain once again. "I am not the same man I was when I left. The people of Trollveggen remember Dag the Destroyer's son. They knew me as who I once was, not the man I am now."

"Why is that a bad thing? Don't you want to go back to who you were before all this happened to you?"

He gave her an unimpressed look. "Do you believe that I could?"

She supposed that made sense. After ten years in the labyrinth, he must have changed in permanent ways. It made her mind stray to her sister. Rose had experienced so much of that darkness as well. If Astrid's experience had only scratched the surface, then her sister was likely feeling the same way Bjorn was.

"I guess not," she said as he finished making the strange saddle that he carried her with. Astrid got into it, helping him as best she could by leveraging herself on his shoulder and decidedly not being distracted by that big hand gripping her leg. "Why don't you tell me who you are now? Maybe that will help you settle into the idea of returning."

He snorted. "No one there wants to hear what I went through."

"Friends stay friends even through hardships. Relationships aren't easy, after all, but we all stay together no matter how hard it gets. That's just what it's like being a good friend."

He headed out, picking careful and intentional steps along the peak of this mountain range. "They don't want to hear what I've been through, or what I've done."

"I do."

"No, you don't."

Astrid thought about the implication there. Perhaps he had done something horrible that would make her fear him. But she had heard much of it. She'd seen him kill countless people now, and she knew he was dangerous. However he'd been kind to her. He'd been soft with her.

"I think I do want to hear it," she murmured. "Maybe not what you went through there, but the things that make you who you are. You said your father was like you? A berserker?"

"Yes. My father was cursed with rage as well." He jolted her up, shifting her a little higher on his back.

At first, Astrid thought he'd done it because he wanted her to stop talking. But then she realized he'd just slid her higher up his back so he could hear her better. Now she was speaking right into his ear, rather than the flat of his back.

This man. She never would understand how every action of his was so intentional.

"Your father sounds like a terrifying man," she finally said.

"He was. But my mother is soft. She is a smoke breather, as I said. She sees the future and always knew that mine would be difficult. She begged my father to help change the path I was on, but Dag was never a man interested in changing the future. He saw it as already set in stone and therefore, something that should never be tampered with."

"So he was the one who wanted you to be like him."

"Indeed. And my mother always wanted a better life for me." Bjorn shrugged again. "Unfortunately, she was never given that choice. My father took me far away from her when they started arguing, and I haven't seen her in many, many years."

"Even longer than you were in the labyrinth?"

His long sigh answered before his words. "Yes. Longer than that."

Astrid wondered what it was like to grow up without a mother. It must have been hard with a father he was terrified of. But then she had to ask, "You said we were going to the other side of the mountain, where there are more witches and people like me. Does that include your mother?"

"It may. I do not know if she still lives."

That was oddly terrifying. She wasn't sure if she wanted to think about that. Meeting his mother was a bit forward, especially considering they were bound and wanted to unbind themselves.

It was like he could feel her nerves. "What has you all twisted?"

"Well, won't your mother think a certain way about me wanting to break our bond?"

He tilted his head back and laughed. "Bright one, if you think my mother hasn't already seen that in the smoke, then you do not understand what I mean when I say she sees the future. The woman knows more than either of us about the coming days. She knows I'm coming, if she's still alive."

Eerie. Astrid wasn't sure how to feel about that. Her power had always just been in manipulating others, and it felt like a rather strong power the longer she'd had it. But to see the future?

A power like that would need to be studied for ages to come. And he made it sound like there were many smoke breathers out there. As though it wasn't odd at all for a troll woman to be able to do that.

"If your mother can see the future, why couldn't she just predict every attack upon your people? Shouldn't their skills make it easier for them to know when the trolls were going to... I don't know. I guess how to win battles and fight wars?"

He shook his head. "It doesn't work like that. They can only see the future of individuals, not of the world. If the individual isn't the person making the choices, then they won't be able to see the rest of the battlefield," he explained. "It's also exhausting to look into the future. They can only seek out so many people's futures before they will collapse. Magic always has a price and a limit to what can be done."

"I suppose so."

Her power never seemed to be that difficult to control, but she had never tried to manipulate more than one person at a time. If she tried to do an entire crowd, Astrid had a feeling she would also collapse.

She let them fall into companionable silence for the rest of the day. He was running, and she couldn't keep yelling into his ear just to have some form of conversation. So instead, she laid her head on his shoulder and watched the world go by. The blur of the mountaintops, the birds that soared along beside them, the clouds that looked so fluffy and bubbly around them.

Until finally, they started going... down.

She sat up, looking at the world that was now revealed on the other side of the mountain. Where her kingdom was full of trees and farmlands, this was rolling emerald hills. So many hills as far as the eye could see. There were trees as well, and winding rivers, but they were far more sparse.

"What is this place?" she asked.

He paused on the nearest peak, holding on to the straps with his hands and staring out at the land that she had never seen before. "Home," he said quietly. "This is home."

And then they headed down the other side of the mountain range, toward the great unknown.

Chapter 18

Home.

He hadn't allowed himself to think about this place in years. It had always been a place where he had been safe, understood, and felt accepted. He had used his magic here. He had proven to himself time and time again that he didn't have to be Dag's son if he didn't want to be. Until that had been taken away from him too.

The memories that erupted through him the moment he stepped foot here were enough to make him dizzy. Bjorn had forgotten all the places that he'd run as a child. He'd forgotten about the emerald hills that made his soul sing, and the wild animals that weren't nearly as afraid of trolls as they should've been.

He'd forgotten what it was like to be tied to the land so closely that he could feel the ground breathing beneath him. What a beautiful thing it was to feel that way.

Taking a deep breath of the fresh air, he made it down the mountain and stood with his feet in the soft waving grass that reached up to his thighs. This was where he was always meant to be. This was where his soul could find some semblance of peace.

"You grew up here?" Astrid asked.

"Yes. This is home to many trolls who do not wish to live in the mountain." Bjorn took the straps off his shoulders, helping her down onto the ground. "You may walk here. We are not in any rush."

"We are in a rush, though. The sooner I can get to my sister, the better." Astrid peered up at him, her eyes narrowed in what might be confusion.

He just grinned. "The trolls here are nomadic. They traverse the fields as the food shifts and changes. There is no set place to find the people we are looking for. Trust me, bright one. They will find us."

All they had to do was wait. The smoke breathers would be the first ones to know that someone had entered their home. And most likely, they would be the ones to send others to find them. But he wouldn't be surprised if a few bone readers had also read the bones and knew exactly where they would be, and when would be the best time to find them. They'd likely send a blood witch to bring them to the famed Grotto.

Blood witches were better at sniffing out others than the rest of them. Something about knowing how to find people by their scent alone. He'd forgotten a lot of it in the time since he'd been gone.

Astrid wandered through the grass that was over her hips, running her fingers along the tops of the greenery. "How long will that take?"

"There is no way to know."

"Shouldn't we stay put then?" she asked as he headed off into the fields.

"They'll find us either way. I say we keep exploring, and then I can show you more of the land beyond the mountain." He grinned at her. "Or did you not want to see more of this place?"

Bjorn could see the curiosity vibrating through her body. She desperately wanted to adventure, but there was still a sense of decorum and reason that held her back. He wanted her to explore, just for a moment. He wanted her to be free to love this land as much as he did.

There was beauty in that. He needed her to see it.

As they walked through the field, he pointed out all the places that he now remembered. "Over there is where I first rode a horse. It did not like me riding it."

"Did it not?"

"No," he replied with a chuckle. "It bucked me off instantly, and then I learned what it was like to kiss the ground. I have not ridden a horse since."

"You know, I don't think I've ever heard of a troll riding a horse." Astrid walked beside him with all the grace of a woman used to people looking at her. Priestesses glided as they walked, he decided, and she certainly was.

Much later, he brought her to a stream where she could wash and relax for a little while. He knew she had to be feeling rather horrid after their journey, but she didn't complain. Instead, she had endured all that he had thrown at her with grace and poise. He was thankful for that kindness, considering how horrible he felt for not providing well enough for her.

"I will leave you here to wash," he said. "I'll be back in a while, but you... take your time."

She turned to look at him, standing beside the area of the stream he had deemed safe. There were plenty of large flat stones where she could lie out in the sun if she wished. It was also a good place to dry her clothes. There were still bloodstains on the white shirt that weren't likely to come out, but hopefully she could at least turn them into a pink streak rather than the brownish smear they were right now.

The stream was fast moving here, but shallow. He could see that the speed had made the stones less slippery than other places, so he wouldn't have to worry about her falling while he was gone.

She was safe here. But it looked like she was going to ask him if that was true or not.

So he interrupted her before she could even ask the question. "No one will bother you here. Humans never come to this side of the mountain, and you deserve some time to clean yourself. You do not strike me as a woman used to traveling like this."

He was rewarded with her cheeks turning that bright, pretty pink. "Was it so easy to tell?"

"Very, Priestess."

With a soft smile, he left her in the stream. But he couldn't make himself go very far. Bjorn had thought he would explore the area a bit. Maybe seek a place to hunt and gather them some food for the evening. He'd thought his own people would find them sooner, but perhaps they were giving them time alone.

For all his mother and her people knew, he was here with his mate. They likely thought he and Astrid would want to be alone for a while before they were forced to meet his family.

He should head out. He should go farther and farther from her, if only to get some clarity, but instead he found himself downstream from where she was. Not because he wanted to sneak a peek at her. He wasn't that far gone into his own madness.

But because if he laid out on his belly on the warm stones, he could smell her on the water. Her soft scent eased his mind and filled the small pool he was suspended over like a perfume in the air. And yes, he could see the dirty water, the blood that swirled in the eddies before disappearing again. No one else would have noticed it maybe, but he did. It eased his soul knowing that he had provided her time to be clean.

He gave her until the sun was far behind the peak of the horizon. He allowed the evening to barrel toward them before he joined her at the water's edge. Bjorn, at the very least, made sure to hunt down some food for her. Arriving empty handed would have been foolish of him.

She was dressed again, seated on the ground with her arms wrapped around her knees. For the first time, he saw her as herself and not the priestess. He'd been holding her on a pedestal this whole time, seeing her as a being who was so revered and talented that he shouldn't see her as anything but. Except now he could tell that she was so much more than that.

She was small, sitting by the water, a bright light in the midst of green and emerald. A small chip of gold hidden in a stream that had caught his eye, glinting in the sun. So pretty, and yet so small.

The world seemed too big with her in it. And he wasn't all that certain he liked that.

Bjorn sat down beside her without saying a word, handing her the water sprouts and apples he'd found nearby. "They will keep you going until we find the rest of my people."

"Thank you, Bjorn. You're very good at caring for me." He could see a spark of something in her gaze when she said it. Something that looked a bit like regret, or perhaps... something else. He couldn't quite tell.

"What is it?" he asked, curious.

"What do you mean?"

"You did not like saying that I was good at caring for you. I want to know why."

"Oh." Again, pink returned to her cheeks. "It's just... I don't feel like I've done that much for you in return."

"You got me out of the labyrinth."

She sighed. "I did, but that was more for me than it was for you. Your people made it very clear that I needed to free you to see my sister again. I wasn't doing it for you, although perhaps I should have. That makes me feel guilty. Even though I have nothing to feel guilty about. My head doesn't feel like it's been put on correctly. You've been going out of your way to make sure I'm well fed and safe and that this journey is as manageable as possible for me, and I've just been entirely useless."

That wouldn't do. She hadn't been useless, she'd been... been...

No, he wouldn't allow her to think that this hadn't been a mutual experience. He couldn't. "Even without you saving my life, the bond between us has rules. Mostly for me, of course. You wouldn't know what it means, but I need to be a good mate."

"You need to be?"

How did he explain this? "A troll wife is honored. I have not been an honorable man for a very long time, and I wish to be. This is a good way to prove to myself that I can still be honorable, even this new version of me."

She finished up her apple, seeming to think about his words before she asked, "What is a troll wife?"

"Being a troll wife is not just being the wife of a troll. They are worshipped by their partner. Loved beyond reckoning, and treated like the treasures they are. Troll wives are protected not just by their husbands, but by everyone who comes in contact with them. They are worthy of that protection." He stood, dusting off his pants before reaching out a hand for her to take. "Come with me. I want to show you something."

She took his hand and allowed him to pull her to standing. "What if she doesn't need protecting?"

"It's not because we think they cannot protect themselves. A troll husband is well aware of his wife's talents. It's that she doesn't deserve to hold that all on her own. His role is to make her life easier, to take the burden off her shoulders where he can. It's not about solving her problems. It's about being there with her."

They were words he'd heard his entire life. Words that he had heeded, and he'd prayed that someday he would put them into practice with a wife of his own.

He guided her away from the stream, under the branches until they came to a small glade. The stream ran through this area of the forest, but only lightly. It was a thin, winding snake, surrounded by thick bushes that likely hid what he was hoping for.

Crouching down, he pulled her to a log and set her on it. "Stay here."

"What are you doing, Bjorn?"

He didn't answer her. A bone deep need had begun deep in his body. It had started from the first moment he'd seen her and then gotten stronger every moment until this point.

He headed off into the bushes, following the need inside of him that said he had a job to do. Until he realized what it was.

His magic had woken. Finally. After all this time, when he'd thought it had abandoned him to his rage, it was back.

The bushes hid a surprise that he now knew was perfect for Astrid. He reached into the branches, gently cajoling the tiny creatures into his palm. Holding his mouth over his cupped hands, he whispered a request to them. And though they didn't know the language, his magic made it known what he wanted.

"I don't like spiders," she said as he approached. "If you hand me a spider, Bjorn, I will start screaming."

"They aren't spiders."

"They?" she repeated, her tone growing more and more frightened.

But then he opened his palms, and all the fireflies lit up. Each of the glowing creatures flew toward her, landing on her hair and around her shoulders, some even along her wrist like a bracelet. She was covered with sparkling creatures, all of them blinking on and off in hues of gold and light green.

"I have failed you as a troll husband," he said. "The first thing I was meant to do is cover you in gems. You should be dripping in jewelry by now, but I have none to give you. I don't even have my own jewels in my ears. Trolls wear their piercings as marks of honor. We earn them through honorable deeds. And you should be covered in them for what you have done."

"I haven't done anything, Bjorn. Not really."

"You saved me. That is more than I could ever have asked for." And yet... the fireflies burst into flight, all of them heading back to the bush where he had gotten them. His eyes tracked them, looking away from her blinding beauty. "But you are not mine. I have struggled with that. I do not know how to be a good troll husband to one who is only with me temporarily."

"You've been keeping me alive. It's more than I could have asked for."

"I should do more," he murmured. "I could, if you were mine."

But she wasn't. He wouldn't even dream that she could become his, because it would only end in heartbreak. They were here to sever the bond. She'd saved him. He would bring her to her sister.

That was where their story ended.

He moved to give her space, but paused as her tiny hand grabbed onto his.

"Your magic is with animals?" she asked, her voice quiet and introspective.

"Yes. I had forgotten. It was dormant in the cells, but there weren't animals there either. So perhaps that was all it was. I thought it had abandoned me."

"You become more and more interesting every day, Bjorn." She used her grip on his hand to pull herself upright. "I'm lucky to have met you. I didn't know what an adventure this would be, or how hard it would be to sleep on the ground, but... I am glad I'm here. I don't regret this."

His heart beat a little harder in his chest. Ducking lower, he told himself it was just to catch a small bit of her scent, not because he thought for the briefest of seconds that he might kiss her. "I am glad it has not been all bad, Priestess."

Chapter 19

She stared up at him, this monster who had covered her in starlight. He wasn't what she had expected. He never was. One moment he was a warrior fighting for his life in a labyrinth, and the next he was sitting here putting fireflies in her hair because he couldn't cover her in gemstones.

Her heart pounded in her chest as she stared up at him. Bjorn looked down at her with that soft expression, a man who by all means had no idea what he did to her. He didn't have the faintest clue how much it meant to her that he cared at all. He wanted her to be happy, healthy, well fed, all the things that people should have done for her since she was a child.

But none of them had. She'd always had to take care of herself and everyone else.

Until him.

She moved before her thoughts could catch up with her. Astrid reached for his jaw, sliding her fingers along the harsh angles there, and tugged him down to her lips.

She'd known kissing him would be a little odd. After all, there were tusks on his bottom jaw that came out from his lips. They weren't entirely compatible, at least in a way she was used to. But she wanted to try. A kiss had always been something soft between people, a thank-you, an I appreciate what you have done for me that went beyond what words could convey.

And because he was a good man who had done so much for her already. She didn't want him to think that she didn't see all his effort. She did. And it had changed how she would see the world for a very long time.

For a moment, he remained frozen underneath her touch. She had intended only to give him a peck anyway, so that was fine. But then he groaned.

The sound was deep and guttural. It came from deep within his chest, like she'd prodded an old wound of his. Then he lunged forward. His powerful arms circled her, clutching her against his warm chest. Her palms slammed down upon him, and the heat of his skin burned.

He kissed Astrid back like she had never been kissed before. There was desperation in the way his lips and tongue moved over the seam of her mouth. But it was so much more than that. It was worship as she parted her lips and he delved between them, tasting her for the first time.

Every muscle inside of her tensed, seizing as pleasure coursed through her from head to toe. A wave of heat made her feel like she would soon start to pant, but she didn't recognize this person. She wanted to beg him to touch her more. Suddenly, all she could think about was the ache in her breasts and the sudden hollowness between her thighs.

She wanted a troll. It was wrong. Deplorable. He was a different species, and she should never have been tempted by him in the slightest, and yet, her fingers clenched harder on his strong shoulders. She leaned into the kiss, kissing him back like she had never kissed another man before.

Because he was ravenous. He kissed her like a dying man who didn't care who or what saw them right now. This was the last kiss of his life, if his touch was to be believed. He was making the most of every second he got with her.

When he pulled away, Astrid was breathless and could barely think straight. She shouldn't have kissed him. He shouldn't have kissed her back.

But she couldn't regret what they had done.

His eyes and expression were so soft. Bjorn tucked a strand of hair behind her ear, then followed the line of her jaw down to her lips. He traced them with one ragged claw. "Why did you do that, bright one?"

She didn't know. She'd wanted to. Because something in her felt like it had been important for her to do it?

Taking a deep breath, she said, "You are a good man, Bjorn. Kind and thoughtful. You have cared for me more than anyone else has my entire life."

"You are a priestess. I did what I was supposed to do."

"But before that, I lived on the streets with my sister. We were orphans with no family, no hope. The kingdom we live in is difficult for many, and a long life is only given to those with money or power." She licked her lips. "I still remember the starving little girl who was kicked away from stalls of food and who barely slept in the gutters while trading the watch with her little sister. I became powerful so that little girl would never experience that again."

At her every word, he seemed to grow more and more angry. When he replied to her words, it was with a snarl. "No child should endure that."

"I will never endure it again. I thought our journey would be difficult, but you have made me remember that I am more resilient than I thought." She took a step back from him, needing to clear her head.

Night had settled upon them. The fireflies were all alight, blinking on and off in the distance. They made Bjorn's features peek in and out of her vision. It was so difficult to see him now that there were trees above their heads to hide the moonlight. But she swore he was angry. She thought she would know the set of his shoulders easily by now.

"Astrid," he said, his voice so low she almost didn't hear him. "I don't think you understand—"

But then they were both interrupted by the rustling of leaves and bushes before another troll walked into the clearing. Astrid couldn't see her well, but she could definitely tell it was a woman. She was tall and lean, with wide hips that clattered with the sound of bones clacking against each other. She was decorated with so many of those gleaming white bones. There had to be at least two hundred of them creating the entire skirt.

Her top was similar to the skirt, although it seemed like it was made out of much smaller flat bones, so at least it appeared to be a little more comfortable than the skirt did. The troll woman didn't look at her at all. She just looked at Bjorn as her face lost all the slate gray coloring and turned nearly white.

"Bjorn?" she asked, her voice croaky with some emotion Astrid couldn't name. "Surely it's not you?"

"It's me."

"But it's been…"

"Years," he replied. He took a step farther away from Astrid and then sank to his knees.

She had no idea what he was doing. Why was he on his knees as though praying to this woman? But then a breeze ruffled the leaves above the woman's head, and some moonlight cast upon her features.

Pretty, broad features, with a strong nose and a wide mouth. A familiar pair of tusks jutted up from her bottom jaw, and twin horns curled over her head. They weren't as large as Bjorn's, and they certainly didn't appear as though they would aid her much in a fight. But it was hard to deny the resemblance.

This was almost certainly his mother. And he now was prostrating himself before her. As though being on his knees just wasn't enough. He laid down with his face on the ground, his arms outstretched toward his mother's feet.

She stood there before him, tall and strong and staring down at her massive son, who was now trying to make himself small before her.

"Mother," he said. "I have been gone too long."

"By choice?"

"Never." The word ripped free from him. "I was taken by Dag the Destroyer, and then…"

Astrid could hear how hard it was for him to even say the words. She almost stepped in to tell his mother that he'd been in the labyrinth, that King James had done horrible things to him for years and that his mother should be gentle with him. He was just learning how not to be in that place.

She didn't need to step in, though. His mother bent down and placed a hand on his shoulder. "I know where you have been, my son. And I have seen what you have done. I needed to hear for myself that you were not there by choice. That is all. I never doubted you, even for a second."

Bjorn got up on all fours, still not looking at the woman who'd birthed him. "I return to you with no decorations, no piercings, no honor. I am not worthy of your love, Mother."

The sound that came out of her was both a howl of rage and a cry of torment. His mother grabbed both of his shoulders, forcing Bjorn to sit back on his heels and look at her. Then she cupped the back of his head, pressing their foreheads together. "You have always been worthy of love. When you were here, when he took you from me, and even in that dark place. I never stopped loving you. Not for a single second. There is nothing you could do that would make me love you less. Nothing, do you hear me?"

Astrid's heart shattered. The moonlight turned the tears running down Bjorn's cheeks into glimmering diamonds, and she wiped her own tears away with the backs of her hands.

What a beautiful moment to witness, and suddenly she felt like she was trespassing. She should fade into the bushes, maybe head back to the stream. Bjorn would know how to find her. He always did. She could give them a few minutes alone and then join them. This wasn't about her. It was about them.

She was just about to leave when his mother turned to her. "You. You are the priestess who saved him."

Why did those words feel like an accusation?

Astrid wasn't entirely sure what she was supposed to do in this situation. If she had been in court, then she would have curtsied and simpered. She'd met quite a few important mothers in her day, but she wasn't in court right now. She was in troll lands, surrounded by their culture, and she had no idea what was polite here.

So she nodded. "I am."

"Why?"

"Because I need his help to get my sister back."

Bjorn's mother seemed not to believe her. She reached for the bones at her skirt, tearing off a few and then whispering to them in her hands. Throwing them onto the ground, she tossed them right at Astrid's feet. "Read them."

"I don't know how."

"Look at them. Read them. Will the words to appear in your mind."

She did what the woman bid her, but she didn't have any expectations. She'd seen bones before, and they had never spoken to her before. They still didn't, but she tried at the very least.

"They say nothing to me," she finally said.

"And the wind? Does it whisper in your ears?"

"No."

"Have you seen sights in smoke? Glimmers of a time that has yet to come?"

"No." What were these questions, anyway? Why was she asking her all this?

Bjorn's mother tsked. "You brought me a difficult one, my son. There are more tests I must try with her, but these are the ones I can ask for now."

Her dark green troll shrugged. "I do not know what she is. They call her priestess, Mother."

"And they are right. I can sense it. Her magic is waiting to break out, but there is something blocking it. I don't know what." Bjorn's mother stood, staring at Astrid with the same intensity as her son.

Astrid wasn't sure if she should be insulted or intrigued by what was being said. Eventually, though, Bjorn stood as well. Astrid noticed how shaky he was as he stood up. She wanted to ask him if he was all right. She wanted to clarify that this was what he wanted, and that was the only reason why he was so shaky. That he'd finally come home, seen his mother, he knew that his life could be put back together.

But she didn't have the chance. His mother barreled toward her, cupping her face and turning her head from side to side. "She is interesting, isn't she?"

"Mother, you may be scaring her."

"It's rare for me to get to see a woman like this. Humans are usually so weak in their magic, or they do not know how to use it." Again, the woman cranked Astrid's head to the side. "I wish I could peer inside you. Perhaps that would give me more clarity."

If she wasn't careful, she was going to snap Astrid's neck. Eyes wide, she looked to Bjorn for help because she couldn't tell his mother to let her go, but the troll woman did not know how fragile humans were.

Bjorn seemed only amused by his mother's actions. He walked over to the two of them and pried her hands off of Astrid's face. "There will be plenty of time to peer into her. But we are tired. We have been traveling for nearly a week now, and at a pace that is not sustainable. If I have any right to beg you for anything, Mother, I request food and a safe place to sleep."

She looked him over and then seemed to agree. "You will have that, my son. It is the least of what I can do."

The troll woman turned and headed out into the forest, as though she knew her child would follow her. And that left Bjorn and Astrid in what seemed like privacy once again. But she swore she could feel eyes on them. It was like they were never alone in this place, and she hadn't realized it until this moment.

He gently turned her head to the side, looking at the marks his mother had left on her skin before sighing. "I apologize. She is... intense."

"You could say that."

"But she will be able to break our bond. If anyone can, it will be her. I am glad to see she is alive." His thumb pressed against the ache in her jaw, tracing the redness on her cheeks that was surely there. "There will be a healer in the camp. I will bring them to you."

"I don't need a healer. The marks will be gone in the morning."

"They may bruise."

Astrid lifted her hand and pressed hers on top of his, holding his hand in place so he would understand that she was not afraid of his mother. "I don't need a healer, Bjorn. If I think I do, I will ask for one. Otherwise, leave it be. Your mother seemed intent on getting to know me, and that is something I will indulge her. But I don't want to find out what magic I have, or what magic she thinks I have. I know who I am. We're here to break the bond, not for any other reason."

Something flashed in his eyes that she couldn't name. Disappointment, maybe? But that didn't make sense. He wanted this to be severed just as much as she did. They couldn't remain bound to each other when their lives were so different.

"Come with me," he said, his voice gruffer than before. "I will show you where I grew up."

As he turned around, she felt a cold wind tracing down her spine. She'd said something wrong, she realized. But she had no idea what that wrong was.

For a moment, she entertained the thought that he wanted to keep her. Because that kiss had been world changing.

Still. A kiss could just be a kiss. Of thanks, of desperation, of hope…all the things that they had both poured into it. But that didn't mean it was anything serious.

Chapter 20

Bjorn hadn't been back here in years. There was a part of him that was nervous to see how much of his home had changed. A childhood home was meant to stay the same as he remembered. Every object in the right place, every person the same age as they had been when he'd left. It was a silly thought. A child's desire to control what little they could.

As he brushed aside branches and leaves, helping Astrid through what were the most tangled brambles he'd seen, he realized a lot had changed from his homeland. The morning light blossomed before them, illuminating a village that he had dreamt of for years.

The witches and the most talented of their women had needed more protection. This he did not understand. There were so many places where they were safe. Humans never came over the mountain, and if they did, they were swiftly dealt with by those who were like him. Berserkers, and others whose rage allowed them to kill without feeling too much guilt about it later.

That was how they had always lived. That was how they kept the blood witches, the bone readers, and the smoke breathers safe. These women were far more important than any others in their society. They were how the future was tamed.

And yet, he did not see more men like him. He saw a few of the talented witches preparing more barriers. Some of them called out to the tangled brambles and grew them stronger again once they were through the thorns that plucked at their skin and clothing. Soon he would get a better dress for Astrid. Something that wasn't just a shirt. And then he would find jewelry for his bride.

No, he reminded himself as they stepped out of the darkness and into the light of his home. She wasn't his bride. She didn't even want to be.

Instead of thinking those darker thoughts, he focused on seeing his homeland through her eyes. The grotto had been built over years and years with creative hands. What had once been a hollow in the forest was now so much more.

A stone path at their feet was dotted with crystals that grew from deep within the earth. They had been cajoled there by the songs of many artists, all of their colors reflected light that danced across the stones. Some of them were amethyst, others quartz, some were even clusters of emeralds and rubies, laid out for all to see that this was a place of beauty and power.

The stone paths spider-webbed around them, leading to homes and spiraling off to shops, then drawing back to small gardens. Everything here had been created by artistic hands, though. The pots that held flowers and herbs had been painted to look like mosaic tiles. The homes were small huts, but their doors were carved to look like swirling magic. The roofs were made out of slate stones, each of them painted in murals that stretched across the entire village. Each depicted a story that was told to children in the evenings.

The air smelled sweet here. Like greenery, freshly cut wheat, and tomatoes when he brushed up against their stems. Just taking a deep breath here felt like he hadn't breathed in years.

And then there were the people. Trolls who were the strangest folk Astrid had likely ever seen. Many here were still very close to their animalistic natures, so they could be guided by the women who were like priestesses to his kind. Most of the trolls were less human with scales, horns, and claws. All of them must have been terrifying to her.

But when he looked back, he could see that her eyes were just wide in awe. A couple of trolls walked by them, one with a clawed hand that looked like the foot of a raven, and he saw her eyes flick to it quickly before looking at the dress the woman wore instead. It was a pretty dress, hand beaded into swirling patterns that looked like overlapping feathers. Homage to the raven that had given its life to bring her from the mud, most likely.

The two trolls were so shocked to see a human in their midst that they froze. They were unable to move, staring at Astrid as she stared at them, and he thought for a moment he'd have to step in.

Astrid plastered on a bright smile and said, "Your dress is lovely. The beading is so intricate, I'm sorry I was staring. I was just trying to find out how you stitched that."

The troll blushed a pretty shade of deep red that matched her umber skin. "Thank you."

Then they skittered off, likely to tell others that they were brave enough to talk to the human captive who had entered with a troll they did not know. Bjorn hadn't seen many of these people since he was a child. He assumed no one would recognize him.

At least, until they approached the training grounds.

His mother used to live on the other side of them, and he knew that was likely where she still was. Dag the Destroyer had never wanted to visit his troll wife unless he could still train for a few days out of the visit. Therefore, they had lived near where the men and women who protected this grotto were trained.

Though he hadn't seen any of them when they entered, he was pleased to see there were people still training there. Six trolls wrestled in the dirt, each of them with gleaming weapons at their waists and snarls on their faces.

But then they paused as one. Their arena was surrounded by a thick fence made of fallen logs, keeping out anyone who wasn't training with them unless they wanted to be drawn into a mock fight. The ground where they wrestled had been turned to dust after years of trampling the earth.

Bjorn could still feel the dust clinging to his skin. He remembered what it was like to be thrown onto his back, the air whooshing out of his lungs as another, larger troll put him in the dirt.

None of them could do that now. They wouldn't have the strength, the power, or the control to make it difficult for him to fight them. Not after years of what he'd been through.

They must have caught his scent, or perhaps Astrid's. All six of them leapt to their feet and headed in their direction. Though they were covered in dirt and sweat, they were an intimidating crew of trolls to be heading straight for them. He'd never been prouder to see them.

"Ho there," one of the young men said. "Do you have permission to bring a human here?"

"From Ylva herself," he said, watching as they all relaxed.

It seemed his mother was more important than he remembered.

Or perhaps that his mother had finally been recognized for all that she did for his people.

Too many years had passed. It was hard for him to imagine all the things that could have changed. He barely knew if his memories of this place were conjured by his mind or if they were real.

One of the warriors in the back pushed forward. She was a scarred woman, her body marked by countless battles that she wore with pride. Leather straps bound her small breasts to her chest and wrapped around her legs almost in the manner of leggings. But there was a scar above her left eyebrow that was familiar. He had a flash of a memory, almost as though he remembered how she'd gotten it.

And then he did. They'd been wrestling just like the others had been wrestling. They'd been children though, pretending to be what their parents already were. His father, her mother, both warriors that were renowned throughout all of troll kind. He'd rolled her a little too hard, and she had ricocheted off into the distance where she'd hit her head on a rock. Bjorn remembered thinking she would cry and that he'd get a beating for being too rough, but she had instead claimed she was proud to wear her first scar so young.

"Tyra?" he asked, the name coming to him unbidden.

She grinned, revealing a chipped front tooth. "I thought that might be you, but I hadn't hoped you actually survived after being stolen from us. Bjorn, son of the Destroyer. You have finally returned to us!"

She reached for him. It was everything he had wanted in a reunion. Bjorn had dreamt of this in his early days in the labyrinth. He'd prayed that when he returned, people would remember who he was. That they would gather around him, holding on to his shoulders and clutching him to their hearts where he could feel that they were alive too. He had desperately hoped that they would give him a chance to be loved one more time.

But now that she had him in her arms, he could only stiffen. He didn't like Tyra touching him. His skin crawled where every point of her fingers lingered, almost as though there was static between him and her. She squeezed him harder, and he could see stars sparking in his vision.

He couldn't breathe like this. She was too close. Panic set in under his skin, and he wasn't sure what to do with it. The beast inside him raged, shouting at him to throw her off because no one could touch him. No one. It was the fastest way to death to let someone hug him like this, when he could grapple them onto the ground and make sure they didn't do it again.

She stepped back thankfully, but only a bit. Tyra grabbed onto his horns, shaking his head from side to side like she'd done when they were children. He remembered her saying that his horns were his greatest strength and weakness, because they were great at battering but also handles for her to throw him.

Right now, every muscle in his body locked, so he wouldn't use them to bloody her face.

He didn't want to. He didn't want to hurt anyone in the grotto. This was his home. He was safe. He wasn't in the labyrinth anymore, and he didn't have to protect himself or anyone else.

But then another fighter grabbed onto him, and all these feelings got even worse. He couldn't think straight with someone holding on to him. Even gently, as they were now. They weren't trying to harm him.

Another troll slapped him on the shoulder, and his mind screamed it was an attack. He knew it wasn't, though. He knew that.

He was whipped into another hug, passed from troll to troll. Then he saw them. The group of trolls who loomed over Astrid. A few of the warriors had gone from hugging him to walking over to her. They were too close, and her eyes were a little too wide. He hadn't seen that expression on her face before, and it made something in his blood boil. They needed to give her more space. Hell, they needed to give him more space.

These trolls might have known him when he'd been a child, but they didn't know him now. They should've known better. Both he and Astrid deserved respect.

One of the troll warriors put his hand on Astrid's shoulder, the massive paw a little too large, the claws a little too close to her neck.

Bjorn saw red.

Shoving the nearest troll off him, he lunged for the one touching her. A snarled warning came out of his mouth just moments before he had the other troll in his grasp. "Get your hands off her."

He didn't think. He didn't even have the ability to do so. One moment he was barely holding himself on a leash, and the next, he had spun the troll around and locked tusks with him. They were close enough that he could feel the younger male's breath fanning across his face. His tusks were larger than Bjorn's, but that didn't matter.

Rage burned between them, so hot he could feel it in billows of heat off his chest. If he wasn't careful, he was going to lose his mind. Berserker rage should only be used in the most dire of circumstances, not among friends who were just happy to see him again. Not among people who had trusted him, who thought he was there to see them again.

But he couldn't reason with the part of himself who had seen another male's hand on her shoulder.

"You brought a human to the grotto," the troll snarled. His bright blue skin had flushed a deeper color with anger. "We are allowed to ask her what she is doing here."

"You are not allowed to touch what is mine."

"She doesn't smell of you. She doesn't wear your jewelry. All I see is the faintest bond between the two of you, and if you came back here, I can only assume you came to break it." He snapped the last two words like a whip.

Bjorn yanked himself away from the other troll. There was a name for the man just out of reach. He remembered him. He remembered the split tongue in his mouth, and the hissed way he used to talk. He was not a kind troll, but he had a sense of honor that was better than most.

This was unlike Bjorn. He should not have been this angry to see his people doing their job.

Staggering back, he blew out angry breaths as he tried to get control over himself. But now, people were looking at him. Staring. Watching every movement like he was someone to fear.

Bjorn knew he was. He knew they shouldn't look at him like the same laughing man who had run through this grotto in his youth. He was not the person they wanted him to be.

And maybe that was the problem. Maybe he didn't want to be who they expected him to be.

"Bjorn," Astrid said, her voice a balm to the heat that made his chest ache.

He looked at her, grounding himself with her beauty, her calmness, and the sight of her. She wasn't upset. He didn't even think she was scared. Instead, she just watched him.

"Yes, bright one?" he asked, his voice lower than it usually was.

"Perhaps you would like to go somewhere quiet? We have had a long journey."

He swallowed hard. In so few words, she gave him a reason to be upset, a reason to have lost his sense of reason. All while making it seem like it was all right that he had done so. Even a few of the trolls around them seemed to relax a bit, their tense postures easing as the words were given life around them all.

Of course he was tired. He had been protecting her for their entire journey, and none of them knew how long he'd done so. They knew where he had been, of course, so they knew that all emotions would be much more heightened.

This woman protected him, just as he had protected her.

"My mother's house is near," he said. Bjorn forced himself to straighten and then face the six trolls who had been so kind to him. One of them was still on the ground where he had pushed her, rubbing the back of her head where it had likely struck the ground. "My apologies. As the priestess said, it has been a long journey."

Only Tyra still wore a frown on her face. "Take care of yourself, Bjorn. You are welcome here."

He could read between the lines of what she said. He needed to watch his reactions, because his welcome could be taken away very easily.

Nodding, he reached for Astrid's hand and tugged her away from the training grounds. Perhaps his mother's house would provide some sense of security. And maybe Astrid was right. Maybe he just needed a little rest to be closer to the man he once had been.

Chapter 21

Astrid tried to keep her breathing regulated until they made it to his mother's home. Ylva's house was apparently a cottage just like the others, although it seemed to have been in this grotto for much longer. The trees just beyond had dipped down, their leaves giving her home a rather lofted looking roof, even though Astrid could tell that wasn't part of the home at all.

Rather than the prominent crystals that had so far decorated this place, Ylva's home had gleaming stones laid beside the rock path. It was pretty. Sparkling. The mark of a woman who lived on her own and who enjoyed delicate things. Not entirely what Astrid had thought she would find in this place.

And still, her mind went right back to Bjorn losing himself when the crowd of people had approached him. She could see his emotions in streaks of color that rioted around him. For a moment, all she had seen was a cloud of red that created a haze between him and the others. She'd known he was angry, far more than she could ever have guessed he would be. Then sickly yellow beams had burst through the red. Shame, she had realized at the moment.

He didn't want to be angry. He didn't want to scare people. But he also needed time, and they weren't respecting that.

Ten years of torment and fighting and anger had turned him into the man he was now. She feared most people here would want him to be the same person they remembered from the last time he had left. The carefree young man she had heard of, and the man he claimed to have been.

There wasn't a hint of that person left in him. The hopeful young man who had left here carrying a warrior's dream had been beaten into the blood and mud of the labyrinth and left there so this version of Bjorn could rise.

He stalked up to his mother's house, red still bursting free from his skin every now and then. He jerked the door open and gestured for Astrid. "Inside, bright one."

Even now, she didn't think the anger was directed at her. He'd given her no reason to fear him, although she likely should. So she walked past him, but paused as his emotions reached out for her.

She didn't know what they wanted. But they were actually reaching. She could almost see the fingers and claws attached to them, stretching out toward her.

What was she meant to do? She reached back. Astrid touched a finger to his anger, shocked as she registered the heat of it on her fingers. She'd never thought of emotions as touchable. But it was so very warm, and it wanted to yank on her hand. When she tugged back, it seemed to follow her, detaching from him for the briefest moment.

His hand wrapped around her wrist, his grip punishing. "I didn't give you permission to take them from me, Astrid."

She blinked, stunned out of her trance only to realize what she was doing. "I'm sorry, I didn't... I didn't realize what I was doing."

"Give it back."

Oh gods, the emotion was still clinging to her. She could feel it slithering up her arm and shoulder, trying to get closer to her skin. Somehow, she knew it wanted to find the coldest part of her body, to allow her to chill the anger that burned through it.

"I don't know how," she whispered, looking up at him and seeing anger for the first time. Not rage, not something that would distract him into becoming a berserker. It was actual anger toward her.

She'd done something wrong again, and this time she didn't know what to do. She was so far out of her element here that it was hard to imagine what a priestess should do in this situation. Astrid knew how to control every aspect of her life and others when she was in a castle, but here? This was not something she knew how to manage.

Swallowing hard, she tried to tug her hand out of his grip. He didn't let her.

Instead, he reeled her closer to him, his voice low and that rumbling tone making her heart race in her chest. "Just let it go, Astrid. It knows you want to help, and that is why it went to you. But those are not your feelings to take."

"I could help you."

"I did not ask to be helped." Again, his hand tightened painfully on her wrist. She didn't think he was intending to hurt her, but it did.

Astrid winced, unable to stop herself from making the expression. Almost immediately, he let her go. Bjorn took a staggering step backward, his eyes on her face and then down to the mark forming on her wrist.

More of the red pulsed again, and the one wrapped around her wrist jumped back onto him. She watched it strike his chest, and he staggered back another step like she'd struck him with it. He even rubbed the space where she'd seen it disappear into his flesh.

"I have to go," he murmured, still rubbing that ache she knew was in his chest.

"Bjorn, I don't know where I am. I need you to stay with me."

"The memories..." He shook his head, and she knew she'd already lost him. "I'm sorry."

Then, he was gone. Racing away from her and this house like he was on fire. The shape of him disappeared through the brambles near his mother's home, leaving behind only a scrap of fabric and what looked like a smear of blood on the branches.

Her heart broke for him, but also, what was she supposed to do here? He'd brought her to this place with the expressed knowledge that these people could break her out of the binding and then they could find her sister. Now he'd left her here?

"That isn't new," his mother's voice said from the shadows of her home. "He used to take off like that as a boy all the time, if you were wondering."

Of course, his mother would be home. Why wouldn't she be here to complicate matters even further?

"That sounds frustrating as a parent," Astrid replied, heading into the home.

"More worrisome than anything. Even as a child, he was big. I never worried about the creatures of the forest with him. What could battle him?" Ylva appeared out of the shadows, lighting what looked like some kind of magical lantern and illuminating the space.

It was so cozy in here. Every bit of the floor was covered in plush woven rugs, sheepskin, and dark brown furs. The furniture was very comfortable looking with a small official seating area, a fireplace that already churned with a fire to keep out the nightly chill, and a small kitchen in the back. This was the first troll home they'd been in thus far with doors that led to separate rooms. Three of them, which Astrid could only assume were two bedrooms and a bathroom.

"Your home is lovely," she said, stepping toward the seating area and taking a tentative seat. She didn't want to be a bother here, and she was suddenly very aware that she was wearing a man's shirt, some belts, and nothing else.

Ylva didn't seem to mind, though. She was already cooking in the kitchen, likely making a hearty meal for the three of them to eat, as any good hostess would do.

It made Astrid feel out of place. She didn't belong. These trolls were doing what they could for each other, and having her here only made everything that much more complicated.

Bjorn should've been able to see his family, his friends, and not worry about her. She folded her hands in her lap and took a deep breath. Maybe that had been the issue. It seemed very likely that he had snapped because that other troll had put his hand on her shoulder, and that was by far an exaggerated reaction. She was fine. The other troll was allowed to touch whomever he wanted. She was used to that kind of treatment as a priestess.

"My son claims you are a priestess in your kingdom," Ylva said. She stood in the kitchen, her hands working through dough. The pounding sound of her fists striking it snapped Astrid out of her thoughts.

"Yes, I am," she replied. "Although it does not mean the same thing to your people as it does to my own."

"I'm certain it doesn't. Humans do not respect the old ways, magic, or very much else these days." Ylva took a deep breath and then planted her hands on the counter beside the dough. "Perhaps you would care to enlighten me on what it does mean to your people."

So Astrid let the words spill out. It wasn't the smartest thing for her to do. If these trolls wished to use it against her own, then they absolutely could. The priestesses were a formidable force in the kingdom, and very few knew they were so talented. Although the trolls didn't seem interested in using people like her to their benefit. If anything, they seemed to just want to be left alone.

When she was finished, Ylva was nodding. "So you use your feminine wiles to control the men who believe they are in control. Very interesting."

"Sometimes, yes. Other times it is very boring. The rules of the kingdom are to be silent and not seen, but my people are also somewhat of a trophy. The more we look like the king's daughter, the more likely we are to have power." She shrugged. "I do not know why. The king has his favorites, and power follows his favorites."

"Likely because the king himself has considerable power," Ylva replied. "King James might be human, but he is not to be underestimated. That man has magic, and that magic spills over to those he begets a child with."

Astrid supposed that was true. She'd only met the princess once, and that woman was also as evil as they came. She'd touched her magic only slightly and the emotions that came with it, and both of those things had made Astrid recoil in horror.

Considering how afraid the prisoners were of the princess as well, she suspected there was good reason for the princess's name to be whispered only in hushed tones.

Ylva got her bread into the right shape and then came to sit with Astrid. She reached for her hands, holding them in her own before turning them over. "I used to know my son well. But now I believe you know him better than I do."

Astrid sucked in a breath as the troll woman traced the lines on her palms. "I don't know about that. I've been traveling with him for a week, and was trapped in the labyrinth with him for a short time before that, but I wouldn't say I know the man well."

"Trauma has a way of building trust between those who may never have trusted each other before. You were both trapped in that awful place. You were both there unwillingly. Clearly there is a bond between you." Ylva pricked a small hole in Astrid's hand. That small prick of pain was nothing compared to the blood that welled out, and the deep violet mist that arose with that bead. "Perhaps more than just a normal bond of two people who have shared experiences."

She swallowed even harder. "We stayed the night in a blood witch's home."

"I saw."

"It was a mistake. One that we must remedy for me to save my sister."

Ylva took a deep breath, sighed, and then leaned back in her chair. "Breaking a bond such as this is dark magic. It takes much out of the person who does the breaking, and those who seek to break the bond."

"I understand that it is a lot to ask."

"Why do you wish to break the bond with my son?"

Why did she? That was an easy answer. "He said it was the only way to save my sister. I would sacrifice my own life if it meant she was safe. Rose is all I have. She's an innocent who couldn't even make it through the training to become a priestess. She deserves more than what life gave her."

Throughout all of her words, Ylva's gaze tightened. Her eyes narrowed upon her, watching every word as it was shaped by her mouth as though she had to believe the words that Astrid said. "What if I told you that you could do all that without breaking the bond?"

"He said it was impossible. That life would be torment for the both of us, so far from our... bonded mates." The words were difficult for her to say. They still seemed foreign on her tongue.

"It is true that bonded pairs do not do well far from each other. But I see no reason why you should leave."

The words stunned her. Astrid opened her mouth, closed it, tried to think of a good reason to leave and then finally blurted, "Wherever Rose goes, so do I. Your people kidnapped my sister to use as collateral so that I would free Bjorn. They threatened her life, and I have no doubt they are keeping her in a prison. I think it's highly unlikely that she would want to stay where she is a prisoner."

"Hm." Ylva shrugged. "And if she does?"

"Is this something you have seen in the smoke?" Again, the words were strange. She asked the questions like no matter what Ylva said next, she would believe them. Like this was the truth that this woman could see the future.

It was preposterous. These were the words of an insane person, and she shouldn't assume that Ylva could see the future. No human could. Why could a troll?

And yet, she still leaned forward ever so slightly, hoping that she could indeed see a time where Rose didn't want Astrid to end this bond.

But Ylva shrugged. "I can only see the future of those who ask. Are you asking me to look into your future, Astrid?"

She didn't know.

Knowing the future felt like a sharp sword that she was holding flat side against her skin. If she tilted it just right, it would cut her.

She licked her lips and then shook her head. "No, I don't think I want to know my future."

"Then don't ask questions." Ylva stood, heading back toward the kitchen. "I can tell you have power in you, but if you have no wish to see how that power can change and grow here, then I will not force you."

Astrid remained on the sofa, not sure that she'd made the right choice. Finally, she clutched her fingers together and said, "I don't know what I want right now. I'm afraid there's much for me to consider."

"Yes, I've given you far more than you wanted to think about." She nodded toward the door on the far right. "That will be your bedroom. If Bjorn returns tonight, I'll send him in to you."

Astrid had already made it halfway to the door before the words registered. "You'll... send him in?"

"Of course. You're mated. Therefore, you will share a bed." His mother raised a brow. "Unless you would have him sleep on the floor?"

She could hear the judgment in Ylva's tone that warned she had only one response that would be appropriate. So Astrid bared her teeth in what she hoped looked like a smile and said, "Yes, of course. How silly of me."

Then she walked into the bedroom, shut the door, and pressed her forehead against it. She hadn't expected life to get so much more complicated here among the trolls. But she supposed she should have.

Now she had to have dinner with his mother alone. How tense would that be?

Chapter 22

Bjorn tried to stay away for as long as he could allow himself. He had known his emotions were going to be a problem. He'd felt them bubbling up more and more the longer they were here.

This was complicated. He wanted to feel like his old self, but he also knew that wasn't possible. He wanted the memories of his time in the labyrinth to disappear, but they couldn't.

He wanted to stay bonded with the woman who made him feel more like a man than he had in ages.

But that wasn't going to happen either.

The forest held no answers for him. He could hear the trees whispering, their leaves shifting against each other as they surveyed the son who had returned to them. But none of them knew how to ease the torment in his chest. They could not move. They had not seen the battle and rage and blood that he had seen.

And when he returned to his mother's home, he did not know what to do with himself. All he knew was that life couldn't be the same as it was before. He would have to be the one to disappoint more people, telling them that he wasn't who they expected him to be.

His mother stepped out of her home, quietly closing the door behind her. He hadn't expected her to still be awake. The moon was high in the sky, nearly rounding the highest portion and then turning down into the later parts of the evening. She should've been asleep in her bed, not worrying about her son.

"Mother," he said, lowering his head and hoping she saw that he was trying his best to respect her. "I should apologize for my actions—"

"You apologize too much," his mother said. She headed toward him, keeping their conversation from her house. "That woman in there is resting, and I expect you should want your troll wife to sleep."

He winced at the term. "This is what I need to speak with you about."

"She told me."

The words hung between them, sharp and unfriendly. He hated that the first person he'd brought to his mother was someone who didn't even want the bond with him. He should have brought a young woman who was just as obsessed with him as he was with her. That was what a troll wife and husband should've been.

But then he looked at his parents, at the hate that had brewed between them, and he couldn't find it in himself to believe that all troll wives loved their husbands. He'd seen the truth of that in his own parents.

"Bjorn," his mother said, "my advice to you, if you wish to hear it, is that you should try. She is a good woman. You are a good man. The match that was made in that blood witch's hut was intentional."

He shook his head. "It was a mistake. She does not wish to be bonded to a troll."

"Are you certain of that?"

"As certain as I can be. She is a priestess to her people, and is used to a life I cannot give her. I have not made jewelry in her honor. I cannot even make her clothing. You should have seen her before all this." He took a deep breath, remembering the glimmering outfit with all those stones. "She was dripping in pearls, Mother. She was the most beautiful creature I had ever seen. All golden and gleaming."

"And yet, you say she must leave you because you have not proven yourself to be a worthy husband. You haven't even made her clothing, so you say." His mother shrugged. "Then make something for her."

"What?"

"Make a dress for her, Bjorn."

Anxiety burned in his chest, and on the tail of it came the rage that always ruined everything. "I have not sewn or even thought of making clothing in years. Ten years of pain have burned away my memories."

"Those memories are still there. You just have to awaken them." She looked him in the eye, peering into his soul. "I will care for your troll wife while you relearn what it is to be a troll husband. This is what I have seen in the smoke. You will do it."

He didn't know what to say. He didn't deserve this chance. Astrid should find someone who would take care of her better than he ever could, and some part of him wanted to argue with his mother. So he shook his head, denying the words.

"I have no money. No ability to pay for anything that is necessary."

"You will figure it out," she replied. "Don't come back until you have something worthy of her, my son. And if I might suggest a path for you? Perhaps you would find yourself in the farthest part of the forest to the north, as you did when you were a boy."

She headed back into the house, and he wasn't all that certain what she was talking about. His memories weren't entirely there. He didn't know what was in the northern forest, but if that was where she wanted him to go, then that was where he would go.

He didn't wait to see Astrid, although every part of him wanted to peer in through the window of the second bedroom just to see her sleeping. To make sure that she was all right.

The grotto wasn't far from many of their resources, so it wouldn't take him long to get to the northern forest. Bjorn put his feet on the path, and started out. He followed the cobblestones until they stopped, and then continued going, keeping the moon on his left so he was headed in the correct direction.

Throughout the short journey, he reminded himself that it was all right to take his mother's advice. She still believed in him, somehow.

The forest appeared in front of him as the sun rose on the horizon. The streaks of pink and hues of bright lavender filled his vision along the darkness of the trees. They were so thick it was hard for him to wander among them, pushing aside branches that were as thick as his arm and ducking underneath leaves that were larger than his head. It was a vibrant barrier to the woods, but then it was so dark even he had a hard time seeing what was in front of him.

Why was he here? His mother had said he'd been in this forest before, but the memories were so thin. He didn't know what reasoning he would have needed to be in the forest. And if this was supposed to get him some form of money to pay for fabric for Astrid's dress, then maybe there was a treasure here for him to find.

Then he heard a sound above his head. A creaking groan that made memories flood through his mind.

He froze, listening to the noises of the forest as the birds went silent and all the bugs stopped their chirping. He stared straight ahead of him, watching in horror as what he had thought was a fallen log, moved out of his way.

That wasn't bark. It was hair. And that log had been the leg of a legendary monster.

He ducked, remembering the stories of creatures who lived in these woods. Massive spiders, orbweavers, who had grown larger than horses. These were their lands, their world, and he'd only come here once when he was a young man on a dare.

Bjorn made sure he was far beneath the canopy of the trees where the beasts lived. Thankfully, it didn't seem like any of them had realized he was here yet. Their webs were farther above his head, and he was lucky that he hadn't stepped on any of the points where they stretched nearly invisible to the ground, waiting to catch prey.

Suddenly, he could hear them speaking as well. Their words were so easy for him to pick out, as though he had always heard them speaking.

"Scarce food lately," one of them said, her voice deep even for a female. "We must hunt, soon."

"There will be food that wanders into these woods. There always is."

"Humans hunt now. Trolls hunt. The lands grow sparse."

The other voice snorted. "Then humans or trolls will wander into the woods. They seek food, then they become food."

Why had his mother sent him here? Just to awaken the magic inside him even more? Perhaps that was the lesson she wanted to teach him. He could pay for the fabric of his troll wife's dress if he remembered how to use his own power.

He needed to leave. That was the only choice. Bjorn turned, then froze as a leg longer than he was tall lowered onto the ground in front of him. The orbweaver heaved itself out of the trees, the heavy abdomen dragging down a nearby tree so hard that it stripped the bark from the trunk. Her body was black obsidian, so dark it gleamed even in the meager moonlight that barely filtered through the leaves.

The legs of the beast were longer than any he'd seen. With fine hair dusted all over them, they helped move her massive form carefully. Right in front of his face, a spinneret the size of a sword waved in the air before she walked a little farther away.

"We need more webs," the spider muttered, one of her massive legs reaching between the others to pull silk out of her spinneret. "More webs mean more food."

"You're wasting your time," the other said, one massive talon waving above their heads. "Rest. Conserve energy for when there is food."

"We haven't had food in ages."

Bjorn watched as she wove a complicated net and then ducked deeper into the undergrowth when she turned to climb back up the tree. If he wasn't careful, they were going to realize where he was. And considering how much they were talking about food, that could end very poorly for him. He wasn't even certain he could fight something that large.

He touched the knives at his side, knowing they wouldn't be enough to fight these creatures if he had to. The weapons weren't long enough to even break through those tough hides. He needed to leave, but as the massive spider belly moved past his sight, all he could do was stare at the beauty of the webbing that was now in front of him.

That was what it was. The orbweaver webbing wasn't sticky like a normal spiderweb. Their webs were long cords, thin, but impossibly strong. You could saw through them with a knife, but they wouldn't stick together.

He'd stolen some of those threads for his mother. As a teenager who was dared to go into the forest, he had run through it and gathered as many pieces of that webbing as he could. She'd crocheted a miniature web out of them, winding the threads into knots, and hung tiny crystal beads off of them to look like droplets of water hanging off the web.

This was perfect.

This was... everything.

Astrid deserved to be covered in gossamer weavings with tiny drops of diamonds decorating the entire dress. She'd look beautiful in a dress like that. Beautiful in a way that he could never replicate, but he now desperately wanted to try.

Be a troll husband, his mother had bid him.

And so he would.

With a deep, steadying breath, he raced out of his hiding place. This would take more than just precision. It would take every ounce of his speed, his effort, his energy. He ran through the clearing to the sound of the spiders gasping in surprise. He sliced through the first strand, yanking it out of the ground where the female had attached it. Then another.

There were five strands in this clearing alone, each of them anchoring the webs that made up the spider's home above him. Their anger and rage filled the clearing as he darted from it, leaping over fallen logs and coiling the threads around his elbow and up to his hand as he bolted. The nests were easy to find when he was now looking for them. He could see them in the trees, and how they were anchored.

Was he ruining their homes? Yes. But he wasn't going to stop now.

He continued, running through the forest and dodging the angry legs that speared down at him from above. One got close enough that he felt the needlelike hairs pierce through the skin of his arm. He'd have to pick those out later, but for now, he would ignore the sharp sting. He just had to get an armful of these strands and then he'd be able to make a dress worthy of her beauty.

"Rage!" a spider female screamed above his head. "Intruder!"

His breath sawed in and out, his heart thundered in his ribcage, but the fear that had gripped him was no more. This was what he was good at, what he'd always been good at. Hunting, seeking, adventuring—this was as much part of his soul as anything else.

And when he'd gathered enough of the silk, he ran free from the forest. There were at least fifteen spiders trailing him now. The sound of their thundering steps as they ran through the forest after him was enough to put all the hairs on his arms on end. He was so close.

The sound of wind whistling over his head made him duck. He tripped, flying through the air and certain he was about to be devoured by snapping jaws that would tear into his flesh with ease.

Bjorn rolled into the sunlight. He palmed his blade, turning onto his side and holding it toward the massive spider that lurched onto its back legs, screeching as the light burned the many eyes dotted across its face.

Breathing hard, he stared as it slunk back into the darkness. It was breathing heavily, glaring at him along with the many, many others who had gathered along with it. They all remained at the edge of the forest, drool falling off their fangs in wet plops.

He held up the bundle of threads that he had stolen, brandishing them like the treasure they were. Breathlessly he called out, "My troll wife thanks you!"

They were already muttering about rotting corpses and hanging him up by his toes.

But he'd done it. He'd proven himself worthy of the material to make a dress that many troll wives would dream of for years to come once they saw his wife wearing it.

Now, he just had to make it.

Chapter 23

Astrid was getting antsy. No one would tell her where Bjorn was, or why it was taking so long for him to come back. A part of her wondered if he was dead. He'd disappeared into the forest, and she had no idea what his anger would lead him to do. He'd proven himself to be slightly unhinged when it came to others.

What if he'd started a fight he couldn't end? What if he had fought his way through another mercenary group and gotten captured again?

She'd sat with his mother for three days. Three full days of eating, resting, thanking others when they brought her items of food or articles of ill-fitting clothing. She'd done everything she could to remain patient with them all, but she was done waiting.

She needed to find her sister. Rose was running out of time, and even though they had sent a message, the bond between her and Bjorn should have been broken by now. If it was even possible at this point.

Ylva was very secretive in everything that she did. Astrid had tried to pin her down multiple times with questions about where her son was, or if Astrid could make the journey to Trollveggen alone. But the smoke reader was very quick in all her responses.

"I will read the smoke for you to guide your journey. Remain here until Bjorn returns."

That was the only response she ever seemed to get whenever she asked too many questions. Otherwise, Bjorn's mother simply took care of her as any good mother might. She made food. She refused Astrid's offers to help with the housework. She brought her outside and treated her almost as if she were a helpless child.

Careful sitting there.

Don't touch that.

Breathe easier, Priestess, this will be more comfortable for you to sit on.

Ylva had even fanned smoke away from her, saying if she didn't want to entertain the possibilities of what she might become through troll magic, then she shouldn't even inhale the smoke. She was tempting fate, Ylva claimed.

By the third day Astrid was losing her mind. If they weren't going to tell her where Bjorn was, then she would find him herself. Before Ylva woke in the morning that day, Astrid dressed herself in one of the many dresses that had been brought to her. This one was a little shorter than the others, but it still hit her at the shins. It was made mostly out of leather, dyed a pretty deep red that complemented her skin tone very well. The troll who had made it was clearly extremely proud of her work.

The only issue was that it was shaped like a box. It was clearly made for a troll woman with far more curves, and someone who was much taller. It barely clung to Astrid's form, one side nearly always falling down her shoulder and off her arm. She'd gathered it around the waist with a belt that was sewn into the dress, but even then it wouldn't tighten enough without bunching rather comically.

At the very least, it stayed on her body, and it wasn't a shirt that she had taken from Bjorn. But maybe she preferred the shirt a little, if only because it was a piece of him.

She headed out along a path, starting in any direction. It didn't matter where she went, because she didn't know where he was. She figured she could go anywhere, and maybe she'd come across him.

Astrid explored for most of the day. She came across the farm that the trolls held most of their cattle in. There were so many gardens she could barely keep track of them all. There were some people who who smiled at her, some who were terrified when they walked by, and countless children that were so adorable it was hard not to pinch their cheeks.

But no Bjorn. And no matter who she asked, they also hadn't seen him in days.

At this point, she was going to ask any troll she could to take her to Trollveggen. She'd done her part. She'd gotten Bjorn out of the dungeons. She'd gotten him into the lands where the other trolls lived. That was as much as she was willing to do right now.

Sometime in the afternoon, she found a path that headed in a direction she hadn't explored yet. It disappeared into the trees, but not in an ominous way like many of the paths that led out of the grotto. This one was just... pretty. Golden light burst through the leaves of the trees, illuminating the path as if she were meant to go this way.

So she did. She followed the path far from the village, meandering through golden light and emerald leaves until finally she came to bright white pillars. Taller than six men high, they were clearly ruins of what used to be here before the trolls had come. They were stunning creations, reflecting the light in a way that made her eyes water.

Astrid strode up to the first one, freezing when she saw the image of a person behind it. But then she realized very quickly it wasn't a person at all. It was a stone carving of an elf.

Taller than her by far, the willowy woman was stunning in her beauty, although her arm had broken off at some point. She'd been carved with delicate fabric pooling along her curves, and gently pointed ears that were tipped as sharp as daggers. Her strangely inhuman face, close enough to be eerie, stared down at her with disappointment.

There were more pillars, Astrid realized as she strode past the first goliath. Ten of them on each side, all of them leading away from the village. She glanced down at her feet, and then she noticed that there were small chips of what might have been a floor long ago.

"Elven," she whispered as she bent down and picked up a shard of the floor. It had once been white marble. This had been a place of worship for the elves, or perhaps a place of revelry. But now, in their absence, it was just the remainder of what had once been beautiful.

The chipped pieces under her feet had been moved by the earth shifting beneath it. Tree roots had popped out in all directions, a stream had meandered through it, and moss ate away at whatever was left. It turned this place into a hidden beauty, a gem in the middle of the forest with no purpose other than to fill the senses with light and wonder.

It was there that she saw his shadow. He was leaning against a pillar, his horns scraping against the white marble and his legs spread wide. He looked... exhausted. Like he hadn't slept since he'd left her.

Sighing, she headed toward him. The poor man needed to take care of himself more. But if he refused to see to his own well-being, then she was just going to have to do it for him.

She frowned as a glint of metal in his hand caught the sunlight. A needle? What in the world was he doing?

Astrid should have announced herself and not snuck up on him, but she also wanted to snoop a bit. Bjorn was still very much an enigma to her. The man was more mystery than he was reality, and she wanted to understand him.

So she didn't announce herself, and instead crept up to a nearby pillar and peered around it. What she saw there was not what she ever would have guessed.

Bjorn had his legs spread wide, his pants down around his buttocks, and his cock in his hand. She got stuck on that for a moment, because what an impressive cock it was. It was slightly deeper green than the rest of his body, but the head was such a pretty pink, it was hard for her to even think about anything else. Not to mention the size.

Astrid had seen many cocks in her life. She was an advisor to a lord, after all. There were so many men around her at all times, it really would have been a miracle for her not to have seen almost every lord's cock in the kingdom at this point. They seemed to love whipping them out and brandishing them at the first opportunity.

But Bjorn's was... large.

No, that wasn't even the right word for it.

Massive. That was more like it.

He gripped his hand around the base of it, holding the beast with his hand, and she sucked in her breath at the thought that he was maybe pleasuring himself. She would sneak away if that was the way of it. The man deserved a little alone time. All the gods knew she desperately needed such a thing herself except... then the needle glinted in the sunlight yet again.

Bjorn put a strap in his mouth, biting down hard on the leather, and she had a sudden flash of what was about to happen. Was he going to hurt himself? What was this mangling of the man who had saved her? No, she should step in.

But if she stepped in, what if she distracted him and he accidentally maimed himself?

She was so indecisive that she missed her opportunity. With a move that looked almost practiced, Bjorn threaded the needle through the underside of the head of his cock, and then straight out the middle of the head. The tendons on the sides of his neck stood out in pain, but he didn't make a single sound after that. Not one that she could hear, at least.

Astrid's hands flew to her mouth, and she held her breath as he immediately picked up a hoop that he then pushed through the same path the needle had gone. Blood dripped from the wound, although perhaps not as much as she had thought there would be. She'd been certain a wound like that would gush blood like a mortal wound. This one did not, although she still thought perhaps it should.

And as though nothing had happened, Bjorn placed what looked like a handkerchief underneath his cock and then started tucking himself back into his pants.

To catch the blood?

What on earth was the man doing?

Finally, a sound came out of her, one half of rage and one of shock. It ended up being a rather squeaky noise that echoed quite a bit.

Bjorn flinched, then stared in her direction. His eyes got wider every passing second that neither of them said anything. But what was she supposed to say? Why did you just maim yourself? What the fuck are you doing?

She settled on the former. "Why are you hurting yourself?"

He blew out a long breath, and she was certain he was steadying himself for the argument that was about to occur. "Trolls have piercings."

"Pierced by others, I would imagine. Not by themselves." But no, that wasn't her issue with it. She stalked toward him, suddenly so angry she could have spit lava. "Why are you mangling your body like that? What could possibly possess you to harm yourself like that?"

He didn't seem bothered. He sat there in the moss, his pants still half undone but at least his cock hidden. Still, it was distracting to see all those abs and muscles on display with his pants undone and the finest bit of hair revealed by them. "My mother advised that I have yet to prove myself as a good husband to you."

"That has absolutely nothing to do with... with..." She gestured to his crotch and then to his face. "Stop trying to change the subject."

"I'm not changing the subject."

"Is it your anger? Is self-mutilation something that soothes you?" She hoped not. Oh gods, what if that was what it was?

Astrid could feel the blood draining from her face. Suddenly she wasn't sure she could stand on her own if she had to think about this. The needle played through her mind, over and over again. The flash of metal in the sunlight, the cords of his neck in sharp contrast to his body, the pain he must have felt.

Bjorn held out a hand for her to lean on, not standing himself. "I told you all great trolls have piercings that they earn, did I not?"

She was hardly following what he was saying. If she wasn't careful, she'd topple right onto his poor abused cock and hurt them both. "You did."

"Husband piercings are earned as well. They are usually done before a bonding, but..." He arched a brow. "The two of us didn't do things all that normally, I suppose."

No, she still wasn't following. Shaking her head, she asked, "What is a husband piercing?"

He looked pointedly down at his cock. "I think you already know the answer to that, Astrid."

Oh.

Why?

"Why in the world would that be a husband piercing?" she asked, perhaps showing a little of her own naivete.

"Probably because troll wives love them so much." His voice was sardonic and obviously a little amused. "I'd offer to show you why, but I think that will be impossible for a little while yet. Trolls heal fast, but not that fast."

She must've looked like a fish standing there with her mouth open, but she really didn't know what to do with this information. Trolls pierced their cocks for their wives? Nothing about that made sense to her. How would a random piece of metal in a cock feel good?

She shook her head. "You did not have to do that for me. This is dissolving anyway. We're breaking the bond—that's what you said."

"And in the meantime, we are still bonded, and I have not been doing my job as your husband. My mother's advice is sound. This may be the only time in my life that I am a husband. I should give it my best effort."

He took his hand away from her, but she wasn't sure if she could manage to stand on her own yet. This knowledge was perhaps a revelation and one that she would need to sit with for a while. Piercings. On his cock of all places!

Her eyes kept straying to his lap, and she needed to pull them away from him. She didn't want to see. She did not. She'd watched the whole process, and that had been more than enough considering the absolute nonsense of what he'd done to himself. He'd put a needle right through himself!

But Bjorn clearly understood what she was looking at. He grinned. "Would you like to see?"

"No," she instantly replied.

"It is quite gruesome right now. And it will swell. If you want to see what it will look like, you should look at it now before it does."

"No, Bjorn."

He shrugged. "If you're curious, I'd let you. That's all I'm saying."

And somehow he managed to make her want to laugh in the midst of all this madness. She caught herself looking down at his crotch yet again before becoming even more annoyed with herself. "Come on, you should get back to your mother's and put something cold on that before it really does swell."

"My mother doesn't need to help. I'll just get in the stream."

"Infections, Bjorn."

"Healers, Astrid." But he took her hand when she offered it to help him stand. "I'm sure there have been plenty of young trolls doing worse things immediately after a piercing than walking into a river to help the pain."

"I'm sure we can find something safer and better than that." Maybe helping him stand wasn't the smartest idea. Neither of them was very steady on their feet, but she managed to get him walking. And once he was moving, he was able to prop her up.

"This is ridiculous," he said with a soft chuckle. "You shouldn't be carrying me home."

"I'm not carrying you home. You're carrying me home."

"We're carrying each other, then." The soft look on his face made her heart skitter in her chest. "Thank you, Astrid. For helping me."

"You're welcome. I still think it's stupid what you did."

She swore he muttered something under his breath like, "I wish I could show you why it's not." But then he was moving them forward so quickly she was having a hard time keeping up.

"Why are you in a rush?" she asked.

"Because I have a gift to show you."

"More than just piercing your cock?"

He grinned, and it was the first time she'd seen a real smile on his face. One that lit up his eyes and his whole features until he was almost... handsome. Traditionally handsome, not just handsome for a troll. But suddenly he looked like a man she wanted to spend lots of time with, just to see him grin like that again.

"I think you'll like this one quite well. I went through a lot of trouble for it," he said.

Well, who was she to deny a gift?

Chapter 24

Bjorn did his best not to look quite as sore as he was. He remembered the pain of piercings, but he'd never pierced his cock before. After all, those were only done when a troll was certain he had found his bride.

Perhaps this had been a mistake. But as they both staggered back toward his mother's cottage, he couldn't bring himself to believe it. The right thing to do was to give this a shot. His mother's advice was sound, but even more than that, he wanted this to work.

In the labyrinth, it had been hard to believe anything could be done about his future. He'd given up on the idea of living because there hadn't been a future to have. Fighting like he had, it had been inevitable he would make a mistake. The time he had been in there had been spent during his youngest years. He'd been a good fighter, and he'd stayed alive. But he'd known those times would dwindle. Someone would've eventually fought better than him, or the king would've given him an impossible task that would've killed him.

Now he was free. He wasn't in those pits with no future and no hope. Perhaps he had feared hope for too long and now he didn't have to fear it anymore.

With Astrid under his arm, he felt like hope maybe wasn't that terrifying. Now, all he could do was pray that what he could offer her was enough to change her mind about the bonding. If he was lucky.

They made it back to his mother's house, and he groped for the door. Opening it while leaning perhaps a little too hard on the hinges, he gestured for her to go inside. "Please."

"What is this, Bjorn? We really need to get something cold for your... your..." The adorable little thing couldn't even say the word, and that made him a little concerned for their future, but he was a patient man. He could figure this out.

If he had to wait a hundred years and still only get to taste her, then it was a life worth living.

Astrid headed in before him and then paused in the doorway, her mouth dropping open. Bjorn had made sure they could share this moment without a single person interrupting them. He'd shown his mother the dress he'd worked on for a good thirty-six hours, and then asked her to give them some privacy. She'd been all too happy to do so, saying she'd stay with a close friend while they figured things out.

Even Bjorn was surprised he'd come up with a dress that pretty. The woven pattern created a bodice that would wrap around her waist and cup her breasts in the same path he wanted his hands to follow. The strands of silk seemed to glisten even from where he stood, with only dim sunlight to illuminate them. The skirt would fall from her hips in a straight, silken line, stunning in quality and woven so skillfully that even he wasn't sure where the pattern started and ended. It had taken him hours to figure out how to do that kind of weaving.

But the best parts were the tiny crystals he'd added to each part, just like his mother had done all those years ago. Frozen water drops in the form of smoothed crystals that he'd carved out with his claws. His hands still ached from the work.

"What is this?" Astrid asked.

"It's for you."

"Where did you get a dress like that?"

He could feel his cheeks heat. "I made it. For you."

The stunned expression on her face was worth all the work he'd put in. She looked back and forth between him and the dress, clearly trying to match the man to the creation. "You... made it?"

"That's where I've been." He leaned against the door frame, trying his best to focus on this conversation over the throbbing between his legs. But still, all of this was worth the pain and the work. "A troll husband does more than just provide jewelry and protection. Gifts are a large part of who we are. Handmade gifts."

"I didn't know you could... could..."

"I had forgotten how to weave, but then I remembered," he interrupted. He was feeling a little awkward with her praise. "Try it on. I'd like to see if it fits."

Then he headed back outside, closing the door to temptation. The longer he was with her, the more he wanted to see of her. Just a few days gone from her side and already his mind had wandered to dangerous places. He wanted to know what it would look like as she slid that ugly dress off her shoulders. Would she blush knowing he was watching?

It was a twisted part of him that even wanted to watch. Trolls and humans rarely mixed, even though trolls often needed humans to create children that were stronger in magic. But it wasn't often that the human woman wished to be with the troll husband.

If they ever bonded.

He knew the history of their people, the torment they often found themselves in. He knew without a doubt that this relationship between them had flaws even he could not control. Tempting each other like this would only end in heartbreak, and yet he was willing to have his heart broken if he got a few minutes with her.

Movement at the corner of his eye caught his attention as a pair of blood witches approached. They were elderly women, even frailer than the usual sight of a blood witch. Twins, he realized as he looked them over. A rarity among his people.

The two old women sat down on the logs outside his mother's home, stretching their legs and massaging their thighs. They both wore traditional clothing, which he hadn't expected. The long red fabric was threadbare, a testament to the many times they had worn the ceremonial garb. Though the threads still clung to their shoulders, the long skirts had been torn multiple times, revealing their thin legs. The charcoal coloring of their skin was broken only by the raised strips of scarring that looked like the pattern of waves.

"Svala," one said, and then pointed to the other. "And Lykke."

"It is my honor to meet you," he replied gravely, only to see more women joining them.

These two were clearly bone readers. The bones rattling on their dresses were in patterns made to make it easy for them to read the bones that twisted against their skin in reaction to those around them. One was burnt orange in color, the other a light blue that rivaled the sky. They were young women, far younger than he'd seen bone readers. But each of them wore necklaces of a different creature. One was a snake, the other appeared to be a rat. They must have been renowned readers, because he didn't expect to see them sitting with ancient blood witches like they were.

And last were two smoke readers—his mother and another, a new mother herself. He was stunned to see the smoke reader with skin the color of pale moonlight and her silver child on her hip. He hadn't seen a baby troll in such a long time. The little one had plump cheeks and bright eyes, along with the tiniest tusks he'd ever seen.

The two of them sat on the third log in front of his mother's fire pit, staring at him expectantly.

He had no idea what was going on.

"Mother?" he asked, his voice perhaps a little gruff. "Why are all of you here?"

"Light the fire for us, my son."

Of course she wouldn't answer him. When did any of their people answer questions?

He tried not to grumble under his breath as he worked on lighting the fire pit, trying his best not to wince and then have them ask why he seemed in pain. The last conversation Bjorn wanted to have with his mother was to tell her that he'd pierced his own cock and that it was sore.

Thankfully, the fire lit quickly, and he could sit down on the last remaining log. Nerves bit at him. He had wanted this moment to be special between him and Astrid. The dress was meant to be a gift that he had made for no reason other than to see her smile. Now, it felt a bit like an ambush.

It was too late for him to change anything or to usher the ladies away. The door opened and out stepped Astrid and he...

He forgot how to speak.

The dress clung to her curves in all the ways he would have dreamt, but also now wanted to hide from the sight of others. The silver threading looked like gossamer. The stones glinted in little flickers that made the eye dance all over her form. She'd let her hair down, so it flowed over her shoulders, melding into the silver of the gown until he was enchanted by the goddess who stood before him.

He was unworthy of even a moment of her time. She was beyond beautiful, stunning, glorious, and he was an animal wallowing in the muck begging for a ray of her attention.

The troll women around him hummed out appreciative breaths. The one with the child said, "Well done, Bjorn. I remembered your weaving, but I didn't know you could do this."

His mother agreed, "He was always talented."

One of the blood witches, Svala, he thought, said, "Now that is a witch if I've ever seen one. There are few like her, I'd guess. Lif, take some of that smoke and see what the rest of us can see."

So that was what they were doing. All these women had gathered together to peer into Astrid's potential magic without asking if she was actually willing to do so. Meddling beasts. They were going to make this so difficult for him.

Astrid walked over to his side, standing right in front of him in the dress he had made, and watched the proceedings of the women before him. "Did you want me to perform in some ceremony?"

He couldn't help himself. Bjorn placed his hand on her hip, turning her to look at him and only him. He wanted to see her for a few moments. Just to look at what masterpiece he had created with time and energy. "You look..." He didn't have the words for it.

A pink blush spread on her cheeks, just as he had hoped it would. "You are too kind, Bjorn."

"Do you like it?"

She seemed to really think about his question, rolling it over in her mind before she nodded. He could feel a knot inside of him ease at her approval of what he had made, and then she placed a hand on his arm. "It's beautiful. I just don't know how to thank you for something that was made by such a talented hand."

"There are no thanks needed from you. Merely seeing you in this is thanks enough."

It was a memory that would be burned into his mind for many years to come.

"Come," his mother said, gesturing with her hand. "Sit with us, Astrid. Now that you look the part."

He could see the little furrow in her brow, and the confusion at what his mother was even suggesting. But she sat, and that was something that he could admire about her. At least she didn't let their oddities bother her too much.

She sat down next to him, her legs so close they could have touched if he moved. He almost did until his mother sent smoke billowing in their direction. Both of them coughed, and he tried to move the smoke away from them with his hands. But there was so much of it coming off the fire, it was hard to get any fresh air near them.

Svala approached them through the smoke, pricking their fingers with jagged needles before disappearing. And then there were the bone readers. It was all he could hear, the rattling of the bones in their hands and how they threw them onto the ground.

"Aha!" Lykke shouted. "Not one of us after all! But similar. Close enough that it would be difficult to tell. Powerful, indeed. I haven't seen a match like theirs in a very long time."

"You think you saw something?" his mother muttered. He saw her blow in their direction, another wave of smoke making it hard to even see the other women. "Oh. You're right. There it is. How did I miss that?"

One of the bone readers shook the bones in her hands, and he saw one of them fling near his foot. She must have thrown them hard. "From Hugr to Fylgja, it's not unheard of. Just uncommon."

"What are you all talking about?" Bjorn coughed, trying to clear the smoke a bit more so he could at least see his mother.

With a snap of their fingers, the smoke cleared.

Astrid and he were left staring at the six women, the sudden silence making it hard to do anything but focus on them.

His mother leaned forward, clasping her hands together with her elbows braced on her knees. "She is not one of us, Bjorn, although I can see why you might think so. Her power affects the Hugr, the mind and emotion of all souls. Your magic is outside of your body. You can speak to and control animals if you wish. Combined, your gift could become very powerful indeed."

But they were here to break that power, not encourage it. He didn't want to know what they could do together if they remained as they were.

Apparently, Astrid did not share the same thoughts. "What do you mean? I know Bjorn said our magic would mix the longer we're bonded, but..."

She trailed off. He wondered if some part of her was concerned about what she would reveal if she went down this path. But his mother immediately jumped into the conversation as though she had been hoping for Astrid to ask.

"Every bonded pair amplifies each other's magic. You are a unique pairing because you are both strong in magic. Given time, and practice, you would be able to access and perhaps even control the Fylgja. They are guardian spirits, often in the form of animals, that guide every living being in our realm. Many cannot see them but will know what they are."

"The Fylgja?"

"Have you ever stood in the middle of a field and heard crows that weren't there?" His mother asked. "Have you ever sat on a stream and listened to frogs croaking that you could not see? These are spirit guides. Guardians who lead us through our lives, sometimes even determining how long we live. You could affect them. Pull them out of people. Use them to your own advantage. You could wield those creatures like weapons, if you wished. Your own and others."

Astrid's eyes grew larger and larger. Even Bjorn wasn't sure if he enjoyed the thought of that. Together, they would be rather impressive if they continued to allow their magic to mix.

"And if we sever the bond?" she asked.

"None of it will come to be. You will return to affecting emotions. He will talk to animals. It will be as if nothing happened." With a shrug, his mother stood. "But the things I see in the smoke... I would suggest you keep the stronger magic, dear ones. You are going to need it."

"Why?" Astrid asked, her voice shaking.

"You said you don't want to know your future. I will respect your wishes."

As the women stood and left the fire, all Bjorn could think was that they had done this on purpose. The sly look in his mother's eye, the way the other smoke breather held that baby who behaved so well, the other four who had only been there to underline what his mother and the other smoke reader had said. They were here to try to convince them to stay together.

His mother winked at him as she left with the other smoke reader and then mouthed words he had no idea how to read. But he knew that this was meant to help them. This was meant to push them in the right direction of staying together.

He was weak enough to accept the help. Bjorn wanted her, damn it. He wanted Astrid to stay with him, and if this was how he got her to do so, then that was what he would do.

"Come with me," he said, standing and ignoring the pain blistering through his body.

"Where?" She took his hand and stood, a furrow between her brows. "And why? Shouldn't we get this bond dissolved and then leave? My sister needs us, Bjorn."

"Your sister is safe under the mountain." And he needed to buy himself time. He needed to think and wonder and beg her to stay with him if that was what it took.

Chapter 25

Her mind was spinning. This wasn't at all what she had thought would happen here in the grotto. The plan had been to get in, break the bond, leave.

But now everything felt jumbled. His family had been so kind to her. He'd made her this dress that fit her better than any dress had back home, and that was saying something. The style he'd chosen, the measurements, they were all so perfect she wondered if he'd somehow snuck in while she'd been sleeping to size her waist.

Astrid knew he hadn't. He was so aware of her every move and all the things that she liked, that he could create a dress out of nothing that he knew she would love.

Then there was that kiss. Of everything that made her head spin and turned her mind, that kiss was the most confusing of all.

She'd dreamt about it just last night. The way his hand spanned her waist. How he had gripped her so easily with his hand tunneling through her hair. The passion in his touch alone had convinced her that he would be equally attentive elsewhere. And now she knew he absolutely would be. Just look at the dress on her body and how long it had taken him to make it.

But she was here for her sister. No one else. Her life didn't matter. Her wants and needs didn't matter. Rose had to come first, before all else.

So while he dragged her through the village, she told herself that she would get ahold of her feelings. She would tell Bjorn they needed to sever this bond right now, and then they would move on with their lives without each other. He would bring her to the mountain. She would free her sister, and they would part ways.

But then she saw where he was bringing her, and the words stuck in her throat. He parted the brambles for her, making sure that not a single one touched her skin or her new dress, and they went out into the fields beyond. The waving grass tickled her hips, so pretty it was hard to believe it was real. The sun shone high in the sky now, warming her skin. And the grin on his face was one she was still getting used to.

Bjorn smiled while they were here. That silly, big grin on his face might've looked dopey, but he was so happy.

She hadn't seen him happy before all of this. He'd been gruff and stern, not this bright eyed man who still had hope in him.

"I've been remembering so much since arriving here," he said as he tugged her through the waving grass. "So many of my memories I kept buried. I didn't want to remember anything. It was too hard to think of all this when I was locked away in the dark."

"I don't think anyone could blame you for that."

"They could. Many in that dungeon clung to their memories. Even Rabbit claimed it helped keep him out of those dark places." His brow furrowed, a familiar frown crossing his features. "They kept trying to stay out of the darkness while I guess I dove headfirst into it."

No, she didn't want him to think of all these things when they were here, of all places. He could work through the memories when he needed to, but he'd just made her a dress. He'd been so sweet and hopeful only moments ago.

"Where did you get this fabric?" Astrid asked, plucking at a bit of her waist. The attempt to change the subject seemed to help, at least.

"Orbweavers."

"Isn't that a type of spider?"

He snorted. "Bigger than you're thinking. They're the size of horses on this side of the mountain. Nasty beasts. They hunt trolls, humans, anything big enough to eat."

Her mouth dropped open the more he talked until she stammered, "Then how did you get all of this?"

"Carefully," he replied, with a grin back on his face. "Come on, we're not far now."

She had no idea where he was taking her, but she realized she'd follow him anywhere. He reached back for her hand, and she trembled as their fingers interlaced. It was like they were the only people who existed right now. Just her and him, with the sun glinting off his horns.

Finally, he placed his hand on her belly, stopping her from moving and dropping lower into the grass. "There they are. I wanted to show you my very first animal obsession when I was little."

Obsession? She frowned and glanced around them. "I don't see anything."

"First, what do you think they are?"

She hadn't the faintest idea. "Horses?"

"No."

"Are they some kind of massive lizard beast that doesn't live on my side of the mountain?"

He snorted. "Absolutely not."

"I don't know then, Bjorn. You're a warrior. I would imagine it's some kind of large creature who could tear my head off if I'm too loud."

The smile never budged from his face. "None of the above. It's them."

He allowed her to peek her head up over the grass to see... pigs. Adorable pigs that were vastly unlike any creature she'd seen before. The wiry hair covering their bodies was rather similar to a boar, but that was where the similarities ended. They were reddish in color, with the most massive floppy ears that she had ever seen. Tapered at the end, they looked rather magical the more she stared at them. Their ears were clearly fairy-like, and the small spots that created patterns on their skin were adorable.

"Pigs?" she asked. The word seemed wrong to say. "You were obsessed with pigs?"

"Not just any pigs. Secret keepers." He reached for her hand again, so comfortable touching her that he didn't even wait for her to take his hand in return.

And she thought that was rather nice. Everyone who had been around her had been hesitant. People didn't touch priestesses without permission. But Bjorn didn't even think of asking her. He just did it because he knew she didn't mind if he held her hand.

They walked toward the small gathering of pigs. She counted six of them all snuffling about in the grass, although they froze when the two of them approached.

Bjorn lifted his hands, murmuring as a flutter of his magic floated through the air. "Calm, friends. We are not here to harm you, but to share secrets."

"Secrets?" she whispered as one of the pigs broke away from the others.

"Trolls call them secret keepers for a reason. I don't need magic to convince them to come to us. They are all very interested in holding what others might not know."

"I don't understand," Astrid replied with a soft laugh.

He leaned down to the pig who approached and whispered into its ear. It took him a little while, but then the pig seemed to... nod. As if it understood the secret he was telling it.

"What did you say?" she asked with a laugh.

"That's the beauty of these creatures. They'll only tell the secret when the person it's about is ready to hear it. They keep secrets for all of us."

The pig wandered over to her, and she bent down. Holding out her hands for it to snuffle, she patted the flat nose as it seemed to deeply draw in her scent. "Bjorn, this is silly. The pigs don't really do that."

But then the pig opened its mouth and Bjorn's voice came out: "I think she's the most beautiful woman I've ever seen."

Two things about that were startling. The first was that a pig had spoken with his voice and the second, that he thought she was beautiful.

Astrid looked up to see how worried he was. A small furrow had appeared between his brows, and his hands were curled into fists against his sides. But he stood there looking at her, watching like he always did. Waiting to see what she would say.

"I..." She didn't know what to say to that, actually. "But I'm human."

"And?"

"And you're a troll. Surely you had expectations of what a troll wife would look like for you. I can see how different I am from everyone here." She lifted her arms as though that would remind him. "Why would you think I'm beautiful?"

In the blink of an eye, he was right in front of her. So close she could smell the sun radiating off his skin. He lifted a hand to her cheek, turning her face so she looked up at him. "How could I not find you beautiful? Would you like me to tell you all the reasons? The grace in your hands when you talk. The sky that I hadn't seen in ten years in your gaze. The sound of your voice eased every angry part of me. There are a hundred reasons and more to find you beautiful, Astrid."

"A lot of people have found me beautiful in my life."

"But none of them see what I see." A flash of anger nearly turned his gaze red, but his hand was still gentle when he cupped her jaw. "I see your strength, your resilience, your ability to put all others before yourself even when it is detrimental to your own health when you do so. I see your loyalty to your sister, and your love for this world. I no longer see the priestess, Astrid. I see you."

Why was that so terrifying? Why did that make her want to not look at him, to crawl out of her skin because that was terrifying to believe?

His thumb crested over the peak of her cheekbone, tracing the lines of her face. "I don't know which god looked favorably upon me to send you into my life, but I will have to find them and worship them until I die."

"Bjorn," she whispered.

"I don't want to sever the bond," he blurted. He almost seemed surprised that he'd said it, but then he forged forward with newfound confidence. "I like you. I can see a future where we are friends. Perhaps more. I know that is not what you want to hear when you desire to find your sister and cannot see beyond that. But Rose has been in Trollveggen for many months now. Perhaps she would wish to stay as well."

"My sister wants a life outside of all this."

"Your sister wanted a life outside of the labyrinth. Outside of the cruelty that revolved around our lives, but I cannot tell you if she would ever go back to your kingdom. Your sister wanted her freedom. Trollveggen gives her that."

"You don't know if that's true."

But it made sense. That had been her fear from the start of all this. Rose had seen the worst of their kingdom, been thrown away to the dungeons where only the worst monsters lived. At least, the monsters who were humans. It seemed that was who the king wished to punish her with.

Would she even want to return?

What would Astrid do then? She certainly didn't want to return to the castle where so many horrible things had happened. She couldn't go back to Lord Tolly or even back to where they trained the priestesses. She was just as lost as her sister now, having thrown herself into finding Rose when she knew there wasn't anywhere for her to go after this.

"I didn't think this plan through all that well, did I?" she asked quietly.

"You saw a way to save your sister," he replied. "And you did. You found me, you released me, and now I will make sure you get to her side. That was your plan, and it was a good one."

"But what do we do after?"

He stared down into her gaze, and she swore she saw a future in his eyes. One where they lived together quietly, growing their own food, raising their own animals. It was a quieter life than she was used to. But there was no more manipulation. There were no expectations of politics or having to control an entire room so a war didn't break out.

Peace. That was what he offered her.

His thumb moved again, this time trailing along her jaw. "We do whatever you want, bright one."

But that was terrifying too. She didn't know what she wanted.

"I need time to think," she said. "I don't know if this future you want is one that I can agree to. I'm sorry, Bjorn."

"Take all the time you need. While you're thinking, I will show you what a true troll husband is like. I will show you what it could be if you chose to stay." He took a deep breath, his chest rising like a barrel in front of her. "May I do that?"

"I don't see why not."

A voice in her head screamed that, yes, she did. She already liked the man. He'd proven to be honorable and trustworthy, and if she wasn't careful, he was going to make this very difficult to leave.

Again that thumb, so distracting as he seemed to memorize the feeling of her cheek. She tilted her head back a bit more, unable to deny him when he was standing there like that.

Astrid's hands found his chest, warm and solid and comforting. "Bjorn... I..."

He groaned, the sound deep and rumbling in his chest as he lunged for her. This time he didn't ask to kiss her, nor did he wait. He just took what he wanted, and she was swept along for the ride.

Massive hands spanned her waist, tugging her harder against his chest. He nipped at her lower lip, drawing it into his mouth and teasing her with his tongue. The shape of his mouth was different from hers, but it didn't make her feel odd to be kissing him. In fact, all it felt was right. Her entire body seemed to heat up at his touch.

Bjorn's hand smoothed up her ribs. She could feel him measuring the span of them, so small compared to him, and then up farther, farther, just until his thumb brushed the underside of her breast. How was it that even that little touch made her entire world light up with desire?

A small moan escaped her, and she almost froze. It was inappropriate for her to make that sound, and yet it seemed only to encourage him. He pressed against her harder, his mouth doing things to her lips that she hadn't even thought possible while his hand moved up again until his thumb brushed against her stiff nipple.

And then suddenly he cursed and lurched away from her.

"What—"

But then Astrid realized his hand was pressed between his legs and he wore the most pained expression she'd ever seen on his face. He hadn't even looked like that when there had been an arrow sticking out of him.

"Oh no," she muttered, reaching for him. "Is there anything I can do to help?"

"Just... don't even look at me."

"Bjorn, that seems dramatic."

"You're so pretty," he groaned, before slapping his hands over his eyes. "Go away, please. You are not helping by being here."

"I could get you something cold?"

"Astrid. The fact that you are breathing near me right now is making this worse. Please."

She bit her lip to not laugh and backed away through the wheat. "All right. I'm leaving."

"Why is that not helping?" he seemed to mutter to himself.

She shouldn't find that quite so funny as she headed back to the village. But she did.

Chapter 26

As much as Astrid felt the pressure to get to her sister, she also felt a strange need to stay here and linger. It was so beautiful in the grotto. Almost impossibly easy to convince herself that Bjorn was right—her sister must've been fine. If the trolls in Trollveggen were the same as the ones here, then they were almost certainly kinder than her initial thoughts of them.

After their moment in the field, she hadn't been able to stop thinking about kissing him, lingering on those warm lips and feeling those strong hands moving over her body. She hadn't thought she would ever be interested in him like that.

But maybe that was a lie as well. She'd thought about it the very first time she'd seen him strung up on the ceiling like he was a feast for whoever wanted to claim him.

He'd slept on his mother's couch since he'd returned home, something Ylva was clearly displeased with. Astrid didn't want the woman to think less of her, but she also wasn't going to rush this relationship with Bjorn. They were still learning each other. Sleeping in the same bed would likely lead to them doing something neither of them wished to rush.

She had the idea of getting Ylva a gift this morning, though. There were markets in the grotto where artisans sold their wares every morning. She wasn't entirely without wealth. Astrid had carried her necklaces and jewels from the pearl gown this whole time in a small pouch that she wore underneath a woolen gown Bjorn's mother had given her.

Now, she was going to put those pearls to good use.

The market was a pretty place to be, where the grotto opened up onto this street that wasn't a street. The houses on either side glowed in the morning light, so green they didn't look real. Cobblestones beneath her feet were already warming as she walked barefoot through the street that had more stalls lined up on either side than she would have guessed.

The first one she ducked into was a small pottery shop. The artist was particularly talented at creating vases. They were each hand painted, painstakingly depicting historical moments that all trolls would apparently know. And though she was impressed herself, she wasn't all that certain that Ylva would be.

Another stall, another interesting feature. This troll seemed talented at growing plants that likely wouldn't grow here on their own. Each of the tiny flowers was so perfectly unfurled, they looked like little art pieces.

But from what she had seen of Ylva, it was unlikely the woman would want a flower either. She seemed hard around the edges. Less likely to take care of something that delicate.

As she exited the stall, a heavy arm wrapped around her shoulder. For a moment, she thought maybe Bjorn had caught her sneaking out, but then she looked up into a decidedly feminine face attached to a massive body.

"Wandering on your own? Probably not the best idea."

She'd seen this woman before. But where?

Astrid searched her memory until she remembered this was one of the women who had been wrestling when they'd first arrived in the grotto. "Oh, Tyra, is that right?"

The troll woman seemed to expand a bit with pride. "Good memory, little human. I'm glad you know who I am."

"I was looking for a gift for Ylva. Bjorn's mother is not very pleased with me."

Tyra tilted her head back and let out a booming laugh that filled the market. A few trolls looked at them with disappointed expressions, but most of them seemed to watch the proceedings with amusement before they went back to their work or shopping.

"Ylva is not known for being an easy person to be around. I'm not surprised you're finding her difficult. What's got her all in a knot?" Tyra started guiding her through the shops, bypassing many of the stalls that Astrid would have originally paused at.

"Bjorn's sleeping on the couch."

"Why?"

The innocence of the question made Astrid hesitate to answer. The trolls seemed far more easygoing with their bodies. They touched each other all the time. She saw so many of them hugging, kissing, always touching each other in some way. They linked arms, held each other's hands, tugged and pulled each other when there was no reason to.

Making Bjorn sleep on the couch would be so far beyond what Tyra would understand. Clearing her throat, she came up with the very first lie that she could. "He snores."

Tyra blinked at her. "What?"

Oh, she was in it now. So rather than preserve her dignity, she just made snoring sounds. Loudly. Very similar to the performance she'd put on in the labyrinth, honestly. Honking, pig-like noises and then she shrugged. "While he sleeps. The whole time."

Tyra's eyes had widened in horror. "You should make him sleep outside then."

"I agree. But still, it angered Ylva, so I thought I'd get her a gift."

"By the gods," Tyra muttered before dragging her into a jewelry stall. "You should get her plugs for her ears. Perhaps she's angry because she isn't sleeping at all."

The lie would haunt her for the rest of her days here. She was certain of it.

The stall they walked into was a good distraction, though. Astrid had always loved jewelry. Perhaps that was part of why she didn't mind so much being a priestess. Some of them had fought very early on to not be part of the order. A few girls hated even the thought of being a priestess, but Astrid had seen how beautiful the older girls were, and how they dripped in wealth, and she had wanted to be like them.

Standing here was a bit like the first moment she'd seen those priestesses. Surrounded by wealth and jewelry so delicate, it looked like they were conjured out of thin air rather than created by a real person.

"These are beautiful," she said, noticing that the woman standing behind the stall was staring at her.

Not just looking at a human, but staring. And the more she looked, the more upset the woman seemed to be. Astrid tried to ignore it by looking at the jewelry, but soon enough, even Tyra noticed.

"Give me a moment," she said, before pulling the other troll woman to the side.

Astrid tried not to listen to their conversation. She picked up a pair of stunning ruby earrings. They were like little drops of blood, suspended by such thin metal it almost looked like there was nothing holding them at all. They would defy gravity in such a way, and she thought maybe Ylva would really like these. Astrid had certainly never seen any earrings like them before.

She placed them in the center of the stall and then started looking at the necklaces. Maybe there would be a matching set, but she had no idea how much they cost. The bag full of pearls should be enough, but she wasn't all that certain if the trolls even liked pearls. They seemed to be more interested in gemstones.

Unfortunately, the necklaces were closer to the other two women, who were muttering loud enough for Astrid to hear them.

"No!" the vendor said, her voice a little too loud. "She slights Bjorn, flaunting herself throughout the market like there is nothing wrong. I will not sell to her."

"She doesn't know our ways."

"Clearly she does! She buys for Ylva, does she not? She is a shameless woman. Walking around without a single piercing. She dilutes his honor, and he shouldn't let her leave the house without bridal piercings."

"Maybe they haven't talked about it yet," Tyra said. "They're newly bonded."

"Then that is a flaw for both of them to rectify. I will sell nothing to a woman who dishonors her husband so publicly." And then the vendor stalked away from the stall, clearly not going to sell anything at all to Astrid.

She waited until Tyra returned. The troll had a sheepish expression on her face. "I guess she had somewhere to be. Don't worry, I have another idea."

"What are bridal piercings?"

Tyra's deep red face paled. "Um. You heard that?"

"I heard most of it."

"I thought humans didn't have very good hearing," she muttered, rubbing the back of her neck before taking a deep breath. "When trolls are bonded, truly bonded, they get piercings. I'm sure he told you that. Women pierce our ears. They're the markings of a troll wife, through the lobes."

Tyra gestured to her own ears, and Astrid could see of all the decorated piercings that marked up and down the cartilage, there were no piercings on Tyra's lobes.

"Ah," she said. "And the vendor was angry that I didn't have them?"

"Guess so."

She took a deep, steadying breath. Piercings weren't on her list of things to do, but she supposed if that was what it would take to get people to trust her, then she would do it. "I think I need to speak with Bjorn, then."

So much for a gift.

So much for anything reasonable.

There was too much rattling around in her head now. Bridal piercings, Bjorn's poor abused cock, not to mention the kiss. He wanted to stay bonded with her, which essentially meant they would stay married as far as his people were concerned.

She hadn't even given that much thought, considering she didn't think they were married. It had been a mistake for her to read a few words off a knife, and then they'd accidentally brushed their cut hands together. It shouldn't be that easy to mistakenly get married!

Tyra must have stopped following her as she headed back to Ylva's, because she was alone as she stood in front of the door. She wasn't even sure what she was going to say to him. Only that there was a strange feeling in her chest that wouldn't go away since the vendor had said Astrid was dishonoring him.

She didn't want to do that. He was quite possibly the best person she'd ever met. And she trusted him. Liked him, even. But was she sure she wanted to dedicate her entire life to a troll? No, of course not.

He had kept her safe. He'd done everything in his power to give her a chance out here, and then he'd done everything in his power to get to her sister. So it felt like... Well, not quite that she owed him. That wasn't the right word.

But it did feel like she wanted to return that trust and favor.

Astrid headed into the house not knowing what she was going to say to him. He was standing in the back, perhaps cooking breakfast considering all the food spread out around him. He had a knife in his hand, a cutting board on the counter, and very much looked like he was involved in something torturous. But he smiled at her the moment she walked through the door.

"Mother headed out already. There was someone who needed her counsel with the smoke, so it's just you and me for breakfast."

"I'd like to go get my sister now," she said, the words blurting out of her before she could even talk to him about what had happened in the market. But then she added, "And why haven't you talked to me about bridal piercings?"

He froze, with the knife held in his hands and a blank expression on his face. "All right."

"All right, what?"

"All right, we can go get your sister now. I wasn't expecting us to be here forever." He set the knife down. "Now what was it about the bridal piercings?"

"A vendor wouldn't sell anything to me in the market. She said I was dishonoring you by flaunting that I don't have anything in my ears. I used to have my ears pierced." She ghosted her fingers over the lobes. "I'm not even sure that I'd need them to be pierced again, honestly. I can put earrings in my ears. I just didn't know it was important."

That blank stare wasn't helping. He just looked at her. For longer than was comfortable. Was he even blinking?

Then finally he blinked, swallowed very hard, and said, "I didn't think you'd want to wear the earrings. They are a sign of a bonded couple, and you want to break the bond."

"But you don't."

"No," he replied vehemently. "I don't."

And that snapped something inside of her. She had been trying so hard to stay away from this, but it was getting harder and harder when this life he offered her was damn near idyllic.

Sighing, she said, "You promised me that you would try to show me what a life with you would be like. I cannot promise anything until I see my sister is safe with my own eyes, but I... I can show you what a life with me could be like."

His hands clenched so hard around the side of the table she heard it crack. "I can accept that."

"And if it means that you are more honored when your..." She slipped over the words, but they were important to say. "Troll wife is wearing earrings, then I will wear them. If you have some. I'm afraid I don't have any."

He nearly tripped over himself as he rushed into his mother's bedroom. The last thing she wanted to do was anger the already angry woman by stealing some of her jewelry. Astrid thought Ylva wouldn't like it if someone had rummaged through her things. But he knew the older woman much better than she did.

When he returned, it was with a pair of earrings that sparkled like stars in the night sky. They were clear crystals, but the way they were cut refracted the light and made them seem like bottomless gems that trapped even the slightest sunlight within them.

"These were the earrings my father gave my mother when they became bonded," he said quietly as he handed them over to her. "I hope they bring us better luck."

"I can't take these. They're your mother's."

"They are mine to give to my troll wife." He wrapped his hand around hers, closing her fist around the sparkling jewels. "I give them to you, Astrid. Please. Wear them for me."

Why did that make a shiver travel down her spine?

She popped the backs off the earrings and slid them into her ears. Thankfully, neither of the holes had closed up and then she was wearing his mark. His earrings. A sign that she was his.

His gaze flicked back and forth between her ears, and then he seemed to take in the entire picture of her wearing all of it. His throat worked in a swallow, and then he winced. "You look too good in those, bright one. Too good."

"The same problem as before?"

"Trolls heal fast. Not the same as before." But the twisted expression on his face didn't change all that much. "I'll prepare us to leave. Trollveggen isn't far, but the journey will be a few nights in the wild again."

"Nothing we haven't done before."

The heated expression he gave her made her entire body shiver. "A little different from before, troll wife."

There it was again. The shiver as she backed toward the guest bedroom to gather her own things as well. But this time, the shiver was nearly impossible to ignore.

Chapter 27

Bjorn packed with blistering speed after that. Some part of him was concerned about the time they had wasted here, but another part feared what it would mean if they lingered for too long.

The grotto had always been home to him, but now it was like poking a bear. Everything that he used to love annoyed him. He didn't like that there were people training at all hours of the day. He didn't want to join them, even though they were kind enough to continually ask him. The sounds of people moving set his teeth on edge, and no matter how hard he tried to be comfortable here, he just couldn't.

There was guilt in that admission. A feeling that he should have been able to handle this and for some reason, just couldn't. Perhaps there was still a lingering part of him that feared it made him weak that he was so incapable of being around others.

Astrid was a good excuse to leave. Especially since he had told his mother that he would try his best to be a good husband. Her family was important to her, and her sister needed her.

He was being a good partner to her. She needed to leave. He would guide her safely to Trollveggen, and argue on her behalf that her sister should be released, and that was all he was expected to do.

Packed and ready to go, he shifted a few items that he had strapped onto his back. His mother had insisted she send them with better care. One of those items was a rather large tent that made it difficult for him to carry much else. Thankfully, the troll maidens here were quick to set Astrid up for the journey as well.

His troll wife had boots on her feet now. They were made for a troll child, but they would work for the journey. The spider silk dress he'd made her was wrapped carefully in her own pack, although she carried little else in it. Another dress had been given to her, a sturdy one made out of wool that would hold up to the test of the journey, keeping her warm on the cold nights as they journeyed over the high peaks of the mountains.

Astrid stood outside his mother's home, waiting for him beside the woman who had birthed him.

Bjorn was surprised to see tears in his mother's eyes. She had never been one for emotions. Even when he'd been a child and his father had taken him away, all he remembered was the rage in her gaze as she'd watched them leave. But now, she reached for him and held him close to her thundering heart.

"My son," she whispered. "You take care of all that the gods have given you."

"I will, Mother."

"And fight for what you deserve." She pulled back, framing his face with her hands. "Because you deserve so much more than you are willing to give to yourself."

He wasn't sure he agreed with her, but he nodded to appease the sadness he could see in her gaze. "We will return to see you."

"Please do. Bring my new daughter back."

Her new daughter? He hadn't even thought she'd liked Astrid. At least, not that much.

But he could still see his mother's earrings glinting in Astrid's ears, and something clicked into place inside of him. She was his troll wife. She was his mother's new daughter. And this was the only way the trolls would accept a woman like Astrid.

Honor. Loyalty. Dedication. That was what their people lived on.

"No more goodbyes," he murmured, reaching out his hand for Astrid to take. "Come, troll wife."

He didn't think he was mistaken in the heat that flared in her eyes. She was intrigued by what he'd said. She wanted more from that as well.

Sometimes it still felt like kissing her in the glade or watching her with hungry eyes was forbidden. Perhaps he was wrong about that.

Things were different now. They weren't going to sever the bond. The oldest and most talented of their seers, witches, and prophetesses had given them a glimpse into the future of what their magic could be.

Her tiny hand fit into his, and off they went. He lifted the brambles for her, headed off into the tall grass, back toward the mountain that had sheltered them from their first journey.

Astrid seemed happy to be traveling this time around. He watched her as they walked, and she didn't show any signs of fatigue. Her arms swung at her side, her hair bounced where she had tied it on top of her head, and she started talking the moment they were a few steps away from the grotto.

"I have never traveled this far from the castle," she said, her voice clearly delighted. "I didn't even know there was another side to the mountain, isn't that silly? All the human settlements and other kingdoms are on the opposite side. At least, as far as I know."

"There are no humans here," he replied.

"I wonder why! Humans like to spread out. Kings don't get along when they are too close together. But I suppose there has always been more room where they already are. No one has needed to go over the mountain and risk angering the trolls." Her brows furrowed. "How strange it is to think. Maybe this is where the elves came from?"

"I don't know." Bjorn had never given it much thought. The elves were fickle creatures who had created his people, and he wasn't all that impressed with their work. His people were exhausted in the pursuit of becoming more like their originators. Why should he give them much thought at all?

She glanced over at him the moment they reached the base of the mountain, amusement twisting her lips into something similar to a smile. "You don't like talking about elves."

"No."

"Why?"

"It's a touchy subject for most trolls." He held out his hand for her to take. He needed to get her up and over a rather large rockfall before they were back on a twisting path that headed up the mountain. It had been used for ages by his people, although it looked more like a goat path than one for people. "The elves were what made us, so we are grateful to them in some way. But they also were cruel masters."

"As they were to most. They considered themselves gods among humans." She hopped over the rocks, dropping down rather impressively for a woman who had been raised the way she was. She glanced back at him to see the surprise on his face. "What?"

"I expected you to be more... finicky. Less capable. Every time I look at you, you surprise me, Priestess."

"Because I was a pretty doll all dressed up for men to look at?" She snorted. "That's what the king wanted everyone to think about us. The training to be a priestess was significantly more than how to make your hair look nice."

"Such as?" He found himself rather interested. His people were specific in how they trained their more powerful women as well, but he knew there weren't any similarities between the trolls and humans. A priestess among the humans was a woman who was used as a weapon but hidden to look like a pretty comb.

Astrid seemed to think for a while. He didn't mind allowing her the silence. The day was beautiful, the sun was in the sky, warmth on their shoulders as they walked through the prettiest part of the mountain. As of right now, the incline wasn't very steep, but it would become very much so by the end of the day.

She took a deep breath and started to tell him a story he never would have guessed. "I told you I was on the streets with my sister. Most of us were. Girls gathered up by people who knew that they had no one else. Some of us looked enough like the princess to actually be used as priestesses. Others ended up working in other ways with the sisterhood. There were a lot of us. Hundreds of girls of various ages, every single one of us hoping that the king would see us to be worthy of more than just living on the streets."

He glanced over at her, clearly surprised. It gave her a bit of strength to continue, because she knew it was surprising.

"Of course, my sister and I were chosen. I thought that meant they would teach us how to use our magic in new and impossible ways. And they did, but not at all how I expected. We were taught the basics like how to cook and clean, and yes, there was an emphasis on using our magic to convince most people, if not all, that we were powerful. But the reality was that they wanted us to control the court system.

"Every good priestess knows how to manipulate a man. That's actually very easy. We're taught how to use our magic to convince others that what they want isn't what they want. We know the ins and outs of the entire kingdom. Secret passages. Who is fucking who. The children who are actually another noble's child. We are the secret keepers of quite literally everything."

And he had known she was powerful in the human realm, he just hadn't realized how powerful she actually was. She knew... everything?

Bjorn stumbled over a rock, realizing in that moment how dangerous it was for them to return to Trollveggen. If King Egil caught wind of everything she knew, the ins and outs of the kingdom, who they could blackmail, everything that she said she could do…?

Hurrying behind her, he grabbed onto her shoulders and spun her around to look at him. "Listen to me. When we make it to Trollveggen, you cannot tell anyone that you know all of these things. Do you hear me?"

"Why would I not tell them?"

"Because my king will use you. I do not know what he will want to do, or how he will extract the information from you, but you must be careful."

She stared up into his gaze, clearly confused by his words. "Why wouldn't I want to help your people after seeing what mine can do?"

He swallowed hard. There was still a part of him that was still twisted from what he had experienced, he realized. His instincts should tell him to destroy the entire human kingdom and all the people within it. And he wanted to. He wanted King James dead, and he wanted the human king's blood to run out onto the very grounds that he had killed so many others upon.

Yet Bjorn's instinct, the fear that ran through his veins, told him to prevent that from happening at all costs.

Bjorn shook his head. "Maybe you're right. We should probably take you to King Egil as soon as we can. You should tell him all you know so that the trolls can..."

He didn't know what they would do. Attack the human kingdom? Perhaps. He had seen it happen in his lifetime, although it had been a very long time since they had done so. The trolls rarely had the resources they needed to do such a thing. But he knew without a doubt that his people wanted to. They would kill hers off in a heartbeat.

She reached up and touched a hand to his jaw. "Why are you suddenly so worried?"

"I don't know how the trolls in Trollveggen will react to you. They are not kind to your people." He could see it now. They would do whatever it took to protect their own families and the people in that mountain. She represented a group of people who had hunted his kind and killed his people in horrible ways for centuries.

She'd been there in the labyrinth, after all. For years before she ever tried to help him. And even then, it had been for her own gain.

Astrid merely smiled up at him, and patted his neck before turning to continue up the mountain. "I know they aren't going to trust me. They have no reason to. But I'm not there for them, Bjorn. I'm there for my sister."

And that was that. She didn't seem to care that she was going into a very dangerous situation with people who could kill her. She'd walk through fire if it meant she got her sister back.

He'd never been more attracted or confused about being attracted to a woman in his life. After that, it was a little hard to talk. The steep incline wasn't all that difficult for him, but it very much was for her. Bjorn found himself stopping more often, waiting for her ragged breathing to even out before he continued. The sound of her breath sawing in and out of her lungs was more than a little concerning. He'd never heard a human wheeze like that before.

But she didn't complain, nor did she say to stop, so they kept going. Up and up until the sun started to set, and finally he determined it was a good time for them to pause. The last thing he needed was to run her into the ground.

"Here," he said, pointing to a rock for her to sit on. "Rest for a moment while I set up camp."

She nodded furiously but said nothing in return. That was his first warning of concern. Bjorn took the skein of water off his side and handed it over to her.

"And drink," he added. "All of it."

"That's the last of our water," she said, still breathless and almost impossible to understand.

"I will find more."

He kept an eye on her while he set the tent up. She weaved a little back and forth, but seemed to be settling in a bit better. Her breath didn't sound so ragged anymore, and she was steadier as she sat there sipping at the water. Enough so that he didn't fear so much that she was going to keel over.

At least he knew she could survive a trip like that if necessary.

Bjorn laid out their blankets and then stared down at them, realizing that there was only one tent and a small space between their bedrolls. He'd have to do something about that. He wasn't all that convinced he could survive the night if he had to be so close to her for that long.

Ducking out of the tent, he headed away from the tent and started setting up a fire. "Are you hungry?"

"I could eat."

So that was what he did. He settled her, gave her water, fed her, and made sure that everything was a little better on this difficult journey. That was what a good husband would do. He knew the right motions, but somehow it still felt like it wasn't enough. This partnership was still a little cold, when he wanted everything to be warmer for her. He wanted to convince her that this wasn't just the right thing, but that she wanted her life to be like this.

Bjorn was perhaps a little stuck in his own head about all of this, because he blinked and suddenly she was standing. There wasn't any food left in her hands, and she stretched her arms over her head with a deep groan.

"All right, I'm heading to bed." She gave him a meaningful look. "You're welcome to join if you're done acting weird."

"Acting weird?" he repeated.

"Yes. Like you're trying too hard."

Then she disappeared into the tent.

"Trying too hard," he muttered as he kicked dirt over the fire to put it out. "I'm not trying too hard."

But maybe he was. And maybe, just maybe, she wanted him to be himself without attempting to be the best troll husband he could be. But even as the thought occurred to him, he shook his head.

It couldn't be that. No one wanted that from him.

Chapter 28

Astrid didn't know what was going on with him. One moment Bjorn was full of lust, kissing her in a wheatfield like he was a starving man who would do anything for a taste of her. But then he had her to himself, and he froze.

She wasn't sure what he was trying to do. With every step he was hovering around her. He helped her over rocks. He gave her water. The man had even pressed the back of his hand against her forehead like he was checking her temperature and then insisted she step into the shade for a little while because she'd felt warm to him.

It had been a slow, arduous journey. She hadn't been prepared for the uphill portion of it, but she could have gone faster on the flatter bits. But he was so concerned about her welfare that it had slowed them down considerably.

Was this what he thought it meant to be husband and wife? That he needed to treat her like a fragile little thing who could shatter at any minute? Astrid didn't want that.

Which was why she'd told him how she had been trained. She

knew how to control people, manipulate them, and get them to do what she wanted. But she wasn't some fragile little doll like everyone wanted her to be in the human kingdoms. Out here, she didn't have to be either.

Sighing, she headed into the tent as a plan formed in her mind. Usually, she would let the man take charge. Sure, the few sexual encounters she'd had in her life had never led to actual sex. The men had been well aware that they could only touch her in a limited fashion, and none of them had seemed all that disappointed by it in the end. She just needed to figure out how to do this and get this man to take the lead if she wanted any of this to end up where it should.

Which was... sex, she supposed.

Astrid had rarely felt this way around men, if at all. Human men were lacking when it came to gaining her interest. No one had made her feel warm and liquidy inside like Bjorn did, and certainly not just by a kiss.

It was their first night alone together. She was sore and tired, but she was doing this.

A part of her needed to know if the kiss was a strange phenomenon that only happened when his lips touched hers, or if there was something far more compelling happening here. What if he could make her see stars with more than just his lips?

Well, she supposed, he was welcome to use his mouth in other places.

She could hear him outside, doing something to put the fire out. It gave her time to prepare herself. The poor man wouldn't know what was about to hit him.

Tugging at the knot that tied the wool dress around her, she pulled it free from her waist. The fabric fell open like a robe, and there was very little beneath it. The troll maidens who had given her this clothing had been adamant that she needed undergarments as well, but the grins on their faces weren't as innocent as she would have expected from young women.

She understood why now. Astrid had come from a culture where undergarments were long, covered most of her body, and were only there as structure for the garment that would cover them. Apparently, the trolls in the grotto did not feel the same. These garments were helpful when it came to moving quickly, but the bindings around her chest pushed her breasts up. And rather than a petticoat, there was only a small strip of fabric between her thighs.

She'd revealed the same amount of skin in many of the dresses she had worn as a priestess, but somehow this made her more nervous for Bjorn to see her like this.

Still, this was what she wanted. Astrid knew she was only nervous because she actually liked him. If it were any other man, she would have scoffed at these feelings and tugged her drooping dress even lower. She knew how to convince a man that she was the only woman in the room that he would ever dare to look at, and yet this troll had her twisted up in knots.

Blowing out a steadying breath, she turned as the flap to the tent opened and Bjorn entered.

"The fire is out," he muttered as he heaved his bag in through the door. "Should be safe enough tonight if we... we..."

His gaze was like a physical touch. His eyes lingered on her feet, sliding up her calves to her thighs. His gaze heated as he reached the small strip between her legs and then heated even more as his eyes wandered up her stomach, to the swells of her breasts perched just so. By the time he met her gaze, his look could have burned her from the inside out.

"Astrid?" he asked. His voice had deepened into a low growl.

Oh, she hadn't planned for this part. How silly. She was shaking as she watched his hands curl into fists, like he was trying not to touch her though he wanted to. And she wanted him to.

Warmth built between her legs, her body flaring with a desire that was as foreign to her as this entire experience had been. She had to call upon all her training to pretend she wasn't so affected that her mouth had gone dry.

"I have a question to ask you, Bjorn."

"Anything," he snarled.

By all the gods, he was big. A hulking beast stood in front of the tent entrance. He was mostly a silhouette with massive horns and a body built out of shadows, like a monster had walked in and she was supposed to tame him. Why did that make a sudden rush of desire slick her thighs? She shouldn't want a beast like him, and yet... all she could think was that she wanted him to lunge at her. She wanted him unhinged, untamed like he had been before.

"Are you still sore?" she asked. "I suppose I'm curious about the speed at which trolls heal."

His hands spasmed at his sides. "I am healed enough for some things. Not for others."

"Care to explain?"

She felt like they were on the precipice of change. If he rejected her, of course she wouldn't push. He wanted to take things slower, and considering his history, she wouldn't deny him that. But she was curious how far he was willing to go.

"Astrid, we have a long journey ahead of us," he said, but she could see how he was barely holding himself in control. He was shaking, standing there all by himself. "I have yet to convince you to be my troll wife."

"That thinking all seems rather outdated." And then she shrugged.

She'd completely forgotten that the dress wasn't tied onto her. She was so used to being clothed in very little around other people that it wasn't surprising she'd forget it. But then she felt the wool slithering off her shoulders, down her body, until it left her standing there nearly naked in front of him. Only small scraps of fabric hid her from his gaze.

It was like he had been struck by lightning. One moment he was standing in front of the tent flap. The next, he was right in front of her. She'd thought he would swoop her up in his arms, tackle her to the ground, have his way with her like an animal. But he froze right in front of her, so close their chests were touching.

And then he stayed there. His muscles shaking, breathing hard, he said quietly, "I do not know the right way to do this. My memories are all from the labyrinth, and I have no wish to treat you like the men treated women there."

Oh. That was why he was so nervous.

Astrid could handle that. It wasn't that he didn't want her. It was that he was afraid he would hurt her. This sweet, wonderful man wanted direction.

She hooked her hand behind his neck, drawing him down until their lips touched. And then she whispered, "I will tell you what to do, husband. But first, kiss me until I tell you to stop."

His hand tunneled beneath her hair, and suddenly this was the man she remembered. The passion in his kiss was enough to take her breath away, not to mention the way he clutched at her waist, his fingers spasming against her skin before he tugged her even harder against himself. She was surrounded by the heat of him, but the desperation in his touch as though he feared they would never touch again.

His kiss scorched her to the bone. She was marked by him, devoured by his lips and tongue, and never again would she be the same person she'd been before. Because with every nip of his teeth, every stroke of his tongue, she became addicted to his touch. She wanted every ounce of him, the good, the bad, even the horrible things he had done trapped in that labyrinth. She wanted it all.

Astrid's fingers spasmed against him, clutching at the muscles that moved beneath her touch as he held on to her just a bit too tightly. When she pulled away, he didn't hesitate to let her. There was no resistance as she pulled back enough to whisper, "If I let you do whatever you want to me, what would you want to do?"

He groaned and pressed his forehead to hers, as though he couldn't stand to look at her while he said this. "All I have dreamt of since the first day I saw you was finding out what you would taste like, bright one."

"Taste like?" She had served men as a priestess, not the other way around. He'd tasted her lips already, but if he wished to taste her skin, then he certainly could. But then something in her mind steered her thoughts in the right direction. The direction he must've meant.

Men did that, she knew. She'd seen it happen when she'd been with her lord, but it was few and far between for men to be interested in such things. They were more interested in women sucking their cocks. Which she would gladly do for Bjorn if he wished. His piercing was intriguing, although she hoped it was healed.

Bjorn slid his hand down her neck, slowly moving down her body. She held her breath as that massive, calloused hand moved between her breasts, his thumb flicking over her hardened nipple, then down to her stomach. She couldn't think as the raspy sensation of his fingers teased the edges of the binding between her legs.

Then her entire world nearly exploded as he whispered, "I will beg, if I must."

She was already moving before her mind had caught up. Astrid drew him with her, or he helped her down onto the bedroll, she wasn't sure which one of them moved first. But soon enough, she was spread out, her legs wide as his claws made quick work of the fabric that hid her from his gaze.

It had been a long day, her mind screamed, scrambling for reasons they shouldn't do this. She was sweaty. She'd hardly had time to clean herself. The very least he should do was—

His tongue found her center and gave her one strong, thorough lick. All the thoughts in her head about why she shouldn't do this scattered. With the sensation of that massive tongue flicking across her clit, delving deeper to her core where he teased her entrance before circling that bundle of nerves again. She would never be the same.

She arched, barely able to control her body as she wanted to grind herself against his mouth. More, she needed more.

He perhaps knew, because the groan that rumbled through his chest was one of pure satisfaction. "Knew you'd taste sweet."

How was she supposed to hold herself together when he said that? Astrid writhed beneath him as he attacked her again. The sensation of his tusks sliding against her legs was smooth now because she was so wet, it had somehow gotten all over his face. Or maybe he'd done that. She wasn't sure. All she knew was that he was devouring her whole, and she was so close to seeing sparks.

Until he moved back for a moment, his thumb pressed against

her clit, and he held it down in a way that had her throbbing. She gasped, looking up to see him biting his nails until they were short enough for him to...

Bjorn plunged his finger into her, sinking it deep inside her body. She bit her lip, eyes rolling back in her head as she rode just his finger that somehow felt so big.

"Gonna have to stretch you a bit," he murmured as he worked her. "That's all right. We'll get there. Can't hurt you."

He wasn't talking sense. All she cared about was the fact that now his finger was inside her and his tongue was on her clit and she couldn't breathe. He was inside her, outside her, everywhere until she finally clenched around him. Her head slammed back, and maybe that was why she saw sparks, or maybe it really was that good when he made her come.

He groaned with her, the sound almost pained, but it was so hard to focus on that right now. Her body had turned to liquid. Her arms wouldn't lift, but she wanted to hold on to him. She needed to feel his skin pressed against hers for some strange reason.

Bjorn knew. He always knew. He crawled up her body, breathing hard and pressing kisses to her torso along the way up. Then, a soft blanket draped over her. The same quilted blanket that he'd said had been his when he'd been a child. It was warm and cozy, chasing away the chill of the air that cooled the sweat that had gathered on her skin.

Then he pressed one more kiss to her lips, with the taste of herself remaining.

"Sleep, bright one," he said.

"What about you?"

He rolled her onto her side and then curved his body around her. She could feel the hard bar of his cock pressed against her bottom, but he made no moves to do anything about that. Instead, he folded himself around her body and wrapped an arm over her.

"Sleep," he grunted again.

"Bjorn, I can feel your—"

"Sleep," he repeated. "The piercing limits what I can do. It is a small price to pay to know reality is even better than dreams. I will watch over you tonight. Tomorrow we have a long day ahead."

Who was she to deny him that? Sleep was rapidly calling her anyway. After being treated like that, she wasn't sure any woman would have been able to stay awake.

But also, she felt like this was one of the rare times in her life she was completely safe. Wrapped up in his arms, Astrid knew without a single doubt there wasn't a person in this realm who could harm her.

Chapter 29

With her tucked against his side, he felt like he could do anything. He felt like a *god*. Astrid was all snuggled up, tucked against his heart, and it didn't matter that there was a distinct ache between his legs. He'd been in pain for ten years. Suffering to have her in his arms was worth every moment.

Bjorn still couldn't believe it. After all this time, he had found the person he was meant to be with. The perfect mate bond, someone who he was worthy of, and all it had taken was ten years of torture.

He almost snorted at his own thoughts. Astrid had come out of nowhere. Fate had been laughing at him, most likely, when she had walked into that labyrinth and seen him tied up like that. The gods had likely been teasing him, dangling what he could not have, while he'd swung from the chains that had reminded him of where he was. But then she had laughed in the face of the gods, telling them that he was hers.

It felt like such a long time ago. He didn't remember the faces of the people who had been in the room, but he remembered hers. He remembered her pearl dress, every single stitch on it, and the mask that had covered her pretty face.

Bjorn would have to ask her about that. He'd only seen a few women of her station before, and they all wore masks like she had. The trolls would never cover up the features of someone so powerful, but he feared that was normal to humans. Why? He did not know. But he wanted to. He wanted to know everything about her life and how she had come to this moment.

He tightened his arms around her, shifting just a bit closer. As if he could get any closer. One of his legs was between hers, an arm draped over her, the other she used as a pillow. She was as tight against him as possible, and it still didn't feel like it was enough.

Hours passed. Bjorn didn't move even when his muscles started to ache and his hand lost all feeling. None of it mattered. He wanted to remember every detail of this moment. How her breath rose and fell in her sleep, the dusting of her eyelashes on her cheeks, and the way her hair smelled like flowers even though he knew that had to be impossible.

He would have stayed here forever if he hadn't heard the telltale signs of movement outside their tent.

At first he thought it was animals. Tiny scratching noises, then a few rocks that had been loosened and fell free. He knew most animals would see a tent like theirs and not be curious enough to risk their lives.

But then, a voice.

"Did someone survive you think?" Male. Obviously pitched low so no one would hear him, but that booming voice would have a hard time being quiet. It carried across the mountain peaks because there was nothing to dampen the sound.

Bjorn tensed. He could feel Astrid waking when she felt his body tense against hers. Carefully, he shifted his hand up from her waist to her mouth.

Clamping down around her jaw and nose, he muffled the sound she made as she woke. Though startled, she rolled to look at him.

Her wide blue eyes were full of fear. It made that rage, that beastly part of himself that he'd never been able to control, rise to the surface.

This night had been perfect, but neither of them was ever truly safe until they were in Trollveggen. Peeling his hand off of her face, finger by finger, he listened to what the men were saying.

"I don't think anyone could have survived that carnage. You saw the remains of those men. Whatever did that was an animal." The sound of movement as another man joined the first. "I think it's more likely that we're looking at hunting down some beast."

"The king said to return quickly and report."

"He also said to make our own judgments." This man was harsher sounding, more aggressive in his tone and words. "My judgment is whoever is in that tent isn't one of ours."

That was more than enough for him to hear. Bjorn would not take risks on their journey. He knew damn well what men like this were like. They would fire arrows into the tent before they would even look at who was in it.

Carefully rolling away from Astrid, he reached for the bags he had left near the door. His weapons were in there, although he always kept a few out as well. The knives he would grab last.

Except his hand wouldn't pick up the knife he'd left beside the bed. He'd forgotten that his right arm had been wedged underneath her, so of course he couldn't hold anything with it yet. The blood hadn't returned to his limbs after being pinned beneath her all night.

That would complicate things. He could wait until the feeling came back, but he wasn't all that convinced the men would wait that long. Soon enough, there would be a battle, and he needed to make do with what he had now.

His non-dominant hand would have to be what he fought with. It wouldn't be the first time. There'd been a battle in the labyrinth where one of the men had stabbed him through the right shoulder. His hand had gone numb then as well, and he'd had to fight with his left. He'd still won, although it had been a little more difficult.

He doubted it would be an issue here. Palming a few more knives, he strapped them onto his legs before turning to Astrid. Pressing a finger to his lips, he made it very clear that he wanted her to stay quiet. She nodded.

The last thing he wanted to do was damage their tent. But those men were clearly watching the front and would yell for reinforcements if they saw him. He cut through the back of the tent with his knife, sharp, silent, and slipped through the small opening so he could get around without being seen.

Crouching to hide behind rocks, he headed toward the sound of the two human men who were still murmuring quietly. They thought they were well hidden.

They were wrong.

He caught the first man by the neck, slicing through his skin with claws that were just as sharp as his knives. Bjorn would have preferred a larger weapon, but he'd already been carrying so much on the journey up here. The last thing he needed was a heavy axe, as he preferred.

The second man whirled, already drawing his sword. But they were too close to each other, and he couldn't pull out a sword without his arm getting caught against Bjorn first. With a swift movement, Bjorn plunged his own blade into the man's gut. It wasn't precisely where he wanted to hit him, but it would have to do.

The man opened his mouth, clearly attempting to scream.

"Don't," Bjorn growled, angling his knife upward toward the man's lung and sinking it even deeper.

He wasn't fast enough. The sound that came out of the man was a dying rattle, but it was loud enough that shouts echoed up the mountainside in response. The damned man. Now they were going to have a fight on their hands, and there was nothing he could do about it.

"Astrid!" Bjorn yelled as he leapt down in front of their tent. "Run!"

It was the only thing he could have her do. Already there were ten more men running toward him, each of them armed to the teeth. And even more behind those.

He ran into the group, enraged and far more dangerous than they were expecting. Or perhaps he was exactly who they'd thought they would meet, because they all seemed far more prepared than they should have been.

Bjorn sliced through sinew and bone, hacking through the men who got close enough to him. Screams echoed throughout the mountain, blistering the air with the sound of pain and torment. This was the symphony he had created over many years. He had listened to the sound of dying men and turned it into an instrument only he knew how to play, but there were many of them, and there was only one of him.

He'd fought ten, fifteen men before. Bjorn would put his own life at risk to fight. Easily. He had for many years.

But everything in him froze when he heard her scream.

Astrid. Four men hauled her in the moonlight toward the rest of their group. She was kicking and screaming, trying her best to get their hands off her when they never should have touched her.

And then he made his mistake. Bjorn should have kept fighting. Every dead man was one less they had to worry about here. Unfortunately, that wasn't what he did. He stepped toward her, forgetting that he was surrounded by people who wanted him dead.

The men took advantage of his confusion. They leapt at him, suddenly not with swords, but with ropes. They tied him up, binding his arms behind him. But he didn't need his arms to fight. He'd always figured out a way to kill people with his horns or his legs. Then his legs were bound, and they forced him onto his knees.

He watched them dragging her away, and something in him broke. For the first time, he wasn't able to save her. This was what he had been made to do. To fight, to destroy, to kill. Now he wasn't even able to do that.

But Astrid's gaze found his, and he felt something blooming inside of him. A connection that he hadn't realized had developed between them. He could feel it. A cord that bound their souls together, twining around him and around her magic until he could feel her tugging on it.

He let her and watched as words fell from her lips. Words that were said in the black tongue, a language she still did not know. They came from him. From deep inside his soul, because he had heard them said so many times when he'd been a child, even if he hadn't spoken them himself.

Their combined magic ripped at the men who held on to her arms. Each of them yelled in response, dropping their hold on her and clutching their chests. Astrid wasn't just peering into the weight of their souls as many blood witches did. She was doing exactly what his mother, and the others had said she would do.

A pale white mist emerged from the men's chests. They were all frantically trying to stuff it back into themselves, unsure of what she was doing, but certain that it was dangerous. That mist seemed to glow in the moonlight, glittering with tiny sparks inside of them until they converged into something alive. One of the men had a white wolf that was meant to be his spirit guide. It turned on him with a snarl, teeth gnashing at the air around him. Another had an eagle that took off into the sky. The last, a snake that slithered toward him, hissing and snapping at the air.

"Parlor tricks," one of the humans said, who still held on to the ropes binding him.

The wolf lunged, grabbing onto the man's arm and twisting it back and forth. He screamed, blood spurting in the air as the creature bit through the muscle there all the way down to the bone. The sound of it breaking crunched through the sudden silence as everyone watched what was happening.

The soldier took off running the moment the wolf released him. It licked its lips, blood covering its white fur before it gave chase.

The other two men ran as well. That left Astrid on the ground, her hands pressed against the stone as she breathed hard. But then she pulled herself together. He watched it happening. The wool dress she had thrown on was loose over one shoulder, falling down to reveal the red marks left by those soldiers' hands. But she stood, anger and rage sparking in those pretty blue eyes as she headed toward them.

"Get her," one of the soldiers said, tugging on his rope so hard that Bjorn's head was jerked back. "Someone grab her! Don't let her get close to all of us."

But no one moved. Perhaps no one dared to when Astrid suddenly spoke.

"I don't need to be close to pull those out of you," she said. "I would tell you to run, but I have no mercy for men like you."

An explosion of smoke shaded his vision. Bjorn couldn't see anything that was happening around him as the humans started screaming. One by one, the ropes fell. He freed his arms first, cursing the men who still held on to his legs and jerked him left and right as they tried to fight off the beasts who were supposed to help guide them.

He supposed they were. Punishment was guidance as much as anything else.

A snake suddenly leapt past him, and he hissed out a breath at how close it had been to biting his face. Then a mountain lion used his back as a spring board, slamming him against the ground.

Damned animals. They needed to give him enough clearance so that he could... could...

Finally. He wrenched a knife free and sawed through the remaining cords attached to his legs. Once he untangled himself, he ran in the direction he'd last seen her. The smoke made it hard enough for him to see, but his feet were sure and true as he burst through the heavy weight of magic and out into the fresh air where she stood.

Astrid's hands were lifted, the black tongue dropping from her lips like she had spoken it her entire life.

And her eyes were completely white.

He'd never seen them look like that before and fear speared through him. She needed to stop using that much magic, or she'd deplete herself. There was only so much anyone could use before that magic would overtake them.

They didn't have time to rest. Not when he now knew King James himself was sending more scouting parties up the mountain.

"Astrid," he said as he approached her. "Astrid, we have to go."

"I can still hear them screaming," she whispered. "I can't stop until they stop."

Oh, his poor, broken creature. Fear was what made her say such a thing, and he needed her to understand that. Carefully, he reached out and grabbed onto her hand. Holding it close to his heart, he hoped she didn't call out his own spirit guide to berate him for not keeping her safe.

"I'm here," he said. "I'm here with you, Astrid. Nothing is going to happen now."

"They came into the tent."

"And that was my mistake for leaving you. One I will not make again. We must go now, bright one, so they do not know where we run to."

"Where are we going?" Those white eyes moved in her skull, and he had the strange sense that she was looking at him. "There is nowhere to go but up. They will see us."

"Trolls are more resourceful than that. I had hoped to go into the mountain taking the usual route, not..." He swallowed. "Trolls have other ways, Astrid. You and I will go in one of the old ways. It is not the safest path, but no one will see us."

She blinked and he saw the white haze over her eyes was more of a film than entirely white. "They won't know where we are?"

"We'll be entirely safe. They won't be able to follow us." He reached for her waist, gripping her side with a strong, sure hand. "Come with me. We'll hide where they cannot follow. Let me take you to the heart of our mountain, Astrid."

She nodded. Once, twice, three times, and then all Bjorn could see were those sky blue eyes once more. "We had better be quick."

Chapter 30

Astrid wasn't sure what had come over her. The magic had just... flowed. She'd never felt so powerful in her life, but she'd also never been so terrified. The magic hadn't felt like hers.

For years, she had known what her magic felt like. It was a warm, comforting friend that she could call upon whenever she needed to. The heat of it would flow down her arms, to her hands that always knew what to do with it. But this magic had been cold. Bitter on her tongue. It had swirled around her mouth, using her lips and tongue as its own.

The language she had spoken was unfamiliar to her. Just like when she had read the words on the talon, she hadn't known what she was saying or what she was calling upon. It had felt like someone else was using her body as a puppet, and she hadn't liked that.

She could still taste it on her tongue. The bitter aftertaste of that power was like she had sipped on oversteeped green tea. She couldn't shake the strange taste or the feeling even as Bjorn lifted her into his arms and darted away from the men.

He stopped by their ruined tent to pick up a few things. Her pack with the pretty dress he'd made her, a few more weapons, and a water skein that he hung off the side of his hip. Then he picked her back up again, and off they went. Running across the ground was difficult for him with her in his arms, but he made it work. It wasn't like any of the soldiers were following them.

The screams had died down, at least. It made the ache in her chest ease. They weren't dead, she hoped. They were just reminded why they shouldn't attack innocent strangers on a mountainside and assume they could do whatever they wanted. Bjorn remained silent throughout his mad sprint. Even his footsteps were quiet as he picked his way over the rocks, crouching low sometimes when his big ears caught something hers didn't, and then making a mad dash toward the next hidden area where rocks would prevent others from seeing them.

She did her best to remain quiet as well. It wasn't like she was doing anything to help, after all. All she had to do was not talk and keep her opinions to herself.

Until they came to a crevice in the mountain that looked like a naturally made crack. She wouldn't have given it any thought if she had walked by it, other than thinking perhaps an animal might make that its home. But Bjorn headed right for it, ducking underneath the stone and setting her down in front of him.

"Go forward," he said. "I want to stay behind you in case anyone follows us."

"Do you think they will?"

"I didn't see anyone, but that doesn't mean we weren't followed." He nudged her. "Go on. I know you can't see, bright one, but there shouldn't be anything that will trip you up. It will get tight, though. Exhale if you get stuck."

"If I have to exhale to get through, how are you getting through?" She started forward though, suddenly terrified of what she would find. Was it that tight in this tunnel into the mountain? Was this even the right one?

He chuckled, and the sound eased some of the tension in her chest. "This tunnel was built for trolls, Astrid. Not for humans. Where you stand can be narrower because it was built for hips, not for chests."

That made sense, actually. She supposed it wasn't all that surprising that she was going to have to fit tightly where his hips were built to go. She took her time, steadily making her way through a tunnel that would have otherwise terrified her.

It still did, at points. The jagged rock was unforgiving as she pushed her body through the tunnel. She had to turn her head to the side, so it wouldn't scrape her cheeks. And there was a small section where her chest simply would not fit through. She did as he said, exhaling long and low until there was no more air in her lungs and through the stones she went.

A small spike of panic had overcome her halfway through that section. Astrid desperately needed to breathe, but couldn't. Rocks held her chest and back compressed, but if she didn't get oxygen soon...

"Easy, bright one," his voice came from behind her in the tunnel. "Don't freeze. Keep moving. If you don't move, you will get stuck. But you can move."

She could move. He said she could, and so she did. She popped free from that horrible spot and inhaled air that smelled like greenery and gardens. That little fact didn't surprise her in her panic to get as much air into her body as she possibly could. Nor did she notice that there weren't rocks on either side of her, and she could bend forward and place her hands on her knees. She just did it because she could, trying to get her body to release the tension that made every part of her shudder with fear.

She had done that.

Really, she'd done that. Some mad part of her had survived sliding through rocks that had tried to clamp down on her in their strong, vise-like grip. She could have died right then and there.

A wild part of her laughed at the thought. She hadn't died. She'd almost died so many times recently, and none of it had stopped her. Astrid was stronger than she had ever thought, and that elation had her spinning in his direction.

"Are you all right?" he said.

She could only make out the shadow of him, coming out of the crevice himself as he wiggled his shoulders free. And the moment she could finally get her arms around him, she did. She climbed his body like a tree, framed his face in her hands, and kissed him.

Bjorn didn't move for a second. His arms were at his sides, apparently surprised that she had climbed him that quickly. But then his arms came around her, and he kissed her back. Fiercely, almost violently. His tusks scraped against her cheeks, but she didn't care. She just needed to celebrate with him, to share the elation of being alive.

His arms closed around her, safe and warm and all the things that she wanted him to be. Bjorn had proven himself time and time again that he was so much more than the broken prisoner she had thought him to be.

"This is a reaction to using so much magic," he murmured against her lips. But she could hear the sound of his weapons dropping to the ground. "You are not yourself."

"I am happy to be alive."

"You used more magic than you ever have, and your body isn't sure what to do with that." Now, there was a heaviness against her back. Rocks, she realized, but not jagged like the stones had been in that crevice. Smoothed out, as though they had been carved to be this way.

Astrid reached back and flattened her hands against the slick surface. His hips braced her now, she didn't have to clutch onto him as much as he leaned all his hardness into her.

And there was so much of him. She was surrounded by his strength, his body, the tiny movements of every twitching muscle as she ran her hands down his torso.

"We can't do this," he said as he ripped his mouth from hers, only to trail his lips down the side of her neck. "We have a long way to go."

"Aren't we safe here?"

"This is just a resting area. There isn't even a bed here." Then Bjorn's tongue traced a pattern against her throbbing pulse, and need shot right between her legs.

She couldn't think when he did something like that. He was clearly suggesting she should argue with him about something, but she had no idea what she was meant to be arguing about. Who cared if they were alone here? Who cared if this place wasn't meant for what she was about to do?

"Why would I need a bed?" she moaned, palming the back of his head as he licked over her collarbone.

He stiffened before leaning back. She couldn't quite make out his face. It was so dim in here, the lighting was near impossible to see his features other than the horned shape of him. But then he lifted his hand, tracing a careful finger along her swollen bottom lip.

"When I fuck you, troll wife, it will be in a soft bed, so I do not scrape your back against the stones, so there is no part of you that is sore." He leaned down, nipped at her ear, and then growled, "Other than your sweet pussy, which will remember the shape of me for days afterward."

She swallowed hard, her eyes rolling back in her head. He wasn't going to allow her to seduce him, that much was clear. But she could do a great many other things.

Unhooking her legs from around his waist, she stood on her own two feet. His lips found hers unerringly, clearly thinking he was going to get away with a repeat of what they had done in the tent earlier in the night. An urgency pushed her to do more, though. They were so close to no longer having their privacy, and she needed to reassure herself.

Once they found her sister, Astrid had no idea what the next steps for her would be. If there was some chance she and Bjorn would be parted, she wanted to make sure he'd remember her.

Planting her hands firmly on his chest, she turned them both. Soon, it was his back slamming against the rocks, and her hips that pressed him into place. The length of his cock burrowed against her belly. The damn thing really was big. It was enough to make her nervous, but she wasn't going to stop now.

"If you won't let me have my fun," she whispered, trailing her lips down his chest. "Then I will find other ways to entertain myself."

She'd seen other women do this, had done it herself, but never with a cock so massive. She tugged at the waistband of his leather pants, wanting to feel it at the very least. His thick leather pants weren't the type to easily come down, though, and that made things difficult.

"Astrid, you don't have to—"

"Shut up, Bjorn." Perhaps that came out a little harsh, but she was tired of his excuses. Right now, she wanted him to feel as good as he made her feel. That was all.

He seemed to understand that she was calling the shots right now. His hands went to the sides of his pants and made quick work of ties.

Why hadn't she thought about the ties?

And then the leather was sagging, and she still couldn't see anything, but she could damn well feel. Reaching out, she grasped his cock in her hand and confirmed what she had been thinking.

He was big.

Really, really big.

Damn, she wasn't sure this would ever work between them, but she was damn well willing to try. Astrid couldn't even fit this thing in her mouth. It just wasn't possible. Her jaw didn't open wide enough to give him what he was likely expecting.

So instead, she licked her way up the shaft of it, measuring the entire length with her fingers and tongue. She heard the sound of his skull hitting the stone behind him, and the long groan that worked its way out from deep within his chest.

His hips bucked a bit in her hands, and she couldn't stop herself from grinning. Finally, she reached the head of this ridiculous cock, her tongue finding the ring at the tip.

"Are you sure you're healed?" she asked, toying with the ring.

He was panting when he responded, "I'm healed."

"This was for me, after all. Wasn't it?" Again another flick of the ring, and she wished she could see his features because his hands slammed against the wall this time.

"Yes," he breathed. "All for you."

Well, if he was going to be such a good boy…

Astrid tried her best to fit him into her mouth. Just the head and slightly more could fit, but that was all. She had to use both hands to work him, moving them in alternate directions, both slow and fast, meandering and hard. She didn't give him enough of anything all at once. The man didn't get to come, not yet.

She wanted to learn him first. To trace the veins of his cock with her tongue and learn what made him gasp. Was it her sucking on the head of him and flicking her tongue, or did he like it even better when she cupped his balls beneath? He seemed to like harder movements, faster than what she was doing. Delicate touches weren't for Bjorn, it seemed. Which was fine with her. She didn't need to be delicate to do what she wanted.

Tormenting him was fun, she realized. She'd always done this just as a job or to convince a man to do what she wanted. But now it was just... enjoyment. She liked the taste of him. Liked the feeling of his ring on her tongue and how he didn't hide his reactions in the slightest.

He was thoroughly and wonderfully loud. Every sound was an answer to something she did, and he didn't seem to care at all that someone might hear him. She'd never been with someone who was so loud, so excitable by everything that she did.

And finally, she gave him what he wanted. Heavy, strong, squeezing him tightly in her hands while she sucked hard on his tip. Her knees had pressed up against Bjorn's feet, and she could feel his toes curl as she did it until finally he let out a groan that made every hair on her body raise.

His come coated the back of her throat, and she swallowed it all down, licking him clean with slow laps.

He sagged against the wall, and then slid down it until he had her trapped between his raised knees. He reached for her, his hands skimming along her face and jaw before dragging her against him.

When had this become a place she was so happy to be? There was no one else she'd want to hold her like this, and he was a troll. A troll!

Of all people, she shouldn't feel so safe and at home in his arms.

But she did.

"I don't think you understand how much I want to lock you up to keep you safe," he whispered against her hair once his breathing settled down. "You are..."

He seemed to struggle to find the words, but even in that silence she felt her heart glowing in her chest.

"I know," she whispered, pressing her hand against his thundering heart. "I know exactly what you mean, Bjorn."

For the moment, they could rest with each other. They could linger in the darkness and in the aftermath of pleasure. Who knew what would happen in an hour, but for now, they were together.

Chapter 31

At some point during the night, Astrid realized there was a light in the cave they were in. She'd opened her eyes to see that Bjorn had found implements to light a fire, or at least torches that lined the wall. She was so tired from their journey, from the fight, she hadn't even thought to look at her surroundings. Instead, she had fallen right back into a dreamless sleep.

But as she woke the next morning, if she could even call it that, there were moments from the night that she wasn't sure had been a dream or had been real.

The vision of him leaning over her, brushing her hair away from her face and arranging her body into a more comfortable position. Opening her eyes, she'd seen him standing before a wall that was painted with what looked like a map, with one of those torches in his hands. The glimmering darkness split open into something blue and purple that surely couldn't have been real. But then she'd closed her eyes again and sunk back into dreams, so she didn't know if any of it had truly happened.

His hand on her shoulder pulled her into the waking realm soon enough. "Come," he murmured. "We wake and we go to the rest of my home."

"Where are we going exactly?" She rubbed the heels of her palms against her eyes, trying to get the grit of sleep off her face so she looked somewhat presentable.

"To the king."

He looked nervous. Almost as though he was hesitant bringing her anywhere. It was sweet of him to think she would be uncomfortable, but a troll king was likely not all that different from the others.

She patted her hand against his chest and smiled up at him. "He is not the first king I have met."

Bjorn stared down into her eyes and then sighed. "I suppose you are right."

"Let's not waste too much time. Although I don't suppose there's any water left, so I might look a little more presentable?"

In the end, she changed into the dress he had made her. Freshly washed, now clothed in spider silk and the most beautiful gown she'd ever put on her body, Astrid was ready to meet a king.

Bjorn walked with her out of the cave. She'd expected a secret crevice in the mountain, perhaps a green area that had light spearing through it. But she hadn't expected... this.

They stood on a small ledge that held them out over the kingdom below, and she feasted her eyes on Trollveggen itself. Bright purple trees with leaves that seemed to glow in the dark filled her vision. The cavern was hollow. The mountain itself was hollow. She stared down into a vast world full of brightly colored forests, a glowing blue river that ran through the center, and dotted buildings that looked like starlight.

Except there was more starlight up above. Dotted glowing worms that she could see overhead stretched ever farther out along the top of this cave. And there were people. Trolls who moved about their day, wearing clothing that was so vivid and colorful that she never would have guessed it was possible to even make them.

This place was beauty. It was full of life and sound. Her ears couldn't quite pick out the individual sounds at all. Only that there were so many different ones. The rushing river. People talking. Singing voices, although that couldn't be right. She must've been dreaming that up.

"This is..." She tried to find the words, but was a little ashamed to admit she couldn't.

Bjorn was staring at it as well. Feasting his eyes on what he had lost for so many years. Then she felt like an ass, because of course he was staring at it. He hadn't been back here in such a long time, and maybe he'd thought he never would.

"Are you all right?" she asked, eyeing him.

He nodded slowly. "I'll be fine."

"That's not really an answer."

"It's just..." He gestured out at what they both were staring at. "It's the same as it always was, bright one. Not a single bit of it has changed, and here I am. A fragment of the man I was before I left."

She couldn't tell him that he was the same person. She hadn't known him back then. Besides, it didn't seem like that was what he wanted to hear from her. He wanted to get moving, and that was the best she could offer as well.

Bjorn found a rope that had been tied to the wall, anchored by heavy iron bolts, and then had her hold on to the side of his neck. Together, they descended into the mountain and headed off down the streets.

They were mostly empty, so she had to assume it was very early for the trolls. But she was able to stare at houses this way. They were so modern. The exteriors of the homes were made with impressive wooden beams, and delicate attention to details like small curved siding and matching rivets that held everything together. The windows were perfect, something she rarely saw in her own kingdom, and the lights outside were mostly will-o'-the-wisps. Although some appeared to be oil lamps, though they were unlike any she'd seen before.

Then there was the castle itself, which was built into the roots of a massive tree that loomed above the entire kingdom. Calling it a tree didn't even seem appropriate. It was a giant that was nearly as big as the mountain.

Together, they walked up the steps that were woven throughout the massive roots, and then she was entering a troll castle.

How strange it was. Astrid couldn't help but compare this place with the human castle where she had spent so much time. It was easy to confuse them. The clean floors, the chandeliers from the ceiling, but this one had many more antlers and furs, and all the other natural elements that made it stand out from the one she was so used to.

Not to mention the trolls. They must've been nobility, considering they were all dripping in jewels. One of the men who walked by was so heavily pierced and wearing so many necklaces and bracelets that she was shocked he could move at all. The trolls came in so many colors. There were bright yellows, blues, purples, every color she could have imagined and yet had never dreamt of as a skin tone.

Bjorn strode past them with his head held high. She watched the others as they walked past, and the eyes that followed them. So many people here stared at him, then whispered the same word over and over again.

Soon enough, she realized it was his name. They said it with heavy accents, some of them still speaking in the black tongue.

News of his escape hadn't reached this far yet, she guessed. Or their king had planned for a grand entrance.

Exactly like they were doing now.

Bjorn led her through the entire hall, all the way to the back of the castle. He pushed the twin heavy doors open and revealed not a throne room, like she had expected, but a room with a long table covered in maps, and about twenty trolls sitting all around it.

These were the kind of trolls she had expected. Warlords with scars that decorated their features. A few of them had horns like Bjorn. Others were dusted in feathers. One man was even missing an eye, which she tried very hard not to stare at.

She had underestimated what it would feel like to not have the face covering over her features. Even with just her eyes visible at times, it had always helped hide her from the stares of so many people. It didn't matter when it was peasants or the working class, but these were people with means. People who knew what it took to look at her expression and know exactly what was going on in her head.

But she was a priestess. She had trained her entire life to do this, and so she would.

Astrid lifted her chin and strode all the way to the end of the table with Bjorn at her side. The hulking behemoth at the end, with his useless wings draped over the back of his chair, could be none other than King Egil himself.

She dropped into a deep curtsy the moment they neared his chair. "Your majesty. I received your letter."

A deep, booming laugh erupted from his chest. "Aye, so it seems."

"As requested, I brought you the troll from the labyrinth that you wished to see freed." She risked a glance up at the man whose mottled gray skin looked more like stone than flesh. "I believe the deal was for my sister's well-being."

The king gestured to his right, seemingly bored with how she addressed him. "Yes. Humans are always so persistent when it comes to getting what they want. Your sister is fine. But I thank you for bringing back my destroyer."

The words stuck in her head. Bjorn wasn't a warlord, or a destroyer, or anything like his father. He was a kind, soft man who wished for a kind, soft life. But then her eyes flicked in the direction the king had gestured, and her whole world rolled to a stop.

Seated on the other side of a massive green troll was a woman with bright blonde hair. There were dark circles under her eyes, and she was painfully thin. But even from this distance, Astrid could see that her eyes were their mother's eyes. Such a light blue that they were almost gray. Haunted eyes, people used to say.

Now she understood what they meant.

"Rose?" she whispered. It felt like the word was so loud. Perhaps because the entire room had suddenly gone silent.

Her sister stood from the table, and they stared at each other for a while. There'd been a time when people used to think they were twins, even though Astrid was older. But time and experience had changed that.

Astrid's hair was golden, her sister's had faded to nearly white. Rose was so pale. Even the veins underneath her skin were visible, making her seem almost bruised as she walked around the table and stood before her sister.

Her heart couldn't stop thudding against her ribs. She could feel it, starting and stopping as hope tried to take flight out of her body. This was her sister. Rose.

"I never stopped looking for you," Astrid whispered. "Not a single day."

Rose swallowed hard, and it seemed like the words she said next had to be ripped out of her mouth. "I know. I always knew you wouldn't stop looking for me. It's just... I knew where you were. But I also knew you would never find me where he put me."

The green troll she'd been sitting beside slumped back in his chair. "Oh, now she speaks."

Without hesitation, Astrid glared at the man. Her look would have sliced through his body if it was a knife.

The green troll wilted in his chair before pointing at her sister with a black clawed finger. "She hasn't talked in weeks."

"Then she wasn't ready to talk," Astrid snapped.

His nostrils flared. She would have gotten into a fight with him if Rose hadn't reached out for her arm. The troll's eyes immediately went to the contact, widening in what she could only describe as shock.

Astrid tried not to think too much about that. Of course her sister would touch her. They were family. Family was different, no matter what happened to a person. Family was safe.

Making a point, she twisted her arm in Rose's grip and laced their fingers together instead. She'd hoped her sister would understand the comfort she offered, and she was so relieved when Rose squeezed her hand back. They were always meant to be together, after all. That had been the plan ever since they'd lived on the streets.

"Come with me," Rose said, and suddenly she was dragged out of the room.

Astrid had only a second to look back at Bjorn. He stood there, a pillar of strength among his people, and she mouthed the words "thank you" as the door closed behind her.

Her sister.

Finally.

After all this time.

Rose took her to what must have been a drawing room, sitting down on a small couch facing each other and all Astrid could do was drink her sister in. She looked at every feature that had changed, every new wrinkle on Rose's face. A story that she did not know, but knew at some point she would.

Reaching forward, she gave Rose time to withdraw but then finally traced her sister's jaw. "You look just like you did ten years ago."

"Do I? I was afraid you wouldn't recognize me if you ever saw me again."

"I would recognize you in pitch black," Astrid whispered. "I would know you if they took my eyes and ears. You are my sister, Rose. How could I ever forget a single detail about you?"

Her heart broke when tears filled Rose's eyes. Even now, Astrid tried to drink in the details of her sister's features. What she wore. How she curved in on herself without a single drop of confidence that she used to have.

Astrid withdrew her hand. "It's been a long time since we have been together. I know this."

"I am not the person you knew." Rose looked down at her hands curled in her lap, and that was when Astrid noticed her sister's fingers.

Dried blood crusted around her nails from picking at the skin there. And the nails were chewed raw, it looked like. She'd seen hands like that before, after horrible tragedies had occurred to a few of the priestesses. They were sent back to the sisterhood, and she didn't ever see them act like themselves again. They were ragged edged pieces of the women they once were.

Some lords were cruel to those they were given. But then again, men were cruel to women.

Astrid risked a touch again, covering her sister's hands with her own. She tried to ignore how her own hands were smooth and lily white, even after traveling for such a long time.

"We will leave this place," she said. "I made a deal with the troll king. They said if I brought Bjorn back, then I could take you wherever you want to go. We don't have to stay here, Rose."

Her sister's hands started to shake beneath hers. "I don't want to go back."

"Then we'll go to another kingdom."

But it was already too late. Rose's eyes stared into her own, wide and haunted and filled with memories that Astrid couldn't fix. "Please don't make me go back. I can't do it again. I can't. I'm rotting away inside, Astrid. It's eating me."

"What is eating you?"

"The memories," Rose gasped. And then her pretty voice twisted into something snarled and tangled, like the roots of a tree had grown into her soul. "Them. They're still eating me from the inside out."

She'd never seen her sister like this before. Both mourning and aching and raw. Rose had always been a delicate girl. Sensitive in a way that Astrid couldn't understand. Her sister was gentle and delicate, and now...

Those shaking hands turned to claws beneath hers. The fingers stiffened and tore at her thighs. "The king wanted to give me to one of them, and I refused. I said I wouldn't go. He pushed, he yelled, he threatened, and then I slapped him." Rose hiccupped. "I slapped him, and he sent me away into the darkness and the shadows, where there were only more hands that took. They took everything from me, Astrid."

Tears burned Astrid's eyes. She didn't know how to help her sister. Her magic swelled inside of her, whispering that she could take away the pain. She pulled on it slightly, tugging at those memories to give her sister some relief, but even touching those emotions made Astrid recoil in fear.

"That's more than enough," a deep voice interrupted them.

The green troll from before strode into the room, looming above them with his arms crossed over his chest. His hair was wild, not bound like many of the trolls here. He glared at her again, and then gruffly said, "Rose, head back to the house."

The snapping order was one her sister apparently could not refuse. She scurried away, her head low, her arms wrapped around her waist. Like she didn't want anyone to see her.

Astrid waited until her sister had left the room before asking, "What happened to her?"

"Years in your labyrinth," the green troll snarled. "It wasn't only the men who were ruined there, Priestess."

He followed her sister out of the room, like a great cat stalking a mouse. Astrid was left seated on that comfortable couch, wondering what had happened to her sister, and how she was going to fix this.

Chapter 32

Bjorn watched Astrid go with his heart in his throat. He was pleased that her sister was here, and seemingly unharmed. It was a relief to know that Astrid would finally get what she wanted. But it made him nervous, too.

What if Rose wanted to leave this place?

What if they both wanted to return to the human kingdom, where he couldn't go? He'd tried to be a good husband. To prove to Astrid that he would be someone worthwhile to remain with. They could build a life together here, even if it wasn't the life she was used to. Now was the moment when he would find out if that was enough.

But he hadn't been given enough time. There was so much more he wanted to prove to her. So much more that he could do to give her the right first impression.

Doing that in Trollveggen was, apparently, going to be much more difficult than he had originally thought. All the warlords around the table stared at him with expectations in those gazes. Even the king himself had called him the Destroyer.

They wanted him to be like his father. They hoped that he would be. These warlords expected a beast of a man who could plow through any and all soldiers that stood in his way, no matter the pain that was caused or the wounds that were acquired. He was expected to be just like Dag the Destroyer. His father had been a renowned fighter simply because of the insanity with which he'd fought.

Bjorn didn't want to be that person. But if he didn't have Astrid, what else did he have? This was his future, no matter the cost.

He squared his shoulders and turned his attention to his king. Slowly, he dropped onto one knee and pressed his hand to his heart. "I have returned, King Egil."

"I'm sorry we couldn't get you out sooner, boy. That is a fault of our own, and one I apologize sincerely for. You should never have been there that long."

Bjorn almost choked when he felt the king's hand on his shoulder. He'd never seen the king touch another like this, not in kindness or deference for what another troll had gone through. It was unprecedented.

Trying hard not to get choked up, he cleared his throat. It was hard for him to accept this kind of treatment. Bjorn had been taken when he was a young man, and he wasn't a young man anymore. But he still wasn't old. He wasn't ancient. He just... felt like it.

The king patted his shoulder again, and then addressed the other warlords. "Our destroyer has returned! With a bloodline from berserkers, we now have our shield. Our people are whole again, but there are many still to save. Together, we will break into the human king's castle, and we will take back all those who are ours. We will destroy this labyrinth once and for all. We will fill it with earth and blood, crumbling it into ruin to send a message to all humans. The trolls will not break easily."

A cry rose from the twenty warlords at the table. Each of them thirsted for blood, and so should've Bjorn.

But even the thought of it made him shudder. Returning to that place would be hard enough, but knowing he had to return only to fight again? Even if it was fighting to free the others, even if it was the right thing to do...

He was tired. Tired of fighting, of battle, of blood. He wanted a quiet life, with a quiet place to rest his head.

He'd been running for such a long time. Even before Astrid had freed him, Bjorn had never felt like he was safe. Even thinking back to when he'd been a child here, he wasn't sure he'd known what safe felt like. His mother and father had always argued. Dag had wanted him to be a warrior. His mother had wanted him to delve deeper into his magic and ability to control animals. Everyone had expectations of him considering who his parents were, and he... he just wanted it all to be silent.

Yet now he stood with the weight of the troll kingdom on his shoulders yet again, with all their expectations as they stared at him and cheered, knowing that he would lead them in a fight they could not lose.

He just wasn't sure they were right. The humans had bested him before. And now he had something to lose.

Perhaps that was why his father had never truly loved his mother. Dag had been pragmatic. The man had always known that a woman could be his greatest downfall.

The king stood along with the other warlords. They all watched King Egil, waiting for the moment they were released. With a snap of his wings, their king nodded his head. "Go. Be with your people now."

Then Bjorn was swarmed. Just like in the grotto, too many people touched him, lingering hands that made him want to snap at them. He would bite through their flesh if that was what it took for them to give him air, but he held himself together.

Barely.

He was near snapping when he saw a familiar face. Lavender colored features and tattoos down his left arm, it was hard to miss Ragnar where he stood at the back of the crowd. His oldest friend had his arms crossed over his barrel of a chest, waiting for all the others to get through.

So Bjorn did the same. He waited, enduring all the touches and well wishes with a nod of his head and what he hoped looked like a convincing smile. Until everyone had filtered out of the room and all that remained were he and Ragnar.

The last time he'd seen this purple-skinned bastard had been in the labyrinth. He'd had a troll wife then, although the redhead was nowhere to be seen at this moment. Apparently, only Astrid's sister was brought along for important meetings like this.

Alone with his oldest friend, he had no idea what to even say. The last time they'd seen each other, Bjorn had been little more than an animal running on instinct. He knew there was no way to sugarcoat that. He'd killed in front of Ragnar, given them the only chance he'd known at getting out, and even then it hadn't felt like enough.

Bjorn had scared Ragnar's troll wife. He'd done the worst thing a male like him could do. Even though he'd tried not to, he knew what state he had been in when Maia had seen him.

The same state he'd been in when Astrid had seen him, although at least she had come upon him when he'd had a little more hope than before. He hadn't been quite so animalistic as he had been before...

well. Before.

Shaking out his hands, he snarled, "Are you going to say anything?"

Ragnar was too silent. Silence was usually a precursor to something horrible happening. Someone was going to attack him, he could feel it. That itch crawled up his spine until Ragnar's arms dropped to his sides.

"I don't know what to say. Seeing you here, in your home, is strange. You are not the young man who used to live here, and yet, I see so much of him in you." Ragnar's face creased into a smile that was supposed to be reassuring, but it wasn't.

Bjorn couldn't parse out why it wasn't reassuring. He didn't want to be here. His soul felt like it was trying to crawl out of his body, as though if he could just get out of his skin then he could find a safe place to rest. To reset.

Then Ragnar was right in front of him, his hand on the back of Bjorn's neck. They were both big trolls, always had been. They had trained together as young men, fighting, rolling, always locking tusks when they were younger.

Perhaps that old muscle memory was why he lunged forward and did just that. Their tusks locked, breath fanning against each other, the very air they breathed battling as they both held themselves just out of reach from fighting. They were not going to lose control just yet, but he could feel that it was close.

One of them was going to snap, and he was almost glad for it. Bjorn needed to fight. He needed to release these horrible emotions so he felt more like himself. He needed this.

But then Ragnar lifted his hand again, gently placing it on the back of his neck, and pulling him in a little closer. It was a gentle touch. Not one meant to fight, but to console.

Ragnar's breathing wasn't out of control like Bjorn's was. He was steady and calm, his heart beating slowly, each inhale calculated and measured. Louder than it needed to be. As though he was trying to guide Bjorn through quieter, steadier breaths.

And it worked. Perhaps he was aided by the cool guidance of Ragnar's magic as well, but he felt his anger simmering down to the place it usually was. Manageable. Just out of reach in case he needed it, but he didn't right now.

Their tusks unlocked. Their foreheads touched. And he stood there breathing with the man who had given up on him. The friend who hadn't spent his lifetime searching for him, when he had been right there.

"You have every right to be angry with me," Ragnar said, his voice pitched low. "I expected that. I knew that if you were going to make your way back to us, there would be a long time where we had to mend what we had."

"You left me there."

"I did. I didn't know you were alive. None of us did. But the moment I found out you were there, I sent people after you. We tried. We tried to get you out, and we failed. I am sorry for that, brother." Ragnar's voice was unsteady at the end of it. As though he was honest in his words, but it was hard to believe them.

"Ten years," Bjorn said. "Ten years of fighting. Ten years of losing myself, bit by bit until I didn't even know who I was anymore. I buried every memory of this place, of the people who loved me. I hid in the violence, and it lives and breathes inside of me now."

"This is not a wound I can heal."

"No, it is not. But it is my reality, and the reality of so many others. You want to attack the castle? You want to take them back?" Bjorn breathed in and separated himself from Ragnar, reeling until his hands were pressed against the table. A map spread out before him, nowhere near detailed enough to get them into the castle the right way. "What if you lose all of them, Ragnar? What if we lose and all of them are trapped in the same place that we escaped?"

"It's a risk we have to take. We could get them back. We could have gotten you back if we had tried hard enough, and we didn't." Ragnar didn't move, but Bjorn could feel his eyes on his back. "You would leave them there?"

"I cannot tell you how many times I believed it would be better to die than return here. It would be better to seek out a bitter end than to know you all had lived and moved on without me." He took a deep, shuddering breath. "And now I fear I may have been right."

There was silence in response. Silence that told him he had stepped over some line that Ragnar could not understand. But his friend couldn't understand it to begin with.

The sound of nothingness burned, and finally Bjorn tried to explain it away. "You don't know what it was like down there. You don't know how it felt to be fighting for my own survival while killing our kind. People I knew. People who meant something to me. Did you know I was taken with Hakon? A good man. They made me slit his throat into a barrel so they could take his blood away. I don't know what they did with it. I will never forget him begging me not to do it, when I knew if I didn't, they were going to make him do it to me."

So many memories. Maybe they were the reason for the rage that bubbled up inside him. They were the reason he didn't want other trolls to touch him.

Bjorn was tainted. The curse had sunk into his flesh, and he feared it would spread to anyone who touched him. He couldn't shake that thought. Not in the grotto. And certainly not here.

"You did what you had to do to survive," Ragnar replied. "No one is going to begrudge you that. They're just happy you're home."

"They want me to be a weapon. Again. They want to wield me like they did my father, and they expect me to do so because I'd want my revenge." He looked up from the table and stared into Ragnar's gaze. "I just want to be left alone, brother. I want to go back to my farm and grow food with my own two hands. I want to finally have pigs. And to live with the woman I love, quietly. Without anyone bothering us."

There was a lot to unpack in that statement. But Ragnar's brows lifted at the end, and he repeated, "The woman you love?"

Fuck.

He did love her, though. He loved every inch of her beautiful body and every spark in that brilliant mind. Nodding solemnly, he admitted, "I've known for a while now. She doesn't, though. So keep your mouth shut about it."

Ragnar lifted his hands. "I wouldn't dream of saying a word."

"Not even to Maia."

"Now, brother, you know as well as I do, a troll wife like mine knows everything and everyone." A flash of his white teeth reminded Bjorn of the boy Ragnar used to be. Teasing. Funny. Always joking about something.

And now look at him. Beaten into a sharp sword that healed as much as he hurt.

Heaving a sigh, Bjorn pushed away from the table. "Look at the two of us. If you had asked me when I was a child who we would be as men, I never would have said this."

"No, neither would I."

"It's a disappointment to our ancestors, I suppose."

"Ah, I wouldn't go so far as to say that." Ragnar gestured for the door, and the two of them headed out of the room. "I was a young man who had a lot of big dreams. But I wouldn't change anything that happened to me, because it led me to her."

The door opened, revealing the redhead Bjorn had met in the labyrinth. He'd carried her to Ragnar and then watched them both disappear through the damaged wall he had shown them. She was still alive. He was pleased to see it.

Her eyes danced over him, and he saw the sheer pleasure in them. "Bjorn!"

His name rang out, echoing too loudly. Trolls looked at him, many of them knowing who he was without question now and it made him panic.

Ragnar grabbed her arm gently, reeling her into his chest and leaning down to murmur in her ear. The redhead, while boisterous, clearly understood that there was going to have to be some time before they had their reunion.

She nodded and mouthed, "Later."

And then she had eyes only for Ragnar as he swept her into his arms, and headed out of the castle. Like no one existed other than the two of them.

Bjorn could only hope his future was so bright. He'd have to wait and see.

Chapter 33

Perhaps Astrid was a lovesick fool, but she immediately went to find Bjorn. She didn't want to stay in that pretty sitting room that looked rather like a lord's parlor. She didn't want to be back in this world that she felt like she had just left. What she wanted was him.

She needed his quiet strength, his resilience against anything and everything that might bother him. She wanted to know that she was safe. And safety had become intertwined with being in his presence. What a strange thing it was to think. Only months ago she would have thought trolls were the most dangerous creatures to be stuck with. She would have flinched away from the mere thought of even standing near one.

Now she was walking through their castle, ignoring all the other trolls who gave her odd looks, and found Bjorn.

He still stood in front of the door leading into that meeting room. His expression was a little odd, his eyes far away as he stared down the hall. She looked in the same direction, but she didn't see anyone who was looking back at him or anything strange.

"Bjorn?" she asked quietly, reaching out to touch his arm.

He shook himself out of whatever stupor he'd been in and looked down at her. His gaze cleared as if he hadn't realized he was staring. "Astrid. I was just coming to find you."

"I figured you were." She glanced around them, trying not to appear so nervous. "I don't suppose you know where we're staying tonight? I would like to get clean and... Well, it seems like your city is far more civilized than I had originally thought. The people here are so elegant, and I feel underdressed."

That seemed to shake him the rest of the way out of his discomfort. His gaze softened, and a small smile crossed his features. "You wish for a bath?"

"If possible. I know that's a lot to ask considering the amount of work it takes."

She used to hate asking the maids for a bath. It took nearly an hour for them to heat all the water and then lug it to the tub, but she knew very well that that was the only way to do it. How long had it been since she'd actually bathed? With all the travel, just dipping her body into a running stream of water wasn't doing it anymore. She needed soap. She needed a sponge. And perhaps some time to soften all the dead skin on her body so she could scrub it all off again.

Bjorn shook his head at her words. "I forgot humans are so backward. We have running water here. Hot water from the springs in the mountain. It takes nothing to run a bath."

"Oh."

Another plus for his side, she supposed. If she didn't have to wait to take a bath whenever she wanted, it suddenly didn't seem quite so difficult to stay here.

He planted his hand on her back, and they started back down the hall. She was rather distracted by a beautiful troll woman with emerald green skin dripping in what looked like diamonds. Literally dripping with them. She had diamonds hanging from her ears, her neck, her arms, pierced through her claws, there were hundreds of them dotting all over her body. It was wondrous to look at.

But then they were out the door, and Bjorn murmured, "How is your sister?"

The world felt like it came crashing down a second time. He guided her back down the steps, returning to the market and the homes that dotted the streets. It would have been so much easier to pretend that the conversation with Rose had never happened, but she knew very well that she couldn't.

Sighing, she shook her head. "My sister is not the same as she was before. I didn't expect her to be, of course. After everything I saw myself in the labyrinth, I couldn't imagine that she wouldn't have some wounds. But she seems almost unreasonable. Certainly not herself."

"The things I know that happened to women like her were cruel, and they broke even the strongest of minds." Someone bumped into her, and his hand flexed against her back as he guided her through the crowd. "You were lucky I could spare you that."

Astrid was still troubled by her sister's reaction. So troubled, in fact, that she barely saw the streets they walked through. Bjorn moved her quickly, but she was used to that too. He didn't like it when people stared at him, and he didn't like crowds forming around them.

Unfortunately, that was all they seemed to get now that they had returned to the troll kingdom. It had made sense in the grotto. Those people were all his friends and family, and they had been terribly worried for his life. Some of them had likely even given up hope they would ever find him again, and that was understandable. He'd been gone for ten years.

She knew a bit of what that was like. For ten years she had prayed for her sister's return. Astrid had never given up hope, because that emotion was the only thing she could cling to.

Hope that her sister was still alive. Hope that their relationship could be mended no matter what had befallen her dear, gentle sister, who had never even harmed a spider in a garden.

Now, she wasn't so sure.

She sidestepped a troll who was heading through the streets with a cart tied to his back. Unfortunately, she wasn't quick enough to entirely get out of his way. Bjorn had to lift her up just to make sure she didn't get run over. The man grunted at her, but he didn't seem to react as much as the trolls in the grotto had. Which was odd, she thought. Considering the trolls in the grotto had been rather surprised to see a human woman walking among them.

But not here. Not in Trollveggen. It almost seemed as though these trolls were expecting to see her kind.

"Bjorn?" she asked, blinking to clear her mind of the dark thoughts. "Do any humans live here with the trolls?"

"Some," he grunted. There was a darker stain on his cheeks as they stood still in a small crowd to cross the busy street. His eyes swept left to right, surveying everyone around them. "From what I gather, King Egil made a statement to all the humans in your kingdom. They would take brides and offer your kind a better place to live than your own kingdom."

Astrid couldn't stop herself from looking now. Every now and then, although it was rare, she would actually see a human woman. There weren't many. She was certain that would take time for anyone in her own kingdom to realize that the offer wasn't a trick. But there were plenty of women who would take anything to get out of the situation they were in.

There were enough priestesses who felt the same. She was certain of that. If she could get a letter back to the sisterhood, she figured she could get far more powerful women here than their king could. After all, there were a lot of priestesses currently laboring under fat, sweaty lords who had no clue what a gem they had been given.

Thoughts swirled in her mind. Rose didn't want to leave here, and that was all right. Astrid didn't really want to leave here either now that she'd seen its charm and majesty. Perhaps even better than where they had come from.

Besides, it was a good excuse to stay with Bjorn. Glancing over at the hulking creature beside her, she realized two things rather instantly.

She wanted to stay with him.

And she wanted him.

It was that easy. Seeing him here, lit by the blue and gold lights of wisps floating around them, he had become rather magical to her. His skin might've been green, and he might've had tusks and horns, but he was still the most beautiful man she had ever seen.

The dark color on his cheeks had spread. Down his chest, up to the tips of his ears. Not a blush, then. Anger.

"Oh, no," she whispered, her eyes darting around the crowd that was already forming around them. "Bjorn?"

He wasn't listening to her, though. His breath came in great, heaving inhalations that lifted his body up and down. He was clearly not in a sane state of mind. Astrid glanced around them, realizing what a terrible situation this was. There were too many people. So many trolls were setting up wares or had already been selling for hours now. He was going to lose control, and then where would they be?

She couldn't let this happen. She couldn't. Because if this happened, then they were going to be kicked out of this kingdom. If she didn't get him under control, then she would have to leave.

Astrid wasn't going anywhere without Rose.

"Bjorn," she said again, sharper this time.

When his eyes turned to hers, she could see they were already ringed in red. He'd thought he was ready for this, to be back home with his people, and he'd been wrong. She could see the despair in him. She could feel it. Astrid tugged a bit on her power, looking through all the anger in him and all the heartbreak that radiated around him.

He wanted to be here. He wanted to feel like he belonged, but then they had disappointed him. Betrayal was strong in the mix of emotions that radiated around him. It was an emotion that she didn't know how to control because it was so strong.

Until she got an idea in her head that maybe wasn't the best she'd ever had. But they were compatible. They had wanted to touch each other for days on end now, and if she played her cards right, he wouldn't be thinking about anything but her.

Glancing around them, she decided an alleyway was good enough. He'd wanted a bed, romance, a soft evening where he wooed her until she could do nothing other than fall into his bed. He was a romantic at heart, but life didn't give him the chance for romance like he wished.

She would have been disappointed if she weren't so excited.

Grabbing his hand, she all but yanked him in the direction she wanted him to go. Bjorn was surprised enough to follow, but she could still hear his heavy breathing and the chuffing sounds he made when he was so angry he couldn't think. It was a dangerous game to play, but she didn't think he would ever hurt her.

Even angry. Even when he was so far gone that he didn't know his own name or the names of others, he knew her. She had to believe that.

Red rage poured off of him in waves that only she could see. It tried to cling to Astrid, to drag her into the depths with him. She refused to get stuck in that with him, though. It didn't want her to calm it or even to speak with it. His rage was uncontrollable.

But she could distract him.

The alleyway was empty. It looked like it curved at the end, and she had hope that it was a dead end. When she found exactly that, Astrid resolved herself to a dead end street to somehow seduce him. Bjorn turned from her and pounded his fist into the building, the stones cracking around the force of his strike. And then quietly, so quietly she almost didn't hear him, he said, "Leave."

She'd left him alone in this quite enough. Instead, she walked up to him and placed a hand on his back. The warmth of her touch always seemed to calm him, even if he was still shuddering under her touch.

Slowly, Astrid smoothed her hands up his back, feeling the ridges along each side of his spine. The power in his back made her shiver with desire. He was very strong. So capable.

"I can think of other ways to use that anger," she whispered, before leaning forward and pressing her lips to his shoulder. Then she slid her hands back down and tunneled them underneath his shirt.

It was like she'd plunged her hands into a fire. Bjorn's skin was so warm, muscles twitching beneath her touch. She wanted to press her lips and tongue to the deep valley between his muscles, to trace all of that power with her lips. He was so warm. So capable. And if this was the time when she could distract him with her body, then... so be it.

Pulling up his shirt, she did just that. Astrid licked him. Which in hindsight probably wasn't the best thing she could have done. She didn't even know if he liked that.

But the deep groan that rumbled through his chest made her see stars at the touch of her slick tongue to his skin. Then he rolled them, and her back was pressed against the wall he had just been punching with his fist.

Breathless, she stared up into his gaze that was still somehow so angry, but also like he wanted to devour her whole. That was exactly what she wanted. She wanted him to devour her, just like he had in that tent.

Somehow, he knew. Bjorn gave her a look that was perhaps a little chiding before sliding down onto his knees before her. He didn't even look to see if anyone could see them. He just tucked his hands underneath the skirt of the dress he had made and pulled it slowly up inch by inch.

"I'm not going to fuck you here," he growled against her skin, his nose trailing up the inside of her thigh as he pushed her skirt higher and higher. "But I am going to tend to your needs. Then I will bring you back to my home and I will fuck you into oblivion, bright one."

The first touch of his tongue between her legs made her see stars. Astrid gasped and grabbed onto his horns, holding on to him just as much as she was keeping him where she wanted him to be.

He was so talented, and perhaps it wasn't even that. It wasn't that his tongue knew where to go or that it was abnormally quick—although it was both things—but Bjorn was so enthusiastic. He groaned at every taste of her, like he had never tasted anything so delicious. He wanted to devour her, lick and suck at her flesh, and listen to the soft sounds of her pleasure.

There wasn't a part of him that shied away from her taste. He didn't make her feel like this was a chore in the slightest. She'd heard so many priestesses speak of an experience like this, and how it was always a gift from someone else.

Bjorn made it seem like he was the one receiving the gift.

The little grunts he made as his tongue flicked her clit made her want to scream. And then he moved away, delving deeper until his tongue was inside of her, and that was wonderful, but not nearly enough.

With a rough grip, she moved his head back to where she wanted him by the horns. He seemed to like that. His eyes stared up at her, his gaze heated because she had made him go where she wanted, and there was some power in that.

Control, Astrid realized. Perhaps she really enjoyed control more than she knew.

Now she held him there, forcing his movements to be almost nonexistent. He could have broken free from her grip at any point. He was strong enough to do so.

But he didn't. He let her use him, let her grind herself against his face until that breathless pleasure threw her off a cliff. Astrid could feel every muscle in her tense, and the sound of his answering groan made her want to tear this dress off herself. She didn't care that they were in an alleyway where anyone could see them. She didn't care that someone might hear their pleasure.

Astrid wanted him. Desperately.

Breathing hard, she looked down where he stared back up at her, his lips glistening. His long tongue licked it away as he stood, never once breaking eye contact with her. Bjorn braced his arm over her head again. Looming, as he always did, but never in threat.

"That's one way to distract me," he growled. "Now, we're going back to my old home, and I'm going to treat you the way I want to."

That didn't sound bad to her at all.

Chapter 34

Astrid didn't remember any of the streets. She didn't even remember how they got from that alleyway up into the higher sections of Trollveggen, but suddenly they were there. He stumbled a few times, cursing and adjusting himself before he'd hurry her along faster. She would have laughed if she weren't breathless herself.

For a man who struggled with anger, Bjorn sure was ignoring every single one of his triggers on the way. People tried to stop to talk to them. There were plenty of shouted, "The Destroyer has returned!" Even a few people grabbed his arm, trying to stop his rapid speed. But he shrugged all of it off.

Higher and higher they climbed until she feared they were actually leaving the mountain. But then he reached a door in the stone that looked like it had been carved there for centuries. It didn't open when he put his shoulder to it. With a sigh, he planted both of his palms flat on the carved surface.

The carvings depicted a battle scene. She could see there were plenty of blood sprays carved in, most of them coming from humans it looked like, before it gave an answering groan and swung open.

He stood in the doorway, staring into the darkness while his barrel chest moved up and down with breaths he couldn't seem to control. Finally, he shook his head and stepped inside.

"Sorry about the dust," he muttered. "I thought someone would take care of it in my absence."

She peered into the shadows, blinking as wisps lit up from every single corner of the room. Suddenly she was faced with a very practical space. The living room and kitchen were one big room, covered in dust just like he'd said. There was a fine layer of gray over all the furniture, the counters, everything. Even the giant fireplace in the back wall that took up the entirety of the space. Astrid could stand in that fireplace if she wanted, could even lie down, and she still wouldn't touch any of the corners.

Was this where he had grown up? It had to be. She had figured, though, that someone else would've taken the place. His father had died. Surely someone else would have used the space after his death? It made little sense to have an empty home like this.

She didn't have time to look around or even think much more than that. Bjorn lunged for her, his hands wrapping around her waist and lifting her. Astrid had to wrap her legs around his waist to not dangle in the air, but the moment she locked her legs around him, all she could feel was the hard bar of his cock pressed against her core.

It was like someone had showered her with sparks from a fire. Everywhere tingled. Her fingers even seemed to go numb at the sensation of him grinding against her as he kissed her. She couldn't think, couldn't breathe, could only feel every point where he touched her.

"I have waited for this moment," he whispered, breaking away from her lips to trail down her neck. He kissed every inch of her skin he could reach. "You do not know how you have tormented me from the very first moment I saw you."

She didn't know if she should say she felt the same. She hadn't. The trolls had been terrifying to her, and she'd seen him as a tool. There was much she had to pay penance for when it came to that.

He opened the door behind her, and they were plunged into darkness again. The wisps here seemed to have a hard time waking. They blinked on for a few seconds, and then the room was black again.

It left her staring at the images that seemed to jump in front of her. One moment he was right in front of her, the next, her back hit a mattress. And yes, there was dust. But all of that dust billowed up in sparkling pinpricks that danced in the light. She stared up at the demon who loomed above her, his horns accentuated by the wisps behind him. Curving and sharp, the tips glinted in the light.

Darkness. The sound of his heavy breathing filling the room, and her need making her squirm on the bed.

Then light again. All she could see was the image of Bjorn whipping his shirt off over his head, and the yellow light turning his abs and pectorals into peaks and valleys. The shadows were stark, showing every single ripple of muscle that flexed over his ribs. Her gaze trailed down to the startlingly hard abs that had stunned her the first time she'd seen them, and then darkness again.

The low sound of his growl echoed throughout the room. "Wisps," he thundered. "Enough."

The darkness had never terrified her, and he knew that. Now she had to use her other senses, and everything seemed so much more than before.

Suddenly she could hear him louder. Every touch made her jump until he soothed her with those big, broad hands. Even the scent of him, warm and comforting and familiar, seemed stronger than she remembered it being.

"Breathe," he murmured into her ear as he slid down her body once again. "I've not even started yet."

But now she could feel his skin against hers. When he draped her legs over each of his shoulders, she pressed her bare calves against the heat of his back. It made all of this seem that much more intimate as he devoured her once more. His lips, his tongue, his fingers pressed inside of her. She arched, hissing out a breath at the tightness of not one, but two fingers as he sank deeper and deeper into her.

The burn of the stretch didn't hurt, though. She welcomed it, breathing deeply as he reached his knuckles. His thumb rubbed her clit, soothing her through the sting into pleasure that was nearly too much. It hurt, in the best way possible.

He moved up her body, his tongue and lips touching everything that he could along the journey. Murmuring in her ear, he said, "I don't want to hurt you, bright one. You're going to have to take a third."

"A third?" she choked.

He nodded against her neck, his lips moving against her pulse as she felt him withdraw and then, yes, there was a third. A third finger that she was supposed to somehow take.

If it had been with anyone else, she would have shaken her head and tried to wriggle away. But Bjorn knew her. He knew how to read her anxiety, and he damn well knew how to distract her. He leaned closer to her ear, that deep, gravelly voice already doing more than he could have guessed.

"You cannot imagine what it's going to feel like when I finally fuck you, bright one. You're untried, untested, and now the first man gifted the beauty of taking you will be the one who worships the ground you walk on. There will be no pain, no ache, only my cock sinking into your cunt that is already weeping for me."

Astrid could feel how wet she was as his fingers pressed deeper. There was that pinch again, the ache, but it immediately disappeared. She was shocked she could take all three, but then she wasn't thinking about that at all. Because he was moving. In and out. Gliding through all the mess she had made and his words continued to make her core tighten around him.

"The moment you beg me to be inside you, I will be living in a dream. You're so wet, bright one. So warm. You take my fingers so well, and I just know your greedy little cunt will feel like I've died in battle."

She hadn't even known he could say those filthy words. He was such a gentleman at all times, but now she didn't want him to be a gentleman. She wanted him to do the exact things he was saying because she was so full of his fingers that surely he would be able to fuck her now.

She'd never expected she would even have thoughts like that. But she was desperate at this point.

"Bjorn," she moaned, her body writhing. Astrid couldn't control herself. She was moving, riding his fingers while seeking out that painful bliss that she knew he could give her.

Instead, he continued to bring her to the very edge, only to back off so she couldn't quite reach that pivotal wonder. She was almost overheated now, her body coated in a fine sheen of sweat. Every time he exhaled, the air from his breath felt ice cold on her skin.

And then finally, finally, he rose above her. She could sense how hesitant he was, but also how desperately he wanted her.

She didn't even jump when his cock pressed against her opening. The piercing at the tip was strange, but no stranger than his claws had been the first time she'd felt them.

"Gods," he grunted, his hips giving a little buck that unseated his cock. It slid up and over her mound, dragging wonderfully against her clit until he notched himself once more. "You feel so good."

The head of him sank into her, the pressure startling because it wasn't like his fingers at all. This was a foreign feeling. A wonderful feeling. A fullness and a tightness that spread throughout her entire body. She had thought she was warm before, but now she was an inferno as he moved at a glacial pace. She wanted more. Wanted movement, thundering slaps as he slammed into her over and over again. She wanted to feel the passion that she could sense simmering right under his skin.

Her magic rose to the surface, pulling and tugging at his desire even as he let out a sound that was all too similar to a whine.

"Don't do that, Astrid." His breath puffed against her neck. "I'm barely holding on to my control as it is."

But she didn't want his control. She wanted...

She just wanted.

So she plucked with her magic, weaving her own need into his until his hips jerked forward and he was flush against her. The tight pain of it was over in an instant, and then all she could feel was him. Breathing hard, she sank her teeth into his shoulder and then rolled her hips against him.

"More," she whispered. "More, more, more."

He was never one to disappoint. Bjorn slid out of her in one smooth glide that dragged his cock piercing along her inner walls.

There was a certain section that made her seize up. It felt so good there, shockingly good, better than anything else had felt before.

She swore she felt his grin against her neck before he plunged into her again. One hard thrust, a feeling she would probably regret tomorrow, but then bliss. Aching, wonderful bliss as he bottomed out again, and that piercing somehow made it better in every way.

"Fuck," he grunted, moving on his own now. There was a pace to it, a rhythm that they found together that made every part of her fracture.

The glide, the slow thrust, it rewrote everything she knew about pleasure. His whispered praises continued to make every part of her vibrate.

"You feel so good."

"Every part of you is... perfect. Gods, Astrid, you're perfect."

At some point she lost track of how long they'd been going, only that his stamina was shockingly high. And somehow, she wasn't tired of it. It seemed like he knew how to build that peak higher and higher. Every time she swore she was about to come, the pleasure only grew. More and more until she was almost afraid to know what it would be like.

Until he snapped. His pace became blistering, brutal, every slap of his thighs against hers suddenly made her see stars and then...

Then.

Finally, she came with a cry that echoed in the room. She grabbed onto the dusty sheets, holding on with all she had so she wouldn't scratch lines down his back even as he bellowed out his own pleasure. She could feel him. Twitching and pulsing inside of her.

The two of them spiraled down together, breathing hard, suddenly realizing that they were lying on a dusty bed, surrounded by the ghosts of his past. She expected him to tense up again.

Instead, he just rolled to the side, threw an arm over his eyes, and laughed. It was a bit ridiculous that he was laughing after what they'd done, but then she couldn't help herself either. Astrid joined him, finding joy in the madness that had overcome the two of them.

The ache between her legs was still shocking, but what had they done? They were like two teenagers, desperately seeking some kind of release before one's parents got home. They had explored each other's bodies. He'd brought her nearly to ruin with those talented fingers and that impressive, massive beast of a cock between his legs.

He hooked an arm around her, dragging her onto his chest, where she lay half draped over him. "I didn't hurt you, did I?" he asked, running his claws through her hair.

"No, of course not."

But Bjorn knew her very well. His other hand slipped between her thighs, gently stroking the mess that was slowly leaking out of her. He noticed how she held her breath as he slid his fingers ever so carefully between her folds. "Ah, you're sore. We'll take care of that."

"What are you going to do to help that?" she said with a chuckle, only to add in a shriek as he sat up with her in his arms.

Then he was hopping off the bed, picking her up like she weighed nothing and striding out into the light. She threw a hand over her eyes at the sudden brightness.

"Bjorn, what in the world are you doing?"

"Providing you with what you deserve, troll wife. After such pleasure, you deserve far more than just this." He pushed another door open and brought her into a surprisingly clean bathroom.

Where all the other rooms were dust-covered, at least this one didn't show quite as much damage. Most of it was stone and very utilitarian. She could see there was a section where one would relieve oneself, a sink, and a mirror. Clearly, it was a home made for a man who lived alone. But in the center of the room was a stunning tub carved out of the stone itself. It sank into the back wall, where there appeared to be a metal bar sticking out of it.

"Here," Bjorn said, seating her on the side and reaching for the bar. With a twist of his hand, water started coming out of a spigot. Warm water. Steam twirled up into the air, filling the tub surprisingly fast.

With a quick motion, he grabbed her and sat down in the water with her back pressed against his chest. "Now," he murmured, relaxing into the water with her. "We relax, bright one. Let the water heal what I broke."

"You broke absolutely nothing, Bjorn," she whispered as she stroked his arm around her waist. "In fact, I think you might have healed me more than you know."

Chapter 35

Bjorn woke with her draped across his chest the next morning, and he could not believe his luck. She was here with him. Still. They hadn't talked about whether or not that meant she was staying for good, but even the gift of her memory would keep him going for ages to come.

Astrid was light incarnate, and she glowed when he touched her. Just as he had hoped she would. He would never forget the way she'd come alive in his arms and how much he had wanted to devour her whole. And then he had.

She'd let him touch her. Him. A man who had blood on his hands and who drifted in nightmares every evening. He knew what he had done. He knew that there were so many ghosts haunting his steps, telling him that he wasn't good enough for any of what he had been gifted. And yet... She still allowed him to touch her. She still graced the halls of this haunted home, and he wanted to do more.

Bjorn was not sure which god had looked down upon him kindly and thought he deserved this, but he still wasn't sure that god had thought it through. He didn't deserve this, and someday soon, he was certain it would all be ripped away.

So he was going to enjoy every single moment that he could.

He didn't sleep while she did, instead taking in the beauty of her eyelashes that dusted her cheeks. She slept so soundly with his arms around her, and he knew she didn't always sleep like this. He had seen her sleeping in the forest. She'd twitched and moved often, startled by any sound that came upon them. He'd even seen a squirrel wake her so forcefully that she'd gasped as she'd sat up.

But lying on him? She slept like she didn't have a care in the world. Astrid had no idea what a gift she was to him, especially after all the darkness that had found him for such a long time.

Eventually, though, he knew it was time to get up. The wisps were back to that horrid blinking, usually a sign that they were trying to turn on and mimic the sun that was above the mountain.

He'd forgotten what it was like to sleep here. Years in the labyrinth had worn away at those memories too, but now he could almost remember the scent of fresh coffee in the air that his father had loved to brew. Dag used to travel for months to get a store of it, dragging Bjorn along with him to see all the trolls who were more animal than man still.

Sighing, he shook his head to clear those memories away. He did not have to travel with his father any longer. This home might've been full of all those haunting memories, but he did not need to linger in them.

"Bright one," he murmured, nuzzling his face into the silky strands of her hair. "We have to get up."

Astrid groaned, tucking her face against his neck. The sound made it seem like he'd asked her to move mountains, when all he needed was for her to get up so he could feed her. There had to be something to eat in the kitchen. Someone must have known that... Well, he supposed no one would have stocked it because no one had known he was returning.

He'd have to go get food. Which was fine, he supposed. He slid out from underneath Astrid, arranging her body on the bed so he could leave without waking her. After all, they'd been busy last night. He'd done enough to her that would tire any person out, and she'd been trying her very best to keep up with him. The poor woman hadn't realized just how creative he was.

And he was quite proud of that.

Bjorn pulled on his pants in the other room, not wanting his movement to wake her, and then headed out the front door. If he was lucky, the market would already be set up, but not with many people. Crowds were still difficult for him, as evidenced yesterday. He'd been alone in a cell for such a long time, having all those bodies surrounding him felt like he was supposed to be fighting. Even though he knew he wasn't.

But the moment he opened the door, he realized he had worried about nothing. Because there were already people walking up the path toward his new home.

He leaned against the door and waited there, watching as a green-bodied troll shouldered his way past the few brambles that had fallen in front of the path. Gunnar's hair was a wild mane around his head, tangled with curls that Bjorn didn't remember being there. He'd always been a handsome young man, but now he was even more so. And then Astrid's sister trailed along behind him, stoically allowing Gunnar to touch her with his hand on her back even though Bjorn could see how much she didn't want him to.

Rose had a lot of work to do, he knew. That poor woman had been through far more than any of them would ever know. He remembered her in the labyrinth. She had always been a shell of a woman, barely there no matter how many times she'd been given to others. Even those men who had gotten her had whispered about how she was a hollow creature.

Behind them were Ragnar and Maia, the two of them fitting far better than he had expected. He'd only seen them together a few times, and now he could see why they were well suited. They were both muscular. Capable. They moved with the confidence of people who knew their bodies well and knew their own limits. He would have been impressed if he hadn't also noticed their arms were laden with food.

He waited until they were within earshot before calling out, "That's quite a lot in your arms there, Ragnar. You sure you can carry that much?"

His lavender-skinned friend snorted. "I'd like to see you try."

"I've carried more than that for miles on end. When was the last time you carried something heavy, healer?" He headed out to help, taking as much of the food as he could in his own arms and splitting the difference of weight.

Bjorn might have added a few more items to his own armload, just in case Ragnar had forgotten how strong he really was.

Maia snorted. "Considering how thin you are, Bjorn, I think you might need a few weeks of eating right before you get into a wrestling match with Ragnar."

"Careful, fire hair." Bjorn remembered the nickname from when he had last seen them together, although he wasn't certain he should call her such a personal nickname. He did so, though, to see Ragnar's cheeks darken with disapproval. "You might end up in the wrestling match, and I don't think you'll hold up against a troll."

With a hiss of sound, Ragnar wrapped his arm around his troll wife and tugged her against his side. "Don't talk about wrestling with my wife."

"Not while you're here. Understood." He heaved the food a little higher and headed into his home.

Depositing the food took only a few moments, and then he made his way into the bedroom to wake Astrid. She was already up though, sliding the spider silk dress over her arms like she had been born for it, and he…

Fuck, she was so beautiful.

Walking up behind her, he helped get the dress on until the hem kissed the floor and then framed her hips in his hands. He pressed against her, holding tightly to the woman he was so enamored with, and pressed a long kiss to her shoulder. "We have visitors."

"I heard them," she replied with a soft laugh. Turning in his arms, she blocked the kiss he would have given her with her hand. "And I heard you flirting."

"Flirting?"

"Joking about wrestling with another woman?" He didn't think she was entirely serious, although there was a spark of jealousy in her eyes that he had never seen before.

Bjorn nipped at her fingers. "It is hard for me to look at anyone else beyond the sight of your stunning beauty, bright one. I teased my oldest friend, saying what I knew would make him angry. But my eyes never strayed from you, nor did my heart ever skip a beat for another. You are without a doubt my guiding star. I would follow you through any darkness, Astrid. I would be a fool indeed to look anywhere else."

The anger in her gaze turned molten. He could feel her using her power to see if he was being honest, and he wondered if she could tell if someone was lying. No wonder the lords of her kingdom had wanted to use her as much as they could. Her power was legendary.

Then she sighed and rolled her eyes. "Fine. As long as you aren't looking at anyone else seriously."

"Why would I? I have perfection right in front of me." He leaned back, staring down at her body in that silk dress and marveling at her beauty. It was hard to not look like a dopey, love-sick moron, but by all the gods. She was remarkable.

"Bjorn, enough," she said with a soft laugh. "You said we have visitors?"

"Your sister, my friends Gunnar and Ragnar, and Ragnar's troll wife, Maia," he replied. "They came with food and, I assume, for some other reasons."

"You didn't ask?"

"Why would I?" He shrugged. "They aren't going to stay long."

"Why would they not?"

"They brought food. We have it now. They can leave." He frowned when she gasped at him like he'd said the sky was falling. "What?"

"They are guests, Bjorn! If they want to visit us, which they likely do, then we are going to let them visit. They can stay as long as they wish, and we will cater to them as is required. Good hosting is a talent I see you do not possess."

Hosting?

Why would he ever be good at hosting people?

Frowning, he trailed after her as she headed out into the main room. He was surprised to see that she was correct. Both couples were still in the main living area waiting for them, although Rose and Maia appeared to be picking things up. He didn't like them doing that. If they were guests, as Astrid claimed, then they shouldn't be working.

Slowly, he leaned over and grabbed a moth-eaten pillow from Rose's hands. She froze like a deer in the sights of a hunter, staring at him with her pulse visibly thudding in her neck.

"You do not have to clean while you are here," he said gently, placing the pillow back onto the couch. "This house has been in disrepair for many, many years. A few more hours won't hurt it."

But then Maia's voice caught his attention, and it made everyone in the room freeze. "My god, she really does look like the princess."

More silence followed that declaration, and Maia's face turned a lovely shade of bright red as she realized what she had just said. She probably shouldn't have blurted that out, considering it was something that all of them knew, and it was likely something that made both Astrid and Rose uncomfortable.

Both of them looked remarkably like the princess, although perhaps Astrid looked more like that horrible woman. His bright one seemed to blink a few times, and then finally said very magnanimously, "It's a good thing I don't act like her."

That seemed to ease the tension in the room. Ragnar scoffed at her words. "The kingdom wouldn't survive that. The princess's ego isn't big enough for the rest of us to exist around. Let alone two of her."

Then Gunnar pointed at Bjorn and said, "You should come with us. We thought you might want a tour of how things have changed since you were here last time, and it'll be easier with two of us. No one will bother you like they have been. I heard your welcome was a little overwhelming."

He didn't want to leave his home. Part of that was the safety this cavern gave him, and the other part was that Astrid had yet to settle in. He wanted to be the one here to help her. To assist her. To show her the entire house and tell her stories about how he'd lived here as a boy and how easy it had been to get in trouble with his father insisting that he be perfect in everything that he did.

But Astrid looked him over and then grinned. "You should go. It might be good for you to reacquaint yourself with the city."

Or it might make him worse. He feared that.

A soft touch of her magic stroked through his body, and suddenly he felt that anxiety lessen. It was like all she had to do was yank on it a little harder than the other emotions, and that was enough for it to calm down. Instead, he was able to feel the excitement that burned within him at the thought. She hadn't made him excited, it had always been there. He just hadn't been able to feel it through the anxiety that made everything so much harder.

"What will you do?" he asked, as though no one else was in the room with them.

She gestured to the other two women. "I assume they are here to help us make this ancient room a home. We'll get things situated here."

"That doesn't seem fair. I shouldn't be out adventuring while you're here working."

He didn't like the idea of all three women cleaning the house while he and his oldest friends were out doing nothing. That was his role. He was supposed to take care of her. He was supposed to make her life easier, and right now, it felt like he was doing anything but.

Ragnar looped an arm around his shoulder and leaned down. "They want to see that you two are settled and comfortable. This home is a tomb, Bjorn. It has been years since your father died. It's not fit for anyone to live in. Let us help you feel better about being back in

Trollveggen, and let the women turn this bucket of dust into a home again. It'll make them feel better."

Bjorn eyed all the women, trying to make sure that was the truth. Astrid nodded a few times, Rose didn't make eye contact with him, and Maia made shooing gestures with her hands. So he supposed it must've been all right.

Sighing, he headed over to Astrid and cupped the back of her neck. Gently, always so gentle, he pressed a kiss to her forehead. "Do not do anything that makes you regret coming here. I just got you to my home, bright one. I refuse to lose you because you didn't enjoy cleaning."

She laughed. "Bjorn, I'll be all right." But then she paused and really looked at him, her magic pushing that anxiety down even farther. "Take care of yourself too."

He planned on it. Because if he didn't, then he wouldn't get to return to this home with her.

Chapter 36

Astrid had forgotten how nice it was to be surrounded by other women. She'd been traveling with Bjorn for such a long time, it was easy to forget. And of course, even back home she'd usually been in the presence of lords who regularly ignored each other unless there was a reason to share secrets.

But the sisterhood had been countless women altogether in wonderful harmony. She'd loved having so many sisters to learn and grow with, people who cared about her well-being, and the feminine energy that always made every room feel beautiful.

Rose and Maia worked rather well together. They moved as though they knew where the other was going to go, politely side-stepping without a word as they went about cleaning. It was so easy for her to fit in with them until it felt almost like they were dancing.

The home hadn't been cleaned in a very long time. Nearly ten years, if she heard correctly about Dag the Destroyer's death. But somehow, it felt like ten years still wasn't enough to build up the amount of grime they washed from the floors and off the counters. It took effort for them to really get the thick dirt off of everything, especially around the front door.

That wasn't from years of being closed up. She knew that.

Whoever Bjorn's father had been, he hadn't been a good one. She was muttering something to that effect, carrying yet another bucket of water to the living room and having half a mind to just empty the whole thing onto the stones and then go back for another without even attempting to mop it.

Rose stood in her way though, and it looked like her sister's gaze was actually clear for once. Astrid froze, uncertain what to do right now. The last time she'd tried to have a real conversation with Rose, it had all gone downhill very quickly.

"Did you want to say something?" Astrid breathed, praying she didn't sound too hopeful. She knew coming on strong would only chase her sister away yet again, but she really was... hopeful.

Rose took a deep breath, and it was very clear she was steadying herself for the conversation ahead. "I don't want to leave this place."

"Okay."

"Okay?"

"I just want to go where you are happiest, Rose. I want to have a relationship with you again. I have missed you for years and..." Astrid tried to think of the words that wouldn't make her sound desperate, and finally ended with a simple plea. "I just hope you still want me in your life."

"Why wouldn't I want you in my life?" Rose sounded like she genuinely meant those words.

Deep inside of Astrid, something started to heal. Bit by bit, piece by piece. "Because I failed. I didn't find you when you were right under my nose. The first place I should have looked was the labyrinth. Both of us knew how cruel the king was, and I knew... I knew he had paired you with a cruel lord. The meeting couldn't have gone well. It wouldn't have gone well for anyone. But I was so wrapped up in everything else that I didn't even think he would send you..."

There, she wanted to say. She hadn't thought he would ever send her sister to the labyrinth. Not when Astrid was a favored priestess, and so powerful.

The king had always been fond of Astrid. Her lord had been a kind man, and Tolly had never tried to touch her when many of the other lords would have. Astrid had been given a rather favored position, when many priestesses had not.

Rose shook her head. "I knew you were keeping yourself safe. You know I saw you once, through the bars of my cage when I was one of the prizes. You were so pretty sitting next to your lord. Glowing like a beacon of hope. I knew you'd have come for me if you'd discovered where I was, but I hid. I didn't want you to know that I was there."

"Why would you do that?"

Rose shrugged, lifting her arms in a defeated gesture. "I'm broken, Astrid. I broke the first few months I was there. I wasn't strong enough to survive what they put me through, and my magic is only good for me. They knew what they were doing. They know how to break people in that place. If you had managed to find me in there, you would've found me even more broken than I am now."

"I wish I had," Astrid burst out, desperately wanting to hug her sister. But even she could see how little Rose liked to be touched. "I would have loved you, no matter what state you were in."

"I don't think anyone could have loved me like that," Rose whispered. "But I'm glad you're here now, all the same. And I'd like to stay here, if we can."

Her heart shattered. This was what she'd always dreamt of, and yet somehow it felt like Rose was begging her to allow them to stay here. She nodded, sloshing water onto the floor and all down the front of her spider silk dress that she'd completely forgotten she was wearing. "Yes. Yes, of course. I would love to stay here too. I was going to pick you over anyone else, but I... I..."

Maia walked by, blowing a red curl out of her face. "You found yourself a troll husband. It's hard to leave them, trust me. I know."

"Well, I've seen yours." Astrid just set the bucket down. Perhaps they could all use a break. "He's huge."

"Bjorn will be bigger once he puts weight back on, I bet. He was massive when I saw him in the labyrinth, but they thought starving him would be a better punishment." Maia set her own mop down and then turned toward them. "What do you say we all head to the market?"

Astrid thought that was a lovely idea. She hadn't been able to explore it yesterday. And while she'd take another romp beneath the sheets with Bjorn over an adventure in the market, her troll husband wasn't here.

Husband, she thought with a giddy laugh. She hadn't thought of him as her husband until this moment, but it appeared they were going to stay together.

She'd have to tell him that when they saw each other next. She was staying, and nothing was going to change that now.

"Is it safe?" Rose asked, her voice so small and tiny that it was almost painful to hear her speak. "I remember the market being unwelcoming to humans."

Maia headed toward the door and grabbed what must have been Rose's cloak. It was a sturdy thing, left outside rather than bringing it into the dust. With practiced hands, Maia wrapped it around Rose's shoulders and firmly tightened it. Almost like a vise. And just like that, all the tension in Rose's body seemed to leak out.

It made something in Astrid's heart twinge to see another woman caring for her sister so well, as Maia lifted the hood of the cloak and draped it over Rose's face. "We need to get your sister something else to wear. Right, Rose? She can't walk around like a princess the whole time she's here, can she?"

The hood of the cloak moved from side to side.

"The trolls are much more used to our kind walking around Trollveggen now. They weren't welcoming to me, but I was one of the first to be here. Even those who had kidnapped human women to improve their bloodline didn't let their brides walk around like we are now. But things are changing, and we are the ones who are going to keep those changes happening." Maia nodded, seeming to like this plan. "Besides, Bjorn still has some money left over from his father, I'm sure. We'll have to spend it."

Astrid jumped in at that. "I'm not sure that's a good idea—"

"He'd want us to spend it. The trolls love adorning their women." Maia didn't seem worried at all about that, so Astrid decided she wouldn't be worried either. This was what these new people expected, and all she wanted was to be a good troll wife.

Maia seemed the best to emulate. She was already a rather good troll wife to a very large troll. So together, they all wandered down the steep side of the cliff that had been worn by centuries of troll feet, and into the market below.

It was somehow much easier to head into the market than it had been to leave it, although it seemed like a shorter trip than she remembered. Perhaps they had been so desperate to touch each other that any trip would have seemed long. Now, though, Astrid got to marvel at the beauty of this kingdom.

Giant mushrooms stretched overhead, the delicate filaments beneath looking like fans. Some of the mushrooms even glowed, casting blue tones all over the ground they walked on. Then there were the purple-leafed trees that were so big, it was almost hard to fathom how they had grown so tall. The troll houses that dotted the landscape were absolutely stunning. Each of them with their thatched roofs melded into the landscape, similar to the homes built in the grotto, but these were made mostly out of stone and thick lumber.

How the humans had no idea that this hollow kingdom was filled with artisans and impressive craftsmen, she would never know. Even the windows were beautiful. Some of them were stained glass, with all manner of murals depicting stories flowing through each building as they walked by them. The streets were carved right out of the mountain, so they were smooth and buffed by years of travel.

The market itself was so full of people it was hard for even her to breathe. No wonder Bjorn had been so uncomfortable. Now that her mind wasn't so busy with everything else, she was shocked to count the incredible number of trolls who had no care if they bumped into each other.

Two young men locked tusks, shouting at each other with so much anger it was almost violent. Bright bursts of color radiated off them before one of the shopkeepers broke them apart. The two young men then seemingly laughed it off and headed down the same street together. Like nothing had happened.

"Troll tempers run hot," Maia said, shrugging as she guided them through the streets. "They deal with their arguments in their own way. You'll get used to it."

"Will I?" she murmured, shocked at the violence that she'd seen. They hadn't even hit each other, and still her heart was pounding. How was Rose? The poor thing must've been shaking like a leaf.

But her sister appeared fine under her hood, wandering from stall to stall until she stopped. Both Astrid and Maia had been watching her, so they both went over when she waved her hand. Apparently, Rose had found the right clothing for her.

This stall was mostly covered by a roof, so she had to walk into it through mounds of clothing and racks of hanging clothes. But inside it wasn't quite as bad as the thick press of bodies outside. It was cool in here as well, which Astrid hadn't even realized she needed.

"This one," Rose said, holding up a pretty blue gown. It was fitted at the waist, and much shorter than anything Astrid would ever have chosen for herself. But the fabric would sway around her knees very prettily with that cut.

Out of the back, a troll woman loomed. She was tall, round, and took up space unapologetically. And, by the gods, she was decorated.

Every part of her body was dotted with piercings. Her ears. Her lips. Her eyebrows. Her nose. Even her collarbone sported glistening gemstones.

The rings on her fingers clacked together as she pressed her hands onto what looked like a table and stood. She was tall too, Astrid realized. This was a substantial woman who had more than enough jewelry to feed an entire kingdom with that amount of wealth. What was she doing here? Selling clothing of all things?

"Ladies!" the troll woman said, her voice booming. "You're here to buy a dress?"

Rose turned, saying absolutely nothing as she held the dress up and pointed to Astrid.

"Ah, a lovely color for a lovely human."

Oh no. The troll woman was coming toward her now. Astrid tried very hard not to cower before the sheer amount of energy that crackled toward her as the shopkeeper thundered toward her with every step.

At least she was dressed beautifully as well, Astrid mused before the woman's hands landed on her shoulders. Because for all her size and space she took up, this troll was incredibly eye catching. Astrid couldn't stop looking at her as the woman snagged the dress from Rose's hands and held it up to Astrid's body.

"Your friend has a good eye," the troll murmured. "This will look lovely on you. Take your dress off. Let's see if we're all right."

Astrid blinked. "Excuse me?"

"You're Bjorn's new wife, aren't you?" The woman seemed impatient. "He'll want to see you in something other than that. Men love variety, especially when it comes to their women. Off with the dress, put this one on. Or were you going to buy it without knowing what it looks like?"

The loud chortle that came out of the woman was a whip crack through the air. Astrid realized she was very serious about changing into the dress right here, right now. Which...

She'd changed in front of many women in her lifetime. There was no privacy for priestesses, but somehow this made her a little uncomfortable.

Astrid stripped the spider silk dress off herself and told herself not to cover her body while the vendor handed her the dress. But the woman made a little sound under her breath, almost like she was surprised.

As Astrid struggled into the dress on her own, the troll woman turned to Maia. "Didn't I hear she's a soul whisperer?"

She watched Maia shrug as Astrid finally got her head through the neck of the dress. "That's the rumor I heard. You could ask her."

The troll woman turned to her again. "Are you?"

"I don't even know what that is."

"A person who speaks to the fylgja. Someone who can see spirit guides and then bring out the creatures inside." The troll woman's brow raised. "Rumors spread quickly here. You'll find that soon enough."

"Oh. I suppose I can. That's what the blood witches said in the grotto." She wasn't going to tell them that she'd done just that with Bjorn. That magic hadn't been entirely hers. It seemed like Bjorn needed to be there for it to happen.

Astrid tried to turn the conversation to the dress, but the troll woman plowed right over her. "Why doesn't she wear the piercings then? If she's one of them, she should be pierced."

"She has the wife piercings," Maia replied.

"That's not what I'm talking about. She's earned the piercings of a priestess. She should wear them with pride." Tsking, she plucked at Astrid's dress, twitching it tighter around the waist and already pinning it. Somehow the woman had needles ready to go. "You've earned them, girl. Why not get them?"

But Astrid didn't even know what piercings the woman was talking about. She tried to look at Maia, but the other woman wasn't looking her in the eye. What piercings were they talking about? And why did she feel like, once again, she was failing Bjorn?

Chapter 37

Bjorn was surprised at how much he enjoyed his time with Ragnar and Gunnar. In the labyrinth, any time spent around the other men was usually a sign that he was about to fight them. But now he could be with others without having to worry about what he'd be ordered to do. There was only the joy at being with them and an ease that he was shocked he could feel.

They took him all over the kingdom, showing him all the old places they once had terrorized as children. He laughed with them, remembering all the foolish things they had done in those days. He was more than a little pleased they even remembered those times.

Ragnar had pointed to a tree that had looked much smaller than it had when they were children. "Remember when Bjorn got stuck up there? His father had been so angry he'd threatened to cut the tree down if Bjorn didn't climb down on his own."

"I'd been so scared he actually would that I climbed down. Who knew it would be that easy?" Bjorn said with a chuckle. "I think the whole tree shook as I half fell down it."

Then they'd found a hidden cave system that only children could get through. But Gunnar crouched, peered into the darkness, and then shook his head. "Bjorn used to dare me to get into that crawl space. I got stuck so far in they had to get another child to come get me. You knew I wouldn't fit, and you left me in there, anyway."

"I was the child who went in to get you," Bjorn had grunted, before shoving Gunnar toward it. "Let's see if your fat head still fits."

The memories were good. Although some of their antics had been perhaps a little dangerous for children, they were still memories with his friends. Moments of fun in a childhood that had been filled with darker times at home, and a family that had split apart when he had just wanted them to stay together.

But his friendships had always kept him together. These two had always made him feel like he was still wanted and believed, no matter what else happened.

Now, they were heading back up the rise toward his home, and he didn't feel the shadows that always seemed to dog his steps. Instead, now there was a bright future ahead of him.

Rose and Maia were already coming out of his home, their laughter bubbling up and popping above his head. This could be a good thing. He could belong here, after all his time spent believing that no one would ever want him to come back.

Ragnar overtook him, heading up the path at an impressive speed toward his troll wife. And Bjorn would have followed his oldest friend if Gunnar hadn't put a hand on his shoulder and held him still.

"You know the king isn't going to change his mind," Gunnar said under his breath. "You will have to fight again."

"I am done with fighting, Gunnar," Bjorn replied, his eyes on the house that hid a bright light that guided him. "I think I would like to rest for a while."

"Egil won't allow that."

"Then I will enjoy every moment I have not fighting, so that I can walk into battle with her beauty in my heart." He headed away from his brother, not even looking at Rose, who flinched away from him as he headed into the house.

There wasn't any particular reason he wanted to see Astrid. He just did. He liked to look at her, to watch her as she moved in that graceful way that made it seem like she was gliding through the air.

And then he saw that they really had made the house a home. The dust was all gone, the grime of years disappearing into a house that looked comfortable. They'd somehow found old quilts that were draped over every piece of furniture. Suddenly the massive hearth in the back didn't look like somewhere his father would toss scraps of meat and threaten to toss Bjorn as well. It looked like a warm space to snuggle in front of with his troll wife, to hold her against his heart on the cold nights that would soon greet them.

The worn sofas in front of it were no longer threadbare. Instead it looked like someone had taken a needle and thread to them. Patchworks dotted them from what he assumed were other pieces of quilts. The kitchen smelled like baking bread, and not a single dust mote floated in the air. It was a new home.

A place to start over.

The door to their bedroom opened, and his heart stopped at the sight of her. Astrid had a small towel in her hands that she was using to dry off her arms, it seemed.

She paused, meeting his gaze with a confused expression of her own. "Why are you looking at me like that?"

"Like what?"

She smiled, and he forgot how to breathe. "Like you haven't seen me in decades."

"A single moment away from you feels like a year," he said, so quietly he almost couldn't hear himself. "The day is not nearly so bright without you by my side."

She fought a smile. "That seems rather dramatic."

"Don't worry." Bjorn walked over to her, grabbing her waist and tugging her into his arms. "The world is bright again."

He kissed her, and the world disappeared. There was only the feel of her melting into him, her hands pressed against his heart. He kissed her with every ounce of love in him. Because he did love her. He worshipped the ground she walked on, yes, but he loved her with every broken piece of him.

Taking a breath, Bjorn leaned back to tell her just that. It maybe wasn't the perfect moment, but there was no perfect moment to tell someone that they were the best part of his life.

Only for her to interrupt him. "We saw a shopkeeper today." Astrid even leaned back so he could notice the pretty blue dress she wore. "She said something about how I've earned new piercings in gaining the approval of your mother and the others at the grotto."

He hadn't expected that.

How did he talk to her about this? She didn't know what she was asking for. He couldn't imagine what his mother and the other of their magical women had told her, otherwise why would she be asking about them? But he didn't know if he should be the one to tell her such sensitive information either.

"Uh..." He released her, taking a step back to rub at the back of his neck. "That is something you have earned, yes."

His mind wandered because he knew what those piercings were.

Throughout his entire life, he had watched young women get them in the grotto. There was usually a ceremony with everyone who lived there. The piercings were an honor. He remembered all the families coming out to watch, and the cheers that would erupt after the young woman's nipples were officially adorned with glimmering metal.

It had never been about anything other than honor and hope. The women were so proud of themselves, and their families would cry. He had cheered with the others, never thinking anything differently.

Until this moment.

The thought of her wearing his jewels, glittering gemstones turning her perfect little breasts even more beautiful? It made him so hard he could hardly think straight.

Yes, he wanted to pierce her. Yes, he wanted to know what she would look like and how he was going to roll those bars in his mouth once he could. He would tug on them with his teeth, giving her even more pleasure than just his pierced cock could give her.

But that wasn't the point of those piercings. He wasn't supposed to think of them sexually. They were an honor that she would wear with pride, not something that he could lust over. His mother would be so ashamed of him.

Still, Bjorn had to clear his throat and adjust himself before replying to her. "These are perhaps not piercings you would be willing to get."

Astrid pointed behind him to the island. "Fortunately, I already know what kind of piercings they are. And yes, you are correct. There was a time in my life that I would have been horrified. Marking my body such as that would have been something that terrified me. But now I am a troll wife. I am here to stay, Bjorn. And if wearing those jewels means I honor you by doing so, and myself, then I will do it."

There was a small box on the table. Shocked, he wandered over to it and opened it. A piercing kit, he realized. With hollow needles blown by a metalsmith in town, most likely. Even a few jewelry options. He had no idea where she had gotten this, but the simple gold balls would not do for someone as stunning as her.

He'd have to go into the mines, he realized. He didn't trust any jeweler to have stones breathtaking enough to match her. He'd find them himself. And when she was fully healed, he would place them himself as well.

Heat flashed in Bjorn's chest, and he turned to look at her with a more calculating expression. He could do this, but he would do it in his own way.

"You are certain you wish to wear them?" He confirmed while making sure he had everything he'd need in the box.

"Yes, of course."

Fine, then. She'd said this was what she wanted, and he would not deny a gift like that.

Bjorn turned, grabbed her by the waist, and set her onto the counter. Like this, they were almost eye to eye. Nerves danced in her gaze, and she licked her lips while staring at him. "Is it going to hurt?"

"Yes, bright one. Nothing I can do will help that."

He gently grasped the straps of Astrid's dress, pushing them down her shoulders so they slipped. The fabric pooled at her waist, and his mouth went dry looking at her. It had been dark last night, and now he could see her. Every inch. Every bit of smooth skin, pretty pink nipples, and the way her chest moved up and down in a rapid breath that betrayed her fear.

"Bjorn," she whispered. "Are you just going to stare at me?"

"No, bright one." He met her gaze and grinned, although he knew the expression looked wicked. "Did you know troll saliva has healing properties?"

"That sounds like something you've made up."

"It's not made up. It won't close a wound, but it certainly will help it heal. Now, let me help you."

He bent and sucked one of those pretty pink beads into his mouth. He'd done this to her before, but still it felt like the first time every time. At her gasp, he couldn't help himself. Stopping was entirely out of the question as he swirled his tongue around her nipple and swore it tasted just like sugar. As obsessed as he was, he wasn't surprised her entire body tasted like some forbidden candy to him.

Astrid's hands came up, gripping his horns as he alternated between her breasts. He should stop. He should focus. He should get her pierced so that the nerves wouldn't overrun her and ruin this moment, but also, he didn't want to stop.

He wanted to taste her. Devour her. Destroy every bit of nerves in her body until all she could do was writhe on the island in front of him. Fuck the piercings. Fuck everything but this moment between them.

Bjorn trailed his hand up one of her thighs, growling low under his breath when she automatically parted them for him. It was so easy to slide his fingers between her legs.

She was already soaked, because of course she was. This perfect creature was made for him, it seemed. And he would worship her until the very end of his days.

The little noises she made drove him wild. The little whimpers, the sounds of her pleasure as he plunged his fingers into her, made him not quite able to think straight. But he had a job to do. A job that wasn't supposed to be just this.

He released one of her nipples, blowing on it so it hardened enough to pierce. They were both breathing hard by the time he pressed his thumb to her clit, gently rubbing back and forth in the way he'd already discovered made her pant.

"The first one is going to hurt," he said, leaning down and biting at her flesh. "But you're going to come when I pierce the second."

"What?" she breathed.

He had done this many times in his life. Not nipples, but he'd pierced more trolls than he could count. All of them had. Bjorn had pierced his own cock. It was very quick for him to snag the needle, line it up, and then thread it through her flesh.

The curse she let out made him wince. It was bound to hurt. This was a sensitive part of her body, and he knew for certain that a distraction was helpful in situations like this.

So he leaned down to her non-pierced nipple and went to work again. He circled her clit with his thumb, his fingers working her once again. This time he took his time, spiraling her higher and higher.

He kept his head about him. Every time her breathing turned ragged, he kept doing whatever had made her excited. He spun her tighter and tighter, feeling her clenching around his fingers until she was right at the edge. Just enough so that he was certain she would do as he told her.

Ducking between her legs, he licked her, devoured her, using his teeth and tongue to keep her right on the edge until he could surge up and kiss her mouth. She clung to him, her hands wrapped around his horns as she desperately kissed him back.

And he was right. She came the moment he pierced the second nipple. Her moans were both pleasure and pain, a memory that she would never, ever forget.

Bjorn leaned back to look at her, thighs wide, cheeks and chest bright red from pleasure, with needles threaded through each of her nipples. Gods, he'd never seen anyone more perfect for him. There was no other woman more beautiful, more brave, more daring in everything that she did.

He was a lucky, lucky man. A man who didn't deserve her, but he intended to spend the rest of his life proving that he could be worthy of her.

Leaning down, he kissed her one more time. Gently, now. Using his lips to ease her back down into reality as she stared up at him in shock.

"Wow," she whispered. "That's not what I thought it would be like."

"I still have to put the piercings in," he said with a chuckle. "That's just the needle."

"Oh." Astrid looked down at her chest, and he had the pleasure of watching her face turn even deeper red. "I didn't think I'd like them so much."

What an utterly ridiculous thing to say after what had just happened. Bjorn tilted his head back and laughed, the sound coming from deep inside him as he shook his head. "Astrid..." He had no idea what to say to her after that declaration. "Hold on to my horns. This is going to hurt too."

He chose the gold bars, even though he didn't like them without stones. Silver wasn't good enough for her. He wanted his bright one to be adorned in gold.

Chapter 38

Astrid had known this little bubble of happiness would disappear. They weren't lucky enough to come to Trollveggen and then simply live out their lives, happy and unaffected by anyone and everyone else around them.

The message came early in the morning. Bjorn didn't even get out of bed. He muttered about a door locked by magic and then rolled over and ignored the pounding of someone's fist on the stone. But Astrid couldn't sleep.

What if something had happened?

What if Rose had run?

She laid there, thinking about all the things that could have gone wrong. Her sister's decisions shouldn't matter so much, and yet, somehow, they did. She was still frozen with the fear that Rose would want to leave and Astrid would lose her all over again.

So she got out of bed, sneaking away from the big man sleeping naked in their bed. She glanced back at him one last time, her gaze tracing over the broad expanse of his back and the naked globes of his ass that made her want to turn right back around and crawl back under the covers with him.

But she couldn't. Not without checking to make sure everything was all right. She threw on a robe, trying to ignore the feeling of the soft fabric as it clung to her newly pierced nipples. They were so sensitive, and she still couldn't tell if that was good or horrible yet. Everything they touched was a sensation. She just couldn't tell if she liked it or not.

Astrid opened the door partly to distract herself at this point.

She'd thought it would be some messenger she didn't know, but it was Gunnar. And her sister. Rose stood behind him with a soft, dreamy look on her face as she stared off into the distance.

Gunnar grunted at Astrid as he pushed past her into the home. "I'll get him up. Watch her."

"What's wrong with her?" Astrid asked. Her sister wasn't even moving. She was standing there, staring off into the distance.

"Nothing's wrong with her. She's just off wandering. She gets herself in trouble when she does that, so don't let her wander without being with her. Yeah?" Then he disappeared into the bedroom as though that wasn't a strange thing to say. She could hear Bjorn cursing and then something breakable being thrown inside the room.

"Right," Astrid muttered, leaving the cave and grabbing her sister by the arm. "Come with me, Rose."

She guided her sister to a rock and sat her down, gently holding on to her ice cold hands. The poor thing had bare feet. Dirt smeared between her toes, but at least there weren't any cuts and scrapes. Astrid reached up and brushed Rose's tangled pale hair away from her face.

It broke her heart to see her sister like this. Wandering in her mind was something she'd always done, but it still made Astrid nervous.

"You did this when you were little, and I'd ask you when you were coming back to me," Astrid said. "Wandering has always been your power, I know that, my dear, but you cannot always disappear into fantasy worlds. You weren't given this gift so that you wouldn't take part in living."

It took a while for Rose to come out of it. Throughout it all, she could hear Gunnar and Bjorn shouting inside. Apparently, her husband had very little interest in coming with Gunnar, if that was what he had been sent for. And she didn't blame him.

A twisting feeling in her gut warned her that they were about to travel again. No good king could know that another was stealing his people, forcing them to perform and die for profits, and not want to do something about it. Her heart ached that Bjorn had to be involved at all, but she had known that he would.

He knew the labyrinth better than anyone else. Astrid had only been there for a week or so, but she'd had help creating a map to escape. Visiting the labyrinth with a lord wasn't the same as living inside of it for ten years.

Rose blinked, and then she was back. Her gaze was soft, her eyes still dreamy, but she was looking at Astrid's face and not into a world that didn't exist.

"Oh," Rose said quietly. "What am I doing here?"

"Gunnar brought you."

"That was nice of him. I had wanted to see you." Rose blinked a few more times, clearly trying to get herself to detach from whatever world she had built in her head. "You know the king wants you and Bjorn to return to the labyrinth? He wants Bjorn to fight for him, and then destroy everything there. He has a plan and everything."

"Of course he wants his revenge. It doesn't surprise me that Bjorn and I are involved in some way."

Rose's eyes filled with tears. "But it means you will have to return to that place. That horrible, horrible place, Astrid. You can't go back there."

Astrid had known there would be some struggle in this. Her sister's memories of the labyrinth were a dark cloud that followed her around. They were the memories she ran from over and over again, but no matter how fast or how far she went, she'd never outrun them.

Squeezing her sister's hands, she watched as Rose realized they were touching. For a moment, she thought Rose would rip her hands away. But then, marvelously, her sister squeezed her back.

"I'm going to go back and I'm going to help them destroy it," Astrid said. Her mind was already spinning with how she could do it, but that was a hard question. "I don't know how yet, but I'm going to. They need me, Rose."

"I don't want you to go through the same thing I did. I couldn't survive it knowing he was punishing you like he punished me."

"Who?" Astrid asked before she thought about it. "The king?"

Rose nodded vigorously.

"Oh, my sweet sister. He cannot trap me. I'm so much stronger than I was when we were children."

Astrid stood when the door to their home burst open and Bjorn came careening out. He had her new blue dress in his hands and wore an expression that was better suited for war than it was this moment.

"Come on," he snarled. "We're telling King Egil to go fuck himself."

The blustering weight of his anger startled even her. But then Bjorn froze, looked at Astrid and her sister, before correcting himself. "Sorry, Rose. Didn't see you there."

Her sister seemed to relax at least a little. "That's all right, Bjorn.

I'd be just as angry."

Astrid had a hard time believing Rose even remembered what it was like to be angry. Maybe that would help her in many of the situations she struggled with these days. What if her sister went with them? Raged at the men who'd harmed her, killed them all, and left victorious? Perhaps soaking in their blood would fix some part of her that was still hiding deep inside her body?

But Rose hadn't even been able to kill a bug. Astrid remembered how hard her sister would work to catch the smallest housefly and release it outside because it wasn't fair of them to murder an innocent. She didn't like harming anything at all, and that... Well, that had always been Rose.

Astrid had a feeling that trait hadn't changed in the slightest since they'd been children. Most likely, her sister would only hurt more if she took part in killing those men.

Sighing, she stood and walked over to Bjorn. "Gunnar is inside, I think. Why don't you join him there, Rose?"

Her sister scuttled off, and Astrid took her place beside her husband. Bjorn looked her over, clearly furious, but at least that anger wasn't directed at her. It never was.

He handed her the dress without a word. Astrid dropped the robe to the ground, pulled her dress on over her head, and then made sure the robe was folded up by their front door. Hopefully, no one had been looking, but really the trolls seemed so much less concerned about the physical form than her own people were. It was kind of freeing.

"Let's not keep the king waiting," she reminded him. And together, they headed back toward the castle.

He took her on a shorter path this time, a strange route that seemed to go through a few small portions of the mountain itself before arriving at the castle on a back path. She was surprised there was even a way for someone to get into the castle from behind. But then again, the trolls did like to have ways to get out of any situation. She'd heard in battle they were almost impossible to pin down.

There were countless people in the castle, yet again. But this time they all appeared to be warriors. She had never seen so many weapons all in one place, nor so many people wearing them all at once.

Every troll ignored them all until she heard the whispers start up again.

"That's the Destroyer's son."

"Bjorn has returned?"

"I didn't know we had a berserker on our side. We surely cannot lose now."

All of those whispers were a weight on Bjorn's shoulders. He grew tenser and tenser the closer they got to the king's chambers where they had met the last time. This time though, Bjorn threw the doors open without asking.

King Egil and a few other much older looking trolls were at the end. One of them was a woman wearing the same clothing Bjorn's mother had worn. Bones were threaded throughout her hair like beads, and she looked Bjorn over with a soft smile on her face that made him pause.

"Vilde," Bjorn said, his voice tinged with surprise. "You still serve the king."

"Of course I do, boy. I have always served the king."

Bjorn leaned closer to her and murmured under his breath, "The king's smoke reader. A very renowned prophetess."

"Ah." Someone to be honored, then.

Astrid carefully bowed to each of them in the room. She was

graceful as always, poised in a way that spoke of how many kings and nobles she had dealt with in her life. But just as she opened her mouth to compliment them, to woo them into telling her what the plan was, Bjorn decided to bullishly shove his way into the conversation.

"I'm not doing it," he snarled. "You want to use me as a weapon, and I understand why. But my fighting days are over."

"We need you to fight," King Egil replied. He waved a massive clawed hand in the air, dismissing the words. "And so you will. Your loyalty is to your people, Bjorn. Always has been. Always will be. You will do what I tell you to do."

"I will not fight."

"Vilde has already seen the future, Bjorn. You will fight, and you are the key to ensuring that we win. You will serve your people as you are best suited. Your bloodline has always led our battles, and we always win when one of you serves us." He shrugged. "We have already made the plans. You will take a warband through the front gates. The human king does not expect us to attack, and there are fewer guards there during the day. It is a solid plan."

Astrid could see Bjorn tensing. It wasn't a very good plan. They all knew that.

But she could also recognize the calculating expression on the king's face. This man knew it wasn't a good plan. He was merely saying it to goad Bjorn into anger, or perhaps, to test her. Because Vilde's gaze flicked to Astrid, not Bjorn.

"You know that is a plan that leads only to death," Bjorn thundered. "You must know the moment we go into that labyrinth, we are never coming out."

They weren't looking at him. They were looking at her. Both the king and Vilde, and now the warlord on his other side as well. They wanted her to step in while Bjorn continued to yell at them about how stupid this plan was.

They were baiting her. But why?

Finally, it hit her. They wanted her to take part in this far more than they were saying. "You want me to open the doors," she said quietly.

"What doors?" Bjorn yelled, turning toward her with his eyes nearly red. He was so close to losing it, and she could already sense there were more people approaching the room, just in case Bjorn tried to harm the king.

"The door we snuck out of. The one that is locked from the inside and spelled so that no one could open it without a key. You want me to open the door and let them into the labyrinth without anyone knowing." She swallowed. "It is a good plan, King Egil."

He tilted his head to the side, oddly bird-like as he looked at her. "But can you do it?"

"Not without support. Not without returning to my post as priestess and making them all believe it." She ignored Bjorn's blustering about how she would not be joining anything. "I would need the lord I left. I believe he could get me in."

"Could he be bribed?" the warlord on the other side of the king asked.

"Perhaps. It wouldn't be my first thing to ask him, though. I'd like to see if he'd do it simply because he feels guilty that he left me in there on my own."

Tolly was a foolish man, and sentimental when it came to her. She could still see his expression when she'd last walked past him. If Astrid played her cards right, she could get him back under her thumb. She was quite certain of it, now that his debts were paid and assuming he hadn't drunk himself into more of them.

Bjorn grabbed hold of her shoulders and forced her attention to him. "No." He wasn't ordering. He was pleading with her. "It's too dangerous, Astrid."

"Who else can do it? I can save so many trolls, and I won't really be risking myself." She smiled, but the expression felt a little thin on her features. "After all, it's the same life I used to live. Nothing changes for me."

Except, everything had changed. Because she loved him, and she hadn't told him that yet.

King Egil clapped his hands. The cracking sound had her whipping her head to look at him, but he was just pleased, it seemed. "This is a plan I like. You will work with your lord and open the door for us. We'll need a message to know when you will accomplish that."

"I do not know how to get a message to you."

"I'll figure it out before the war band leaves. You will send us a message confirming when the gate will be open, and my warriors will enter the labyrinth unseen. We'll destroy it from the inside out." He pointed at her. "I want to leave your human king a message. I will rip open the labyrinth and expose the ugly underbelly of his kingdom to all who live there. It is the last chance for the people in his kingdom to prove to me that they are worthy of their lives. No more games between us. One last chance, or I will turn the rivers red with their blood."

She nodded. "Understood."

"Not understood!" Bjorn hissed. "She is going nowhere near that place again."

"Bjorn," Astrid put her hand on his shoulder, tugging at his anxiety until it gave way to clear headed calm. "You know as well as I do, this is the only way any plan works."

His expression tore at her heart. "I cannot lose you, bright one."

"And you won't. But this is to help me too. Let me fix all the things inside myself that I didn't even realize were broken." She gestured around them, as though there were answers in the air for him to see. "I am part of that world. I was there when the labyrinth fights were happening, and I did nothing to even try to stop them. I should have. A good person would have. This is my way to help, to show all of you that I have more remorse for being there than I can ever put into words. Let me help you tear that horrible place down."

He seemed to understand. The anger faded for him to realize that she needed to do this, just as much as he did.

Bjorn nodded. "Then you will fight by my side."

"As I always should."

417

Chapter 39

A war band. Bjorn hadn't been part of one of these since he'd failed in battle and had been taken by the human king. It was strange to lace himself up in armor the same way he had done all those years ago.

Trolls like him wore different armor than the rest of them. He was their bulwark. The wall that stood between the others and the swords of humans that could bite through flesh. While many trolls chose to go into battle with very little armor on their bodies, he was completely covered. From his chest to his thighs, he strapped on thick hide that was harvested from wyrms deep within the mountain. Even his forearms and the backs of his hands wore some of the scaled material.

He had his choice of weapons made by the finest craftsmen, and picking up his double sided axe again was like coming home. He hated how easily it fit in his hand, and how well his muscles remembered how to swing it. It would be so simple to cleave heads from shoulders with the sharp edges, even without thinking about what he was doing.

Every part of him was made to kill. Every bit of his body was a weapon that had been honed and trained by the labyrinth itself.

Now he was going back. Back to the place that had turned him into the monster his father had always wanted him to be. Because his people begged him to go. They wanted him to be a monster as well.

His soul ached with this burden.

Heading out of the armory, he pulled the pieces of the person the other trolls expected onto himself like more armor. He became the Destroyer they all wanted to see. The son of the man who had led them to victory countless times.

He would too. But not for them. Bjorn was not his father, who'd fought for glory and honor and the recognition from a king who was so willing to throw him to the wolves. He did it instead for the children he could save who lived here in Trollveggen. He did it for his bright one, who risked her life along with the rest of them. He fought because it was the right thing to do.

His father had never possessed the ability to fight for others. This was what set them apart.

Astrid waited for him. She stood with her sister on the precipice of a steep cliff, both of them gleaming, golden beings who looked more like royalty than any other human here. They were stunning together, beacons of light in a dark time.

He was shocked to see them hugging. Rose had been so touch averse, it was almost startling to see her do so. This was a marked improvement.

Gunnar stood next to him and snorted. "Oh, sure. She'll hug her sister but not the troll who's been providing for her for ages now."

He glanced over at the other man. "You?"

"Who else?" Gunnar shrugged. "What can I say? I'm a bleeding heart. You handed her to me in the labyrinth and I... I haven't let go of her since, you know? Just hasn't felt right when she's been struggling."

Bjorn eyed him a bit more, seeing right through what his friend said. There was something else at play here. Something that wriggled beneath Gunnar's skin and wouldn't let him go.

"You haven't touched her, then?"

"Gods, no. She doesn't even like it when she notices me looking at her. I've got her set up somewhere nice. I bring her food, run a bath for her every night, and buy her new clothes. Just little things to make her life easier." He rubbed the back of his neck. "I find her when she wanders off, which is often. She's just... really broken, Bjorn."

"Broken things have pieces to pick up."

"I don't think she even has a clue where all those pieces are. She hides them every day, scattering them to the wind so no one can put her back together." Gunnar's gaze was haunted as he looked at Astrid's pale sister.

Where Astrid was golden, Rose was nearly white. She was losing more color every day, it seemed. Fading like all of her magic was draining out of her. Pale hair, pale skin, nearly like a star that had fallen into their realm.

"You'll figure something out," Bjorn murmured. "We all do when we love someone."

"Love?" Gunnar scoffed. "I barely even know the woman. Like I said, I'm just a bleeding heart. Don't know what's good for me."

He stalked off, but there was a nervous set to Gunnar's shoulders now. He knew without a doubt that Bjorn was onto him. No one put that kind of effort into another unless there were feelings involved.

Poor man. He was going to have his work cut out for him.

Bjorn headed over to the sisters who had finally parted. Their quiet, murmured words filtered through the air as he approached.

"I'm going to be fine, Rose. I won't even be in any dangerous situations."

"You stay away from the king. He'll steal you away from all of us, and I don't know how I'll get you back." Rose wrung her hands, clearly nervous about her sister leaving.

"I'm not going to get taken, Rose."

Bjorn stood behind Astrid, looming over both of them and casting a horned shadow that seemed to stretch across the ground. Rose's face somehow paled even more, but then he saw determination square her jaw.

She looked right up at him—the first time she might have ever done that—and said, "You take care of her."

He nodded solemnly. "It will be my honor."

Astrid said one last goodbye before turning to him. Together, they headed toward the rest of the war band.

The waves of trolls, all armored and armed to the teeth, rippled around them. There was so much flesh spread out before them, countless men and women who were so strong that he knew Astrid had to be a little frightened. They all lifted spears, swords, and axes into the air at the sight of him. Their whooping calls echoed throughout the hollow mountain until even those in the far reaches would hear the sound of their battle cry.

"Destroyer!" they called out as he held Astrid's hand and weaved through the masses of them. "The Destroyer fights with us!"

The name dropped onto his shoulders like a weight. He was the one who would kill for them, just as he had killed for all those who had forced him to perform.

But then, a tiny hand squeezed his own. He could hear her above all the other shouts, perhaps only because he knew her voice so well.

Quietly, Astrid said, "You do not battle for those who tell you to do so. You battle for those who cannot."

Her words stuck with him as they made the way to the front of the war band. Ragnar waited for them there with a few other generals, and they headed out from the mountain. Astrid had worn a cotton dress split at the sides that would make it easy for her to hop onto his back, although she would have to change before meeting her lord. She didn't have appropriate clothing for that, but there were many tasks for them to figure out as they moved forward with this plan. He only cared for the sensation of her thighs squeezing around his hips and her arms around his neck.

They would do this together. They would fight as they always had, and they would make this work.

He'd keep her safe, he reminded himself. That was his only role in all of this. Keep her safe and get revenge for both of them.

For all of them.

The trolls ran long and hard away from the mountain. King James had sent plenty of soldiers all around their home, still trying to find a way inside that would give them the advantage. It was hard to get into Trollveggen without knowing where they were going, though.

Instead of attacking those human encampments like many of the trolls wished to do, they headed down a steeper side of the mountain and then around the back of the castle. It took them all night, running at full speed, to find a place nearby that would allow them to remain in secret. They set up camp quickly, lighting no fires to give them away.

Poor Astrid was pale and shaking when he pulled her off his back. He wanted to ask her what was wrong, but she beat him to it. She lifted her hands to her arms, running them up and down as a way to show him that she was cold.

He wouldn't have that. Not for long, at least. Bjorn set up their tent as quickly as he could. Many trolls traveled with the war band who did not intend to fight. They were the ones who brought the supplies. Food, water, the tents, and bed furs that would keep them all warm in the coming days while they were waiting for Astrid's message.

Bjorn took extra furs from the nearest troll who had them. He didn't care that others gave him dirty looks, or clearly wanted to complain. His troll wife was cold, and he wasn't going to watch her suffer. Human skin was so much thinner than a troll's, and he refused to be the person who didn't take care of his wife.

Once the tent was set up, he waved for her to head in before him. He'd get inside as soon as he could, but he wanted her to eat.

Bjorn should have brought snacks for her. He should have thought of it before they'd headed out. The last time they'd traveled like this, he hadn't brought nearly enough food for her. He would learn from this.

Once he grabbed the meager offerings, just a few slices of bread, meat, and cheese, he headed back toward his tent. His plan to snuggle up with her was thwarted only by Ragnar, who stood just outside his tent.

His oldest friend was waiting for him. Quiet conversations were still sparse among the trolls, but the lookouts were now heading to their posts. Theoretically, they would be able to have a quick chat without anyone scolding them.

Who was he kidding? No one would scold him anyway. He was the Destroyer.

"What is it?" he asked.

"I was making sure you were getting food for your wife. Humans are fragile." But Ragnar's expression gave away that there was more he wished to say. He just wasn't sure how to say it.

"And?" Bjorn pushed.

"This…" Ragnar sighed and then blurted it all out so quickly, Bjorn almost didn't catch all the words. "This is likely the last night you will see her for quite some time, perhaps ever. I would suggest making the most of it, brother."

No, he would not think like that. He would not assume that he would never see her again, or he wouldn't be able to let her go. Bjorn would end up keeping her in this tent, and they would have to figure out another way to enact their king's plan.

He nodded though and headed into his tent. He didn't turn around until he was certain he heard Ragnar leave, because he knew the moment he saw her, he'd lose his breath.

And he did. He turned to see her stretched out on their furs, those long legs bare after she'd removed her dress. Astrid wore nothing but a few strips of fabric covering her breasts and ass from his view, but not much else.

All long limbs, smooth skin, and a grin on her face that made him see stars where he stood.

Bjorn set the food down near the door so it wouldn't get ruined and started stripping off his armor piece by piece.

She shifted on the furs, and the sound of her movement seemed so loud. "You took long enough."

"I was getting you food."

"Thank you for that," she whispered. "I don't think we're supposed to be talking."

"We aren't." Piece by piece fell onto the ground until he was free from their weight. Bjorn didn't hesitate to shuck off his pants as well, letting them drop onto the ground along with the rest of his clothing as he prowled over to her.

The things he wanted to do were downright villainous. Not to hurt, or break, but to show her that every inch of her body deserved to be worshipped and all the other gods could be damned. He had never cared for them, anyway.

Dropping to the furs, he prowled between her legs. Kissing up one thigh, then changing to the next, he dragged his lips and tusks over her hips, between her breasts, and then to her stunning face that was still almost difficult for him to look at.

Reverently, he pressed gentle kisses first to her cheeks, then the tip of her nose, then underneath each of her eyes.

"Are you sure we should do this?" she asked, although her arms had already wrapped around him. Her legs spread, and he settled between them.

In a sharp moment, he realized that he had never felt more at home than he did right here. In her arms. With her smiling up at him and all that emotion shining in those pretty blue eyes.

"I love you," he said, the words ripping out of him before he could stop them.

Then he just stared at her. Like the fool he was.

Now wasn't the time to say it. He knew that. She knew that.

But he wanted her to know. Because if Ragnar was right, then he might never see her again. Bjorn would make sure she got back to Trollveggen to live with her sister, but the odds were far less likely that he would make it.

Breathing in deeply, he said it again. "I love you. I have for a long time now. Your strength, your resilience, your kindness, all of it has made me fall deeper and deeper in love with you. No one else could ever compete with you, Astrid. No matter how old you get or how sick you become, I will still worship the ground you walk on, savoring every mark your feet leave behind."

Tears gathered in her eyes. She pressed her palms to his cheeks, holding him in place so he had to look at her when she said, "Against all odds, I love you as well. Bjorn, son of the Destroyer, you are my salvation."

How was he supposed to do anything other than worship her after that? He loved her quietly and without any rush for hours on end. Slowly relearning the shape of her body, all the parts of her that made her gasp or shake with pleasure. Over and over.

Because if he might never touch her again, then he was going to make this night feel like it lasted an eternity.

Chapter 40

Astrid was shocked at how simple it was to get into Lord Tolly's home. She went with a small group of trolls, Bjorn included, to the back of the house. In the late hours of the night, most of the city was asleep. They avoided the taverns and any of the streets where there were brothels.

It was all too easy to stand at the back of Tolly's home, staring up at the building she had seen countless times in her life. This quiet, opulent street now felt stifling and dull after she'd experienced the wide open space of Trollveggen.

"What are you going to do when you get in there?" Bjorn asked.

"I don't know," she replied. "Make it work however I have to. He'll be glad to see me, I think."

"He gave you up."

He had. And Astrid had been kind to Tolly for all these years because he had promised to help her find her sister, but now? She didn't have a drop of kindness left. Astrid was going to do what she had always wanted to do with this fool. She was going to look him in the eye and demand that he help her the way he should have when he'd first heard her story. The way a good man would have.

Squaring her shoulders, she gave Bjorn one last kiss before she headed into the kitchens. No one would be there this time of night. She used to sneak down for evening tea when there might be a little peace and quiet.

Even the acolytes would be asleep. Tolly himself would be in his library or tucked into his room. But she'd noticed there were still a few lights on in the house, which led her to believe that Tolly was still awake.

Why? She intended to find out.

The kitchens were empty, just like she thought. Astrid snuck upstairs to what had been her old bedroom, but she had assumed it would already be occupied. She'd assumed correctly. A new priestess slept there, completely unaware that she was being watched by the woman she had replaced. The room itself had even changed. Someone had gotten rid of all the furniture she had used.

The bedroom had once been golden, just like her. But this priestess had dark hair and milky skin, a downgrade in the eyes of the sisterhood. It made sense. Tolly had lost his last priestess to the labyrinth.

Heading down into the storage areas, Astrid found her old things. It was so easy to slip into a garment that had once defined her. She chose a golden dress that spilled down over her shoulders, dripping like molten metal and clinging to her curves. It was entirely one piece of fabric, not a single seam to make it look like she hadn't just dipped herself in metal. Beautiful, just like she wanted to look. She eyed the mask that went with the dress, then decided to leave it where it lay. Astrid no longer had to hide her face. Never again.

Then she headed for the library, where she already knew he was.

Tolly was seated in the same place as always. He faced the back of the library, seated at his desk with a book open on the surface, but he stared out a window. Lost in thought, she assumed.

"You haven't kept up with the ledgers," she murmured as she slipped into the room behind him. Astrid made sure to close the door in her wake. No one was going to interrupt them. Not this time. "I thought you'd be more responsible considering what happened last time."

He froze, his shoulders stiffening before he turned around to look at her. All the blood drained out of his features, almost as though he was seeing a ghost. He compressed his pale lips, his breath coming in soft pants as he continued to stare at her, saying nothing.

"You don't have a single word to say to me?" she asked as she strode closer to him. Astrid reached out her hands, combing her fingers through his silver hair as she had done so many times when he was upset. "You usually have a lot to say, Tolly. I thought you'd be excited to see me again."

"Astrid?" he asked, his voice shaking with emotion. "Surely it's not you?"

"It's me. I made it back to you."

But that wasn't true, and they both knew it. She'd never had any genuine emotion for him. Sometimes, she'd thought he understood that. He'd look at her, and his expression would grow a little wistful, and then angry. As though he'd wanted her to feel something for him even though he was twice her age.

Apparently, he wasn't thinking the same thing. His expression was still twisted with horror. "I... I... You were given to the troll. They said you were murdered in the dungeons during a brawl. Alongside the Bull who had claimed you."

"You should know I wouldn't die that easily. No, my dear. I got out. But I need your help." She trailed her fingers along his face, lingering on the rounded edge of his jaw. "They wanted me to die, just like you said. That place is a horrible pit of torment and pain. I need to go back to it, Tolly. And I need to tear it all down."

He shook his head. "No, you can't do that. They'll catch you. They'll know I was the one who helped you."

"If you help me do this, then I'll come back to you. Forever," she lied. "I know you have the means and the connections. I'll stay right here, where I have always belonged. By your side."

There was a time when this would have worked. The lord would have done anything to keep her attention, to feel like she saw him and only him in her life. And yet... something had changed.

Because his gaze flicked to the door, not to her curves. He was looking for a way out.

Her hands curled into claws, gripping his face so he couldn't get away from her. "Tolly. You've been keeping so much from me."

"I have no need of a priestess any longer," he replied. "Your services, though remarkable, are not..."

She waited for him to finish the sentence, but he didn't. He couldn't. So she did it for him. "No longer necessary, is that what you were going to say?"

He firmly nodded. "You can try to manipulate me if you wish, Priestess. But I will no longer fall under your spell whenever you desire to trap me. Harwick informed me of all your witchcraft. He told me how you manipulated my mind and how none of my mistakes were my own. You made me make them."

So that was what it had been. Harwick had gotten into his ear, telling him that the priestesses were witches or that they were controlling the entirety of their realm and he should fear them.

Harwick was right, of course. But in circumstances like this, priestesses were always told to do the same thing. Sometimes, it was best to cull the herd when one of them realized they were being controlled.

Astrid was done trying to convince him to do the right thing. She would just make him.

The whispering sensation of her magic pulsed out of her hands, tugging at his fear of her, and his hesitation to even be near her. In that magic she could feel a bit of Bjorn as well, a need to pull a spirit animal from Tolly's flesh. She wanted to show him how right he was to fear her.

She was angry about how he had treated her. And she wasn't afraid of how he was going to react because he couldn't use her sister as an excuse. He couldn't use anyone other than himself as an excuse.

Tolly wrenched away from her with a wild shove that sent her careening away from him. She caught herself on another desk in the library, her hip banging against the wood painfully as he lunged up with a letter opener in his hand. "You don't get to control me anymore," he said.

But his hand was shaking. He gestured wildly with the letter opener, but it wasn't with movement that was controlled in the slightest. He was terrified.

"Don't do that!" he yelled. "I can feel you trying to change how I'm thinking! You always did that."

"I helped you," she said. "I always made you more confident. I helped you in becoming a better lord every time I used my power."

"You were making me someone I'm not!" he insisted. His hand shook even worse. "This is exactly what he said you would do. You are trying to manipulate me. You want to take over my mind, and it's not right. It's not right."

"Not right? Tolly, you're saying that like I'm some kind of abomination. You weren't saying that whenever you had me use my power to get you what you wanted, so I have to admit, I don't entirely believe you." She stood up straight, pointing at the ceiling above them. "You were quick to replace me with another who has the same talents I do."

"Talents? They gave me a priestess who's only good at moving things with her mind. She can't even move anything heavy. A cup. A letter. She's far less dangerous than someone who can twist another person's mind and get them to do whatever she wants." He took a deep, steadying breath, and his hand stopped shaking. Now, the letter opener was pointed at her with obvious intent. "You were always a threat to this house."

"Who told you that, I wonder?"

"The king himself. He said he never should have made you a priestess. That you weren't worthy of the title because you were always too powerful and that power was going to go to your head." Tolly took a menacing step toward her. "But he also said that you couldn't change anything about how I feel. Only amplify it. So tell me now, Priestess. Now that he prepared me for what you would want when you returned, can you change my mind now?"

This man. How had she ever stayed as long as she had?

She'd never seriously thought about killing anyone in her entire life, but now that she'd been around Bjorn this long, the thought of it really didn't bother her that much. A man like this deserved to die. He deserved what she was going to give him in just a few moments.

"Tolly," she said, shaking her head. "I don't have to reach into your mind to change it. You aren't a killer. You have never been a killer."

"How would you know that? You don't know me."

"But I do." She took a step toward him, challenging the mere thought that he could follow through with this. "And I have been around killers now. You left me in that labyrinth. You locked me up inside it and you made it very clear that nothing you did would change the debt. You were willing to use my body, my life, to pay for your own mistakes. Do you know what that did to me?"

She lunged for the letter opener, grabbing his wrist and trying to twist it out of his hand. But he was bigger than her. Maybe there was some part of him that wanted to kill her.

With a quick jerk of his arm, he tossed her across the room. She hit a bookshelf hard, heavy tomes raining down on her head as she tried to cover herself from their strikes. And then he was on her.

Tolly grabbed her forearms, wrenching her away from the precariously tilting shelves. He gripped her so hard she was certain there would be bruises. The metal of the letter opener crushed against her skin, threatening to break through it before he even stabbed her.

"Why would you do this to me?" he hissed, shaking her so hard her teeth rattled. "Why did you ever believe that you could control me?"

He needed to be controlled. Because he was like this if she didn't. Paranoid. Filled with fear for himself and his own life when he should have been focusing on ruling his people and those who looked up to him. Instead, he hid in the city, ignoring that there were tenants who paid him taxes, all to fuel his ridiculous lifestyle while he ignored their well-being.

He shook her again, even harder this time. "I'm going to get rid of you once and for all," he snarled.

The door flew open to the library, and so many things happened all at once. Both she and Tolly looked over to the door to see his new priestess standing there. Her dark hair hung in clumps over her eyes, and then suddenly the letter opener twisted in his hands, plunging into his chest right through his heart. Blood didn't spray as Astrid thought it might, but it did leak out over her hands in bubbling spurts as his heart tried to continue pounding around the foreign object.

Astrid opened her mouth, a little shocked at what had unfolded. She hadn't done that. She was certain she had not done that.

"You…" He coughed and blood bubbled up through his mouth. "You made her do that."

The new priestess strode into the room and grabbed his hands. "Let her go."

"You didn't… You didn't want to," he said to her as his hands released Astrid's arms and he fell onto the ground. "It's not your fault."

The woman spat on him. "Priestesses always choose each other. You laid a hand on one of our own. You gave her to the labyrinth where you knew she would be attacked, raped, and killed. You deserve every bit of this. Whose power is weak now, little man?"

The life drained from his eyes, and Astrid was faced with a rather complicated dilemma. She was supposed to get Tolly to help them, and now he was dead at her feet. Not that she cared all that much. He'd been trying to kill her.

She waited until the other priestess met her gaze and then said, "Thank you for that."

"You're welcome. I didn't want to serve him, anyway."

"I did need him, though."

"For what?" the other priestess tilted her head to the side, ravenlike in her mannerisms.

"I need to get into the labyrinth. I intend to reveal it to the entire kingdom, and show the ugly underbelly of what the king is doing to all the people."

"That doesn't help any of our sisters if you do that."

"Doesn't it? They will no longer be at risk of the same punishment that I suffered," she said. "I wasn't the first one sent there. My sister was as well. The king punished her for not allowing a neighboring lord to touch her when she hadn't even been given to him yet. No one should be able to touch a priestess unless she is bound to serve her lord."

No, that wasn't right. Those were the old words, the ones she had been taught but never believed. Astrid squared her shoulders and looked the other woman in the eye. "No one should be able to touch a priestess without her permission. Ever."

Again the head tilt, as though the other woman was eyeing her. "I agree."

"But I needed Tolly to get into the labyrinth."

"I think the right bribe would do it too. All we need is one guard at the gate. You tell him exactly what is going to happen, and then give him... Oh, ten times his salary should do it. Tolly has that in his safe. Tell him if he helps us, then the trolls will allow him to get out of there. He can leave town and never look back."

The priestess headed out of the library and toward Tolly's chambers. Now, Astrid wasn't going to turn down such an impressive gift, but it felt a little odd that the woman not only killed him, but was also helping her.

"Excuse me?" she asked. "Why are you helping me?"

The priestess glanced over her shoulder and shrugged. "I'm tired of being touched, too."

And that was all the answer Astrid needed. "Do you think there's anyone else in our order who might help?"

"Plenty," the woman replied with a feral grin.

Chapter 41

Bjorn hated waiting. It had always been the worst part of the labyrinth, too. Standing there, waiting to know what kind of creature would fight him, or what kind of fight it would end up being. The other trolls around him didn't understand where his nerves were coming from, but how could they?

Hunkered down in the bushes after getting Astrid's message, they were so certain this was a battle they could not lose.

The raven was one of the troll king's own. The bird had been trained to carry messages all the way across the realm to where King Egil had hidden his son. None of them had seen the prince in a very, very long time. But they understood why the king hadn't wanted him here.

Humans were too dangerous. Sons were lost all the time, just like Bjorn had been lost. The message the raven brought had been very easy to read, though.

MIDNIGHT IN TWO NIGHTS.
THE DOOR WILL BE OPEN.
STAY SAFE. ALL OF YOU.

Astrid

Part of him hadn't wanted to believe the message had come from her. She was so certain in her message, so short. There wasn't a declaration of love or anything to let him know that she was still fighting to be with him. He would have taken anything. Another "I love you", perhaps.

They both knew he was going to fight like he had in the labyrinth. Surely she understood that meant he might not come out. And yet, the message had been short, brief, and to the point.

Damned woman. It was like she wasn't even worried about him.

Now they were all waiting outside the door for it to open, and he was getting antsy. There were too many things that could go wrong. She hadn't even informed them if Tolly had been willing to help, which Bjorn somehow doubted. The man was self-serving and wanted nothing to do with any troll. He'd even tried to get Astrid's favor back through the barrier between the noblemen and the trolls, as if that would let him assuage his guilt.

The door swung open slowly, creaking too loudly. All the trolls around him winced, staring in the town's direction that was so close surely someone had heard the door opening. He didn't remember it being so loud when he and Astrid had made it out of there.

Bjorn was the first one on the path, so he was the first to see the man who poked his head out. The human was scraggly at best. He wore no armor, although he had the build of a soldier. His brown hair was slicked with sweat to his skull, suggesting he had just been wearing a helmet. And he went pale at the sight of the wall of trolls waiting for him, but then he cleared his throat. "She said you'd be here."

"And so we are."

"She didn't bribe me enough for this," the man muttered. "I'm to open the door, walk down the path, and not look back. That's all she told me."

"Is she with you?"

He shook his head. "She headed off into the labyrinth by herself. Her and a bunch of women." Then his eyes widened. "Shit, I wasn't supposed to tell you that."

"Why did they enter the labyrinth?"

The guard shrugged. "Don't know. There's not much in the direction they went, really. Just the women's holding cells."

Of course, that was where she had headed. Astrid was supposed to stay out of all this, but he had the sneaking suspicion that she had learned something none of the rest of them knew. Likely something that had to do with Rose and all the other women that were locked up in there, ready and prepared to be gifts for anyone who had won a fight.

He took one large step to the side, but not big enough that the man wouldn't have to touch him as he passed. Bjorn stared down at the smaller guard, who paused right before he reached all the other trolls.

"I saw you fight once," the guard said. "It's like you weren't the same person you were in the cells. Like you became something else entirely."

"I do."

"How do you do that?"

"I am Bjorn, son of Dag the Destroyer. I come from a long line of berserkers who have fought and won, no matter the pain or the cost. I watched my grandfather fight to his death, missing an arm. His blood coated all of his victims, and he refused to die until they all did." Bjorn could almost taste metal on his tongue. He knew who he was, and what his line was. "I protect my people. I stand between them and torment. Even here."

The guard slipped away, perhaps one of the first human men who had walked through an army of trolls and never once been touched. That was what his Astrid had done for this guard, and he could only hope she had picked the right person to do so.

The man could run to the other guards. He could tell them where they were. But Bjorn had a feeling this man wasn't going to do that. He was going to take his money and run far, far away from this place.

"Come," he said to the other trolls, knowing that the heat at his back was likely Ragnar. "Follow me."

"What is the plan?" Ragnar asked.

"Kill every human in sight. Spare no one unless they are female. Otherwise, kill them all. Release every troll you see. Any humans in those cells? Leave them."

He thought of the man who had been across from him, the human who had made comments about Astrid and who had made women cry when they were gifted to him.

Bjorn would love to tear that man apart with his claws. He would love to see his blood dripping from the walls of his cell, but he also knew leaving all of them there was death itself. Starvation took time. A long, horrible period of time.

Perhaps men like that deserved to wait and wonder why they hadn't been freed. They deserved to panic, to fear what would become of them, to realize that no one was going to find them.

And then they deserved to die alone.

The first group of guards found the trolls almost as soon as they entered, and by that point Bjorn had already worked himself up to near berserk already. He could feel it pressing down on him, even though he knew it wasn't yet time. He needed to guide the other trolls to the cages first.

So he held himself in check as they rushed toward the guards. None of those men stood a chance against the cleaving motion of his axe, nor did they seem to understand the danger they were in. Some of them must have recognized him, but they didn't have time to even blink before he was on them.

Oh, it felt good to use this weapon again. Somewhere in this pit was his father's axe, where it would remain buried as it should be. But he couldn't deny it was far more pleasing to swing this weapon in both directions and slice heads from shoulders with every movement of his arms.

Soon enough, blood splattered the walls of the tunnel, and he turned the trolls into the hall where the cells were. There were many of them, though. That was the problem.

Breathing hard, he tried to speak though he knew it would be difficult. A berserker didn't think. He wanted to fight, to make things bleed. He wanted to hear the cries of the dying begging for mercy that he would not give.

But he was still himself. He was still Bjorn.

For now.

He pointed to five of the splintering passages. "Each of these has warriors in it. Get them, and bring them to the armory."

"Where is the armory?" Ragnar asked.

He... Shit, he hadn't brought them to the armory. He was already losing his mind, and he couldn't remember where the damn room was. Lips twisting around his tusks, he tried to remember the mental map he had built over the years.

But the walls were closing in on him. The smell of mud and blood only reminded him of all the things that had happened. He'd been little more than an animal in this hovel, and just being here made him feel the same. He needed Astrid's cool touch to ground him. He needed the touch of his woman, who had always seen him as more than just a beast to be pointed in a direction and loosed until everything was dead.

One of the trolls moved past him into the hall, and his shoulder struck the light hanging from the ceiling. Unfortunately, that made it swing wildly, and all Bjorn could do was try to focus on the ground that seemed to be getting closer and closer.

He would not pass out. He was Bjorn the Destroyer.

No, he was just Bjorn. Bjorn, who wanted his family and friends to never fear that they would face the same horrors he had. He would not stand by while they had to suffer.

This place would be destroyed. He would honor his father's memory in that sense, but he would never go too far. Not like Dag had.

"This way," he growled, the words getting harder and harder to say.

Ragnar followed him as they both stalked down the lines of cells. There were fewer trolls than what he remembered. A sign that something terrible had happened here. He blamed the king, but of course he did. The king would need to put on much more complicated shows than he ever had before. He'd lost his favorite troll, the one everyone knew they could bet on. Losing Bjorn had likely cost the king an exorbitant amount of money.

He had his eye on one cell in particular. His stomach twisted on the way, though. What if something had happened? What if Rabbit was dead? All the questions bubbling in his mind came to a halt as he paused in front of the doorway to the man's cell, who he might even call friend.

Rabbit stood in front of the small slot with bars. He held his arm at a strange angle. Bjorn could see that even through the tiny space between the metal. Rabbit was alive, though. That was all that mattered.

"Bjorn!" Rabbit said, shock and relief in the sound of his voice. "You made it back."

"Of course I did."

"I doubted you. That pretty little thing could easily have been a trap. I thought the king was going to tempt you into something even worse than this place. Glad I was wrong." Rabbit leaned a bit to the side, trying to see around him. "Who did you bring with you?"

"Ragnar."

"No idea who that is."

Ragnar huffed out an angry breath behind him. "You didn't even talk about me in this place?"

"Rabbit was brought in years after me. I stopped talking about my life outside of these walls long before that." Bjorn grabbed onto the bars of the window, then nodded toward the bar that served as a handle. "Pull with me."

"You think these can be removed by sheer force?" Ragnar shook his head. "I doubt that. They were built to hold trolls."

"They were built to hold trolls who were injured, drugged, or nearly dead. They were built, so that they were impossible to open from the inside. Grab the fucking door, Ragnar."

Together, they heaved against it, pulling and pulling until the stones around it gave. Bjorn grabbed it and then threw it across the hall. The metal and wood hit the neighboring cell and cracked through the door of that one. The other troll would let himself out.

Rabbit let out a low whistle. "You've gotten stronger."

Shaking his head, Bjorn stepped to the side to make some room for them. "No. Just angry."

"Fuck," Rabbit said, drawing out the word. "We should all get out of the way then."

"Armory."

"Why?"

He was already struggling to make sense of why he wanted anyone to go to the armory. Thankfully, Ragnar stepped in quickly. He even stood in front of Bjorn, blocking the view of his friend, who had gotten even thinner.

"There are a lot more trolls waiting to get inside here. Plenty of them to fight. We're getting all of you out, and those who can fight with us will need weapons." Ragnar kept explaining while Bjorn shook his head, trying to get the memories out of his mind.

All he could see now was how thin Rabbit had gotten. And he had already been a very thin man before Bjorn had left. It looked like the king was now completely starving the trolls, and that made him see red. He couldn't just destroy this place. He couldn't just bring it down, revealing all the horrors to the people who lived here. Would it even matter to them? Would they even care what their king had done?

He had to try. He had to make sure that no one would ever return to this place, no matter what happened.

"Bjorn?" Rabbit said, his voice hesitant. "You know these halls are too tight. You can't do that here."

"Do what?"

"Do what your father taught you to do." Rabbit reached for him, his skeletal hand surprisingly strong as he grabbed onto Bjorn. "You have to stay with us. We can get everyone out, and then you can do whatever you want to do. But you know you can't win if you fight them like this."

But he could. Because he had. Every battle he had ever fought like this was one that he had eventually come out victorious. Just like his father and his grandfather. Like all the men in his bloodline who had forgotten what it meant to care for themselves in the end.

Because other people mattered more than them. Their world was more than just a quiet, calm life. It was protection and honor and pain.

Striding away from them all, he ignored Rabbit's call for him to stop. He couldn't. If he looked at Rabbit one more time, then he was going to lose his mind. He was going to kill anyone and everyone who stood in the way between him and the king, who should know that Bjorn was coming for him.

"Free them all," he called out, his voice echoing through the halls. "I hunt."

And though they were supposed to be quiet, a cheer rose behind him. A whooping, haunting war cry that would make every human guard in this place know what it was to feel terror. They would know he was coming for them, but they would never see him before it was too late.

Bjorn the Destroyer hunted through these halls now.

And he was going to make them all bleed.

Chapter 42

The amount of priestesses startled Astrid. Sable, the priestess who had taken her place, had sent a message out to the sisterhood. She'd told Astrid to trust her and allow her to pen the message that would potentially change all of their lives, so Astrid had done just that.

Deep inside her gut, something said that priestesses could be trusted. The sisterhood had perhaps never been particularly kind to her, but they had only been preparing her for a life they knew she could control if she had the strength to do so. None of them wished to be in the position they were in. But they made the best of what life had given them, and they would do whatever it took to grasp some semblance of power.

This was a chance for them to grab a lot more of it.

Now she stood within the labyrinth itself, in the room where the nobles had gathered, and was shocked to see so many of her sisters here. There were more than she had even thought were still in this city, considering the priestesses were also sent out into the wilds and to other kingdoms that sometimes worked with King James.

Clearing her throat, she tried to think of something to say when they all turned their attention to her. She felt like this was a pivotal moment, and she wasn't sure how to use that to her advantage.

"Most of you know this place," Astrid finally said, feeling the words deep in her heart. "You have come here just as I have. With a sour stomach and the knowledge that no matter what you did, you couldn't stop the horrors from happening here. Like me, you turned your face away from the gore and violence and told yourself it was better that it happened where it was contained. I thought the same as you until they put me in the games."

One of the priestesses still wearing her face covering murmured, "So it is true. She was here."

"My lord traded me to clear away gambling debts, like I was nothing. His slate was wiped clean, and all I had to do was give up my body and life. I will not lie to you. I went willingly. I had heard that my sister had been taken by trolls and that I needed to free one to get her back. But what I did not know was that my sister had been held in this labyrinth as well, for ten years."

The shocked gasps that echoed throughout the room mirrored her own feelings. Because it was so incredibly wrong.

"My sister was training to be one of us. She was a good girl, who said no to being raped by a lord. She did what she could to fight them off, and they put her here, where even worse happened to her for years on end. The trolls took her away. They gave her a safe place. She is happy there. Or... Well, as happy as a woman could be after what she has suffered." And that still made her heart bleed. "Now I am asking you to help me."

"How can we help?" Another priestess asked.

"We will show this underbelly to all who live here. We will reveal the horrors that have persisted right under their noses for too many years. I want this entire kingdom to know what has happened."

An older priestess, one Astrid vaguely remembered from her training, pushed to the front of the crowd. "They won't care, Astrid. They won't. The nobles who make their money here will continue to turn their faces to the sides, and therefore so will the rest of their people. Money and power has always run this hideous place."

She'd been afraid of that. She'd been so terrified that she wouldn't be able to do anything to change what had happened here. But then something settled in her mind.

Something whispered there was more she could do. More she could force if she had to.

"Then we tear it down," she said. "We make it so they can never rebuild. This place is unique and hidden. We make it impossible for them to continue after we release everyone in here."

More murmurs bubbled up from among her peers, but they weren't murmurs of disapproval. She could see there were plans forming from all the women who surrounded her. Each of them bundled into groups, perhaps women who regularly worked with each other as they served the many ranks of noblemen who made this kingdom prosperous.

The older woman turned back to Astrid and nodded. "And so we will. The sisterhood has been tired of this royal line for a while, and it is long past time we send the nobles of this kingdom a message. We are the ones who rule. Not them."

Astrid felt her spine straighten. Because this old woman was right. They did rule this kingdom. The priestesses always had. And maybe Astrid hadn't been very good at controlling her lord in the end, but she had affected more than anyone would ever give her credit for.

Now, they were all going to do even more together. They were going to turn this entire kingdom upside down.

"Does anyone know where they keep the women?" she asked, clarifying as she settled into what the plan was. "I know they must be somewhere around here. They wouldn't keep them in the cells with the others, considering they were always clean when I saw them."

"They're in some other cells," another priestess said. She'd ripped off her mask, revealing pretty features underneath blue eyes. She almost looked a little similar to Astrid and her sister, strangely enough. A powerful priestess, then. "My lord... borrowed one, once. We had to come here, and he went into the cells with a guard for a while before coming back."

God, it made her stomach turn. "Do you know which way he went?"

"No. But my magic is in memories. If you give me but a moment, I can pull it from him." The woman walked out of the room, and Astrid had to wonder if she'd brought her lord with her. A rather strange thought indeed.

The older priestess walked up to her as they all waited. "You have to know that this could all fail. I'm not wishing that it does, or advising that it will. But the king is a wily one."

"Then why are you helping?"

"Because someone needs to stop him. And I believe that you are uniquely capable of doing so. A woman scorned is a dangerous beast indeed, but be careful, Astrid. The king is many things, but a coward is not one of them. The moment he finds out that we are here is the moment we should all run."

It was a warning she would take to heart. They all gathered together when the missing priestess returned, looking more than a little troubled. She didn't answer any of their questions as they asked why she looked so pale. Instead, she just took them down a corridor and into the darker parts of the labyrinth.

Not a word was shared among them. Astrid remembered walking here her first time. She'd been so scared and had to fight so hard to not look as though she were trembling. She hadn't wanted any of these people to know she was actually terrified.

But now she didn't have to be afraid. Now she was the one with the power, and she would release all these women from their torment if it was the last thing she did in her life.

Soon enough, they made it to the cells where the women were kept. It was so eerily quiet in these corridors, like no one beyond wanted to move a muscle in case attention was cast upon them.

Another priestess, this one with long red hair, walked up to the first door and waved her hand over it. The lock clicked audibly, and then she moved down to the next, and the next.

Astrid waited as some of the other priestesses went into the rooms, but then she went into one herself.

The woman inside had likely not been here long. Though her dark hair was greasy and lank, she was still far cleaner than some of the other freed women who walked by. She sat on her cot with her hands placed in her lap, staring at the door with some sort of expectation.

"You knew I was coming," Astrid said as she walked to the woman's side.

"I did. There were a few others here who can see the future, and they said you were going to set us free today." She looked up at Astrid with a soft smile on her face. "You are a surprise to all of us. I don't think anyone believed them when they said you were coming."

"I couldn't leave any of you here."

"Because of your sister?"

Astrid smoothed a hand down the woman's head, brushing her hair back from her face. "Because none of you deserves to be here. This is not a fitting punishment for any crime."

"Where do we go from here?"

"The sisterhood will hide you. I can't promise it will be better than where you came from, but it won't be here."

The woman nodded. "It will be better no matter where they place us. But what if we don't wish to stay in this kingdom?"

Astrid hadn't thought of that. Her own sister hadn't wanted to return, knowing what had happened to her. Many of these women likely wouldn't be able to look men in the eyes or even find the help they needed when they knew so many people were aware of what had happened to them.

Some would have been traded to wipe away debts, just like Astrid had been. Some of their families might have been the very ones who sold their lives to darkness. Perhaps some of them had committed crimes, but as Astrid had said, this was not a punishment worthy of any crime.

So she answered for the trolls. "If you wish to go to Trollveggen, they will take you. I don't know if any of you heard the declaration from months ago, but the troll king has set a decree that if you wish to live with the trolls, they will take all women who wish to do so."

The woman smiled, and it was a bright, bubbly expression that broke Astrid's heart. "I think I'd like that. I can tell the others, if you wish. There's a lot more you need to do."

"More I need to do?"

"Of course. You're going to destroy this place." Then she stood and wandered out of the room, gliding like a priestess was trained to do.

As Astrid followed her, joining the others, she saw a small group of priestesses who had set themselves off to the sides. They were the ones with physical magic, and their anger boiled around them. It stretched, sticky and powerful in all directions. Red veining spliced through the air, wanting to harm and maim and tear.

They were the ones who were going to turn this entire labyrinth upside down with the magic that boiled inside of them. Astrid could choose to go with the others, get them settled, be safe. Or she could stay here.

Whooping calls flooded the halls around them. It sounded like the trolls were surrounding them on all sides. Their shouts and cries of anticipation were surely because they were about to fight, which meant Astrid had run out of time.

"Start on the upper levels," she told the other priestesses. "Tear it down from the top to the bottom so you don't trap anyone within. Make sure there are obvious escape routes so we don't leave the trolls behind, do you hear me?"

They nodded and darted away, each of them looking for the structures that supported the labyrinth. Soon enough, this place would be nothing more than rubble.

Astrid joined the women escaping, rushing through the crowd so that she was ahead of them all. "Let's go, ladies. This way!"

She remembered how to leave, but she didn't anticipate running into a wall of guards. Apparently, they'd caught wind of the escape plan. These men were far too prepared, and she knew without a doubt this was going to cause a problem she could not control. The guards all had swords in their hands and hard expressions that made her nervous.

She skidded to a halt, feeling the tension radiating at her back from so many women who had power they had yet to use. "You will let us pass," she told the men.

"Those aren't our orders."

"Whose orders?" she hissed.

"The king himself. We are to contain the problem within the labyrinth." The man bared his teeth in a feral smile. "And you are definitely a problem. Weren't you supposed to be in a cell with the rest of them?"

That was enough.

Astrid lifted her hands, weaving magic with every gesture of her fingers. She pulled the spirits from their bodies, feeling the anger of their guides, who knew damn well these men shouldn't submit to a king who was so selfish and cruel. The beings who were meant to guide each of these men were so angry it was hard for her to even breathe.

Then she released them and watched as the animals all turned on the men. Suddenly, there were glowing blue beasts all around them. Wolves that hunted, gnawing through armor to the flesh beneath. A bear that stood on its back legs and roared so loud she had to press her hands to her ears as it echoed. A horse thundered past her, rearing up and kicking at the air near one of the guard's heads.

"Come on!" Astrid shouted over the clamoring madness. "We have to go now!"

The women rushed with her, all of them trying to get through the teeming mass of guards who were trying to fight off the creatures that Astrid had summoned. It was their only shot, though, and it seemed to be working. Until Astrid careened around a corner and came face to face with her own nightmare.

The king himself stood at the exit of the labyrinth, surrounded by even more guards. These were men to fear. The guards at the labyrinth were trained and capable, yes, but they weren't the people who had won the right to keep the king alive. The most talented, most hardened men in the kingdom were given that role. Now they all stood in front of her.

Clapping his hands, the king walked through his crowd of guards to stand before her. "Impressive, Priestess. For a moment, I almost believed you could do it."

So had she.

Chapter 43

Bjorn learned many things while he was in the red haze of battle. First, the guards here in the labyrinth had never been prepared to handle an uprising. All of their training had been to prevent anything like this from ever happening. They didn't know what to do when a full grown troll, hardened by years of battle, came barreling at them down a hall that was entirely too small for them to do anything but hold their ground.

Second, he knew without a doubt that revealing this place to the people of this kingdom was not going to be enough. The problem was deep within the core of the human kingdom.

The men who worked here were regular people. They were guards, yes. They were trained to fight, and the average human was likely better suited to a garden than they were to a battlefield. But these men weren't noblemen making a profit off the sale of other people's bodies. They weren't even making much money at all.

He had to assume they weren't, considering how quickly they tried to run. None of them had stood to fight against him with any sort of bravery. They all ran for their lives, begging him to spare them when he had absolutely no intent to do so—not when they'd stood by and allowed the atrocities in here to happen for years.

But as he cleaved through them, slicing through their soft flesh, that led him to the realization that the problem was so much higher up than these men. Showing the dark underbelly to the average person in this kingdom would only make them hate living here, but where would they go? The poor could not escape this place any more than he could.

The nobility were the problem, those men and women who had gorged themselves on food and drink while others starved right next to them. Those were the people he needed to target. They were the ones who funded the labyrinth, and who likely sent people into it as well. He needed them to suffer, but those were not the people he fought. They weren't anywhere near this place.

Bjorn imagined them dotted all across the kingdom, each of them in more and more elaborate homes, beautiful and guarded. It would be hard to kill them. Harder to change their minds about this place. They made money here. They enjoyed being here, and that meant...

Fuck, that meant this might all be for very little. He might only be able to free those who were here already, but no vengeance would be served.

It made him fight even harder. It made the deaths he dealt even bloodier and more cruel. He couldn't tear at the people he wanted to tear at, nor could he make an impact with this fight.

He would return to his king, beaten again.

"Bjorn!" The voice shouted through the red haze of his mind, but it was hard to focus on that when all he could see was blood. He wanted to listen, though. He needed to. This was no place to not hear those who were trying to help him.

He could hurt another troll. Just like his father had.

"Bjorn!"

But he couldn't hear that person now. He was stuck in the old memory, the one where his father was killing all who made noise and Bjorn just had to stay quiet. Or he had to fight back.

Suddenly, in his mind he was larger. The size he was now. Facing his father as he had only done a few times in his life before the old man had died a glorious death. But now they were both berserkers, both of them lost to the rage that controlled all of their bloodline. He had feared what would happen if he had challenged his father like this, when the old man had been alive. He'd never even thought to challenge him because what would have happened? Would they both have died?

"Bull!" the shout sliced through the thoughts and pulled him back into the present. He blinked, and suddenly the world was in front of him again. He could see all the bodies that littered the ground, all the guards who had lost their lives trying desperately to fight him off. And as he stood there, he also noticed that Rabbit was way at the end of the hall, staring at him from around a corner.

Bjorn snorted, trying to clear the scent of death from his lungs.

"You with us again?" Rabbit asked.

"You have too much experience getting me out of that," he muttered.

"I'm aware. We've got a problem."

"Which is?"

"The king himself," Rabbit growled. "He's here, and he's got your woman."

Bjorn's entire body went cold. What did he mean the king had Astrid? No, she was supposed to be tucked away somewhere safe by now. Clearly, she had some reason to come into the labyrinth itself, but she should have left by now. Shouldn't she?

Breathing hard, he stalked toward Rabbit and headed down the hall his friend was in. "Where is she?"

"At the front entrance with the rest of the women. The king isn't letting any of them leave."

"She tried to go out the front?" he swore. "Why would she do that?"

"Probably because she got it in her head to save all the other women who were trapped in here. Brave but not entirely smart." Rabbit shook his head, darting ahead of him and leading the way. His friend had always had a better hold over the patterns of this labyrinth. Sometimes he'd thought if Rabbit could have just gotten out of his cell, then he would have been able to go anywhere.

He should apologize for leaving without Rabbit. His old friend didn't deserve to be left behind. None of them did. They were all good men and women who had been trapped here for horrible reasons, and he should have released them all when he'd been freed.

He should have fought to come back here, but Bjorn had been such a coward it had been hard to return. He hadn't wanted to come back to the labyrinth, even though he'd known they all needed him.

"Rabbit," he said as they stalked through the halls. "I should have taken you with me."

"There wasn't time."

"No, but I still should have tried."

"You couldn't have. If you had taken me with you, then you would have been caught. Then we all would have been stuck here forever, or one of us would have died by now. You did what you had to do." He peered around a corridor and then headed down it. "Focus on what you're going to do to save her."

"Rabbit. Can you stop for a second?"

"We don't have time for this!" Rabbit's shout echoed through the halls, startling Bjorn into silence as the yellow troll went on a rant. "You started all of this, Bjorn. You helped the others escape. You got out yourself. No one is mad at you for doing so. It's a good thing you were able to get out of here and a very good thing that you came back. There is nothing you need to apologize for. We all know where we are, what happened, and how hard it is to get out. So just be thankful you were one of the few who managed."

They were still charging through the halls, with nothing to bother them other than the trail of blood that made the stone floor slick. "I didn't want to come back. Not for you. Not for anyone. I feel guilty about that, my old friend."

"None of us would have blamed you for leaving us here. You got out, and your life started again. That's the best thing that could have happened. If you hadn't come back at all, I would have gone on assuming that you just... lived, Bjorn. That's all any of us want. Just to live and allow ourselves to live while forgetting this whole place ever existed." Rabbit kicked a wall as they headed out and then paused. "We're getting close. What's your plan?"

"Kill them all." He stalked forward, ready to do exactly that until Rabbit's hand landed flat on his chest. He froze, looking down at his much smaller friend. "What?"

"You can't go into it like that. The king brought his best, and you are not up to the same standard. Bull, you have fought a lot of different people and creatures, but you haven't fought the king's best with far more of them at his beck and call than we have."

"What would you suggest then? Try to bargain with the man who trapped us all?"

"No, of course not. I would suggest that you think about this plan before you hurt yourself."

There was nothing to think about. He could barge into all of them. It didn't matter if they injured him or hurt him. He would fight as no one else had ever fought before because Astrid was there.

If he heard her scream, heard her call out to him for even a moment, it would all be over. Bjorn wouldn't be able to control himself, not in the slightest.

"Rabbit," he snarled. "You only have a few seconds to convince me of another plan."

"She's your troll wife, isn't she?"

"Yes."

"Then use her magic."

He couldn't use her magic. They amplified each other's magic. That was all. "She has the amplification. All I could ever do was talk to animals, Rabbit. That's it. I'm not good with magic anyway. It all gets jumbled up in my head."

"If she can do it, so can you, old friend. What I need you to do is use whatever that is." Rabbit pointed across the hall to another that split off from the main area. He could see there were other trolls there.

A lot of them.

Trolls who had fought beside him long ago, but who were now used to fighting together. They were willing to battle beside him, knowing that he would take the brunt of the pain and injuries for them. Ragnar was there as well, his lavender features hard to miss among the others. All Bjorn had to do was... was...

He could feel her, he realized. The brightness of her magic stretched into his until he could almost feel the glow in his palms. She wanted him to use that power. She wanted him to spread it, coil it around the trolls...

Oh, he realized what the plan was.

"I'm going to pull out their fylgja," he murmured. "They'll fight with us, not just against the person who had ignored it."

"You're what?"

He grinned at Rabbit. "There are many benefits to having a troll wife, my friend. Someday you will see."

Rabbit made a face. "Do not curse me with a woman, Bull. I have no interest in one."

Of course he didn't. But Bjorn was quite certain that, whether troll wife or husband, the magic was still spread to each. Regardless, he was quite certain he could convince the spirits to fight with them. Sure, he'd only seen her summon them to battle against their own person, but... surely they would fight together as well. It had to be possible.

So he wove the magic, pulling it from the first few trolls across the way. It took some doing. After all, the spirits were only there to guide the troll they were connected to. But he could speak with them, unlike Astrid. He could tell them why it was so important that they fight alongside the person they guided and protected. This was about protection, after all. It was about keeping all of them safe.

More and more he pulled. Wolves and beasts from the woods. Giant spiders, elk, monstrous crocodiles, over and over again. Until finally he turned to his dear friend and reached for the creature within him.

Rabbit sighed, reached down, and lifted his spirit animal up by its very long ears. "Really, Bjorn?"

He shrugged. "I don't make them, you know. I just pull out what is already there."

"A rabbit? What am I supposed to do with this?"

"Tell it to bite?"

Rabbit held it out to him and said, "Bite."

The little creature was highly uninterested in that option. It just hung there, dangling from its ears and twitching its tiny little nose. Probably not a very good guardian spirit but one that fit his friend.

"Stay behind us all," he said, trying very hard not to chuckle. "The last few of them will be terrified of your beast. I am certain of it."

"I will kick you the first chance I get."

"If I'm still alive, yes. You may."

Then, Bjorn walked into the hall. Just himself, subtly motioning for everyone else to stay where they were. He didn't want the king to know that there were more of them. At least, not yet.

He stared down the hall to see the room where it opened up. There were plenty of guards, at least twenty men pointing crossbows at him and even more ready with swords and blades.

"You brought a lot of soldiers to fight me," he said, meandering ever forward.

He couldn't see the king or Astrid yet, but he was glad for it. It was already hard to keep ahold of himself. Seeing her, and the fear he knew he'd recognize in her eyes, would make him lose his mind.

But then he saw the king. He was hidden among all the gleaming armor and all the nonsense that he'd brought with him. Did they really believe flimsy metal armor would keep Bjorn away from their vital organs?

The king stared him down. "You were a dog ready to take any order I gave you. I told you to bark, and what did you do? You barked."

"I did what I had to do to stay alive," Bjorn replied. "And now, I am back for revenge. Where is my woman?"

"Your woman?"

"My wife," Bjorn snarled.

The crowd of soldiers parted to show her, with a sword at her throat and her posture straight as an arrow. She stood there, unafraid of anyone who touched her, because she was looking at him.

"You have one chance to let her go," Bjorn said. "One."

"Slit her throat," the king said, his tone bored. "Then kill them all, even the ones hiding in the next passage. Will you?"

Bjorn's entire world slowed down to the motion of the sword that was already drawing across her throat as the familiar red haze tore through his eyesight. He heard the shouts of his own men, the trolls behind him who raged at the thought that one of their own would be injured. He heard Rabbit shouting at him, but he didn't understand the words.

They'd touched her. Now they would all pay.

Chapter 44

She would always remember this moment. Everything happened so quickly, it was almost impossible to track it all. She was being held by a guard, likely as a way to antagonize Bjorn.

The other women had been able to run, though. They slipped away while the king had been talking to her, and he hadn't cared all that much. Women like them were dispensable, after all. He could find more. It would take so little for him to find as many women as he needed as prizes. They had no choice, because he was king.

But Astrid was different. Astrid had the attention of a troll that the king very much wanted. And that meant she was useful. She knew how men like this thought, and she knew that she was going to suffer just because he wanted to use her pain.

Watching Bjorn walk down that empty hall had nearly broken her heart. She'd thought there would be countless trolls helping him, representing him. Trolls who fought alongside him and instead, he was all by himself.

Maybe he'd done the same thing as her. Maybe he had sent away the trolls and all those who had been captured, so they would all remain safe. It sounded like something he would do.

She didn't pay attention to what they were saying. The words didn't matter. All that mattered was that she got a single moment to look at him before they died.

But she wanted to live. She wanted to live with him, to grow with him, to see everything unfold in their lives as they grew a garden and a family and all the other beautiful things that had been a potential in their future.

Then a sword lifted to her throat, and she knew that wasn't going to happen at all. The king had other plans.

"Slit her throat," the king said, and she could hear how little he cared about any of this as he spoke. "Then kill them all, even the ones hiding in the next passage. Will you?"

Astrid felt the cold metal pressing more firmly against her throat, and something in her just snapped. She didn't care if there were so many soldiers that the odds seemed insurmountable. She didn't care if they served the king and therefore felt as though they were in the right. They were not innocent.

Magic boiled at her fingertips at the same time a boom echoed throughout the entirety of the labyrinth. It was sheer luck that the other priestesses had chosen that time to blast through another level, but the floor beneath their feet shifted.

The soldiers let out angry sounds, some of them reaching for the king at the same moment Bjorn slammed into them. The rage she saw pouring off of him was something she could use. She took it from him, an unending, vast amount of anger that she then poured into all the men around her. They were suddenly enraged too. They wanted to fight, and it didn't matter who they fought.

The guards turned on each other, all of them battling without thought of who or what they were hitting.

All except for the few closest to the king. He glared at them all, and she swore she heard him mouth something along the lines of, "Weak."

He turned with the closest guards, six men who were the largest of them all. They started down a corridor at the same moment Bjorn stood in front of her. She could see there was nothing left of him. Just the berserker, who had killed hundreds, or perhaps even thousands of people at this point. He was rage and glory, venom and vice. He wanted to destroy the entire world before him, and it didn't matter whose death he counted as long as he was covered in blood.

"It's me," she whispered. "It's me, Bjorn."

Then she had the marvelous and miraculous sight of his berserker recognizing her. She could tell when it did. The beast inside him knew exactly who she was. It blinked, and then it turned away from her.

Instead of fighting her or trying to harm her, it stood between her and pain. It was a shield as the guards fought, some of their weapons coming so close that they might have clipped her. Instead, he protected her.

Heart in her throat, she prayed to any god who would listen to keep him safe. She wanted to see him still in one piece when all of this ended. And apparently, he felt the same way.

He did everything he could to keep himself safe. Instead, he took hits meant for her. He was bleeding from multiple places, and throughout it all Bjorn remained stoic and calm, blocking any attack effortlessly and then killing the man without hesitation.

She blinked, and suddenly there was a flood of other trolls. Men, women, and their spirit guides, all of them rushing into the fray. They didn't come just to her aid, but it felt as though the trolls were here to protect her.

Then she saw a flash of yellow rushing toward them. A very familiar yellow that had her gasping and racing out from behind Bjorn. She trusted him to protect them both, and he did. Somehow. Somehow he was controlling himself even though historically he had never been able to do that before.

Rabbit caught her up in his arms, laughing with her and then framing her face with his massive hands. "The king?"

"He took off in that direction."

"Take your berserker and go. He cannot get away, Priestess. He needs to be punished. For all of us."

She nodded, then looked up at Bjorn. "Will you come with me to hunt the king?"

He tilted his head down to look at her, nearly no expression on his face. But then he nodded slowly, and she conversed with the berserker perhaps for the very first time. His voice was lower, gravel rumbling in the depths of the mountains. "Let us hunt, Priestess."

She didn't think about it, didn't hesitate. She just turned with Bjorn and chased after the king.

But the farther she got from the other trolls, the more she questioned whether this was the right thing to do. The king could have any manner of tricks up his sleeve. Likely he had a plan that would keep him away from the trolls, but she feared what it would mean. Did he have some kind of hidden weapon in these corridors? Or was he leaving another way she did not know was an exit? Perhaps he would bring them out to an entire army of people who were waiting for them on the other side.

It was the second option.

They finally caught up to the king at the end of this corridor with all his guards working on a complicated looking structure that had many wheels and dials. A hidden secret in the wall, she suspected. A door that was likely never meant to be opened unless under dire circumstances. Which, of course, this was.

After all, the troll he had been torturing for years was hunting him, and he was the fool who had trapped himself.

Another echoing boom rocked through the labyrinth, and earth rained down on their heads. Astrid wasn't sure how long this place would even stay standing, but it seemed appropriate given the circumstances. The last battle between the man who had created this terrible place and the people he had hurt.

The king turned to see him, and she could tell there was fear in his eyes. Fear, because he had seen how Bjorn could fight, and because he had no idea how powerful Astrid was.

"You should never have come down here," she said. "Why you would ever come yourself, I will never understand."

"I have always handled things myself."

"You are the monster that causes nothing but pain and suffering. You are the one who should hide," she spat.

The king lifted his arms as though he was not surprised by what she said. "I know. You all think I am horrible, but I just know what's going to happen. I know when everything is going to happen."

So that was his power. He could see the future. But how far ahead could he see it?

She narrowed her eyes, planning out something that would end his life very quickly. But she saw him react almost immediately. He snapped his fingers, and the guards surrounded him, a wall of human flesh that would do very little to stop any of them but would buy the king enough time to get out of that complicated door.

There were two men still working on it. The gears ground against each other, rust and age making it hard for them to turn, but they were managing the massive puzzle behind them swiftly.

"To think," the king said. "It would be you in the end. How poetic."

"Me?"

The guards parted just enough for her to see him. Those icy blue eyes captured hers. "Haven't you always wondered why you look so much like the princess? Why do all of the most powerful priestesses look like my daughter?"

"Because you hunted us down in the streets. You chose the girls who look like your daughter so you could pawn us off. The lords all want your daughter, but you would never give her to someone like them, so you chose instead to find little girls who looked like her." Astrid's voice dripped with rage. "You were wrong for that."

"I didn't have to find you. I always knew where you were." He grinned, and that expression made every hair on her body rise. "You're mine, after all. All of you. I found the most powerful women in this kingdom and I created power. So much power, and all the kind I could gift to those who I deemed worthy. My mother was the one with blonde hair. She looked just like you, and your sister, and my daughter, and all the other golden women I created."

Astrid felt like the floor had dropped out from under her. Surely he lied. Surely no man was so twisted that he would do that.

And then it all hit her. She'd believed no man could be so evil that he would do what he had done to Rose. If he was telling the truth, not only had he tried to sell off his daughter to a lord who had wanted to defile her, but the king had punished his own blood in the labyrinth.

Her words turned ragged and raw. "You could do that to your own child?"

"Do what, exactly?"

"You could condemn your own child to a life in this darkness? You did it not just to my sister, but to me, likely to others as well. We are your daughters."

"You are an experiment," he hissed. "Not my children. You do not get to have that name. I have one daughter, and she is the most powerful of you all. Her mother was half elven, and she has more power in her pinky than you could ever dream of. I created perfection. The closest being to an elf that is alive. You are nothing but scraps that I threw out onto the streets because you were not as powerful as she."

Astrid's heart shattered. Not just for herself, but for all the priestesses who looked like her. All the priestesses who had cried as children in the sisterhood, wondering where their parents were and if they had been loved before they were given up to that place.

"You..." She didn't even know what to say.

What was there to say to a man like that? A man who should have loved her. A man who had tried to kill her rather than care for a child he had helped create.

And who was her mother? What woman had been forced to bear a child, likely under duress? The king wouldn't take no for an answer, not from any woman. What had happened to her mother?

These were answers she would never get. The king watched every expression on her face before he shook his head in disapproval.

"Now, girl, you know the truth. And you are likely the only one to ever know it. You can take that to your grave, as payment for letting me go."

"I don't want to let you go."

"You have no choice. You should have been dead back there, after one of my soldiers slit your throat. I'm letting you live now, so it's a trade. You wouldn't want to kill your own father, would you?"

She felt something cold growing in her chest. Something that was so unlike her she almost didn't recognize this part of herself.

After all, she had spent so much time dreaming up what her father would be like. All the while, she'd been the perfect priestess. Astrid had known everything that was happening in every part of the kingdom. She'd kept secrets. She'd played out every opportunity for what the future would be so she could appropriately prepare for whatever happened.

But right now, she didn't want to prepare. She wanted revenge.

"I wouldn't want to kill my father," she replied, straightening her shoulders. "But you made it very clear that I am not your daughter."

Bjorn lunged forward, as though her words untethered a leash that held him in place. Astrid did not hide her face this time. She watched as he tore through the guards, one by one. It didn't matter that they stuck swords in him, that they slashed at his skin or that they tried to shoot him with arrows. He did not stop until he loomed above the king.

Then Bjorn grabbed him by the back of the neck and twisted. Slowly. She could see the panic in the king's eyes, and the way he tried desperately to get away. But she could also see the realization that he wasn't getting out of this one. He peered into the future, his eyes going white, and then all she could see was despair. There was no future where he survived.

The snap of his neck echoed through the hall, and he fell limp in Bjorn's grasp.

Her beloved troll let the body drop and wiped his hands on his already bloody pants, as though he could clean them.

The angry energy seemed to drop from him, then he listed to the side, reaching out one massive arm to brace himself upon the wall.

"Bjorn?" she asked, rushing to his side and planting her hand on his chest. She couldn't hold him up, though. He was too massive. "What do you need?"

"Ragnar," he breathed.

"Where is he?"

"Back with the others. Tending to the wounded."

Ragnar's voice boomed through the corridor. "I am not, in fact. Astrid, I need you to move. Time is of the essence."

She stood to the side, wringing her hands as she watched Ragnar work. His cool magic immediately healed many of the wounds dotting Bjorn's body, but there were still so many oozing blood. She could hardly see where they were because he was so covered in red, and how much of it was his? How much of it was others?

Their gazes met, and Bjorn gave her a little sad smile. "I'm all right," he said, giving her a firm nod. "I'll be fine, Astrid. I'll be fine."

She wasn't so sure he was correct. But she would stand here waiting for him to get better. No matter what.

Chapter 45

So we are at war," King Egil murmured, seated upon his throne.

The troll king never sat comfortably, but Bjorn supposed that was partly due to his wings. There wasn't a way for Egil to sit that didn't twist his wings to the sides or turn his entire body in the opposite direction. He ended up looking like a giant bird stretched across his chair, with his wings draped painfully around him.

The strange look of him was terrifying, to say the least. King Egil was horrific and powerful and had every right to end Bjorn's life. He had gone against every single order, and perhaps every single sense of reason as well.

Sure, he could argue that the berserker within him had made the call. The human king had been prey. He'd been running away from someone who was designed to hunt and kill, but that wasn't why he was dead. Bjorn loathed liars. He had been in control in that moment. He had known every single thing he was doing when he had his hand wrapped around that weaselly little man's throat.

Humans were so easy to kill. So much easier than they should've been. Bjorn had only needed to twist his hand before death had come for King James.

Unfortunately, such a tiny action had led them to this point.

He knelt on the cold stones before his king with Astrid at his side. The others were behind both of them. Ragnar, Rabbit, Gunnar, and all the trolls who had fought with them. They were the ones who had survived and been saved. Though they had lost a great number, he was relieved to see it was even less than he had thought it would be.

Technically, they had been victorious. They'd released their people from that prison, and they had brought them all home. They had destroyed the labyrinth. They just hadn't anticipated the human king getting involved.

King Egil tapped his foot on the ground, the only thing that Bjorn could see with his head lowered. The long talons on his bare feet scraped along the floor as the king thought.

"It was bound to happen someday," King Egil finally said. "The humans have been begging for a war for ages. They have been hunting on our mountain, depleting our food supply. They have kidnapped and taken our people, making them fight for sport while their own made money from death. This future has been barreling toward us, and I have heard it in the night. The drums of war pound throughout our mountain, begging us to fight for what we should always fight for. Our freedom."

A few of the warband leaders thudded their fists to their chests. It almost sounded like drums as they did so. And Bjorn knew, for the moment at least, he was going to stay alive.

"You, Destroyer."

He lifted his head, nervous for what he might find waiting for him. A glare from the king was as good as a death sentence.

He was surprised to see the king appear kind. Or, at the very least, he didn't seem angry.

"You have helped our people as only your bloodline can. I have heard from our healer that you were gravely injured."

"Not gravely, your highness. Injured yes. But I would have been fine." He thought, at least. Gravely made it seem like he was on his deathbed, but he hadn't been that. He'd even have been able to get home if he'd needed to. It wouldn't have been a pleasant journey, but he'd been injured worse in his early years in the labyrinth.

The king cocked his brow. "I have heard from the healer what his official opinion of it was, and I know that you took many swords that were not intended for you. While you might have plunged us into a war, you still brought home all those trolls we thought were lost. The lives you saved today are valuable. Not just to their families, but to all of Trollveggen."

The weight of it all released. Bjorn had done something good, unlike his father, who had hurt so many with what his blood carried. The beast, the Bull, had helped people, and that... that felt good.

But then the king leaned forward, and Bjorn knew he would not like what his king had to say next. "I will forgive you if you agree to fight with us in this upcoming war. We have need of your abilities, Bjorn. Our people need to be protected by one such as you. No more fighting me on this."

And there was that weight again. Lying flat across his shoulders and pushing him down until he was kneeling once more before the king. Bjorn pressed his fists into the stone hard enough that his knuckles ached.

"I agree," he said, the words grinding out between his teeth.

Although he didn't want to fight, he couldn't lie and say it didn't feel good to do so. He had been born for this. He struggled against himself every step of the way, but perhaps it wouldn't be so bad now that he could control the beast.

Astrid had helped him unlock that. Just as she helped him now with her hand pressed over his, easing the anger and anxiety that churned in his chest. Instead, all he could feel was pride that he had done something right. He'd saved people, and he could focus on that now.

Turning his head, he mouthed, "Thank you," to his troll wife.

Astrid smiled at him, and that soft expression healed so much more than he could ever say.

The king once more leaned back on his throne. "Warlords. We prepare for war. The princess has taken control over the kingdom, along with a cabinet of battle hardened men. We fight the humans, no matter what they bring next. I refuse to sit here and wait for them to attack us. Kill them if they are on the mountain. Hunt them down. Make it clear that we were the ones who killed their king and we will not stop now. We will no longer stand for the mistreatment of our people."

Boisterous cries rang throughout the entire hall. It was then that Bjorn realized these trolls had been waiting to fight. They weren't angry cries over him starting a war. The trolls were elated. They had been wanting to do this for countless years, but the king had never allowed them to do so.

Finally, the meeting was over. The king dismissed them, standing and striding toward the hidden chambers in the back where he would meet with the highest warlords. They would decide where and what the next step was.

For now, Bjorn wanted to gather up his bright one and head out into the sun. Even if it was a little dangerous.

"Astrid," he said, helping her stand. "Would you—"

"Before you run off again, might I have a word?"

They both looked over at Rabbit, who stood with them. His friend from the cells already looked better. Just being out in the fresh air, traveling over the mountain with them and eating more than his fair share of the rations, had made him look more like a troll and less like a prisoner. His yellow skin was still perhaps a sickly color, but his hair was no longer greasy. He wore traditional troll clothing, leather straps over his chest, which was perhaps a little broader now than it had been only a few days ago.

"What is it, Rabbit?" he asked.

"It's actually Torben," he corrected. Rabbit's chest puffed up a bit with pride. "Now that we're out of the labyrinth, I think it's better if we call each other by our true names and not the names that place gave us."

Bjorn felt something in his chest creak. It wasn't entirely his heart feeling soft toward this other troll, but it was... something. He grunted. "Torben. I am Bjorn."

"It's nice to finally meet you, Bjorn." He gave a soft smile. "But I thought... Well, I wanted to thank you for coming back for me after all. I'm still looking for a place to live and remembering how to be a troll after everything that's happened, but it's still better. Everything is so much better." Torben pressed his hand to his chest. "All of us want to thank you for that, Bjorn. You should take a moment and talk to them. They remember you from those fights. They remember the monster they were all terrified of. But now they get to see you as a man."

Perhaps someday. Perhaps even soon he could talk to them. To speak with all the others who had been trapped just like him.

But right now he wanted to be alone with his troll wife, and to show her how much she meant to him.

He shook his head and patted Torben's shoulder. "You are a good friend. Always were. We will mend our friendship here until we forget there was ever a time in that labyrinth. I promise you that. There will be new stories to tell, and excitement for us to rejoice in. But today, I am going to focus on my wife."

Torben blew out a long breath. "I had a feeling you would say that. It's a good thing to do as well, I suppose. Just take some time soon to see everyone again, will you? It'll be good for them to see that you have made it out and are happy. Some of them are feeling that they might never be happy again."

"It's a long journey. One we will make together."

He gave Torben one more squeeze before glancing down at Astrid. She was staring up at him with tears in her eyes and a soft expression that made his stomach twist. He liked it when she looked at him like that. All soft and quiet, as though she was proud of something he had done.

And she was, he knew. She was proud that they were here, they'd survived, and that they were together.

"I have a surprise for you, bright one. Would you like to see it?"

"A surprise?" Astrid asked, her brows furrowing. "When did you have time to get a surprise for me?"

"It's not exactly one that I got, but one that I pulled some strings to..." He didn't know how to explain this. "Just come with me."

He guided her out of the castle and into the forest beyond. The purple leafed trees here were nearly bare. Even though the hollow mountain was safe from the weather up above, their kingdom had always shown the same seasons. Winter was coming hard and fast.

Soon enough, there would only be icy air for them to breathe, and they would be holed up in their homes much more. He was so excited to cuddle up by the fire with her and listen to her read him stories from countless books that he would soon buy her.

Their life would be quiet until it could no longer be. He'd already decided that.

Past the trees, they followed a stream, and Astrid was already asking him questions. "Where are we going?" She chuckled, laughing as he shook his head and pressed his finger to his lips. "Bjorn, you have to tell me."

He didn't. And now they were going uphill. Farther and farther up, until he could hear her harsh breathing and the way she kept stopping to put her hands on her hips. He needed to get her outside more. At least then she might keep up with him.

Bjorn hid the smile on his face and the laughter that continued to bubble up his chest as they reached the small tunnel that would lead them outside. This was where he had been leading her, although the tunnel had clearly not been used for a very long time.

He brushed aside a few cobwebs, then headed in before her. At least he would be the one to deal with the cave spiders that were as large as her hand. She would scream and send the whole mountain rushing up to help them if he didn't. Besides, he'd never minded a few webs clinging to his face and horns.

Finally, he lifted his hand and brushed aside a waterfall of ivy to reveal a small glen before her.

It was a small outcropping on the side of the mountain. The hunter's cabin that was there had survived and weathered the times. Made of massive timbers, it was a log cabin that was well suited to surviving the winter. A small brick chimney came out of the top, and

Bjorn knew it was connected to a fireplace just as large as the one in his father's Trollveggen home. The difference was that this log cabin was surrounded by flowers.

They were late bloomers, so the pretty autumn petals were intensely vibrant. He remembered his mother staying here a few times when she'd visited his father. He'd been captivated by all the flowers she planted, and how she'd told him that they would last for years to come. "These are flowers that will survive," she'd said as she'd put them in the ground.

"This is my mother's cabin," he said. "Or at least the one my father built for her. She would never come into Trollveggen because she hated being underground, and hated not seeing the sun every day. So he built this for her here, where she could be wild and free."

"But wouldn't the humans find her?"

"Unlikely." He gestured all around them. There were walls of stones so high, he doubted anyone could climb down or up them. And the sheer cliff on the other edge disappeared so far down that anyone would die if they fell. "This is not where the humans look. No food grows here, no animals drop down. It's a hidden place. Secretive and safe. And if anyone ever made it here, there's a direct path into Trollveggen where she would have been safe very quickly."

He turned to look at her and the sunlight that danced across her features. "For my golden bride, I wanted to give you the sun. Because there is never a time, place, or jewel that is as beautiful as you with the sun shining in your hair."

"Bjorn," she breathed. "You can be such a poet when you want to be."

"My love, I am but your humble servant." He took her into his arms, smoothing her hair back from her face so he could gaze upon her. "And now, all I wish is to make a life with you. To live with you here, in the mountain, wherever it is you wish to be."

"All I want to be is with you," she said with a soft laugh. "Wherever that might lead us."

He leaned down to kiss her, and finally his soul felt at peace. Even though someday soon he would fight again.

Now he had something to fight for.

Chapter 46

Astrid had never thought she would be excited to explore a log cabin, but here she was. Excited to walk into what would have essentially been a hut to her not all that long ago. Now she thought it just might be the home she'd always dreamt of. Because he would be in it.

She reached for his hand, tugging him with her as they headed into the cabin. It really was adorable. A sizeable space where more than a few people could live. Gardens dotted along the exterior, wild and unkempt, but they were made with a loving hand. Flowers and vegetables, even a few pumpkins that were already quite large and ready to be harvested. There were three windows on each side, which made her think that perhaps it would be bright and sunny within.

As she opened the door, she prepared herself for the prospect of more cleaning. If his father's other home had shown her anything, it was that there would be a lot of work in this place waiting for her. And yet, when she stepped inside, she was surprised to see that it was very clean.

The living room was far more comfortable than the one deep

within the mountain. There were more couches, patchwork quilts that were made with loving hands. There were paintings on the wall, of flowers and landscapes. The massive fireplace in the back was obviously familiar. She was certain his father had built both of them. But this was almost a formal parlor rather than a utilitarian room with an area for seating and cooking.

"It's so clean," she marveled.

"I had Maia and Rose help while we were gone. I knew there was a chance I wouldn't come back, but I still wanted you to have somewhere comfortable for yourself. I knew..." Bjorn cleared his throat. "I knew it would be hard for you if I were gone, so I wanted to do something special for you."

This man. Her heart shattered at the thought that he'd been planning to never return while she'd just been planning to keep him safe. He hadn't feared his own death. He'd feared her being lonely and sad in the mountain without him. So he had created an oasis of safety for her.

Her breath caught, and she turned to look at him with her heart in her eyes. "You did all this for me?"

"I want you to be happy here," he replied. "I don't want you to regret coming with me, or giving up all that you did. I know you lived a life of luxury, and I am ashamed to admit there are other trolls here who could give you the same kind of life you are used to, but I am not one of those trolls. I hope perhaps that this will be enough."

"You foolish man," she whispered, walking up to him and planting her hands on his chest. She stared up at his confused expression. "They could never give me what you do. Because there is no man in this realm who would love me like you do."

His expression softened, and he leaned down to kiss her. She could feel every ounce of his love in that gentle, delicate kiss. He took his time, lingering at the corners of her lips and on the swell of her cheeks. He kissed her eyes, as he always did, two sweet kisses that pressed onto her like he knew how much she loved it when he treated her so gently.

Astrid took his hand, tugging him through the room. "I assume there is a bedroom here?"

"There is, but I thought you would want to see the rest of the house first."

She shook her head meaningfully. "No, there's something else I'd like to do before all that."

Immediately, fire burned in his gaze. She knew that he understood her meaning, and that he would worship her soon enough. He had time now, and yet there was no need to rush. They had battled, and they had won. Now she wanted to celebrate that they were both still here.

Bjorn led her to the bedroom in a whirl of movement. She wasn't even sure that she paid attention to where they were going or any other room they walked through. All she saw was a massive bed, one that was circular in shape, with no visible frame.

He backed her knees up to it, breathless already as he stared down at her. Without a word, he started unbuttoning every single button down the front of her dress. Carefully. He took his time, teasing her with little touches as the backs of his fingers toyed with her skin. Never enough, but that feather light brush of his knuckles made her skin burn.

First, he lingered at her breasts, and the tips hardened to near pain. Then down her belly, which clenched in anticipation. And then finally she felt his fingers between her thighs, just barely as he undid the last few buttons.

Bjorn got down on his knees before her, sinking until he could stare up at her with all that awe in his expression making her feel like a goddess.

"There are many beautiful things in this world," he murmured, then pressed a kiss to her thigh. "Wisps floating above a pond. Moonlight peeking through leaves. Stars so bright in the sky that they illuminate the universe. I would give up every single one of them if it meant I could gaze upon your beauty for even a second."

"Bjorn," she whispered, running her fingers through his hair.

He moved the dress from her shoulders and let it fall onto the ground. She stood before him completely nude while he remained on his knees. Her hands found his horns, guiding him between her legs where she knew he wanted to be most.

A deep groan echoed through his chest, vibrating through her entire being and shaking through her hips as his hands came up to grab her ass. With a firm grip, he held her steady as his tongue gave her one long, slow lick.

Astrid's head fell back. She would never, ever get used to that long troll tongue. So flexible, he found every part of her that made her shudder and quake with his touch. He groaned again, and this time the sound seemed to vibrate his tongue as he flicked it over her, again and again.

She moaned out his name, already shaking with need. She was desperate, but he was so apathetic to her desperation.

"What do you want, wife?" he asked, his fingers replacing his tongue as he asked the question.

"Make me see the stars."

"So soon?"

"Please."

He always seemed to love it when she begged. Two massive fingers suddenly plunged inside of her, stretching her near to bursting. A little shocked gasp escaped her even as his tongue found her clit once more. He circled it, so lightly she swore sometimes she didn't feel his tongue at all until suddenly he pressed down hard.

She exploded. Her inner walls clenched around his fingers, gripping him tightly, and she swore she could hear him making the same sounds she was making. A moan of pleasure, a grumbled curse as he sucked so hard it made a second orgasm chase the first.

He was holding her upright at this point. So he guided her onto the bed and laid her out like a banquet for him to feast upon.

She lifted her arms, reaching for him. But he stood instead of lying with her, Bjorn took off his shirt, revealing miles of muscle that made her want to sink her teeth into him. All that green, rippling muscle did was make her feel even more rabid for him.

But it was hard to do anything after he'd made her come twice. The languid feeling that filled her body made her muscles soft and her plan to seduce him even harder.

"Aren't you coming here?" she asked, arching a brow and trying to look sexy on the bed while also feeling a bit like her limbs were made of water.

"I'm joining you, but I'm not done with you yet."

"What?" Her brain wasn't keeping up.

He crawled between her legs, dragging his tongue up her stomach and between her breasts. "I haven't played with these yet," he murmured against her skin. "And they do look so pretty on you."

Her piercings? What did he mean play with them?

His tongue toyed with one, then the other, and it didn't take long for her to realize what he meant. Pleasure spiked from the tips of each breast, zinging right down to her core. She hadn't thought it was possible for her to be so riled up this quickly, but he played her like an instrument. Within minutes she was writhing beneath him, shocked at how much pleasure could come from two metal bars.

She'd never felt like this. Ever. There was pain and pleasure, mixing together until she couldn't see straight. Astrid grabbed onto his horns, thankful for something to grasp at because her hands needed something to do. Her body wasn't listening to her. She wanted... needed... something. Anything. Friction in every part of her body because what he was doing was only winding her up tighter and tighter, beyond what she had thought she could do.

She feared she'd break if he kept going. Her mind or her body, one or the other. She was going to shatter into a thousand pieces and never put herself back together. She'd die if he kept going because she so desperately needed to jump off that cliff, but it just kept getting higher.

"Please," she whimpered, unsure of what else to say.

"Please what, wife?"

Astrid was incoherent. She didn't even know what she was asking, but then she felt his fingers between her legs and that—that was what she needed. Again he sank them into her, the tips of his fingers curling to press against a spot deep inside her that only he had found.

She arched, her back coming off the bed as she splintered into pieces once again. A third time, this one so much stronger than the other two. She'd thought her orgasms would get softer, but no. This one was so much more powerful.

Breathing hard enough that it felt like her heart was beating out of her chest, she finally blinked to see him staring at her with a pleased expression.

"What are you doing to me?" she whispered.

"Waiting for you to look at me so we can keep going."

She swore her face went white. "Keep going?"

"I'm not done with you yet."

And he wasn't. Astrid lost track of how many times he made her spiral out of control that night. Over and over again, never even thinking about himself until she was begging, pleading for his cock.

Maybe that was what he wanted. Once she was a whimpering mess, he stood again and took off his pants.

The cock he revealed was so hard, it had to be painful. The veins stood out in stark relief, and when he palmed it, white dripped from the tip to land on her belly. She wanted to rub it in, even though that thought shocked her.

Bjorn pressed his hand flat to her belly, holding her still as he notched the massive head of his cock between her folds. She could feel cool metal against her skin, and knew exactly what it would do to her once he slid home.

She'd thought he would ram it in—she would have welcomed that—but instead, he leaned down and pressed a kiss to her lips. "I love you," he said as he slid just the tip inside of her. Allowing her to get used to his size once again.

Then he slid in a little more and kissed her again. "I love you."

More and more he fed her his cock, bit by bit, repeating that he loved her with every single movement. She was blinded by him. They could have been attacked again, and all she would be able to think about was how much he loved her, and how much she loved him back.

By the time he was fully inside her, stretching her to the point of almost painful fullness, she was radiating love from every pore. She wrapped her arms around his shoulders, holding him as tightly as she could.

Then he moved. Sliding out of her until he was all the way out before drifting back in. Slowly. Like the sea ebbing and flowing against the shore.

His pace was maddening. When she wanted him to slam into her, to hear the resounding slap of their flesh against flesh, he built her back to that starlit place with the slow patience of a man who knew he had all the time in the world. He didn't rush her. He didn't rush himself.

Bjorn took his time getting to know her body and to allow hers to get used to his. He breathed her in, whispering encouragement that made her very soul glow.

"You are perfect for me."

"Look at how well you take me."

"There is no better troll wife."

"Fuck, bright one. You undo me."

She'd never felt more powerful than this moment, when she decided enough was enough. Astrid pushed on his chest, forcing him to stop as she turned around beneath him. With her back to his chest, she arched her spine. She knew he wouldn't be able to ignore such a sight. Bjorn palmed her ass and let out a little curse before he was inside her again.

This time, there was no soft pace. He surged around her, consuming her even as his hand came around to frame her throat and pull her back against him. He rode her hard, slamming in and out at the pace she had been wanting since the beginning.

They both came together, shattering around each other as she rippled around his cock, feeling him pulsing inside her body, jetting out so much come that she could feel it leaking out between her thighs even as he continued to groan in her ear.

And then they fell together onto the mattress, breathing hard and more tired than she had ever been in her life.

But there was nothing better than feeling his arm wrapping around her waist and tugging her tightly against his thundering heart.

"I really do love you, you know," he whispered against her hair, pressing a kiss to her head. "More than any troll has ever loved a woman before."

She didn't think he could claim that, but some part of her soul whispered he had to be right.

"I love you just the same," she replied. "You call me bright one, but you are my sanctuary, Bjorn. My safe place in this world."

Chapter 47

"B jorn, darling, can you bring the blankets outside as well?" Astrid called out, her arms already full with a basket of food that she was moving.

The entire plan had been to host their friends here, but then it had rained. She'd spent the morning trying to prepare their home for the amount of troll bodies that were going to take up the space, but then the sun had come out again. It had even dried out the new fire pit area that Bjorn had spent a ridiculous amount of time working on.

It really was pretty. The logs surrounding the stones were carved into comfortable seats with animals playing along the bottom. One even had rolling acorns that somehow looked like they were moving. She still wasn't sure how he'd done that. And the fire pit itself was surrounded by stunning crystals larger than her head.

He'd made this place a home, and they continued to add more and more to it. She'd never thought life in the troll kingdom would be so quaint, or that she would like it so much.

Astrid was trying her hand at gardening. She wasn't very good at it, but Maia made the trek up to visit her once a week so she could give

Astrid tips on why her plants were dying. Having someone who could talk to the plants helped.

And she was learning how to bake. Never in her life had she thought she would be cooking so much, but at least she had some familiar training for that. The priestesses knew how to cook, and it was a nice way to get Rose out of her hidden places in her mind that she still often found herself.

Bjorn walked by her, a mound of blankets in his hands as he grumbled about people visiting when he didn't think it was necessary.

"We want visitors," she reminded him.

"You want visitors. You enjoy seeing other people."

They were working on that as well. He didn't like being in crowds, and she didn't blame him for that. After all, ten years had been stolen from him. Ten years spent wondering who he was going to have to fight next. Now, he had the chance to make relationships with them, but Bjorn was better at doing it on his own terms.

Soon, she'd have a good reason to have people over. They were going to get some pigs from his mother and her people. The grotto trolls had claimed the fairy pigs, as Bjorn called them, would thrive on the mountain even in the winter. It would give her husband not only something to do, but an excuse to distract himself when visitors became overwhelming.

Heading out of their quaint little cabin, she was accosted by sound.

Countless people had been invited, and now she got to see all the trolls celebrate. It had been a long time since she'd seen that happen, and Astrid hadn't even had time to be introduced to anyone. She'd been in the troll kingdom for all of five minutes before they were back out to war.

Maia stood waiting for her outside the door with two troll women who were nearly seven feet tall and ridiculously beautiful.

"Astrid!" Maia called out, grabbing the basket of bread from her arms. "This is Inkeri and Rota. They are good friends of mine. I thought they'd be helpful."

"All hands are helpful," Astrid replied with a laugh.

Inkeri was a lovely dark blue, and she stepped forward to grab the blankets from Bjorn. "The troll wives have been waiting for a moment to get their hands on you, Astrid. Your husband has been hiding you from us."

"I have been hiding from everyone, not just you," Bjorn grumbled before heading through the crowd. They parted around him as if they were terrified, but she knew he would stop as soon as he found Rabbit.

No, Torben, she reminded herself. She was supposed to call him Torben now.

Rota laughed, the sound the tinkle of bells chiming throughout the clearing. "You might have the worst husband of them all, I'm afraid. He's good underneath, but that gruff exterior doesn't soften him much."

"No, it doesn't. Though he has a good heart." She kept her eyes on him until she saw he was with Torben and Gunnar and then turned her attention to the other women. "It sounds as though the troll wives stick together, is that correct?"

"It is. We have a gathering place that we would love to bring you to. A glen, if you will, where there is a stream and many of us practice our magic."

A wounded part of her soul healed a bit. Astrid pressed a hand to her chest, the ache there easing at their words. "I come from a place where I was a priestess. My sisterhood got me through a significant amount of pain. I cannot tell you how glad I am that there will be a similar place for me here, if you'll have me."

"We'll have to," Rota said with another laugh. "There's so many of you arriving every day. Whatever you said to the priestesses? They listened. We have many powerful women coming here, so many that I'm certain the king will want to do something about it."

"The king?"

Rota was already heading off. She stole the food from Maia's hands and then danced through the crowd, bringing it to a table someone had set up that Astrid had not yet seen. It was brimming with food, though. She was glad they wouldn't be hungry.

But Astrid wanted her question answered. She looked at Maia and Inkeri, a frown on her face. "Why did she bring up the king?"

The other two women looked at each other, and then Inkeri cleared her throat. "I'll go help Bjorn with all those blankets. He's just standing there with them, and I don't think anyone is going to ask him for one if he keeps wearing that frown on his face."

Maia was the only one to remain and reluctantly answered her question. "The king is concerned that there are many women here who are unwed. The promise was always that if the trolls gave them a safe place to stay, the women would consider marrying a troll. That's how it's always been. The trolls have a plan in mind for marrying people like us."

"Which is?"

"Similar to what you reported, the human king wanted everyone to be as close to an elf as possible. The trolls would be dark elves, and the humans apparently think they could be the light version of that." Maia shrugged. "Anyway, King Egil has decided that if we continue to get a population of powerful human women with elven bloodlines that are as strong as the priestesses, then there should be some kind of guidance for such things."

Astrid didn't like that. "Guidance?"

"A…" Maia clearly struggled to find the words. "It's not a ball. He doesn't want to host a grand party, apparently, but bridal games are certainly an option. Trolls are used to performing for their wives. They want everyone to look at them. They're very flashy. That's rather obvious with all the gemstones they wear. Such things used to convince their wives to marry them, and that is something they wish to continue to do. But we know nothing about that, so the king would like to create a more formal way for them to meet."

"He's not going to force them, is he?" Astrid asked.

"No, of course not. All he's asking is that people try, and how are they meant to try if they don't even know how it works?" Maia still looked uncomfortable even talking about this. "I know it's odd. Trust me. I've been struggling with it myself."

She would have continued to argue if she hadn't seen her sister wandering toward the garden. "Excuse me," Astrid said, then turned to point at Maia. "I'm not done talking about this."

"Neither am I! Together, we might be able to help them avoid scaring everyone away."

It sounded like a plan, but right now, her sister was tromping through a patch of cabbage like it wasn't even there, and Astrid was quite certain she knew what that meant. Rose had disappeared from them again. Off on a journey where none of them could follow. What Astrid didn't understand was what had caused it this time.

Were there too many people? She glanced around, finding only thirty trolls here. The space wasn't large, but she'd made sure that all the seats were far apart. Yet, something had still triggered Rose.

She just didn't know how to help her sister, or how best to make this comfortable for her.

Sighing, Astrid headed off toward the garden. It took a few minutes for her sister to stop, but at least she did. Sometimes she wandered off so far that it was impossible to catch her. Someone always had to be with her. Always. Where had Gunnar gone? Wasn't he usually doing this?

When she looked, she found the handsome troll laughing with his friends. Something in her heart twisted. He deserved that. After all these trolls had been through, he deserved more than watching after a young woman who refused to give him any sort of attention in return. Maybe these bridal trials would be good for both of them. Some time apart, another priestess to catch his eye. Then, at least, he wouldn't be barking up a tree that might never notice him.

She guided her sister over to a bench that Bjorn had carved so Astrid could look out at her garden. There was peace here, and it was quieter even though she could still hear the troll voices.

"You are safe, Rose," she murmured, repeating it over and over again. "You can come back. I would never let anything happen to you, nor would anyone else here."

The words seemed to cut through Rose's mind, at least a little. Her sister came back to herself, blinking as though the sun was a shock even though it had been sunny all day.

"Oh," Rose said, blinking so fast it was almost like she was trying to dash away tears. "I'm sorry. I did it again, didn't I?"

"Where were you this time?"

Rose's expression turned dreamy. "A garden just like this one, except it was so much bigger. The cabbages were the size of my body, and I was just a little ant wandering among the other animals. Did you know caterpillars are very talkative?"

They might've been in her dream world, but not in the real one. Astrid just smiled and brushed a strand of Rose's hair behind her ear. "What was it this time? I didn't think this was too many people for you, but I'm sorry if it was."

"I just overheard what you were all talking about. The king wants to pair us all off." Rose's pale cheeks somehow turned even paler. "I don't know if I'm ready for that."

"No one will force you."

"No, I suppose they wouldn't. But it was easier to drift away than it was to think about everything that came with that thought." Rose shook her head. "I'm sorry. I didn't mean to make it awkward. Your party is so pretty, Astrid."

"You didn't make anything awkward at all."

Something stuck in Astrid's mind, though. Her sister was so adamant that she didn't want to be paired up, but she knew there was one particular troll who would take care of her. Not that Rose ever had to be paired with anyone. But it might be easier if she were cared for by a troll who adored her.

"Can I ask..." She shouldn't. Astrid should keep her mouth shut and not scare her sister back into her mind. But the words kept coming. "Why are you so against giving Gunnar your time?"

"I spend time with Gunnar."

"No, you don't. He's very interested in you, Rose. And he's put a lot of effort into making sure you are safe and happy. I guess I'm just confused why you aren't willing to allow him to be more."

"He's my friend." Rose's nose scrunched. "He wouldn't want to be anything else."

"I think he very much would like to be more than that. You keep putting space between the two of you, though. He's..." She struggled to find words that wouldn't scare Rose. "He's trying, Rose. And it sounds to me like he's been trying for a very long time."

The sound of footsteps approached through the garden, and she could hear her cabbages bursting beneath their giant feet.

Gunnar headed toward them with an almost wild expression on his face, like he was terrified. "Astrid! Oh, good. You found her. I took my eyes off her for just a second, I swear. Then she disappeared on me."

"Not the first time, and likely not the last," Astrid replied with a smile. She stood, dusting off her skirts before moving out of the way. "She's fine, and she's back. I noticed her wandering off through the garden and thought I'd catch her before you had to."

He blew out a long, blustering breath. She could see how badly he wanted to scold her sister. It was the same way she'd felt when they'd been children. Sometimes she'd get so scared that she would yell at Rose when she found her, screaming how it wasn't fair for her to have to take care of a child who lived in daydreams.

Astrid had the thought to warn him that Rose didn't enjoy being scolded, but he didn't do it, anyway. He took another deep breath and then turned to her sister.

"You worried me," he said quietly. "I didn't know where you were."

"I'm usually fine."

"Usually. But the one time I take my eyes off you is going to be the time you walk off a cliff." He gestured with his hand for Rose to stand. Never touching her. Never even offering to touch her. "Let's join the party. I found you a seat that's far off from the others and thought we could try Astrid's bread."

Rose's nose scrunched again. "Astrid's bread is terrible."

At least her sister had found her sense of humor again. Astrid quipped, "I'm still here."

But then she headed off to find her husband. Her sister was well taken care of. That much she knew for certain. She only hoped Rose figured out how much Gunnar was doing for her before it was too late. After all, the king apparently wanted to match up his best trolls and... Well, Gunnar was certainly one of those.

If Rose wasn't careful, she was going to lose a very good man who just wanted to see her happy.

Astrid shook her head, deciding that now was not the time to ruminate on such things. She headed straight for Bjorn, tucking herself underneath his arm as he talked with his friends. Torben and Ragnar laughed at some joke he'd said, and Bjorn looked decidedly proud of himself.

For a moment, she allowed herself to look around and see all that had changed in such a short amount of time. She had so many friends now. People who were willing to eat and drink and laugh with her. She wasn't beholden to politics, lords, or anything other than her own life.

Bjorn tightened his arm around her shoulder, looking down at her with a fondness that made her heart sing with joy.

"Happy?" he asked, low and quiet so no one would hear the question but her.

"Blissful," she replied, before kissing him in front of everyone.

If the trolls cheered, well... they were right to do so.

Epilogue

Gunnar had started to develop a sixth sense about where Rose was. Maybe that was because he constantly had to chase her down. Every time she drifted into that made-up world of hers, she wandered. It could be in the middle of the night, sometimes in the middle of a party, but he had gotten pretty used to it.

Right now, he was in the middle of a meeting with King Egil. Most of the marriageable men were here, and he frankly wasn't interested in whatever the king was going to say. He hadn't been this morning when he rolled out of bed, and he sure wasn't now.

Egil was talking, and Gunnar was worried about what Rose was doing. He could feel that she was wandering. Somehow, he always knew. Maybe it was because he'd become so familiar with her, but he knew when she went on her walks.

"There are more marriageable women here than ever before, and you lot don't have the faintest idea how to woo them," the king said, his tone disgusted. "We are going to be hosting the bridal games again. It has been nearly a hundred years since we've had enough people to do it. But we are finally going to host them."

One of the women next to him piped up, "What about us? Is this just for the men?"

"There have been plenty of human men arriving with the women as well. There are countless of them, and they are all with varying degrees of power." The king stared pointedly at her. "Did you believe I would leave you out of this? Children are good for all of us. Power built into the troll kingdom benefits the whole. You and your sisters will compete alongside our men."

Gunnar could feel the swell of happiness from the women around him. They'd been awfully frustrated lately. More troll men had their eyes on human women than they did on troll women, and even he had noticed how difficult that was for them.

But the human women, especially the priestesses, were shiny and new. They were pretty bright things who wandered through the streets with a sense of awe that made even him look at his kingdom with fresh eyes. Their newness would wear off, though. He was certain of that.

Crossing his arms over his chest, he tried to focus on what the king said. "The bridal games will consist of many competitions to show how strong you are. That will be physically, mentally, and magically. Of course, the human women and men will choose who they are interested in. I don't think it's likely that the humans will compete with you, but stranger things have happened lately. You don't all have to compete for anyone's attention. It is a true bridal game, not just for our newcomers."

Interesting, but he did not care. Rose was wandering farther and farther from him as they spoke. He had left her in the hall outside, so what had set her off this time?

He lifted his hand, waiting for the king to look at him.

"And if we are not interested in competing?"

"All of you are competing."

"I already have a human I'm interested in." He had no shame in announcing it. Most here knew already, considering how often he and Rose were tied together.

But the king did not care. "Everyone will compete," he repeated. "Even you, Gunnar. You are one of my best fighters. I will not lose you to someone who is uninterested. You will at least have to participate and try."

"I have no interest in trying."

"Then I have no interest in funding any of your adventures." The king cut straight to the heart of what Gunnar was best at. He scouted for them, but also researched many plants, animals, and enjoyed being outside of Trollveggen. If the king was going to limit that, or deny him entirely…

Shit. Well. He supposed he was competing then.

Gunnar nodded, but he didn't have to be happy about it. He'd go through the motions, pretend that he was even invested enough to be there, and then he would return to figuring out his way underneath Rose's shield. The woman had proven to be impossibly difficult thus far, but he enjoyed a challenge.

He waited until the first moment he could slip out and then ran out of the room. A few trolls were waiting for him, already pointing in the direction that Rose had headed off. Most of them were used to her behaviors, but really the woman needed to stop doing this and just tell him what was upsetting her.

He worried when she wandered. She was going to hurt herself one of these days because he couldn't tie her to him.

Although now that he was thinking about it, it wasn't a terrible idea. If they were literally tied together, then she couldn't get too far without him knowing where she was. And then maybe people would leave him alone in these bridal trials. They would see that he wasn't interested in anyone but her, and they would then turn their attention to other trolls.

That would work. He'd have to get her to agree to it. Which would be easy. It was Rose. The woman didn't know how to say no, and even though he was trying very hard to anticipate what she wouldn't like, at the very least he could take advantage of this.

He was doing it for her own good, after all.

Heading out of the castle, he tried not to look too frantic when he didn't see her. More trolls pointed in the direction she'd headed, and off he went, through the forest. His heart rate spiked. Why was she in the forest, of all places?

Thankfully, Gunnar caught up with her quickly. He knew better than to grab her. It seemed only her sister could do that, so he walked beside her and started talking.

He was good at talking. Always had been. He was a storyteller by nature and knew how to spin a wild tale that usually caught the attention of everyone around him. It didn't take long for him to snap her out of it. In just a few minutes, she breathed more normally before stopping.

"Why are we in the forest?" Rose asked, ignoring the story he'd been spinning, which had been quite good.

"Because you went wandering again."

"Oh." She blinked a few times, then frowned.

It was the first time he'd seen any kind of negative expression on her face. She looked prettier like that, without the dazed or glazed expression he was used to.

"What started this wander?" He couldn't help asking.

"I don't like the idea of the bridal games. It seems like they're going to force people to... to..." She shook her head. "It makes me frightened."

"You won't be frightened watching me compete." He flexed for her, lifting his arms and trying to pretend he wasn't sincerely hoping she would look. "You'll see all this all the time."

She shook her head at him, turning to head back toward town. "It's not that."

"You don't want to see all these muscles working for you?"

There was innuendo there he hadn't meant. But he did mean it, actually. He found her stunning, and he liked the few conversations they'd had where she wasn't some daydreaming princess stuck in her own mind. She was an interesting person, his Rose. He found her more interesting every day.

But then he caught her reply, and everything in him froze in shock.

"I wouldn't mind," she said, her voice airy and light. "I just don't like the idea of everyone else looking too."

Follow me on socials or Amazon to keep your eye out for the next book!

Acknowledgements

No book is the same without all the people who help work on it. From my beta team, to my editors, to my dear friends who worked with me through every nonsense question - I adore you.

About the Author

Emma Hamm is a small town girl on a blueberry field in Maine. She writes stories that remind her of home, of fairytales, and of myths and legends that make her mind wander.

She can be found by the fireplace with a cup of tea and her two Maine Coon cats dipping their paws into the water without her knowing.

For more updates, join my newsletter!
www.emmahamm.com

www.ingramcontent.com/pod-product-compliance
Lightning Source LLC
Chambersburg PA
CBHW031551310726
48971CB00008B/2711